Quotidian Tales

Everyday stories of the Paranormal

By
David Vernon

MAPLE
PUBLISHERS

Quotidian Tales

Author: David Vernon

Copyright © 2024 David Vernon

The right of David Vernon to be identified as author of this work has been asserted by the author in accordance with section 77 and 78 of the Copyright, Designs and Patents Act 1988.

ISBN 978-1-83538-234-9 (Paperback)
     978-1-83538-235-6 (E-Book)

Cover Design and Book Layout by:
     White Magic Studios
     www.whitemagicstudios.co.uk

Published by:
     Maple Publishers
     Fairbourne Drive, Atterbury,
     Milton Keynes,
     MK10 9RG, UK
     www.maplepublishers.com

A CIP catalogue record for this title is available from the British Library.

Contents

About the Author

Dr David Vernon is a psychologist whose research into the paranormal has covered areas such as the theory of morphic resonance, telepathy, precognition, scopaesthesia (the feeling of being stared at), as well as energy healing and mediumistic communication. He has published numerous scientific papers on the topics of telepathy, precognition, and energy healing and his recent award-winning book '*Dark Cognition: Evidence for psi and its implications for consciousness*' has become a core text for those interested in studying the paranormal. He hosts regular monthly online webinars for the Society for Psychical Research and has been a guest speaker on paranormal topics at scientific conferences around the world.

For Annie,
with infinite love

∞

Note from the Author

Ever wondered if telepathy is real?

What about psychokinesis, energy healing or precognition?

I have.

And, as a psychologist, I've spent more than a decade researching and lecturing on these topics, among others. I've also been fortunate enough to have conducted experiments exploring some of these topics myself, sometimes finding evidence of effects that are often referred to as *anomalous*. This is the standard scientific way of saying that we don't understand what these effects are, why they occur, or how they work. But there's no doubt that they exist.

However, what is interesting about this is that, despite the deep and wide-ranging fascination for these topics, very few people are aware of the research that's been done, or the evidence that's available. As someone who's talked about such topics in public, I'm often met with surprise, when I present evidence relating to a particular effect.

It took me some time to understand why this might be the case. Eventually I realised that it's because the various topics, along with the evidence, are hidden in plain sight. By this I mean that the information is invariably published in scientific journal articles or in academic textbooks. This made me aware that there seemed to be a mismatch between interest and information; although many people are interested in such phenomena, they may not always be aware of the scientific information available.

It was with this thought in mind that I decided to try something different. Rather than write another lecture, or textbook on the subject, I thought I'd tell a selection of stories. Each story would focus on a particular aspect of what is often referred to as *parapsychology*, such as associative remote viewing, precognition, or after death communication. Whilst the stories and characters would all be fictional, the underlying concepts would be very real indeed. The final story attempts to look at what all this could mean in terms of the nature of consciousness.

There are notes for each of the stories, pointing the way to evidence, research, references and/or additional sources of information.

I hope you enjoy my stories.

With very best wishes

DJV

1

Lost and Found

Lucy leant down and carefully placed her violin back in its case. Ensuring the bow was safely clipped in its holder and the rosin was placed back in the small felt padded compartment. She gently closed the lid and zipped up the case, lifting it by the long shoulder strap she turned to the conductor. 'Thanks Mr Woodall,' she smiled and waved goodbye.

The conductor, a tall, slim, well-dressed man in his late thirties, looked back and smiled. 'Well played today Lucy,' he said. Raising his finger towards her he continued, 'remember what I said about working on your vibrato.'

'I will,' she nodded, smiling broadly as she made her way to the exit.

It had been a good practice session and Mr Woodall had told her that if she continued to play as well as she had today, she'd easily make the orchestra. Her smiled broadened as she thought about the possibility of playing in the orchestra. She couldn't wait to tell her parents. As she made her way out of the music school, she could see her mum waiting in the car just a little way up the road. She quickly walked up the road towards the car and opened the back door to place her violin on the back seat before getting in beside it.

Her mother was already looking back at her, 'how did it go darling?' she asked.

Lucy was beaming, 'it was brilliant! Mr Woodall said that I'd played really well and that I might be able to make the orchestra'.

'Oh, that's great news,' said her mother with genuine affection. 'Why don't we stop off at the supermarket on the way home to get some treats?'

Lucy's face brightened, 'ooh yes, can I have M&Ms?'

Her mother grinned wryly, 'I was thinking more along the lines of getting some pizza for dinner,' she said.

Lucy screwed her face up. 'Ohhh,' she grumbled.

Her mother attempted to maintain a serious outlook for a moment and then relented. 'We'll have to see,' she said with a sigh. With that she turned back in her seat and started the car. 'Are you buckled in?' she asked looking at Lucy in the rear-view mirror.

Lucy rolled her eyes whilst nodding her head, 'yes mum,' she groaned. It was a routine she found annoying. Her mother always asking if she'd fastened her seat belt. It made her feel like the child she so desperately wanted to grow beyond.

The car pulled out onto the main road and headed west towards home. Her mother drove carefully but not slowly. Part-way home they detoured to the local supermarket, found an empty spot, and parked up. As soon as the engine had stopped Lucy quickly called out, 'can I come?' Knowing full well that her mother could very easily forget about the M&Ms.

'Hmmm, ok,' said her mother nodding.

They left the car and made their way inside, her mum taking the lead and picking up a wire basket as they walked through the large main doors. They made their way through the fruit and vegetables towards the dairy isle which contained the fresh made pizzas. 'What topping . . .' she began.

'Pepperoni of course,' Lucy interrupted.

Her mother smiled indulgently and picked up a large pepperoni pizza, placed it in the basket and then walked on towards the isle containing the biscuits and sweets. Half-way down the sweets isle Lucy reached out and picked a bag of peanut M&Ms off the shelf, placing it in the basket, whilst carefully avoiding the gaze of her mother. Her mother looked down at her, head to one side, tight lipped in thought.

'Ok,' she said, 'but you can't have these *and* chocolate biscuits.'

'That's ok,' breathed Lucy quickly, 'I just want these.'

Her mother raised her eyebrows. 'Are you sure?' she queried.

'Yep.'

'And you can't eat the whole bag.'

Lucy attempted an innocent smile and shrugged a little, as if to indicate that such an idea had never occurred to her. Secretly, she was pleased that she was simply allowed the M&Ms.

'Hmmm,' said her mother, as if still contemplating whether the M&Ms were a good idea. 'I'll just get some wine for your father and I, to go with the pizza.'

Once they had all that they needed they made their way to the self-checkout area. The slight delay, caused by having to wait for the operator to confirm it was ok for her mum to purchase alcohol, gave Lucy a little time to think some more about what playing in the orchestra could mean for her musical career. For as long as she could remember, playing violin in an orchestra had been her life's ambition. She thought what this would be like as she watched her mum bag and pay for their goods. Her mum then picked up the semi-full bag and they made their way back out through the large sliding doors. As they walked across the car park her mother stopped sharply causing Lucy to look up. 'What's up mum?' she asked.

Her mother didn't answer immediately but just stood there frowning, concern and bewilderment emanating from her like mist on a frosty morning.

'Mum?' asked Lucy, becoming a little concerned herself.

Her mother looked confused. 'I could've sworn we'd parked over here' she said, pointing to the empty spaces by the trolley shelter.

Lucy hadn't really paid any attention to where they'd parked but looked around now to see if she could identify their car. Her mother was also looking from side to side trying to see where the car was. The two of them stood there in the fading light looking desperately around, trying to find a car that was no longer there. Her mother asked Lucy to stay where she was whilst she just double checked the rest of the car park, just in case she'd mistakenly parked in another bay. It took her mother less than five minutes to walk the length of the car park and back again. As she returned she was mumbling something under her breath that Lucy couldn't quite hear, but it sounded like her mum was swearing. Something she very rarely did and because of this Lucy felt a sinking in the pit of her stomach. Her mum dug into her handbag and pulled out her mobile phone, her hands shaking as she punched in the number. As the call was answered she turned away from Lucy.

'Yes, hello. Police please.' She waited for a few moments as the operator put her through to the relevant services and then continued. 'Hello, yes. My name's Mary Adamson and I'm with my daughter at Sainsbury's, off the Park road, and we've just come out of the store to find our car's been stolen.' There was more silence as the voice at the other end of the phone went through a series of rehearsed questions. This time however her mother's agitation clearly showed. 'What! Are you kidding,' her mother's voice rising as her anger began to match her frustration. 'No, no, I understand,' she continued more calmly now, attempting to placate the voice on the phone, 'yes of course I've checked the rest of the car park,' she growled. 'It's a bloody car!' she cried, 'I'd hardly miss it would I.' There was a moments silence as her mother hung her head listening to the voice on the phone. 'No, no, I do understand, I'm sorry, but its rather stressful to come out of the supermarket and find that someone's stolen your car. Yes, just me and my daughter.' Another short silence and then 'ok, thank you,' she said.

Her mother turned back to Lucy. 'The police are on their way,' she grimaced. 'But it will be about ten minutes before anyone can get here,' she added.

Lucy took a step towards her mother and then leant in and wrapped her arms around her. 'Are you ok mum?' she asked, her voice muffled by her mother's coat.

Mary wrapped her arms around Lucy and bending down kissed the top of her head. 'No,' she said truthfully, 'but I will be.' They stood there locked in each other's arms offering one another scant comfort when her mum suddenly looked up, 'oh Christ,' she moaned, 'what's your father going to say about this.'

Then it dawned on Lucy what this meant for her. 'Oh no,' she cried, stepping out of her mother's embrace, a look of shock registering on her face as tears began to well up in her eyes, 'my violin!'

The car had, like so many before it, been stolen to order and was now sitting in a smart, well-lit garage in a suburban region of west London, undergoing a series of alterations and modifications to ensure that it would not be recognised by its previous owner whilst being eminently suitable for its new one. The young man who'd stolen it was receiving his payment in an office on the first floor of the building from the woman in charge of the organisation. Her name was Katya, she was a large grim woman with a seemingly eternal frown on her face that helped to make her gaze seem both intense and dangerous. Katya was currently sitting behind a large desk counting out a pile of cash. 'Thirty-five hundred,' she said, placing the last fifty-pound note on the pile.

'Thanks Kat,' said the young man, leaning over the desk to scoop up the pile of bills. He didn't bother checking them. He simply folded them in half and put them into an inside pocket.

'That was good work Alex,' said Katya nodding gently. 'Quick,' she added approvingly.

The man called Alex simply stood and waited. He'd dealt with Kat before and knew she didn't do small talk, which meant, he hoped, that this might be leading to another job. The moment stretched between them as if each was waiting for the other to speak. Katya then shifted some papers aside on her desk, pulling up one and looking back at Alex.

'I have another,' she waved the pieced of paper, 'commission for you,' she said. Then added, 'if you're interested.'

Alex, still standing, cautiously responded, 'might be.'

Katya pushed the piece of paper she was holding towards Alex. 'I need a Range Rover Velar,' she said, as if ordering an item from an online shopping site.

Alex frowned slightly and thought for a moment. He knew Range Rovers were a bugger to get hold of and the new Velar model would be especially so. But he also knew that this would mean a good price.

'It needs to be in white,' added Katya pointing to the image of a white Range Rover on the sheet of paper.

Just then one of the mechanics from downstairs knocked on the office door and entered without waiting for a response. 'Sorry guv,' he said looking directly at Katya, 'but we've just cleaned out that Beemer that was brought in earlier and found this in the back.' He laid a small black case on her desk.

'What is it?' asked Katya with a frown.

The mechanic unzipped the bag and lifted the lid to reveal a beautiful violin inside. The three of them stood there for a moment staring at the instrument. Whilst none of them were musical it was clear to all three that the instrument was one of quality and could be worth something.

Katya looked up and smiled slightly, 'ok, Mickey,' she said to the mechanic, 'leave it with me.'

Mickey simply nodded. 'guv,' he said, turning and making his way back downstairs.

Katya turned back to Alex. 'I know the Velar will be. . .' she thought for a second, 'challenging to get hold of. But, if you take the job, you can have this,' she nodded towards the violin on her desk, 'as a bonus.'

Alex looked from her to the violin and then back.

'You should be able to get a good price for this on the market,' said Katya.

Alex clenched his jaw in an effort not to smile and attempted to remain thoughtful. He knew the perfect person to offload the violin to and judging by the quality it would fetch quite a good price indeed. 'Ok, deal,' he said nodding.

∞

Two weeks later Paul and Mary Adamson were still dealing with the aftermath of their car theft. Despite Mary having reported the car stolen within only a short time of its disappearance the Police were not optimistic that they'd be able to recover it and encouraged the Adamsons to pursue their insurance claim without delay. Whilst Mary was the one most affected by the loss of what she still called, her car, Paul seemed to be the one who was most aggrieved by the loss. Early conversations between the two had, at times, reached very heated levels as Paul, seemingly oblivious to the irritation caused, asked Mary again whether she'd remembered to lock the car or not. On the third time of asking this Mary had simply looked at him with anger flaring in her eyes and a hint of steel in her voice. 'Don't,' she said. 'Just don't.'

Paul at last seemed to pick up on the clues he'd previously ignored and wisely decided to let the matter drop.

However, whilst the parents were angry and annoyed at the loss and frustrated by the inherent bureaucracy of having to deal with all the various forms, questions and requests from the insurance company, Lucy was devastated by the loss of her violin. A loss that was compounded when her parents told her that the insurance company would not cover the cost of the lost instrument. Worse still, that the costs inherent in getting hold of another car, and what with one thing and another, buying another hand-made violin just wasn't on the cards.

True, Lucy had a second violin. It was her old practice one that she'd used to complete her grades with. However, for her, it simply didn't have the same feel. The tone was slightly off, and it just didn't have the light brightness of sound that her hand-made violin had. Most musicians are keenly aware of the subtle but definite connection that exists between player and instrument. At such levels they know that it's more than a relationship, it's an interrelationship. During heightened moments of play the two separate parts, musician and instrument, would become a single part of something greater. Most good musicians felt it. Two parts working together in synchronous harmony to produce something that could transcend the everyday.

Unsurprisingly, the loss of her violin had negatively affected Lucy's playing and this in turn had brought into question the possibility of her playing in the orchestra. Whilst Mr Woodall, who was both her music teacher and the conductor, had been sympathetic to Lucy's loss, he'd also made it clear that they couldn't sacrifice the standards required for public performance and that if Lucy could no longer meet these standards, then her place in the orchestra would need to be reconsidered. All of which seemed to push Lucy into a downward spiral of frustration and despair.

These losses hung over family dinners like a pall of grief, dulling the taste of the food and stifling the usual light conversation. After one such dinner Lucy moved disconsolately to sit on the nearby sofa as her father quietly cleared away the plates and cutlery whilst her mother picked up the local paper to look again for a possible replacement car. A few minutes later her mother folded the paper and called over to her father as she said, 'look at this.'

'What is it?' asked her father as he stacked plates in the dishwasher in the nearby kitchen.

'It's an advert for finding things,' answered Mary.

'What do you mean, finding things,' queried Paul.

'Well, look,' indicated Mary pointing at the folded page of the newspaper, 'it says lost items found.'

Paul came back into the room and leaned over Mary's shoulder to read the advert she was pointing at. In a small box advert, in bold black letters it read: "**Lost items Found: Initial consultation free.**" Underneath was a telephone number.

Paul made a wry face looking sceptical. 'Probably just some scam,' he said.

Mary looked thoughtful, 'you never know,' she said optimistically. The unspoken question in her voice was clear.

'You're joking,' Paul scoffed, 'it's probably a scam,' he repeated.

'It says the initial consultation is free,' responded Mary hopefully.

Paul grimaced, shaking his head, 'nothing's free.'

Mary cocked her head to one side and raised her eyebrows as if to say, have you got a better idea?

'Oh, you've got to be kidding,' he groaned.

Mary pointedly looked over at Lucy and then back up at Paul saying, sotto voce, 'we need to do something.'

Paul screwed his face up in anguish but bit back the sarcastic response that filled his mind. He looked over at his daughter and shook his head slowly. He loved her dearly and knew how much her music meant to her and he also knew that, unlikely as it was, if this could help in any way then he should grab the possibility with both hands. He stood for a moment thinking and then shrugged. What had he got to lose from a free consultation he thought. He looked back at Mary, 'ok,' he said, 'give it a call.'

Mary brightened immediately and called over to Lucy, 'what do you think Lucy, should we try this out?'

Lucy, who hadn't been following their conversation asked what it was that they should try. Her mother briefly told her about the advert and said, 'well, what do you think? After all,' she added, 'we've got nothing to lose.'

'True,' said Lucy slowly, not fully convinced this would help but not wanting to give up hope either.

'No harm in trying,' said her mother as she reached for her mobile phone. Five minutes later she put the phone down and looked at them both. 'Right,' she said, matter of factly, 'we have an appointment with,' she looked down at the notes she'd made on the margin of the newspaper, 'a, er, Mr Gary Stevenson next Tuesday evening at six-thirty.'

The following Tuesday evening found Paul taking the family to see Mr Stevenson for their free consultation. They hadn't talked about it much since Mary had made the appointment the previous week. Paul, because he couldn't see what help one lone individual could be, and still thought that it sounded like some sort of scam. Mary, because she was concerned about offering false hope to Lucy who seemed more withdrawn since the loss of her violin. The three of them sat in the car lost in their own thoughts as to what this might mean. The silence was broken by the electronic voice of the sat-nav telling them to take the next turning on the right into Sycamore Close and that their destination was half a mile up the road on the right.

As Paul turned into the road he was looking around at the surrounding houses lit by the early evening street lights. 'Seems normal,' he said.

Mary laughed quietly, 'what were you expecting?'

Paul shrugged, 'don't know. Just,' he nodded at the surrounding bungalows with their neatly trimmed front lawns and well-kept flower beds, 'er, something a bit more unusual.'

Mary smiled, 'perhaps they're lulling us into a false sense of security,' she mocked.

Paul briefly looked over at her and frowned. It was a bone of contention for him that this was a waste of time, and he was just there to make sure his family wasn't scammed and it annoyed him that Mary didn't seem to be taking it seriously.

'Here we are,' he said as he pulled the car over to the right and parked in front of a small semi-detached bungalow which, like all its neighbours, had a neat and well-kept front garden.

The three of them got out of the car and made their way up the dimly lit pathway to the front door. As they arrived at the door Paul looked at Mary and Lucy with an air of overstated authority, 'now just let me do the talking,' he said. Mary instantly groaned. Paul clenched his jaw and with deliberate effort said, 'look, we don't know how this works or what they'll want, or. . .'

Mary interrupted, 'the initial consultation is free.'

'Of course it is,' said Paul in exasperation. 'That's how they lure you in. The first bits free then they tell you that they *may* have some relevant information, but they need to just do a bit more work and then they charge you £100 a day.'

'Let's just see how the consultation goes shall we,' said Mary leaning past Paul and pressing the doorbell.

Paul flashed a look at Mary, pressing his lips together in firm disapproval. The last thing he wanted was to start an argument, but he just wished Mary would see the sense of what he was saying. 'I'm just saying,' he said for the umpteenth time, 'that we need to be careful because it's probably a scam.'

As he was saying this the door quietly opened to reveal a slightly overweight gentleman in his early sixties with thinning hair and dark rimmed glasses. The man had clearly heard what Paul said and made a point of looking past him at Mary and asking, 'yes, can I help you?'

Mary quickly took the lead, 'I'm Mrs Adamson, I phoned last week about a consultation regarding a lost item,' she said brightly, as if trying to overshadow Paul's comment.

'Ah yes,' smiled the man, 'Mary, isn't it?'

'Yes,' replied Mary, 'and this is my husband Paul and our daughter Lucy.'

'Well, I'm Gary,' he said in an affable easy going way reaching out to shake each of their hands in turn. 'Come on in,' he said, leading them into a short hallway. 'If you'd like to hang your coats here on the hooks and leave you shoes here,' he said, indicating a short shoe stand, 'and come through into the lounge we can chat in comfort.'

All three took off their coats and shoes and made their way into a brightly lit and comfortably furnished lounge. Once they were all seated Gary began.

'Let me tell you what I do,' he said, 'and then you can tell me about your lost item and we'll see if we can work something out.' He took a moment to settle himself comfortably in his armchair. 'I'm a remote viewer[1],' he began.

'A what,' burst out Paul frowning. Mary flashed him a quick look entreating him to be quiet.

Gary sat for a moment looking at Paul and then said, 'I wonder sir, if I could ask you to wait in the kitchen for us.'

'What!' exclaimed Paul.

'It's just that your negative energy is disturbing the balance of my chakras,' said Gary seriously.

Paul looked like he'd just swallowed something unpleasant. 'Your what?' he asked, in a mix of bewilderment and disbelief, as his feeling that this was some sort of scam intensified.

'If you could just wait in the kitchen please,' repeated Gary mildly, indicating a door at the far end of the room.

Paul looked to Mary, concern clearly showing on his face.

'We'll be fine,' said Mary in response to his unspoken question.

Slowly, with clear reluctance, Paul got up and made his way towards the door at the far end of the room.

'We'll call you as soon as we've finished,' called out Gary as Paul went through the door to the kitchen. Once Paul had closed the door behind him Gary sat back and looked at Mary and Lucy.

Mary frowning a little, her head to one side asked, 'does it?'

Gary seemed momentarily taken aback. 'Does what?' he asked.

'Does his,' Mary nodded towards the door Paul had just gone through, 'negative energy upset your, eh, your chakras?'

'Ah,' Gary smiled, his eyes sparkling mischievously. 'No idea love,' he winked at Lucy, 'I just made that up.'

An unexpected burst of laughter erupted from Lucy. It was the first time she'd laughed in some time. The sound lightened Mary's heart.

'I know people are sceptical,' continued Gary, 'and I can understand that. And I know that some people think that I'm going to go into some sort of trance, or talk about chakras, or wave a crystal over a picture of the lost item, but I don't do any of that. I just try and remotely view the object question,' he said matter-of-factly. 'But I'm not a scam artist,' he added with emphasis.

Mary was smiling to herself and momentarily looked down at the floor feeling slightly ashamed of Paul's comment.

'Ok,' said Gary, settling himself again, 'let me give you a bit of my background and then you can tell me about the item that's missing.' With that he told Mary and Lucy about his time working as a detective in the London Metropolitan Police force and how over the years he'd trained himself as a remote viewer and how the process worked. He also told them that he was a member of an international organisation for remote viewing[2], and that they could check this out online if they wished to be certain about his credentials. He said that he could provide them with a list of references on the subject, which would include books and scientific articles, if they were interested. He also made it clear that remote viewing wasn't an exact science. He wasn't going to be able to give them the sat-nav coordinates of the item they'd lost. It was more about impressions he'd receive that he could then use to sketch out possible details regarding the target. They would have to take and use any information he could obtain to help them in their search for the item. Both Mary and Lucy warmed to Gary as he told them about his training and some of the work he'd done. As he finished both Mary and Lucy were feeling a lot more relaxed and ever so slightly hopeful.

'So,' said Gary, 'tell me about the item that was lost.'

Mary looked over to Lucy who bowed her head for a moment. Then Lucy looked up and said, 'it was my violin.' There was a moment's silence before she added with a harsh edge to her voice, 'and it wasn't lost, it was stolen.'

Mary gave a brief account of how their car, with the violin on the back seat, had been stolen.

Gary nodded in silent understanding and waited, giving Lucy a moment, before signalling to her to continue.

'It was handmade,' Lucy began slowly, 'specially for me, once I'd passed my grade eight. It was made out of spruce and maple wood, and it was made by Anthony Fitzgerald,' the pace of her voice increased, becoming slightly breathless as she rushed to get the words out. 'And it had catgut strings, which Tony, I mean Mr Fitzgerald, said would give it a warm and supple tone – which they did,' she added. 'And I called her Terpsi.'

'Ah,' said Gary with a smile, 'after Terpsichore, the Greek muse of music and dance.'

'Yes!' said Lucy in surprise. She briefly looked over at her mum who nodded and raised her eyebrows to signal that she too was impressed at Gary's understanding. Lucy continued, 'when I got her we were doing Greek mythology at school and I thought it sounded sooo cool.'

Mary smiled slightly as she heard the joy in Lucy's light and slightly breathless voice as she talked about her instrument.

'And it really helped with my playing,' continued Lucy, determined to make it clear just how important the instrument was to her. 'Mr Woodall said that it if I kept playing as well as I had,' she interrupted herself, 'Mr Woodall is my music teacher, and he conducts the Ravensfield Orchestra. He said that it was very likely I'd make the orchestra.' As she finished her shoulders slumped in defeat, and she looked back down at the floor. 'But now it's gone,' she said quietly.

'What piece were you practicing?' asked Gary.

'Oh, it was Mozart's violin sonata number twenty-six in B-flat major,' she responded rather disconsolately.

Gary sat back in silent thought for a moment. As he sat there, he rubbed his chin in contemplation. Then, seeming to come to a decision he looked over at Mary, 'do you have any pictures of the instrument?' he asked her.

'Yes,' Mary replied with a wry smile, 'lots. Of course, they're mostly of Lucy playing it.'

'That'll be fine,' said Gary, 'I just need you to send me a few pictures of the violin, as it'll help me establish a connection.' He sat forward. 'Ok, I'll do what I can to help you,' he said. 'I'll work on it next week if that's ok with you and try to get something to you by the end of next week.'

Lucy brightened, looking hopeful. Mary responded more cautiously. She pursed her lips, well aware that it was only the initial consultation that was free, she tentatively asked about fees for additional sessions.

Gary smiled in response to the question. 'Ah yes,' he said, 'let me tell you what it will cost,' and spent a few moments explaining what his fee would be. Once he'd finished both Mary and Lucy agreed and in an air of general agreement that the meeting had reached its natural conclusion Gary called out for Paul to re-join them. Both Mary and Lucy rose from their seats as Paul, tight lipped and frowning returned from the kitchen. The three of them then made their farewells to Gary as he led them back out into the hall to collect their shoes and coats.

The mood in the car as they drove home was divided. Mary and Lucy seemed at ease and relaxed, whereas Paul was still annoyed at being excluded from the consultation. His annoyance showed in his sharp and erratic driving. Keen to know what went on he asked in a terse voice, 'how'd it go?'

Beside him Mary nodded, 'I think it went well.' Then she added, 'he said he'd try and send us something by the end of next week.'

'Hmmm,' intoned Paul, the disbelief in his voice evident. 'So, what did he do. Wave a crystal over a picture of the violin?'

Both Mary and Lucy looked at one another and then burst out laughing.

Paul looked bewildered and annoyed by their response. 'What?' he asked in an aggrieved tone.

Retired colonel, Sandy Hewitt, a widower at 62, now spent his free time browsing the antique stores and flea markets of London. It had become a hobby of his to buy and sell the odd item, particularly antique furniture. He had a good understanding of wood, and a keen eye for detail. He knew what to look out for. The unusual or unique carving motif, the uncommon use of a particular glass colour, or some other atypical design, all hints that the piece in question could be something interesting. And interesting often translated into valuable. It wasn't that Sandy desperately needed the extra cash, he didn't. He simply enjoyed the process. He liked the serendipitous nature of not knowing whether today was the day he'd find something interesting. He also enjoyed haggling over the price. Something very few Englishmen are comfortable with.

Sandy was tall and lean, with a well-tanned face and a good head of silver-grey hair. He always wore a jacket and tie when out and about and his upright bearing and clear confident manner all helped to identify him as ex-military. Today, he was strolling around one of London's flea markets browsing the various stalls of pre-loved china and silverware. Looking at the seemingly vast array of bight shiny objects, he smiled as he thought to himself that this would be a magpie's dream. He browsed in a non-committal manner left and right as he weaved in amongst the various vendors and customers. Listening to the ambient noise of bargains being offered, prices being discounted, and deals being made. As he made his way past stalls offering ceramic jewellery, retro-clothing and a selection of old paintings he came across one that held a range of wooden instruments. There were recorders and oboes hanging from mounts, rows of acoustic guitars, upright in their stands and a selection of violins, some stacked in their cases with a few laid out on a felt covered table. As he was walking past, one of the violins on the table caught his eye. He changed direction and strolled over to the stall, making a show of looking at one of the recorders hanging from the top bar of the stall whilst surreptitiously looking down at the violin.

'Pure rosewood those are sir,' said the vendor appearing by his side and nodding in the direction of the recorders.

'Hmm, very nice,' nodded Sandy in agreement. He stood for a moment and continued to gaze around at the various instruments. Then as his gaze wandered over the violins laid out on the table he seemed to notice the one on the left hand side, reaching over he picked it up. Turning it over he quickly scanned for a maker's label, also noting the combination of wood. He reached out to check the price tag. It was priced up at £650. He stood for a moment looking at the instrument. He was sure it was made from spruce and maple, with the maple highly flamed, and it had gut strings as well. He worked to keep his face expressionless whilst he felt the familiar tingle hinting that this could be something. Turning to the vendor he said in a nonchalant manner, '£650 seems like a lot.'

'Well,' said the vendor with a leering smile, 'it's a lovely piece of wood . . .'

Sandy interrupted him, pointing to the marks he'd seen when he'd first picked it up, 'oh,' he said with mock surprise, 'it seems to have sustained some damage here.'

'Well,' responded the vendor, 'it's probably been around a bit. Had a few knocks here and there, but nothing that would affect its playing.'

Sandy tightened his jaw a fraction and pursed his lips as if in thought. This was something, he could clearly see that, and the marks he'd pointed to were those made by the tools of a luthier. Which meant this was a hand-made piece. Definitely a something. There followed a short period of negotiation where Sandy worked hard to bring down the price based on perceived and illusory faults whilst the vendor worked hard to retain the original price by pointing to the quality of the wood, stressing that any minor defects were unlikely to impact on the quality of the sound. Eventually, they both settled on an agreed value and Sandy found himself to be the new owner of a beautiful violin. Placing it gently back in its case he could see it had been well cared for and he wondered about its history, and where it had come from.

∞

It had been a couple of days since Gary had been visited by the Adamsons and he'd now printed out the pictures Mary had sent him of the violin. He was sitting comfortably in his lounge with the pictures resting on his lap. He sat back, closed his eyes, and took a deep breath, allowing his mind to settle. Each remote viewer went through a series of stages during the remote viewing process, and each gave their own sequence of stages different names to help them with the procedure. Gary called this first part the "getting out of your own way" part. It was really just an attempt to settle his mind and quieten things down. Once he felt comfortable, he opened his eyes, reached over and pressed the play button on the stereo remote control, and gently looked at the pictures of the violin on his lap as the first notes of a violin sonata emerged from the twin speakers. Here, Gary worked to immerse himself in the target and connect to what he called the signal-line. The signal line is what remote viewers call the stream of information that they receive during their attempts to remotely view something. When he felt ready Gary switched off the stereo and sat back in silence, once again closing his eyes and focusing now on any sensory information that came to mind. This included colour, light, smell, texture, taste and sound. After a few minutes of this he then focused on the dimensionality of the target. In this case, the height, width and shape of the violin. After a few minutes of this he then allowed his mind to settle back and waited for any impressions to come to mind, any information, or concepts relating to what had already come up or emerged to filter out into his conscious mind. He then opened his eyes, took up the pencil and pad beside his chair and began to make a series of notes and sketches based upon the images and impressions he had. Once he'd done this he would rest for a couple of hours and then repeat the process over again. In the coming days he'd try to do this at least three or four times. Until he felt that he'd exhausted every possibility.

Towards the end of the week, he distilled his notes and sketches into a more coherent summary. This ended up being a sketch of a church tower with a broken clock, a sketch of a small country cottage and the words "Winchester" and "military – but not a gun". He packed these up, along with his rough notes and ideas and placed them in a large envelope that he then posted to Mary Adamson.

It was the following week when the package arrived at the Adamson household. Mary had been the one to pick it up as it was addressed to her. As she made her way towards the kitchen, she tore open the package and peeked inside. As she did, she let out a little cry of surprise which brought the others in to find out what was going on.

'It's the notes and things from Gary, the remote viewer,' she said by way of explanation as she held the package up for them to see.

'Well let's see it then,' demanded Paul.

The three of them moved to the dining room and Mary pulled out the contents of the package and laid them out on the table, with both Paul and Lucy peering over her shoulders.

There was a selection of pages with notes scribbled on them, with various words crossed through and others underlined. There were a few rough sketches and a couple of much better ones, as if more time and effort had been taken over these. One was a church with a clock tower and the words "broken clock" beside the tower with a small arrow drawn, pointing towards the clock. Another was a small country cottage with the words "Winchester" and "military" next to it, both underlined multiple times.

Paul frowned, 'what does it all mean?' he queried.

'Well,' said Mary moving the pieces of paper around and selecting out the clearest sketches, 'perhaps we should be looking for either this church, or that cottage and maybe, they're in Winchester.'

Paul snorted, 'yeah, right.'

Mary slowly turned to look at him. Her thin lips were tightly pressed together as she made a motion of raising her eyebrows and looking briefly in the direction of Lucy. She then gave him a look that clearly said, 'you're not helping.'

After a moment's hesitation Paul lamented, 'ah, we'ell, I suppose we could always drive out to Winchester on Saturday to see if we can find these places.' As he said this he looked sideways at Lucy who'd not uttered a word, but it was clear from the expression on her face that she was clinging to the hope that this would lead somewhere. Paul frowned as he thought about how she might react in the very likely event that this led nowhere. It pained him to see her so despondent about the loss of her violin and he was concerned about taking a trip that offered nothing but false hope which would, in all likelihood, be dashed away again. Nevertheless, he knew that there wasn't much else he could do right now except try and show his support.

Hence, on Saturday morning Paul drove the family to Winchester, in search of a church with a clocktower that housed a broken clock, and a small country cottage. Despite the feeling that they were looking for a needle in a haystack there was a general sense of optimistic hope as they set off down the M3 towards Winchester. Unfortunately, several hours later as they crossed and criss-crossed the same roads again and again, without spying either a church or cottage that looked in any way like those in the drawings, patience was wearing thin, and tempers were beginning to fray. The atmosphere in the car deteriorated as they began to retrace their routes in and around Winchester. The early optimism now replaced by a bleak cloud of despair. Eventually, Paul brought the car to a stop at the side of the road and looked over at Mary and Lucy. Shaking his head with regret he said, 'I'm sorry, but we've been down every road and street. We've driven past every church we could find and none of them look like that,' he said pointing in frustration at the sketch that Mary had been holding for the past hour.

Mary huffed despondently and shrugged. 'Well, at least we tried,' she said.

Paul could see the glistening of tears in Lucy's eyes and his heart ached. He reached out tenderly and placed a hand on her leg, squeezing it gently. 'I'm really sorry love,' he said.

Lucy, not trusting herself to say anything, simply remained tight lipped and nodded in understanding.

Paul sat back in his seat and took a deep breath. 'How about we head down to the coast for some fish and chips by the sea?' he asked in mock cheerfulness.

'Good idea,' said Mary. 'It'll save me having to cook when we get home.'

And so, they turned around, again, and headed towards Southampton in a search of fish and chips. A search, as it turned out, that was both easier and more fruitful than their attempts to find the church or cottage had been. Later that evening, as they arrived back home after what had turned into a long and frustrating day in the car, they sought the relaxation and mindless entertainment of the television. Lucy sat staring at the screen, not really noticing what was on, whilst her mum fetched some drinks and her dad sat beside her flicking through one of his magazines. As she sat there, she slowly became aware that on the screen they were showing the image of an old church. The camera then followed the presenter around the garden of the church and panned up a clocktower beside it. It was a very picturesque setting but something about it gave Lucy a distinct feeling of déjà vu. The picture on screen, somehow, looked so familiar. Her eyes widened as it dawned on her.

'Dad!' she cried pointing at the screen. 'Mum!' she called, 'come and look at this.'

Her father looked up as her mother came into the room asking, 'what is it?'

Now, all three of them were staring at the screen. Paul quickly reached over and picked up the remote to increase the volume on the set. The presenter's voice quickly became loud and clear, '. . . raise another two thousand pounds to get the clock working again,' he said as the camera panned back to show the clocktower and broken clock. The scene shifted quickly back to a studio shot with the newsreader sitting behind a desk.

'What!' cried Paul in disappointment.

'Shhh,' interrupted Mary, waving him to silence.

The newsreader looked into the camera. 'Thanks there to Jonathan McGuire for that report from Garnham Green. And we wish them all the best with their fund raising efforts.'

Paul turned the volume back down and the three of them looked at one another. It was Mary that broke the thoughtful silence first. 'It did look like the one in the drawing,' she said.

'It even had a broken clock,' chimed in Lucy.

'Hmmm,' said Paul cautiously. He was reluctant to say too much just in case Lucy got her hopes up again and this turned out to be another fool's errand.

Mary looked at them both, 'what was the name of the place .. ?'

'It was called Garnham Green,' interrupted Lucy quickly. Breathless hope evident in her voice.

Mary looked at Paul and he lowered his head, closing his eyes, as he thought for a moment what the effects on Lucy would be if this was another dead end. However, after a moments reflection his shoulders sagged in resignation as he also realised that there was no way that they could not check this out. He looked up with a forced smile, 'ok, how about tomorrow we go . . .'

He got no further because Lucy launched herself at him, flinging her arms around him and crying into his chest, 'oh dad! Thank you, thank you.'

∞

The following morning all three of them were back in the car heading towards Garnham Green. Again there was a feeling of optimism, despite the numerous times Paul had made it clear that this might lead nowhere and that they shouldn't get their hopes up. It was around lunchtime when they arrived at the village, which consisted of a selection of pretty cottages and well-built houses, along with a pub, all neatly placed around a large green. Off to the left of the green, between two cottages, stood a church, with a clock tower. The clock was obviously broken as the time on it read four twenty-five.

Paul parked the car outside the pub and they all made their way over to the church. Mary made sure to bring the sketch and was continuously comparing it to the church as they walked towards it.

'It certainly looks like the one in the drawing,' she said, holding up the image and looking from one to the other.

Paul and Lucy stood beside her, moving their heads back and forth as they too made the comparison. Paul nodded towards the sign over the entrance to the churchyard, 'St Mary the Virgin of Garnham Green,' he read out.

The three of them stood for a moment looking at the church.

'So, what do we do now?' asked Paul.

Mary shrugged, 'let's have a wander around and see . . . what we can see,' she finished lamely.

With that the three of them walked through the entrance to the churchyard and up to the main building. As they approached the main door there was a notice board to the right, which they stopped and examined, just in case.

Fifteen minutes later, after they had checked and found the main door closed and locked, and had walked around the church and tower twice, Paul voiced his concern. 'Do you think it could just be a coincidence?'

Mary shrugged, as if not wanting to voice her doubts. Lucy meanwhile continued to stare up at the clock-tower as if the clock hands could, in some way, point the way to the lost violin.

Paul turned back and looked over at the car. 'How about we stop in the pub for a quick drink?' he asked. 'We could always ask the barman about the other sketch,' he said in a voice that held little hope.

Mother and daughter looked at one another and both nodded in agreement.

The pub was warm and welcoming, with what must have been a selection of regulars dotted about at tables, and around the central bar. The level of ambient noise, interspersed with the odd chuckle of laughter, was comforting and not too loud. As Lucy sat at a table Paul and Mary went to the bar. Paul to order the drinks and Mary to ask about the sketch. Once Paul had ordered small glasses of wine for Mary and himself and a coke for Lucy, Mary laid the sketch of the cottage on the bar and asked the barman if he recognised it. The barman reached down and picked up the sketch to look at it more closely. Looking back at Mary he said, 'hummm, looks like Winchester cottage to me.'

Paul and Mary looked at one another in astonishment.

'Colonel Hewitt's place,' added the barman, 'just out to the right and up Banbury Road a few yards.'

Mary smiled broadly, 'out to the right of here,' she checked, pointing back to the door they'd just come through.

'Yes,' said the barman, now pointing with his free hand, 'just to the right and then up a bit you'll see Banbury Road. Just go up there a bit and it's on the right.'

'Oh, thank you,' breathed Mary.

'You relatives or summit?' queried the barman.

'Ah, no,' replied Paul. Then added, 'it's ah, sort of a treasure hunt.'

The barman nodded, 'ah.' Then, handing the sketch back to Mary he moved away to serve another customer.

Paul and Mary took the drinks and the information back over to Lucy. All three eagerly finished their drinks and then, as they quickly made their way out of the pub called back their thanks to the barman. A few minutes later they were standing outside the front door of Winchester cottage, which looked exactly as it did in the sketch Mary held. As they stood there Mary said, 'let me do the talking.' Paul was about to object and then thought better of it and simply nodded. This agreed, Mary leant forward and knocked on the door. A minute or so later it was answered by a tall lean, well-dressed man of military bearing with a clear parade ground voice.

'Yes, hello,' he said as he opened the door. Looking at the three strangers on his doorstep he asked, 'what can I do for you?'

Mary smiled weakly. 'This may sound a bit odd,' she began, 'but we're looking for a violin.'

'A violin,' echoed the man, taking a small step back, his face frowning.

Mary continued, 'yes it was . . .'

'Ah!' the man interrupted as realisation dawned. Now, smiling broadly he said, 'a violin you say. Astounding. Won't you come in dear lady,' then quickly added, 'all of you please,' as he stepped back into the hallway, waving them in.

Once inside and made comfortable Mary re-told the story of the stolen violin and how they'd been searching for it using the help of a . . . friend. She didn't want to complicate matters by trying to explain what remote viewing was to this kindly gentleman.

'Well I'll be,' Sandy chuckled aloud after hearing the story. 'Simply astounding. Knew there was something special about that violin the moment I laid eyes on it.'

'You have it!' cried Lucy, unable to stop herself.

'Yes m'dear,' answered Sandy rising from his chair to fetch the instrument. As he returned from the next room holding the case containing the violin he said, 'for some reason I just couldn't bring myself to part with it.' Now however, he walked over and placed the case on Lucy's lap. 'The instrument to its rightful owner,' he intoned with cheerful solemnity.

Lucy yelped upon seeing the case. 'Oh Terpsi!' She hugged the case to her chest as if she'd never let it go again. Then quickly unzipping the lid checked to see if the instrument was intact.

'All present and correct,' said Sandy with a brief nod of acknowledgement.

Paul and Mary were so thankful, and more relieved than they could say to see Lucy back to her old self. They also made it clear that they would cover any costs to ensure that Sandy wasn't out of pocket. Sandy was affably good natured about the whole affair and said that he was pleased to have been a small part in what he considered to be an astonishing story. The meeting ended well with all three adults taking some pleasure in seeing Lucy reunited with her instrument.

The following week Paul had to be coerced into driving Mary and Lucy back to see Mr Stevenson. He couldn't understand why they had to visit the man in person and argued that surely a cheque in the post would cover any fee, and that it would be much easier. Mary ignored his complaints, cryptically telling him that it was essential, but not why. This didn't seem to ease matters with Paul, despite the fact that they'd now recovered the stolen violin. Mary thought it was him just being stubborn and there was an element of truth to this. However, it was also because Paul felt distinctly uncomfortable about going back to see a man he'd maligned as a fraud. He was also a little shaken when he thought about how the sketches that the man had produced were so remarkably similar to the buildings they eventually found. The whole thing seemed to give him the uneasy feeling that perhaps there was more to life than he was prepared to admit, and that maybe there really was something to all of this remote viewing stuff after all. Attempting to suppress such thoughts it was with a distinct sense of duty that he drove them all back to Sycamore Close the following Saturday. On arrival Lucy took the lead and rang the bell. Within moments the door opened, and Mr Stevenson stood in the doorway.

'Ah,' he said, with a broad smile as he looked at Lucy holding her violin case, 'your mum told me you'd be over today.' Looking at them all he stepped back and waved them in eagerly, 'come in, come in.'

The three of them entered the hallway, divesting themselves of their coats and shoes before being guided into the now familiar lounge. Gary was a genial host, making no mention of Paul's behaviour during their last visit, and provided them with tea and biscuits, asking to be told the story of how they'd found the lost violin. Mary provided a detailed account of their adventure at the end of which, Lucy stood up and with a resolutely serious face said, 'and now I've come to pay the fee.'

Paul's concerned face shifted from Lucy to Mary as he wondered what had been arranged.

'Ooh, just let me get comfortable,' said Gary settling back into his armchair.

Lucy unzipped her case, took out her violin and stood.

A few minutes later, the beautiful sound of Mozart's violin sonata, number twenty-six in B-flat major, floated out of the house and drifted on the late summer breeze along Sycamore Close.

2

Silver Futures

The soft background music of the funeral parlour and the hushed conversations created an atmosphere of quiet serenity, as Diane made her way down the walkway between the two groups of mourners. Despite her seventy years, she still managed to retain an air of understated elegance that was reflected in her slender stature and the simple but expensive black dress she'd decided on. As she walked along the aisle, she nodded in recognition at those family members she knew, gently smiling at those she didn't, all the while scanning for the one person she wanted to see.

There! Seated on the left of the walkway with other friends was Sylvia.

Whilst there were a good number of people in the crematorium it wasn't full. Nevertheless, it was clear that Sylvia was saving her a space because as soon as she spotted Diane, she waved her over with a hand holding a damp tissue like a flag of truce. Diane smiled to see her and made her way along past those already seated, making her apologies as she squeezed by. Eventually, she reached Sylvia and sat in the vacantly held spot. As she sat down she looked at her friend and smiled. 'How are you?' she asked quietly.

Sylvia dabbed at her eyes with a now soggy tissue, 'oh ok' she sniffed. 'I'm no good at funerals,' she added with a weak smile. Then brightened a little. 'Nice dress by the way, is that from M&S?'

'No, Fenwicks,' said Diane, pleased that she could still evoke a compliment about the way she looked. 'You know what they say. Once you get to a certain age you need to invest in a good black dress because. . .'

' . . . you'll be going to a lot more funerals,' finished Sylvia with a weak laugh.

The two friends leant in towards one another and hugged. Diane lowered her head towards Sylvia saying 'you look lovely by the way. Very smart.'

Sylvia shrugged a little, 'I don't really like black. Not sure why we always have to wear black at funerals, it's not as if there isn't already enough to make you feel sad at these things without having to wear black.'

Diane just smiled, nodding in sympathy. She knew there was a growing trend to wear more colourful outfits to a funeral nowadays, particularly amongst the younger generation, but she still thought that there was something about wearing black to a funeral that conveyed the proper level of respect. Also, not having to think too much about what colour to wear meant she could spend a bit more time, and money, on buying a more stylish black dress. Diane reflected to herself for a moment wondering whether thinking about how good she could look in a black dress was really the sort of thing she should be thinking about at a funeral. It wasn't as if she didn't miss Margaret, but, she thought, you get to an age and realise that life is simply for living and you need to take every moment of joy you can, because it doesn't last long.

As Sylvia reached for her bag to extract another tissue the vicar walked to the front and took up his position behind the podium. He cleared his voice in a weak apologetic manner to gain their attention, 'Ah, er, ladies and gentlemen, thank you.' The congregation stood.

'We are gathered here today,' he continued, 'to celebrate the life and passing of Margaret Jane Oakwood.' His voice and liturgy faded into the background as Diane shed a silent tear and Sylvia sniffed noisily into another tissue.

After the service they both met briefly with family and friends outside to pass on their condolences and offer support where they could. When the offers of support and shared memories of Margaret reached a natural lull Sylvia turned to Diane and asked, 'are you going on to the wake?'

'Yes, I think so,' Diane responded with a gentle nod. After all, she thought, I've got to get as much value out of this dress as I can. Then said, 'I think it will be nice to share some of our memories of Margaret with the family and let them know what a wonderful person she was and how much she cared for them.'

'Not to mention the free food and drink,' said Sylvia with a smirk.

'As you say,' Diane replied with an air of mock indifference.

'Good,' said Sylvia. 'Can you give me a lift then?'

Diane looked down at her friend and smiled with genuine affection. 'Of course.'

Ten minutes later they were both seated in Diane's car and Sylvia quickly broke the short silence by asking, 'what's going to happen to the syndicate, now Margaret's gone?'

Ah, thought Diane as she let the hand brake off and gently accelerated the car out of the car park, I wondered when we would get to this. But all she said was, 'hmmm,' in a thoughtful but non-committal manner.

'Does this mean we will have to disband now?' asked Sylvia, the concern in her voice clearly evident.

'Nnoo,' said Diane slowly. 'I don't think so.'

'Good,' said Sylvia relieved, 'because I've got used to the money.'

'We don't just do it for the money,' reproached Diane mildly.

'Oh, I know, I know,' Sylvia responded quickly, working to quell any potential disharmony. 'I like the challenge too, and it gets me out of the house and despite my worries early on that it was a bit bonkers it really is fun.'

Diane smiled indulgently. A bit bonkers she thought. Yes, that nicely sums it up.

'But,' continued Sylvia, 'I do also like the money,' she said, her smile turning into a grin.

'Hmmm,' said Diane thoughtfully. 'Well, I've had an idea.'

Sylvia waited. This is what she'd hoped for. Diane was good at ideas. Afterall, the syndicate was her idea in the first place and a damn good idea it'd turned out to be as well.

'Do you know Rowena Stevens?' asked Diane.

'Lives at number 32,' responded Sylvia quickly. 'The one with the gnomes in the front garden, husband died last year.'

Diane nodded, 'yes, exactly.'

Sylvia waited expectantly.

'Well,' said Diane, 'I've been thinking that she would be a good person to have in the syndicate because she's on her own, now that her two sons have moved out. So, she'd have the time and if she's living on her widow's pension, she might also be glad of a little extra.

Sylvia smiled nodding in thoughtful agreement.

'And,' Diane continued, 'I hear that she runs a meditation class at the village hall on a Thursday evening and I'm sure I read on the ARV website, or one of the blogs somewhere, that meditation was a good thing for remote viewing.'

'Ooh, good,' responded Sylvia, pleased that she'd also remembered that ARV meant Associative Remote Viewing. Though the blogging thing still left her a bit uncertain. 'Could even improve our scores,' she added with a grin.

'Hmmm,' Diane murmured, 'possibly. I was thinking of using the meditation as a way in. You know start with that and try to lead on to remote viewing.'

'Sounds like a good idea to me,' agreed Sylvia. 'When do you think you'll speak to her?'

'Oh soon,' responded Diane. 'I'd like to get the group sorted so we can start up again next month if possible.'

Two days later Diane found herself standing outside the small bungalow of Rowena Stevens, her tanned leather document holder in her arms, having just rung the bell. As she waited by the front door she turned a little and looked back over the well-kept front garden with the various gnomes in playful postures spread about between the colourful flowers. Hmmm, she thought, definitely someone with time on their hands, which could be a good thing. The noise of the lock being turned, and the door opening, brought her back to the present and her mission as she turned to face the woman at the door. Rowena Stevens was a little shorter than Diane. She would, Diane thought kindly, be called petite. Also, like a lot of Asian women she had lustrous golden-brown skin which made it difficult to get a clear idea of her age. Somewhat unexpectedly she was dressed in a loose-fitting hooded sweatshirt and grey leggings. It was this seemingly odd attire that momentarily threw Diane for a second and it must have shown on her face as Rowena smiled broadly and said apologetically, 'oh sorry about the outfit. I've just been taking my online yoga class.'

'Oh, I didn't mean to interrupt,' started Diane.

'Not a problem,' said Rowena before Diane could continue. 'It finished ten minutes ago, I just haven't bothered to change yet.'

There was a moments silence as the two women carefully sized one another up.

'Sorry,' apologised Rowena, 'where are my manners. Would you like to come in?'

'Oh, thank you,' said Diane smiling gently.

'You're Mrs Aston, aren't you?' enquired Rowena as she closed the door behind Diane and led her along the hallway to a small kitchen at the back of the house.

'Yes, but please call me Diane.'

'Well Diane, please come on through,' she said in a gentle melodic voice. 'I'd only just put the kettle on if you'd like a cup of tea?'

'That would be lovely,' Diane answered. 'If I'm not interrupting.'

'Not at all. As I say, I'd finished my yoga class about ten minutes ago and was just thinking about what to do next. Have a seat,' she indicated a chair at the small kitchen table, 'and I'll sort out the tea. Is Earl Grey ok with you?'

'Ooh yes,' answered Diane smiling, 'definitely.' She sat down and placed her document holder on the table.

The next few minutes were taken up with Rowena gliding about the kitchen sorting out cups and saucers, pouring milk into a small jug and placing a selection of biscuits on a delicate plate. As she did this Diane looked around, noting that the kitchen was spotlessly clean and the few ornaments on show were both tasteful and elegant. She also noticed the various pictures of family adorning the walls.

'My sons, Adam and Peter,' said Rowena, nodding in the direction of the pictures Diane had been looking at. 'Both moved away now,' she continued in a voice that failed to hide the sadness of this remark. 'Makes the place seem extra quiet since I lost Alan last year.'

Diane winced a little as she heard the popular euphemism. It was one she particularly disliked and couldn't understand why people used it. After all, it's not as if the person in question was really lost, wandering about down a supermarket isle somewhere, unable to find his wife or way out. They weren't lost, she thought irritably, they were dead. Her husband, Stephen, had died five years ago and she knew exactly where he was. Or at least his ashes. Still, she mused to herself, at least she didn't say he'd 'passed'. As in, my husband has passed. Diane always wanted to ask passed what, with what grade and does that mean life really is some sort of test. And what does that mean for those of us left behind – that we've failed?

Rowena's gentle rising voice brought her back to the conversation, 'I said, would you like milk?'

'Oh, I'm sorry,' apologised Diane, 'mind wandered a bit there I'm afraid. What, hmm, milk? Ah, no, thank you.'

'So,' said Rowena, now that the tea had been served and both ladies were seated comfortably at the table, teacups in hands. 'Are you collecting for charity or is it volunteering?'

Diane smiled, looking down at her lap and trying to think about how best to approach this. She frowned in thought for a moment and then looked up at Rowena, 'ah, well neither actually.'

Rowena raised her eyes in mock surprise.

Diane continued, 'it's more of a proposition.'

Rowena frowned a little and turned her head onto one side, looking now at the document holder on the table.

Diane hesitated for a moment as if she were trying to decide what to say. She pursed her lips and decided to just try her luck. 'I know you run the meditation class on Thursday evenings at the village hall.'

'Ye'es,' responded Rowena cautiously.

'And I'm sure over time you've probably had people tell you that meditation is all a lot of nonsense.'

'Yes,' answered Rowena, a bit more firmly this time.

'But to get the real benefits of something like meditation you'd need to be a bit open minded' continued Diane. 'Be open to trying new things and open to the idea that we don't know everything that there is to know.'

'Hmmmm,' agreed Rowena.

'Well,' hesitated Diane, 'how open minded are you?'

Rowena placed her cup and saucer gently back on the table and sat upright, her eyes alight with curiosity. 'Now I am intrigued.'

∞

Diane reached across the table picked up her document holder, opened it and took out a small selection of papers, a couple of magazines and a book. On the top of these was a printed A4 sheet containing a list of websites and other details. Diane gathered them together neatly and then looked up at Rowena.

'I've created a list of resources' she began, 'and put together a selection of scientific papers, a couple of magazines from the society that I'm a member of, and what I think is a useful book introducing the topic.'

Rowena frowned, looking a little confused and cautiously said 'and I need all this because?'

'Because' said Diane smiling with the knowledge of what was about to come, 'you are going to want to check that what I'm telling you is real and not just the deluded ramblings of some mad old woman. And they'll also give you access to a wider selection of information that you can look at in your own time. And' she went on, 'because it can sometimes take a while for what I tell you to make sense and sink in.'

Rowena leant forward asking, 'Diane, precisely what are you telling me?'

'Ok,' began Diane, 'have you heard of clairvoyance?'

'Err, yes,' answered Rowena looking more confused and beginning to wonder where this odd conversation might be going.

'What is it?' Diane asked.

Rowena frowned again. Was this some sort of test she thought. She leant back a little in her chair as she worked to put together an answer. 'Well, I think it's when someone whose psychic is able to see things, or people, or events that aren't really there.'

Diane smiled in encouragement. 'Well, I want to introduce you to a term called remote viewing.'

'Remote viewing,' echoed Rowena. 'What does that mean?' she asked.

'Well,' continued Diane, 'it's similar to clairvoyance because a remote viewer is someone who's trained themselves to try and see things such as distant events, or people.'

'It sounds the same to me,' said Rowena.

'It is very similar' conceded Diane, 'but the remote viewer is fully awake and not in any form of a trance. Not that all clairvoyants need to be in a trance,' she added quickly. 'Also,' she continued, 'there are different types of remote viewing depending on what it is that you are trying to see.'

'Ok,' nodded Rowena, still not sure where this was taking her.

'In particular there's a form of remote viewing called associative remote viewing[1].'

Rowena simply nodded, still looking cautious and unsure.

Feeling a little more sure of her ground now Diane continued, 'this is where an individual tries to remotely see a target that is associated with some sort of future activity or outcome.'

'What!' burst out Rowena with a snort. 'Seeing the future. Are you kidding?'

Diane was unsurprised by Rowena's reaction. She'd been involved in remote viewing long enough to have heard people tell her what was and what wasn't real or possible. She also knew that most people simply thought that reality consisted only of what they'd experienced themselves. And that anything falling outside of their experiences was either deeply suspicious or nonsense. 'I know how this sounds,' she said. 'But it is real and there is genuine evidence for it.'

There was a moments silence.

'Is that what all this is?' asked Rowena waving her hand at the materials Diane had brought along.

'Yes,' answered Diane. She took the book from the pile of papers and handed it to Rowena. 'This for instance is a good introduction to the area from someone whose been involved in remote viewing for the military in America.'

Rowena took the book looking at the title. The large black letters read '*The essential guide to remote viewing*[2]' by Paul Smith, a retired army Major it noted underneath. She flicked through the pages briefly scanning the images and text. On the back she noticed the highlighted text stating "*our minds are more than just our brains"* something she'd always felt was true when talking to people about the benefits of meditation.

Diane then handed her a couple of colourful magazines.

Rowena read the titles, '*Aperture*[3]' and at the bottom of the front page it read 'magazine published by the International Remote Viewing Association.' Again, she flicked through them browsing briefly at the editorials, feature articles and various book reviews. She skim read some of the articles, flicking from page to page. What she read made her head spin a little. It all seemed so unreal. It was as if someone had come along and told her magic was real. When this thought occurred to her she smiled slightly as she could see the first review on the back cover of the book Diane had just given her saying "it sounds like magic. It's not."

Rowena nodded her head towards the remaining papers in Diane's hands asking, 'and those?'

'These are just a few scientific articles on the subject. They are a lot less fun to read,' Diane said with a short grimace and apologetic tone, 'and a bit dry in places but they've all been published in peer reviewed scientific journals so might help to convince you that I'm telling you the truth.'

Rowena put the magazines down and said cautiously, 'and why is it important that I'm convinced you are telling me the truth?'

'Because I run,' and then Diane stopped and did a quick re-take. 'I *used* to run a small syndicate where we used associative remote viewing to predict the outcome of the silver futures market to make money.'

Rowena's mouth fell open as a look of mild surprise spread over her face. She shook her head a little as if to dislodge an uncomfortable thought. Then a broad smile began to spread across her face, 'wait a minute, you're not. . .'

'No,' interrupted Diane gently shaking her head. 'I'm not joking. Everything I'm telling you is the absolute' she hesitated for a moment, 'ok, I'm not sure there is an absolute truth as such but everything I've told you and all this,' she indicated the book, magazines and papers, 'is all true.'

'Hold on,' said Rowena, 'you said "used to", does that mean you no longer do it?'

'Well,' conceded Diane with a little sadness in her voice, 'the group consisted of me, Sylvia Winchester and Margaret Oakwood.'

As soon as Margaret's name was mentioned Rowena bowed her head slightly and said 'ah, yes.' She reached across and placed a comforting hand on Diane's arm, 'I heard about her passing. I'm sorry if she was a good friend of yours.'

Diane let the euphemism go without comment and simply said 'thank you. Yes, she was.'

'And you used association . . .' Rowena asked, the confusion in her voice clear, 'what was it again?'

'It's *associative* remote viewing,' answered Diane emphasising the word associative. 'It's where you associate a specific future outcome, in this case the rising or falling prices on the silver futures market, with an object.'

Rowena still looked a little sceptical, but her interest was also beginning to show as she asked, 'and you made money at this?'

'We did'.

'And you're telling me this because . . . ?'

'Because,' said Diane looking into Rowena's eyes, 'we would like you to join us and become part of the syndicate.'

'Why me?'

'You're smart, active and open minded.'

'Hmmm,' responded Rowena sounding unconvinced. 'But why do you need another person? Why don't the two of you. Who was it' she said working to recall the names. 'Ah yes, why don't you and Sylvia just carry on. Surely, you'd earn even more money if it was split between the two of you.'

'Three is an optimum number,' said Diane. 'It helps deal with uncertainties because then there's always a majority view. If only two people decide we could end up in a situation where one person thinks the price will rise and the other thinks it will fall. This just leads to a stalemate. Also,' she added before Rowena could interrupt, 'it's not just about the money. It may sound odd but there's also an important element of fun.'

'Fun,' repeated Rowena, her eyebrows raising in mild surprise. It had been a while since she'd had any fun.

'Yes,' said Diane nodding and smiling broadly this time. 'It's definitely fun.'

Rowena sat there smiling a little but shaking her head. 'I . . . I, er, don't know what to think'.

'Look,' said Diane, 'let me leave these here,' she indicated the book, magazines and papers, 'so you can look through them at your leisure and get used to idea. Then, in a week or so if you're interested in finding out more just let me know.' As she said this she wrote her number on the bottom of the A4 sheet. 'This is my mobile number so you can either call me or text me.'

'And if I'm not interested' queried Rowena.

'Then I won't bother you again.'

'And all this.'

'Keep them,' said Diane with a small shrug, 'I've lots of materials and have copies of all these.'

Rowena raised her eyebrows but didn't say anything.

Diane got up from her chair and Rowena automatically stood as well. 'Errrm' hesitated Diane initially looking down at her feet, but then reluctantly continued, 'look. One more thing. If you do read the book, you'll come across something called project stargate[4]. Please try to keep an open mind as I'm rather afraid it reads rather like an episode of the X Files.' As she said this she smiled weakly and shrugged a little in seeming embarrassment.

'Ha ha ha,' Rowena burst out, 'this whole thing feels like an episode of the X Files.'

Diane looked a little shamefaced, 'I know,' she said with an apologetic shrug.

Rowena laughed good naturedly, 'don't worry,' she said, 'I can keep an open mind.'

'That's all I ask,' said Diane thankfully. 'And now I'll leave you in peace.'

They both made their way back along the hallway to the front door. As they reached it Rowena leant forward, opening the door and stepping aside to let Diane out. As Diane went to pass she stopped and gave Rowena a brief hug 'thanks for listening' she said.

'Thanks for coming,' answered Rowena smiling. 'I'll be in touch' she added nodding goodbye and closing the door. As the door clicked closed Rowena turned and leant back against the door. She shook her head gently still feeling slightly bewildered. She wasn't sure whether to laugh or . . . what. Then she remembered the materials Diane had left on the kitchen table and pursed her lips in thought as she made her way back to the kitchen intent on finding out what this was all about.

∞

It was two weeks later when Diane received a text message from Rowena asking her to come round that Friday evening for a chat and a glass of wine. Diane took this as a good sign and smiled to herself when she read through the message hoping this meant that Rowena was interested in becoming the third member of their little syndicate. Later that evening Diane found herself once again waiting outside the front door of Rowena's house having just rung the bell. This time the door opened after only a brief pause suggesting that Rowena might have been waiting for her. The two women smiled in greeting and briefly hugged one another as Rowena then led Diane into the lounge.

As they entered the room Rowena indicated one of two armchairs, 'please have a seat' she said taking the other chair.

'Thanks,' said Diane, noticing the wine bottle in its ice jacket in between two glasses with a bowl of nibbles on a tray between the two chairs. She smiled to herself briefly thinking that this boded well.

'Is white wine ok?' asked Rowena as she reached out to pour them each a good measure.

'Yes, that's fine,' answered Diane.

'It's one of the organic ones from the local wine store,' explained Rowena. 'I thought it might be a bit nicer.' She held out one of the glasses to Diane.

Diane smiled politely and took the proffered glass and raising it slightly said, 'cheers.'

'Cheers,' responded Rowena who sat back in her chair and took a long sip of her wine. 'Ah, that's better,' she sighed, smiling.

Diane took a small sip of her wine. It was good, and nicely chilled. 'Hhmm,' she agreed, 'yes, nice and fruity.' She took another small sip and then placed the glass back on the table between the two chairs then sat back comfortably. She smiled at Rowena but said nothing. She thought the signs were good but wanted Rowena to steer the conversation. She didn't have to wait long. After a brief pause Rowena laughed delicately shaking her head, 'you were right' she said, 'all that stuff,' she waved her arm towards the kitchen to indicate the materials Diane had previously left. 'It did read like an episode of the X Files'.

Diane made a wry face and nodded saying, 'I know.'

'I,' began Rowena hesitantly, 'I . . . I still can't believe how much information there is out there'.

Diane waited.

'Talk about hiding in plain sight,' Rowena continued as she took another sip of her wine. 'I checked out the website you recommended. You're a member of the organisation aren't you?' she asked.

'Yes,' answered Diane. 'It's called IRVA, the International Remote Viewing Association[5].'

'How long have you been a member?'

'Just over four years.'

'Why did you join?' asked Rowena genuinely intrigued.

'After Stephen died' answered Diane, 'I wanted,' then she stopped. 'No,' she corrected herself after a moment's hesitation, 'I *needed* something to do. I'd always been interested in the esoteric and the unusual and I'd attended a couple of meditation retreats and it was at one of these that I came across a book in one of the libraries there that mentioned remote viewing, along with lots of other things.'

'Was it the one you leant me?' asked Rowena.

'No, it was called "The Conscious Universe[6]". I remember it well because at the time I was thinking a lot about Stephen and whether his consciousness, or whatever, still existed or not and the title just seemed to call out to me. Anyway, in that book I remember reading a bit about remote viewing and how some people had tried to use it to make money on Wall Street.' Diane hesitated for a moment before continuing in a conspiratorial voice, 'I don't know if you know but Stephen started out as a trader so I had some understanding of how these things worked and it piqued my interest. So, I decided to find out more.'

'And that led you to the IRVA?' asked Rowena.

'Yes,' answered Diane. 'I became a member and enrolled on some of the courses and over time improved my understanding of remote viewing, especially associative remote viewing, and eventually this led me to set-up our little ARV syndicate along with Sylvia and Margaret about two years ago and ever since we'd been working together, having a bit of fun and making a bit of money.'

'I read,' Rowena said cautiously looking carefully at Diane for her reaction, 'that a group of researchers made over $100,000 in stock trading back in the 80's and that this made the headlines of the Wall Street Journal[7].'

'True,' nodded Diane.

'But not everyone's been so successful,' continued Rowena still watching Diane for her response. 'I also read that some of those who'd tried to replicate the earlier successes lost all their money[8].'

'Also true,' agreed Diane.

'So, this isn't a guarantee then?' asked Rowena.

'No,' responded Diane smiling. 'There's only one guarantee in life,' she said.

Rowena nodded in understanding. 'So, what makes you think that if I join your syndicate, we'll be successful?' she asked leaning forward slightly.

Diane was pleased to hear Rowena use the term "we" when describing the syndicate. It was a good step forward. She pursed her lips a little as she responded, 'attitude and practice.'

Rowena frowned a little, took another sip of wine and sat back.

Diane leant forward to explain. 'The right attitude is essential. You need to be conscientious, committed and open minded. It also helps to know that the technique is completely real and that it works.'

'Is that what all the introductory materials were for?' asked Rowena.

'To an extent yes.' She paused and then added, 'let me try and explain.' Diane paused for a moment, pursed her lips in concentration as she tried to come up with a useful analogy that might help clarify the situation and make sense. Still thinking she added, 'you see, there's no point in training to improve performance if you're not even sure the technique itself works.' Her face brightened a little as an idea occurred to her. 'It would be like learning to play the piano but never being sure that when you hit a key with your finger that this would cause the hammer to strike a string sounding a note.' Diane looked at Rowena in the hope that this made sense and was relieved to see her nod a little in understanding. Encouraged, Diane continued, 'never being sure a note would play would undermine your practice.'

'Ok,' said Rowena now beginning to sound both more convinced and more interested, 'what does the practice involve?'

'Time, motivation and a sense of fun,' Diane answered with a smile.

'Can you give me an example?' asked Rowena.

'Yes, of course. Pick two objects that you know really, really well, and that are as different as they could be from one another. For example, one could be soft the other hard, one light the other dark, one light the other heavy, you get the point. It helps as well if you've had the objects for some time as this'll mean your very familiar with them.'

'Ookay,' answered Rowena slowly. She thought for a moment and then said with a slight air of triumph, 'ok, got them.'

'What are they?' asked Diane.

'A bright red silk scarf that Alan used to wear when we went to the theatre together.' Rowena answered, then bowed her head for a moment and smiled a little wistfully. She looked back up at Diane, 'and a dark purple amethyst crystal that the boys gave me for my fortieth birthday.'

Diane nodded in approval as she pictured the two objects in her mind's eye. They certainly seemed to capture the essence of two different objects. 'Ok,' she said, 'make one of them a "yes" object and the other one a "no" object.'

This only took Rowena a couple of seconds before she responded, 'the scarf is yes and the crystal no.'

Diane continued, 'now imagine that it's a Monday morning and you're trying to remotely see into your future to find out which of these two objects you'll be holding as you sit here on Friday afternoon.'

Rowena looked a little dubious at this but decided to go along with it. After all she thought, it can't be any more crazy than what I've already come across, so she nodded slightly to show she was playing along.

'For the sake of argument,' continued Diane, 'let's just say you call the scarf making it a "yes" response. This means that the price of silver futures will rise over the week which means that we,' she paused for a moment, 'that is the syndicate - will purchase stock on the Monday and then sell it at the end of trade on the Friday.'

'And I suppose,' interrupted Rowena, 'that if I call the crystal this means "no" which means what? That you, I mean we, buy stock?'

'It can do,' responded Diane, 'but not always. If the price goes down at the end of the week it simply means we don't sell that week but we may buy more stocks depending on the amount of capital left.'

Rowena thought for a moment. 'Oh,' she nodded in understanding. 'And because you sell at a higher price than you bought, you make money?' she said.

'Essentially yes,' answered Diane. 'However,' she continued, 'the important bit is that on the Friday afternoon when I contact you to let you know whether the stocks went up or down you then sit in that chair and hold the relevant object in your lap trying to connect with yourself on the previous Monday morning.'

Rowena sat still for a moment remaining tight lipped and tried not to laugh at how ludicrous this sounded. 'So, each week on a Monday morning I'm trying to guess. . .'

'Not guess,' interrupted Diane, 'remotely view the correct object.'

'Oh yes, sorry,' apologised Rowena. 'I remotely view the object I'll be holding on Friday.'

'Yes.'

Rowena frowned slightly for a moment lost in thought and then cried out. 'Ah, I've got it. And because each object is associated with a different course of action, such as yes-no or sell-buy, that's why it's called *associative* remote viewing,' she finished, feeling rather proud of herself.

'Exactly,' nodded Diane.

'But then,' Rowena frowned, 'if this works,' and then she added quickly, 'and the evidence you've shown me, and what I've seen online seems to indicate that it does.' She paused as she looked directly at Diane, 'then why aren't more people doing this?'

Diane sat back in her chair and smiled. 'Well,' she began, 'first, how do you know they're not?'

Rowena looked a little taken aback.

'After all,' continued Diane, 'if you were using this method to make money would you tell anyone about it?'

Rowena thought for a moment. 'Oh, err, probably not,' she agreed quietly thinking how people might respond if you told them you were trying to make money by seeing which object your future self might be holding.

'Also,' continued Diane, 'in all likelihood most people either haven't heard of this, or even if they have, they probably don't believe it works so just ignore it.'

'Ha ha,' laughed Rowena weakly taking another sip of her wine, 'now that, I can believe.'

Diane went on, 'and I've been on enough training courses and workshops to know that even when the small minority of people who do come across this take the time to figure out whether its real or not and try it out, most of them give up within a week or two.'

'Really,' asked Rowena, 'why?'

'Because it requires commitment, practice and patience and people generally want instant results,' said Diane in a slightly exasperated tone. 'And, when they don't get them, they become disheartened and give up.' As she said this she leaned forward and picked up her glass taking another small sip of wine. 'Hmm,' she said appreciatively, 'this really is very good.' She took another small sip and put the glass back down on the table.

Rowena smiled, pleased to know that her wine selection had been a good one. 'So how come you didn't give up?' she asked.

'That's where the syndicate helps,' said Diane. 'Having a group of friends to share the experience with helps to keep you motivated, when the going gets tough as it were.'

'Hmm,' Rowena nodded in understanding.

'Also,' added Diane 'with a group of friends meeting on a regular basis there is definitely a social element to it which helps to make it feel a lot more like fun.'

There was a short silence during which Rowena thought about all that they'd discussed. After a few moments she broke the silence by asking, 'so where do we go from here?'

'That depends on you,' said Diane.

Rowena sat in thoughtful silence for a few minutes. As she sat there she shook her head slightly as she thought how bizarre the whole thing still sounded. Even so, she thought to herself, she knew the topic was real. She'd just spent the last two weeks reading all the materials Diane had left and even spent time reading about the research that the IRVA was involved in. She frowned a little in concentration thinking about what she should do next, even though deep down she already knew the answer. She smiled a little as she realised she was simply stalling and that she was definitely hooked. Her smile broadened as she thought of becoming part of the syndicate. The regular meetings, the chance to try something new. A part of her also wondered how good she'd be at remote viewing. With these thoughts running through her mind she reached out and picked up the wine bottle topping up first Diane's glass and then refilling her own. As she put the bottle back down she looked across to Diane and raised her glass. 'I'm in', she said with a broad grin.

Diane picked up her glass and toasted the newest member of the syndicate. 'Welcome to the ARV club,' she said smiling.

∞

It was many trials and months later that the ARV club were having their end of year meeting to agree their annual pay-out. The three women, elegantly attired in long evening dresses, were at the cocktail bar of the local Hilton Hotel. As they sat in the stylish black leather chairs Rowena looked around at the modern art on the walls and the smartly dressed waiters and waitresses serving the equally well-dressed clientele, all with seemingly understated efficiency. She also noticed they were all young and good looking, adding to the air of elegance. She'd never been in here before and thought she might feel a little out of place but in fact she felt quite thrilled by the glamour. Looking across at Diane and Sylvia she realised that they seemed to be quite at home in the plush surroundings which made her wonder if they came here every year to divide up the winnings. This last thought brought her mind back to the many ARV trials she'd now completed, and she thought back to her initial meeting with Diane all those months ago. The weekly trials had certainly been challenging, particularly in the early weeks as she was keen to show that not only could she do it but that she could do it well. After a while she'd settled into a sort of routine and developed a real knack for figuring out which object she'd be holding on a Friday afternoon. It helped, she admitted to herself, that she got on well with the other members of the group. As she thought about the other group members, she realised that each of them brought something different to the group and that perhaps in this way it made the group more than the sum of its parts.

Just then a smart young waiter interrupted her thoughts by asking whether they would like to order.

Diane leant forward, clearly happy to take charge of the situation, 'we'd like three French 75's please,' she said as if this were something she ordered regularly.

There was a little squeal of delight as Sylvia said, 'ooh, one of the fizzy ones, oh I do like those.'

Rowena smiled at them, happy to let Diane take the lead in this situation.

As the waiter left with their order Diane reached into her small black leather clip bag and took out a couple of slips of paper, handing one each to Sylvia and Rowena.

Rowena looked down at the slip of paper in her hand. It showed a reasonable figure made out in pounds sterling. Looking up she asked 'is that the figure for the group?'

'No,' said Diane shaking her head slightly. 'That's the dividend we each receive after deductions and expenses.'

Rowena's face brightened, 'are you sure?' she asked just wanting to be certain.

'Yes,' Diane answered. 'Absolutely sure.'

'I have to say' continued Rowena, 'it's more than I anticipated.'

'Good,' Diane said a little smugly.

Sylvia however seemed perfectly content with the figure as if it was what she'd been expecting. 'Looks like we had a good year' she said.

'We did' answered Diane.

Sylvia looked over at Rowena 'what will you do with yours?' she asked.

Rowena shook her head a little. Still a bit stunned by the amount. 'I'm not sure' she replied. 'I was hoping to get enough for a small holiday' she faltered, 'but, but. . this is more than I'd hoped for' she finished, a smile spreading across her face. She looked back at Sylvia, 'what will you do?' she asked.

Sylvia beamed back at her. 'Well, for a start there'll be some nice presents for the children and grandchildren and then I'll be having Christmas at Claridge's.' She looked across at Diane, 'how about you Di?' she asked.

Diane sat in thought for a moment. 'Definitely a Christmas trip to Fortnum's' she began, 'and then possibly one of those Mediterranean cruises' she said with a wistful smile. 'Certainly, somewhere warm for the winter.'

Just then the waiter returned with their drinks. He placed the three nicely full champagne flutes on the table between them, each glass delicately placed on its own little decorative paper coaster. Beside the glasses he placed a small stand with some petits fours. Then he looked up and asked if there would be anything else to which he was told no thank you and so left discretely.

As one, the three women leant forward, each selecting a glass of the sparking cocktail. Then they looked across at each other and Diane, raising her glass, said 'to bright futures.'

Rowena laughed a little and interrupted, 'to silver futures,' she said with a broad smile.

The three friends laughed happily as they clinked their glasses in unison.

∞

3

Spinning Wheels within Wheels

Dr James Preston straightened his light blue silk tie and smoothed down his jacket as he made his way along the large open corridor of the Home Office building, to the office of Sir Carmichael Harrington, his new boss. James was a young man of 28, tall at just on six feet but slim, with light sandy hair, blue eyes and a bright intelligent face. This was his first post since completing a PhD in psychology at Oxford and he was interested to find out what project he'd be working on. As he walked along the corridor his mind wandered back to the initial disappointment and protestations of his PhD supervisor, Professor Andrews, when James had made it clear to him that once he'd finished his PhD he wouldn't be pursuing a career in academia.

He'd told Andrews that the short-term rather poorly paid academic positions on offer didn't really appeal to him, and he wasn't at all keen on the idea of trying to teach disinterested undergraduates. Neither of which seemed to have gone down well with Andrews. However, he had said how much he'd enjoyed research and if possible, he was going to try to find a role outside of academia that could in some way incorporate this. Professor Andrews had initially tried to persuade him to re-think his decision. However, once it became clear that James really had no intention of becoming an academic Andrews mentioned a research position that he'd heard of on the grapevine that was based within the civil service, somewhere in the Home Office. He wasn't sure what the project was, or even if there was a specific project, but he did know that they were seeking someone with good research skills and a background knowledge in human psychology. James said that this sounded much more the sort of thing he'd be interested in, and Professor Andrews put him in touch with a civil servant by the name of Henry Cavendish who arranged an interview. The interview had gone well, and after various background checks James had been offered the post of researcher. Arriving now at the large wooden door of the outer office James knocked politely and then entered. The outer office was simply laid out and bright. There was a desk to the right, behind which an young woman in a dark trouser suit was efficiently typing at a computer, to the left there was a row of three comfy chairs beneath tall windows and at the end was another door, presumably into the main office.

As he entered, the woman behind the desk paused her typing and looked up, 'Dr James Preston?' she enquired.

'Yes,' said James with a smile.

'If you'd like to have a seat,' she said, indicating a row of seats opposite with a nod of her head, 'Sir Harrington will be with you very shortly.'

'Thank you,' said James taking the end seat nearest the inner office door.

The woman resumed her typing and James took a seat, wondering what sort of project he'd be working on. He'd raised the matter a few times during his civil service induction training, but each time he asked about the nature of the research he'd be involved in he was told, firmly and politely, that once his induction was over he'd be allocated to project by the head of the department, Sir Carmichael Harrington. He smiled a little thinking to himself how this clear adherence to procedure reflected the nature of the way things were done in the service. Sitting here now he looked over at the inner door and wondered what sort of man Sir Carmichael Harrington was. He'd vaguely heard of Harrington before but wasn't sure what his background was. He knew the man must come from a wealthy background, you only had to look at his hand made Savile Row suits to work that one out. There was also some speculation that he'd served abroad somewhere but no one was quite sure where. However, all were agreed that he was intelligent and got things done. Interestingly, he was also known for being extremely polite. Which somehow, thought James, made him seem just a little more ominous. As these thoughts were milling about in his head the inner door opened and small balding man neatly dressed in a dark grey suit emerged. The man stood to one side, holding the door open as he looked across at James with a smile. 'Sir Harrington will see you now Dr Preston,' he said.

James quickly rose from his seat, 'thank you,' he said, walking into the large office. As he did, the man left, closing the door behind him. James looked around the spacious office. To his right he could see a small coffee table set between two large black leather chairs. On the table he noticed that two places had been set. To his left was a broad oak desk and a man rising from the dark green leather chair behind it.

The man was about five foot ten, well-tanned, slim with sharp grey eyes and thinning grey hair. He was elegantly dressed in a silver-grey three-piece suit with white shirt and a dark striped tie. He rose quickly from behind the desk and made his way around to the front to meet James. His movements were efficient, fluid and precise, giving James the impression of a wellspring of energy, tightly controlled. As he reached the front of the desk he held out his hand in greeting and smiled politely, 'Dr Preston, I do apologise for keeping you waiting' said Sir Carmichael Harrington in a calm voice of authority.

They shook hands and James noted the firmness of his handshake and smiled a little inwardly thinking how all this seemed just a little too old school. However, James could also feel the energy of the man. It was like standing next to a coiled spring.

'Please,' indicated Harrington with a brief sweep of his left arm, 'sit.' It wasn't an order, but it had the distinct note of command beneath it.

James turned and sat in the nearest chair to his right.

'One moment,' said Harrington pausing and returning to his desk, leaning over he pressed an intercom. 'Anna, could you bring in the files on Project Veritas please,' he asked.

'Certainly Sir Harrington,' was the bright response. There was a moment's pause followed by a gentle knock at the door.

'Come,' Harrington called out. The woman from the outer office entered holding two files, one large the other small and handed them to Harrington. 'Ah, thank you Anna,' he said taking the files and watching her leave again.

Hmm, thought James, project veritas, perhaps this will be the project I'm going to be working on. It had been a long time since he'd studied Latin, but he knew veritas meant truth.

Harrington, holding both files in his manicured well-tanned hands walked back over to James and sat in the chair opposite. As he sat, he nodded at the expensive looking coffee pot and cups that were laid out between them, 'please,' he said, 'help yourself to coffee. There's milk in the jug and sugar in that small pot,' he indicated a small china pot to the left. 'No biscuits I'm afraid,' he said with feigned regret and a brief smile.

James smiled in response and poured himself some coffee, adding just a smidgen of milk to leave it as dark as possible but not quite black. 'Shall I pour you a cup,' asked James.

'Yes please,' answered Harrington. No, no milk thanks' he responded to James' polite query.

James sipped his coffee delicately. It was good. Hot and bitter, just how he liked it. He smiled.

'Its good coffee,' said Harrington seeing James' response.

'Hmm, very nice,' agreed James.

Harrington was still sitting holding the two files the woman had brought in. He placed them on his lap, leant forward to pick up his cup and took a sip of coffee. Then, returning the cup to the table he took both folders in his hands and sat back. 'Dr Preston,' he began, then hesitated briefly, 'would it be ok if I call you James?' he asked.

'Of course,' James responded, thinking as he did, I wonder if I'm supposed to ask him if I can call him Carmichael. After only a moments reflection he thought probably not.

'Right, James,' began Sir Harrington in a clear and confident voice, 'what can you tell me about the field of parapsychology?'

There was a moments silence as James did a quick retake. He was a little stunned by the unexpected nature of the question and frowned in thought. He wasn't sure what to say and part of him wondered if this was some kind of test. He quickly tried to rally his thoughts, working to recall what he knew about the topic, which he admitted to himself wryly wasn't much. He looked back at Sir Harrington and said with a great deal more confidence than he felt, 'as far as I can recall it's a fringe area within psychology that focuses on things such as telepathy and precognition.' Then added rather weakly, 'among other things.'

As he said this Sir Harrington was watching him intently. Not unkindly, but certainly with interest. Upon hearing James' explanation Sir Harrington made an effort not to let his disappointment show on his face. Then he asked James, seemingly with genuine interest, 'What makes it fringe?'

'Well,' responded James slowly, 'it's not seen as real science . . .'

Sir Harrington groaned inwardly when he heard this and interrupted James gently but firmly asking, 'and what is real science?'

James reflected for a moment. He squared his shoulders a little, feeling slightly more confident. After all, the nature of science was something he felt naturally able to talk about. He relaxed a little and began in a clear steady voice. 'Science is really just an agreed method,' he said. 'A way of doing things.'

'Can you elaborate a bit?' asked Harrington.

'Well,' James hesitated for a moment gathering his thoughts. 'As I say it's an agreed upon method for conducting research. Scientists, that is researchers like me, come up with hypotheses or ideas that they can test in controlled situations and then they analyse the data using various statistical techniques which allows them to make inferences, or interpret the outcome.' He sat back, feeling quite pleased with his response.

'And those inferences, or interpretations,' continued Harrington in a gentle querying tone, 'are what scientists then publish in their academic papers?'

'Exactly,' agreed James, nodding enthusiastically, and feeling a little relieved that he was now on more familiar ground.

'Then why,' asked Harrington seemingly puzzled, 'is parapsychology not a science?' He watched James as he said this, thinking to himself, now we'll see whether he'll be able to cope with this or not.

James sat for a moment, feeling his mouth go dry. He couldn't understand why Sir Harrington kept bringing the conversation back to this odd topic. He thought for a moment not sure what to say and all the while trying to remember anything he could about the field of parapsychology. Unfortunately for James, like most of those who'd studied psychology at university, the findings of parapsychology are rarely if ever examined or discussed. The silence continued as he thought hard about what to say next, but could only manage, 'I, er . . . well, it's not a topic . . .'

He got no further. 'Because,' Sir Harrington interrupted, 'from my understanding of the literature those in the field of parapsychology make predictions, test them in controlled situations, examine the data using the same statistical techniques and publish their findings in scientific papers.' He waited for a moment, then added with a wry smile, 'albeit rather more obscure ones.'

James sat there with a slight frown feeling as though he was being put on the spot but not quite sure what it was he was supposed to say next.

'That sounds like science to me,' pointed out Sir Harrington, watching James to see how he'd respond. He knew he was being deliberately provocative, but he was trying to tread with care, despite his disappointment with the way James had responded to his initial questions. He had rather hoped for a more open minded or informed response.

'Well,' James admitted with some reluctance, 'as I said it's not an area that I'm very familiar with.'

'Indeed,' agreed Sir Harrington, 'and that's because less than a handful of universities in the UK deign to cover the topic.'

This statement was followed by another brief silence as James sat wondering what it was he was supposed to say now.

'However,' said Sir Harrington in a tone that strongly suggested some sort of reconciliation was about to occur, 'wouldn't you say that a good scientist is someone who is critical yet open minded?'

James thought for a moment and then slowly nodded in agreement, 'yes, that sounds sensible.'

'Good,' smiled Sir Harrington as if they were now in full agreement. 'Well, I know you can be critical, but can you be open minded?' he asked.

'Ye'es,' nodded James cautiously wondering where this was going.

'Excellent,' responded Sir Harrington with more enthusiasm. He separated the two files he was holding and held out the smaller of the two to James. James put down his now empty coffee cup and took the file carefully, reading the title on the cover as he did so. Across the front was printed in large black letters *'Project Veritas'*. He opened the file and looked at the selection of research papers. 'What you have there,' said Sir Harrington, 'is a selection of meta-analyses.' He stopped for a moment, 'I'm assuming you are familiar with what a meta-analysis is?' he queried.

'Oh yes,' replied James, frowning a little and nodding. It was only after a moment's silence that he noticed Sir Harrington had paused and he looked up to see him sitting expectantly, with eyebrows raised. 'Ah, oh, sorry,' said James realising that he was supposed to provide more detail. 'A meta-analysis is where an individual or group of researchers examine a number of different research studies that have all focused on the same thing in order to see if there is a common result, or if any trends emerge.'

'Excellent,' nodded Sir Harrington. 'As I say, you have there a number of meta-analyses from the field of parapsychology[1].'

When he heard this James' frown deepened a little and he looked more intently at the titles of the research papers in the folder, briefly flicking through them.

'What I want you to do, at least initially,' continued Sir Harrington, 'is to read through and familiarise yourself with the results of these papers. You'll also find at the back of the file a list of potentially interesting websites, academic societies and books that you may also want to explore.'

James looked up. Hesitantly, he asked, 'is there a specific reason I'm reading this material?'

'Yes,' smiled Sir Harrington, 'and this will become clear when we meet again on Friday at 4pm to discuss what you make of the findings.'

James caught the undertone in Harrington's voice which indicated that their meeting had now come to an end. Sir Harrington then stood, still holding the other folder. James immediately stood as well taking his lead from Sir Harrington.

'If you have any queries or questions about anything you come across, make a note of them and we'll discuss them at our next meeting,' said Sir Harrington in a tone of mild affability. James simply nodded not quite knowing what to say. The two men then shook hands and James made his way out of the large office closing the door behind him as he left. Once outside and walking back along the corridor towards his own office James reflected on what had just taken place. He shook his head frowning and looked down at the folder of papers in his hand. He was still a bit bewildered as to why he was being required to read this material but, he thought with a hint of resignation, at least it should be relatively straightforward.

A view, which he later realised, had been somewhat overly optimistic.

∞

It was just after 4pm that Friday afternoon when both men were once again sitting facing each other in the comfy leather chairs of Sir Harrington's office. Sir Harrington, this time dressed in a dark double-breasted suit with matching dark shirt and tie, sat empty handed across from James, his hands gently clasped in his lap. He smiled slightly as he wondered to himself what the psychologist had made of the evidence he'd been given. He could see that James seemed a little less sure of himself. That, he thought, could be a good sign. 'Well James,' he began brightly with just the hint of a smile, 'what did you make of the papers?'

James looked down at the folder. He certainly seemed less confident and appeared to be struggling to come to terms with what to say. Shaking his head slightly he finally answered, 'I'm not sure.'

'That,' said Sir Harrington, 'is encouraging.'

'Why?' asked James, still feeling unsure what to make of it all.

'Because it suggests that you've at least remained open minded.'

James placed the folder on the coffee table between them. 'As I said before, this is,' then he hesitated for a moment, 'this was,' he corrected, 'not an area that I'm very familiar with. However, over the past week I've read these,' he indicated the folder of papers, 'and a variety of other sources including online articles, I've also checked some textbooks as well as a few of the more traditional scientific journals.'

Sir Harrington smiled, pleased to hear of the efforts James had made in trying to get to grips with the topic. This, he thought, bodes well. Then said, 'and what's your conclusion?'

'Well, from what I've read,' said James still somewhat cautiously, 'the evidence seems to suggest that these . . .' he faltered for a moment. 'These, behaviours, are not only real but that they've been replicated under tightly controlled conditions.'

'What behaviours?' asked Sir Harrington. He knew that they both knew what James was referring to, but he wanted, no, he needed this to be made clear. He needed James to be able to accept and understand what they would be working on before they could proceed.

'Errm, well,' James answered slowly with some reluctance, 'telepathy, energy healing, clairvoyance, and psychokinesis, though this is also sometimes called direct mental influence.'

'So, your saying telepathy and psychokinesis are real?' enquired Sir Harrington. He knew he was being deliberately provocative.

'Well,' responded James, 'It's not that *I'm* saying,' he hesitated for a moment, then changed his approach. 'If we accept the evidence,' he continued indicating the folder of papers, 'then these effects are both real and they've been replicated.'

'Empirical evidence under controlled conditions which replicates,' said Sir Harrington brightly, 'key cornerstones of the scientific method are they not?'

'Yes,' said James quietly whilst nodding.

'So,' asked Sir Harrington, 'where does that leave us?'

James shrugged. 'I'm not sure.' Both men sat for a moment and then James added, 'it would help if I had a clearer understanding of the context in which I'm supposed to be thinking about these. . .' he hesitated slightly as he'd been about to say "things" but knew that he should be more precise. 'These aspects of behaviour,' he said finally.

'A very good point indeed,' responded Sir Harrington leaning back in his chair and staring up at the ceiling. After a moments reflection he continued. 'Tell me, what's the primary role of the Home Office?'

James answered easily, 'to ensure the security and prosperity of the United Kingdom.' It was a by-line he'd seen so many times since joining the HO, as it was printed on every poster and letter heading in the department.

Sir Harrington smiled at the quick almost verbatim response of the departments by-line. 'And what do you think the implications are of the,' he hesitated, recalling the words James had just used, 'the aspects of behaviour that you've just read about?'

James sat thinking for a moment. 'Well,' he answered after some reflection, 'there could of course be security implications and maybe even economic ones.'

Sir Harrington nodded in mute agreement.

'Is that what all this is about?' asked James with dawning realisation. 'The potential security implications of,' he hesitated briefly, 'psychic behaviours?' the scepticism in his voice clearly evident.

'I grant you,' responded Sir Harrington, clearly aware of how James felt, 'it does sound rather like a poor cliché but it's the simple truth. And believe me when I say that a number of our foreign counterparts are quite a way ahead of us on this issue.'

James hadn't really given this any thought, but as Sir Harrington mentioned it, he realised that, given the situation, it was obvious that it wouldn't simply be a UK issue. Every country in the world would be interested in this. He began to wonder what other countries might be doing about it. His thoughts were interrupted by Sir Harrington saying, 'I'm sure you would agree that the evidence you've now examined, which by the way,' he added, 'is but a tiny fraction of what's available, clearly answers the question of whether such effects are real or not.'

The rising intonation of Sir Harrington's voice made it clear that this was a question and required some sort of confirmation. James nodded in agreement, 'yes,' he said.

'Hence, we are left with questions that ask why some people exhibit these behaviours whilst others do not, and perhaps more importantly how do these behaviours work and is it possible to control them?'

James nodded again in mute agreement.

'Which brings us to Project Veritas,' said Sir Harrington rising from his chair. 'No, please stay,' he said in response to James' movement, 'I'm just going to get a file from my desk,' he said by way of explanation. He rose quickly and made his way back over to his desk picking up a buff-coloured folder and then returned to James. As he sat he began to explain, 'Project Veritas, as the name suggests, is concerned with finding out the truth about these . . . let's call them anomalous behaviours,' he said with a smile. 'The aim of the project, which I want you to lead, will focus on how and why these anomalous behaviours work. You will be based at a facility called the Behavioural Research Labs, just outside of Cambridge, and be able to pick your own small team to help.'

James realised now why someone with a background in human psychology was needed. Also, despite his seemingly cautious responses to Sir Harrington earlier, he also knew that he'd become strangely fascinated by the findings he'd read about and the opportunity to explore them more fully sounded both exciting and challenging.

Sir Harrington looked at him carefully. 'However, before we proceed any further, I need to know,' he said with deliberate caution, 'whether or not you're interested.'

James looked back at him, 'yes,' he responded quickly. 'Yes, very much so,' he added with emphasis. He felt a little giddy as he thought of himself leading such a project.

Sir Harrington smiled gently, 'excellent,' he said.

Keen now to show his interest and commitment James asked, 'is there a plan on how we proceed with this?'

'There is indeed. Once you have your team in place you'll begin by recruiting a Mr Barry O'Donoghue as your initial. . .' he was going to say subject, but quickly changed it at the last moment to, '. . . protégé.' With this he handed the buff-coloured folder to James and said, 'in here you'll find all you need to know about Mr O'Donoghue.'

James took the folder and asked carefully, 'what makes you think this Mr O'Donoghue will want to take part?'

Sir Harrington sat back in his chair and smiled tightly. 'True,' he said, folding his hands in his lap, 'there's no guarantee that Mr O'Donoghue will want to get involved with our project. However,' he continued in the tone of one very sure of the outcome, 'events have been arranged so that Mr O'Donoghue will be given the opportunity to exhibit his. . . shall we say, particular gift. This will provide him with the much-needed vindication he so very desperately seeks. Unfortunately, for Mr O'Donoghue at least, we have an operative in place to ensure that events do not favour him, and that the outcome is less than he would have hoped for.' Sir Harrington looked over at James to gauge his response to this stratagem. He was well aware that this would breach every ethical code normally required for research but hoped that James would see that in matters of national security ethics often had to take a back seat.

James was following Sir Harrington's explanation with intense care. He was fully aware of the ethical issues that such an approach raised and whilst he didn't mind the deception he was clear that a line would be drawn if any physical harm were mentioned.

'This,' said Sir Harrington seeing that James had so far not contested the proposed plan, 'will lead our Mr O'Donoghue to feel rejected and ignored and that is when you,' he nodded at James, 'will offer him a way out and redemption.'

'In the form of . . .?' queried James cautiously.

'It will be at this point,' continued Sir Harrington, 'that you offer him a prestigious and well-paid research position in your facility to help you explore and understand his . . . ah, skill. An opportunity I am quite sure he will grasp with both hands.' Rising from his seat he said, 'and that's about all for now.' Upon hearing this James also stood. 'Familiarise yourself with that file,' said Sir Harrington nodding to the folder James held, 'and keep me updated with how things progress.'

James noted the emphasis on things progressing. As if progress were the only possible option. The two men shook hands and James left carrying the folder, determined to find out more about Mr Barry O'Donoghue.

Barry O'Donoghue was a young man of 24, short and wiry with thick dark hair and intense green eyes. He'd been working in the warehouse just outside Hammersmith for a little over eight months. It was now Friday afternoon and he'd come to the end of his shift. He was making his way to the lockers to get rid of his gloves and overall and pick up his things when Bruce, his shift supervisor intercepted him and said, 'Robinson wants a word with you in his office.'

Barry groaned inwardly, nodded his thanks to Bruce and then turned back to the main office. Donald Robinson was the warehouse manager and not a very pleasant person. He was a large man who seemed to be perpetually sweating despite the fact that he spent most of his time sitting behind a desk. Barry had a good idea this would be about his picking rate. Picking rates reflected the number of items each warehouse operative was able to select and process in an hour. It was company policy that all warehouse operatives should have a picking rate of between 70-80 items per hour. There were various financial incentives for those who managed to exceed the target rates and there were a variety of measures that could be put in place to encourage those whose picking rate was below company expectations.

Barry knew his picking rates were on the low side compared to others. In part this was because he wasn't that fussed but also because, as was widely known but never acknowledged, many of the other operatives cut short their breaks in order to have a bit of extra time to pick, which meant that their pick rates would look better. Barry objected to the idea of cutting his breaks short just to reach the unrealistic targets set by the management. The wages were low enough as it was, cutting your breaks short just meant you were working for even less.

As Barry approached the manager's office, he could see that the door was open. Despite this he still knocked politely and then waited for a moment before Robinson looked up from his desk and said in a deep weary voice, 'come in O'Donoghue.'

He didn't ask Barry to sit so he remained standing in front of the desk. Feeling as though he were back at school standing in front of the head teacher having to explain his bad behaviour.

'I've just got the picking rates through from last month,' said Robinson, indicating the sheaf of papers on his desk. 'And once again, lo and behold, your rate is the lowest.' He added, in a voice dripping with sarcasm, 'you managed the massive total of 71 items per hour.' He waited for a moment looking at Barry with ill-disguised contempt.

'I thought we were ok so long as we picked seventy items an hour,' said Barry.

Robinson snorted in disgust. 'How is it everyone else manages to pick over 80 items an hour.'

Barry stood there not saying what they both knew. That others managed a higher pick rate because they gave up their free time. Despite his annoyance he couldn't really see what the problem was. To him it seemed obvious that when you measured any work-based performance there would be someone at the top of the list and someone at the bottom. It stood to reason. If it wasn't him at the bottom of the list it would be someone else.

'Well, we've just had a new directive from head office,' smiled Robinson maliciously, 'the picking rates have just been raised to a minimum of 80 items an hour.'

Barry shook his head sadly. This, he thought, is what happens when too many people reach the target earning bonuses and costing the company money. The target is raised.

'When?' asked Barry his voice quite with resignation.

'As from next week,' said Robinson with what seemed like glee. 'So you, sunshine, will need to up your game, otherwise we'll be putting you into special measures.'

Barry couldn't be bothered to argue. He knew it wouldn't lead anywhere. Robinson, despite his sour penny-pinching attitude was as much a slave as the rest of them. It was simply the system. Barry found the seemingly relentless drive for ever more of everything both tiring and bizarre. What, he thought, was wrong with simply being satisfied.

'I've asked Bruce to keep a special eye on you as from next week,' said Robinson with a smile that contained no humour. 'I just wanted to . . .' he'd been about to say *warn* but did a quick re-take and said, '. . . make sure you knew about the new targets. After all, we don't want any misunderstandings about what's expected.'

No, thought Barry, that way it'll be much easier for you to either, *let me go,* or figure out some other way of getting rid of me.

Robinson waved Barry out of his office, his voice full of malicious sarcasm, 'have a good weekend.'

Barry left the office and made his way back to the lockers. There he exchanged his gloves and light brown overall for his black coat and then made his way out of the warehouse. The early evening air was chilly, and damp and he stuffed his hands in his pockets trying not to think about Robinson. He didn't hate the job. He couldn't bring himself to waste that much energy thinking about it. He just didn't care about it. It was simply a way of earning enough money to pay the rent on his bedsit and allow him a little extra. He wondered if he should start looking for another job now whilst he had this one. The chances are Robinson might give him a good reference if he thought he was going to get rid of him. With these thoughts passing through his mind he made his was along the Hammersmith road to the tube station. There he caught the next Piccadilly line train to Alperton and home.

On reaching the station at Alperton he got off the train and made his way out onto the street. Turning left along Ealing Road and then up and along to turn right into Sunleigh Road. He lived in a first-floor room at number 31. Turning his key in the lock he made his way through the door and looked on top the meter cabinet to see if there was any post for him and was surprised to see an official looking envelope with his name on. He picked it up and turned it over, there was no return address. Hmm, he thought, doesn't look like a bill. He took it and made his way up the stairs to his room. Once inside he hung his jacket neatly on the back of the door and made himself a cup of tea. Waiting for the kettle to boil he opened the envelope, took out the letter and began to read.

It was some minutes later but Barry was still standing by the kettle, which had boiled a while ago. His empty mug still by his side. He read the letter through again for the third time. He was shaking his head slightly as a smile began to appear on his lips. He couldn't believe it. His smile turning into a grin.

The letter was from the television programme *Exploring the Edge*, which dealt with paranormal phenomena and was hosted by the gorgeous Kerry Greenaway. He'd written to them months ago explaining what it was he could do but since he'd never heard back, he'd stopped thinking about it. And now, they were inviting him to come along and show them what he could do. He couldn't believe it. *Exploring The Edge*, Kerry Greenaway. It sounded too good to be true. His natural doubts rose for a moment, he checked the letter heading again and the name of the person who'd sent it. It was from someone called Mandy Stirling, an executive producer on the show. It all seemed legit. There was a phone number in the heading so he decided to call it just to make sure. He dug out his mobile phone and punched in the number, his hands shaking slightly with nerves. The phone range twice then a female voice answered 'Mandy Stirling, how can I help?'

Barry gulped, took a breath.

The voice called out again, 'hello, this is Mandy Stirling can I help?'

'Err. . .' said Barry, 'my name's Barry O'Donoghue and I've just received a letter from you . . .' he got no further.

'Ah yes,' interrupted Mandy brightly, 'Mr O'Donoghue. We were interested to read your letter. Sorry that it's taken us so long to contact you, but as I'm sure you can imagine we have a very large postbag to get through each week. Anyway, we thought it would be good if you'd be willing to come along to the studio and show us what it is you can do.'

There followed a brief conversation where dates and times were agreed, and Barry outlined the conditions needed for him to perform. The conversation over, Barry hung up the phone and stood there for a moment not moving, still standing next to his empty mug. The grin on his face seemed to get wider. Wait till I tell the others at the Kulagina Club about this, he thought elatedly.

∞

The Kulagina club consisted of Barry, as founding member and unacknowledged leader, Steve, and Alice. They usually met on a Thursday evening at Steve's place because he owned a small flat on the edge of Ealing and was the only member with enough space for the three of them to meet and practice. The Kulagina club, or KC, had been going for just over two years now, and all three of them enjoyed the sessions. Needless to say both men were infatuated with Alice the yoga teacher, who was slim and ethereal, with long fair hair and light blue eyes. She was into meditation and all sorts of psychic phenomena but not, it seemed, into either Barry or Steve. It was interesting to see Alice working hard to develop her second sight whilst remaining oblivious to the feelings and raging hormones of the two men she would meet with on a weekly basis to sit in a darkened room meditating. However, through some form of tacit agreement neither man had asked her out, or made any move, which always meant their weekly meetings held a frisson of excitement for both men. Something they both seemed, at the moment anyway, to be satisfied with.

The following week at work had been a particularly trying one for Barry, with his supervisor Bruce seeming to watch his every move, as Barry worked extra hard to ensure his pick rate would meet the new target. He'd felt a mixture of relief and excitement when, at last, Thursday came around, as he'd been looking forward to the next KC meeting. He wasn't sure yet how, or even if, he'd tell the others about his invitation from the *Exploring the Edge* TV show.

As he arrived at Steve's flat that Thursday evening, he was surprised to hear laughter as he reached the door and knocked. He waited for a few minutes and then a grinning Steve opened the door and greeted him. Steve was slightly taller than Barry with fair hair and light hazel eyes.

'Hey,' Steve said in recognition. 'Good to see you.' Then adding sotto voce, 'Alice has brought someone else along – she's called Helen.' He took Barry's jacket and hung it on one of the hooks by the door and then led Barry back along the short hallway to the lounge-diner.

The first floor flat was open-planned and had a nice airy feel to it, helped by the large windows opposite which looked out over the main street. The short hall led directly into the main living area which contained a lounge on the right, with a dark brown three-seater leather sofa and a pale wooden coffee table in front of a large black TV screen. On the left was the small kitchen area and across the other side of the lounge, set beneath the windows, was a round dining table with four chairs.

There, sitting on the sofa was Alice, with the new girl beside her. The new girl looked a bit shorter than Alice, with a dark bob of hair and a wide smiling face. The two girls seemed to contrast one another. Where Alice seemed light, slender and ethereal the other girl was darker and somehow seemed more solid.

'Hi Barry,' said Alice nodding and smiling at him. 'This is Helen,' she said, indicating the girl next to her with a nod.

'Hi,' said Barry nodding to both the girls.

Helen smiled openly, 'hi,' she said. 'I hope you don't mind me coming along but when Alice told me about this, I really wanted to see if for myself.'

Barry shrugged, 'sure,' he said smiling, as he worked, and failed to contain his exciting news.

'You look happy mate,' said Steve. 'What's happened, you won the lottery?'

Barry's smile turned into a broad grin as he reached into his jeans pocket and took out the letter from *Exploring the Edge*. Handing it to Steve he said, 'read this.'

'What is it?' asked Alice looking over at them.

Steve took the letter, unfolded it, and began to read, moving his head in a side to side motion as he scanned the words.

After only about ten seconds he said in a loud voice full of disbelief, 'No way!'

'What – what is it?' asked Alice again, not happy about being left out.

Steve looked up at Barry once he'd finished reading through the letter. 'Are you joking,' he said, 'you didn't just type this up yourself?'

Barry, still smiling, shook his head. 'Nope.'

Steve, now also smiling broadly, handed the letter to Alice, 'have a look.' He reached across and clapped Barry on the shoulder, 'well done mate. This will be sooo cool,' he said.

Alice was now scanning the letter, mumbling out the words as she speed read it, 'Mr O'Donoghue . . .blah. . . blah. . . blah – responding to your letter – blah. . . blah -,' then she stopped and looked up at Barry. 'You're kidding,' she said, her voice rising an octave. 'You've been invited onto *Exploring the Edge!*'

'Oooh,' interrupted Helen sounding impressed, 'isn't that the programme with Kerry Greenaway? The one where she looks at paranormal phenomena an' stuff?'

'Yeah,' answered Alice also sounding impressed, 'wow! As she handed the letter back to Barry she asked, 'can we come?'

Barry was taken aback a bit. He hadn't given any thought as to whether his friends could come along or not. He wasn't even sure he wanted them there, they might be a distraction. He folded the letter and put it back in his pocket shrugging as he did so to indicate that he didn't know, and said in a noncommittal voice, 'I don't know. I can ask – if you want?'

All three responded immediately that they did want.

Then Steve asked, 'what're you going to do?'

'Well,' said Barry cautiously, 'I thought I'd show them my work with the psi wheel[2].'

Steve nodded thoughtfully as if reflecting on all the things Barry could do, 'good idea.'

'Yeah,' added Alice with enthusiasm, 'they'll love that.'

'What's a sigh . . . thingy?' asked Helen.

Alice turned back to Helen and attempted to offer a short explanation. 'It's one of the tools we use to help us focus our mind's energy.' She sat silently for a moment and then frowned a little in concentration before continuing, 'it's probably best if Barry tells you about it, 'cause he can tell you about the history and how it came about.' She looked back at Barry, 'is that ok with you?'

'Yeah, of course,' said Barry eagerly.

Alice got up from the sofa, her slender form moving with grace and ease. She walked over to Barry and gave him a brief hug, smiling as she said, 'well done. This is gonna be great.' She then turned to look at Steve and said, 'if you get a couple of psi wheels we can go over to the table,' indicating the dining table at the other end of the lounge with a nod of her head, 'and start our meditation, then we won't be disturbed by these two.'

Steve smiled in response. 'Sounds good to me' he said moving towards a cupboard where he kept various bits of kit, mostly home-made, which included a number of psi wheels. Kneeling beside the cupboard he began sorting through a variety of odds and ends, pulling out a selection of corks, some long needles, and four large clear plastic boxes. As he did this he called over his shoulder to Barry and asked, 'err, do you want my tablet?'

Barry thought for a moment and thinking that it might be useful to show Helen some video clips said, 'err. . . yeah, ok – thanks.'

Steve got up and quickly left the room for a moment returning a minute later with his tablet which he handed to Barry and then going back to the cupboard he selected some of the materials he'd just laid out on the top and moved to the other end of the room to sit at the dining table. Alice was already seated with her eyes closed, taking deep regular rhythmic breaths and looking very relaxed. Once Steve had placed the materials on the dining table, he too closed his eyes and began to take deep, regular breaths.

Meanwhile, Barry had moved over towards Helen and now sat beside her on the sofa. He smiled as he asked, 'so, how much do you know about PK?'

Helen screwed her face up a little in consternation, 'err, ... nothing really.'

Barry smiled slightly. He didn't mind that Alice had brought along a complete novice because if there was one thing he liked to do it was talk about parapsychology. Over the years, since he'd first developed an interest in the field, he'd tried to read as many books as he could on the subject. He also spent as much time as he could on various online forums and chat rooms talking about psychic phenomena. As he sat and looked at Helen, he realised that whilst she wasn't what might be called pretty, she was certainly attractive. His smile broadened a little as he felt buoyed up by the fact that he'd be spending time talking about his favourite subject to an attractive woman.

'Ok,' he began, settling himself beside her. 'PK refers to psychokinesis.'

Helen looked on with rapt attention.

Barry continued, 'the word psycho relates to the mind and kinesis refers to movement so essentially it's about the ability to move things with your mind.'

'No way,' she said instantly, laughing slightly. Then, with a little less scepticism and a bit more interest said, 'is that real?'

'It is,' Barry nodded smiling. 'Here, let me show you, this clip might help a bit.'

He opened the YouTube app on the tablet Steve had given him and tapped in some details, then looked up at Helen.

'This is an old clip of a woman called Nina Kulagina[3].'

'Ah!' Helen interrupted, 'Alice said you were called the *coolag -* ' she struggled hesitantly.

'The Kulagina club,' said Barry. 'Yes. We named it after her.' He tapped play and handed her the tablet.

Helen watched the grainy black and white footage of a middle-aged woman, with dark hair tied into a bun, wave her hands around a silver salt cellar that sat on a table. After a moment the salt cellar began to move across the table, seemingly of its own accord.

'Wow!' said Helen clearly impressed and a little awed.

The clip continued playing. Switching now to one where Kulagina was waving her hands around a matchbox, a small bundle of matches and some other small items. Then some hands came in from the side of the frame and placed a large clear plastic container over the items.

'That's so she can't use her breath to blow on the objects or use hidden strings or threads,' said Barry knowledgeably.

Helen looked up at him, clearly impressed but still sceptical. 'Is this real?'

Barry simply nodded slowly.

The video clip ended with the woman clearly being able to move the objects under the plastic container without touching them, seemingly by waving her hands back and forth.

'Wow! – that's amazing,' said Helen. 'But ...,' she hesitated frowning slightly, 'how do you know it's not some sort of trick?'

Barry shrugged. 'We don't,' he said simply. 'But that's not really the point. The point is that it shows you what PK is.'

There was a moments silence before Helen asked with interest, 'and you can do that?' nodding towards the tablet to indicate the clip she'd just seen, as she handed it back to Barry.

'Well,' admitted Barry a little uneasily, taking hold of the tablet, 'not as good as that. But it's what we train to do with our psi wheels.'

'A sigh ... what?' queried Helen.

'A psi wheel,' said Barry. 'It's spelt "p-s-i". He continued. 'When people first tried to do PK, or move objects with their mind, they'd often use a needle suspended above circle of card or paper with numbers on it. So that if, or when, the needle moved it'd be easy to see. Over time others tried using small wheels with markings on that were finely balanced on a needle, allowing it to move easily. The idea, again, was that the markings would make it easy to spot any movement.'

'Amazing,' said Helen attentively, who seemed genuinely interested in what Barry was saying.

'Since then,' continued Barry, keen to show his expertise of the topic, 'people have used all sorts of props, including random number generators[4]. But a couple of years ago a French group showed some really good effects using these small clear plastic dome shaped mobiles,' he gestured with his hands to indicate something small and round. 'The plastic dome is balanced on a needle stuck in a cork, and ideally you'd want some markings on the dome, so you'd be able to see if it moves.'

'But that's not really a wheel is it,' said Helen in mild protestation.

Barry shrugged and smiled. 'I know, it's not a "wheel" as such,' he said, making the quotation marks with his hands, 'but it's really simple to make and the dome spins round just like a wheel and,' ... he faltered, 'well, the name just stuck.'

Helen smiled at this seemingly honest admission.

'So, you try to spin these . . . plastic dome-wheels with your mind?'

'Yes,' nodded Barry.

'How does that work?'

'With a lot of practice and effort,' answered Barry.

'Oh,' said Helen a little disappointedly.

Barry smiled knowingly at the clear disappointment on Helen's face. People always wanted it to be easy he thought. To be able to do it straight away. He knew all too well that the idea of being able to spin a wheel with your mind might sound like a lot of fun, but the notion that it would likely involve hours and hours of practice and effort generally didn't sound like much fun at all.

'Think of trying to learn a musical instrument,' said Barry invoking his favourite analogy. 'You wouldn't expect to be able to pick up a guitar and play a song straight away. It takes time and practice.'

After a moment's thought Helen slowly nodded in agreement and understanding. 'So, how *do* you do it?' she asked.

Barry didn't answer right away but stood and said, 'hold on a mo' and I'll get a couple of sets.' With that he made his way to the cupboard and the materials that Steve had laid out earlier. After only a couple of minutes he returned with two clear plastic boxes, each about eight inches across, containing a cork, a needle and a small plastic dome with markings drawn on it in black felt tip pen. He placed them on the coffee table beside them and said, 'before we begin with these we need to try and settle our minds with a short meditation.'

'Is that important?' queried Helen.

'Yes,' said Barry, now all seriousness. 'We've found that a short meditation before the session really helps to you to focus your mind.'

'Just sit back and relax,' said Barry sitting back on the sofa, 'and try to repeat a short single word mantra in your head over and over. It doesn't really matter what the word is – just use one that'll help you relax and focus. I just use the word "calm" to help me.'

'Ok,' nodded Helen, sitting back and closing her eyes.

Barry closed his eyes and began to recite in his mantra in his mind, *calm . . . calm . . . calm*, over and over. Within minutes he could clearly hear his heartbeat and recited the word in time with each beat, relaxing as he did so.

After about fifteen minutes of this Barry took a deep breath and brought his mind back to the living room, the club, and to Helen sitting next to him. He opened his eyes and turned to look at her. Feeling his movement Helen also opened her eyes and smiled gently.

'That was harder than I thought,' she said. 'My mind kept wandering onto other things.'

'Don't worry,' said Barry, 'that's normal. It just takes time, and practice.'

'Ok, you take that one,' Barry said pointing to the plastic box nearest Helen, 'and I'll take this one.' He moved down to the coffee table kneeling beside it and then looked up at Helen. 'If you take out the bits, I'll show you how to set up your psi wheel.'

With a little squeal of delight Helen moved down to the coffee table picking up the plastic box nearest her and taking out the cork, needle, and the round plastic dome shaped cup, placing them all gently on the coffee table.

Barry then indicated that she should follow his lead. Taking the needle first he stuck it firmly into the cork and stood it on the coffee table. Then he balanced the domed shaped cup on top of the needle. This took a couple of goes as it slid off the first time.

Helen also seemed to be having a bit of trouble getting her domed cup to balance on the needle.

'You've got to get it in the right place for the mobile-wheel to balance,' said Barry encouragingly.

Once they both had their mobiles set up Barry took his clear plastic box and, upending it, placed it over his mobile. As Helen tried this she again knocked the side of her mobile and the domed cup fell off again.

'Arrrgh,' she said in frustration, reaching for the domed cup as it rolled across the table. 'Why do we need to put these box things over them?' she asked.

'Because you want to be sure that when the mobile moves it's not because of some puff of wind or draught. Don't worry,' he said soothingly, 'it usually takes a couple of goes to get it set up.'

Once Helen had her mobile set up and had covered it with the clear plastic box, following Barry's lead, she looked up expectantly.

'Now what?' she asked.

'Now,' said Barry, placing his hands vertically either side of his plastic box, 'you've got to try and get the mobile to move just by thinking about it.'

Helen placed her hands vertically either side of the clear plastic box, mimicking the movements of Barry, and concentrated. A small frown appearing on her face.

After five minutes of concentrated effort Helen sighed and sat back shaking her head. Barry still had his hands in place and a light smile on his face as he continued to concentrate. Helen looked over at his mobile. She stared at it with interest. It was moving. Slowly, but it was clearly moving without being touched.

'Bloody hell!' she said in a loud voice full of disbelief. 'It's moving,' she said, pointing at Barry's mobile. 'It's bloody moving!' She looked up to her left to see Alice and Steve sitting at the dining table, both now working with their own mobiles. Alice looked back across at her and smiled, raising her eyebrows and nodding as if to say, 'see, I told you.'

Barry looked up from his mobile, relaxed for a moment, and said, 'practice and effort.'

'Hold on,' said Helen sitting up quickly and reaching out to grab Barry's hands. She held them both in her hands, turned them over and then ran her fingers through his. Looking up she shrugged, smiling weakly, 'just wanted to check you didn't have any strings attached.'

Barry smiled in understanding. 'No problem.'

They all continued to practice with their respective mobiles for the next twenty minutes, which felt a lot longer to Helen who struggled to make any progress. The others however seemed to have varying levels of success. At the end of the twenty minutes Steve sat back with a loud sigh and said, 'ok, who's up for a cup of tea?'

Helen sat back frowning slightly and feeling more frustrated said in a voice, weary from the unsuccessful efforts, 'anything stronger?'

'Alcohol interferes with your ability to focus your mind,' said Barry sternly.

'Oh,' said Helen, feeling a little guilty.

As Steve made his way to the kitchen to organise tea Alice said 'don't worry Helen, it takes time. It was months before I saw any movement in my mobile. You've just got to stick with it.'

'It really is about time and practice,' echoed Barry encouragingly.

Helen nodded in understanding but was still a bit annoyed and dismayed at not being able to get the mobile to move.

'Biscuits?' asked Steve, returning from the kitchen with a large plate of biscuits which he placed on the coffee table between Helen and Barry.

'Yes please!' responded Alice brightly. So saying, she moved over to sit on the floor beside the coffee table in order to pick at the selection of biscuits on offer.

'Not for me thanks' said Helen with a hint of sadness in her voice as she eyed the plate of sweet treats. 'I'm trying to watch my weight.'

'Oooh, chocolate biscuits, yum!' said Alice. With, what Barry thought was unnecessary zeal.

Whilst Barry would normally have been happy to munch his way through a few biscuits, he felt a little sorry for Helen and so decided to side with her and refrain from the biscuits.

'I don't put weight on,' said Alice, as if she'd been asked. 'I can eat and eat but I just don't put any weight on,' she shrugged, smiling as if gaining weight were somehow a failing.

Helen looked up, and with a completely straight face said, 'perhaps you've got worms.'

Barry almost chocked on his tea. He caught Steve's eye and both men quickly turned away trying hard, and with only limited success, not to laugh.

∞

Barry blinked, taken aback a bit by the bright lights of the television studio. He'd just arrived at the studio for *Exploring the Edge,* or EtE as everyone on the set seemed to call it. It consisted of an interview area on one side which contained a large wall mounted screen and two small sofas facing out towards where the live audience would be, and then a smaller flat spaced area where Barry was told that he'd be demonstrating his talent.

Barry was currently being given a short tour by Jo, one of Kerry Greenaway's many assistants. Jo was an athletic looking young woman in her late twenties with short blonde hair, dressed in jeans and a t-shirt which had the show's logo emblazoned across the front. She seemed nice enough but almost always had a faraway look in her eyes when Barry spoke to her because she was either listening to instructions through her headset or responding to questions via the attached mic she wore.

Jo pointed in the direction of the two colourful sofas set behind a light wood coffee table, 'you'll come on over there from behind that screen,' she indicated the gap behind the screen, 'and Kerry will introduce you to the audience. Then she'll bring you over here to do your stuff,' she said pointing towards a nearby table set up with one of Barry's psi wheels. Hanging above the table was a stationary camera set up to face down so that it would be able to relay the image of the plastic mobile to the wall mounted digital screen.

Just then a small group of people came in from the left-hand side all talking at once, and walking towards him, in the middle of the group, was Kerry Greenaway. She smiled at Barry as she approached and held out her hand, 'Gary, is it?' she enquired.

He was definitely starstruck and it took him a moment to say, 'err. . no, it's Barry.'

'Oh yes,' smiled Kerry Greenaway without acknowledging her mistake. 'It's really good of you to come and show us what you can do. I'm sure the audience will love it.'

Barry shrugged a little, not knowing what to say.

'Jo here will take good care of you,' said Greenaway, reaching out and gently touching Jo's arm.

He then remembered his conditions for appearing on the show and hastily asked, 'you do know I've got to have some time to meditate before I can . . .'

Kerry Greenaway held up her other hand and interrupted, 'don't worry, Jo will sort all that out for you.' She looked back at Jo, 'you've got the change in running order, right?' she asked.

Jo checked the clipboard she was holding, 'yes, Barry will come on after we've had the Portsmouth poltergeist and then head into the break.'

'Good,' said Greenaway seemingly satisfied. Then turning back to Barry and reaching out once more to shake his hand said, 'ok, well I'll leave you with Jo for now and then see you on the set in about an hour.' With that she left, swallowed up quickly by the small group she'd come with as they all began talking again.

Barry stood still, a little stunned. He'd just met Kerry Greenaway. He smiled a little gormlessly as it took a moment for what just happened to settle in. Damn, he thought, then looked back at Jo.

'Do you think she'd let me take a selfie with her?' he asked.

'No,' said Jo quickly. 'But if you want, I'll try and get you a signed photo.'

He nodded, 'ah, err – yeah ok,' he said, feeling somewhat let down and dejected.

'Now, if you'd like to come with me,' said Jo briskly, leading Barry off to the left and behind the scenes. 'I'll take you to your room.'

Jo led Barry along a series of corridors where people seemed to be constantly coming and going. Arriving at a door marked '12' she turned and said, 'if you'd like to make yourself comfortable here, I'll come back in a bit to take you over to make-up.'

Barry frowned a little. He'd never worn make-up in his life and wasn't sure he needed any now, but he knew such things were the norm on TV so decided to simply nod and go through the door in the hope that he'd be able to get some peace and quiet so he could prepare himself for the coming show. Inside the small room was a single comfy chair and a small coffee table. Once Jo had left and closed the door, he seated himself in the chair and closed his eyes. He wanted to try and allow himself plenty of time to relax and focus his mind. Breathe, he thought to himself as he began to repeat his mantra in his head over and over . . . *calm . . . calm.*

He got no further as Jo burst back in the room interrupting his meditation. 'Sorry,' she said looking down at her clipboard, 'I've got to move you to another room, this one's just been reallocated.'

A little irritated, Barry rose reluctantly from the chair and followed her out into the corridor.

'Sorry about that,' said Jo again with a slight shrug. 'It's always a bit manic just before we start recording.'

He simply nodded and smiled as if in mute understanding. However, he didn't understand at all. Surely, he thought, they should know which room he was supposed to be in.

Jo took him along the busy corridor to the end where they turned left and then went along another somewhat darker corridor. Half-way along Jo stopped and put her right hand to her headphones tilting her head to one side – 'what?' she said into her mic. 'Oh, what! – but I thought he was going to be –'

Barry stood behind her in the corridor listening to the one-sided conversation as people moved past them in both directions. He moved slightly to the side, backing himself against the wall in an effort to keep out of people's way.

'Ok,' continued Jo still speaking into her mic, 'I'll take him to nineteen, that's still free.'

She looked back at Barry, 'sorry about that, another change of plan.' She turned back, 'we're this way now,' she said leading them back the way they'd just come. This time she led him along a maze of corridors and through various back rooms. It felt to Barry as if they were going around in a large circle. Eventually, after about ten minutes Jo stopped outside another small door.

'Here you are,' she said. 'Sorry about the mix up. You have a rest here for a bit and I'll be back in a tick to take you to make-up.'

Once again Barry walked through the door and into another small room that looked almost identical to the one he'd just left. Part of him wondered what the point of moving him was, but he was becoming very aware of the time, and knew he needed to get back to his meditation. He moved over to the chair and sat down. He'd only been sat in the chair for about three minutes when the door opened and Jo came back in.

'Ok,' she said smiling brightly, 'got to get you to make up.'

Barry was becoming irritated at the interruptions, 'you know I need to meditate before I go on?' he said, the frustration and annoyance beginning to show.

Jo nodded her head in understanding, 'don't worry, just need to get you set up and then you'll be able to…' she hesitated for a moment, '… get yourself sorted,' she finished.

Unfortunately, Barry found himself being taken from one place to another without having any time to rest. First, he arrived at make-up, after what seemed another round-about journey, and had to wait for ten minutes only to have some foundation powder lightly dusted over his face. Following this, Jo informed him that he needed to be 'mic'd up,' which meant another meandering journey and a wait whilst someone fitted him with a clip-on mic and fixed a small amplifier to his belt. Meanwhile, he was becoming more and more anxious about having enough time to settle himself and prepare for his piece on set.

'Don't worry,' said Jo with bright nonchalance, as Barry said for the umpteenth time that he needed to have some preparation time. 'You'll still have plenty of time,' she said, leading him to yet another room.

Barry found this room to be furnished just like the others with a small coffee table and single comfy chair. Unlike the others however it seemed to him uncomfortably hot. He began to feel stressed and unsure.

Just then, the door to his room opened quickly and Jo poked her head, 'five minutes before call,' she said and quickly closed the door before Barry could respond.

'Wha'… hey, hold on!' Barry flustered. He got up quickly and walked over to the door and opened it to find Jo outside talking to someone on her headset – again.

'Yeah, ok, ok, right,' she was saying, all the while nodding and checking her clipboard. 'Yeah, of course,' she added and then looked at Barry.

'You ok,' she said seemingly concerned.

There was a moment's hesitation as Barry thought – no, I'm not ok. Despite my asking several times and making it crystal clear that I needed some time to relax and focus before I go on, I've not had five minutes peace. What with bloody wandering about to find a room that I can't relax in, and then make-up, then being fitted with a microphone, and now you've stuck me in some kind of sauna! These thoughts screamed loudly through his mind, but he said nothing. He stood there meekly starring at her. He knew it would be unreasonable to vent his anger and frustration on her. After all, it wasn't her fault, she was just doing her job.

Little did he know, that is precisely what she was doing.

'You, ok...' said Jo again with mock concern in her voice as Barry stood there not responding.

He looked down in defeat, then up at Jo, 'it's really hot in here,' he said nodding back towards the room. 'Any chance you can get me a glass of water or something,' ... then added, 'please.'

'Course,' she said brightly. 'Come on, I've got to get you to your walk on point.'

Before he had time to say anything she grabbed his arm and, half pulling, half pushing, directed him very firmly along the corridor whilst at the same time tapping her headset and saying, 'can I have a drink please for the guest at entry point C before he goes on.' There was a moments silence followed by her saying, 'ok, thanks,' into her mic. She turned to Barry.

'Just along here,' she said, 'and there'll be a drink for you when we get there.'

Barry allowed himself to be guided along until at last they reached a spot behind the large screen. They stopped with Jo still holding his arm. He looked around and recognised some of the setting and could hear Kerry speaking to the audience on the other side. He began to feel very nervous indeed.

'Aaamazing!' Kerry Greenaway was saying smoothly, 'what a really interesting case ladies and gentlemen. It just goes to show, that despite all we know, we still don't have all the answers.'

There were supporting cries and applause from the audience.

'And now!' Greenaway was saying, with the clear indication that she was about to introduce something new, 'we've got a real treat for you.'

Behind the scenes a much younger assistant came rushing along to where Jo held Barry whispering loudly, 'drink for the guest.'

Jo took the cup handed it to Barry and said, 'quick have some of this and then you're on.'

Barry took the cup and gulped down a mouthful. He coughed and spluttered immediately; his eyes watered, and his throat burnt. It wasn't water, it was some sort of alcohol. He was about to say something when Jo, still smiling, turned him deftly and shoved him gently but firmly in the direction of the set saying, 'go, you're on.'

Barry walked slowly out onto the set, blinking in the bright lights as the audience applauded.

As he made his way over to meet the show's host Jo smiled in satisfaction and felt the buzz of her phone in her pocket. She pulled it out and read the message.

'*How did it go?*' read the message. The caller ID at the top read, Veritas.

Jo turned, shielding the phone, and wandered further backstage as she typed in her response. '*Good, no time to rest –*

lots of distractions and even managed to give him some alcohol. He's just gone on.' She finished typing and pressed send and then waited. A few seconds later another message appeared.

'Good work. Time for you to clear out.'

'On my way,' she responded pocketing the phone as she headed out of the building without looking back.

Meanwhile, Barry had now reached Kerry Greenaway and she was enthusiastically shaking his hand as she introduced him to the audience and the cameras.

'Here we have Mr Barry O'Donoghue.'

Barry blinked, smiled weakly and waved, all the time feeling a little sick from nerves and worry about whether he'd be able to perform, especially as he could see Alice, Steve and Helen waving vigorously at him from the front row of the audience.

'Well Barry,' said Greenaway full of bright enthusiasm, 'what are you going to do for us today?'

'Erm,' Barry's mouth was dry. He had to swallow and then with effort said, 'I'm going to give you a demonstration of PK.'

'And for those in our audience, and out there,' indicated Greenaway with a sweep of her arm which took in both audience and cameras, 'what exactly is PK?'

'It's psychokinesis – it means moving an object with your mind.'

This led to a number of pleasurable ooohs and aaahs from the audience.

'Wow ladies and gentlemen!' enthused Greenaway. 'The ability to be able to move an object,' she paused for dramatic effect, 'with your mind.'

There were gasps of pleasure and a ripple of applause.

'Well Barry,' said Greenaway leading him now over to where they'd earlier set up his psi wheel on the table, 'over here we have set up a,' she hesitated for a moment, 'a psi wheel, is that right?' she asked with fake puzzlement.

Barry nodded, then realised he was supposed to answer for the audience and cameras. 'Oh, er yes, that's right.'

'And could you describe this for us?' asked Greenaway, smile still fixed in place while she was thinking to herself – Christ this guy's hard work.

'As you can see,' responded Barry pointing down at the kit and feeling a little more relaxed to be talking about something he felt familiar and at home with. 'It's essentially a plastic domed mobile with markings on, balanced on a needle, which is stuck into a cork base. Then the whole thing is covered in this clear plastic case to make sure . . .'

'Why has the little round plastic bit got markings on it?' interrupted Greenaway.

'That's so we'll be able to see if it moves.'

Greenaway made a surprised looking face, as if to indicate how impressive this seemed, and looking over to the audience said, 'you mean *when* it moves.' This got a ripple of laughter from the audience. 'Ok,' she said, and with another look at the audience raising her voice asked, 'are we all ready to see Barry move this psi wheel with his mind?'

This received a number of loud whoops and cheers from the audience.

She looked back to Barry, 'ok Barry, do your stuff,' she said.

Barry, now feeling very nervous again went around the small table and stood so that he could place his hands on either side of the clear plastic box containing the psi wheel whilst still facing towards the audience. He briefly looked up and could see members of the audience shifting their attention between him and the large screen on the other side of the studio which relayed the image from the camera held above the table. He looked down quickly, trying not to think about how many people were there watching him. He closed his eyes and took a deep breath trying hard to calm himself. Repeating over and over in his mind his mantra of *calm . . . calm . . . calm.* After a few seconds he opened his eyes and focused on the psi wheel in the box.

Nothing happened.

Everyone continued to watch. The tension in the room seemed to rise along with people's expectations.

Nothing happened.

There was a feeling now as if everyone in the studio were holding their breath. Waiting, willing the psi wheel to move.

Still, nothing happened.

'Well, let's leave Barry there for a moment,' said Greenaway in a loud stage whisper, 'whilst I just come back over here to meet someone who says he can tell us how this trick is done.'

At the word 'trick' Barry's attention snapped away from the psi wheel and over to where Kerry Greenaway was now standing by one of the sofas facing the audience. He frowned in annoyance. It's not a trick he fumed silently.

Greenaway leaned forward a little into the nearest camera and said in a loud voice, 'please give a warm welcome to Professor Andrew Wells!'

As she said this a late middle-aged man in a navy-blue suit pranced nimbly onto the set to a generous round of applause. On reaching the sofa area he and Greenaway shook hands and then each took a seat.

'Professor Wells,' said Greenaway with over played deference, 'thank you very much for coming along.'

'Thank you for having me,' he said. His voice clear and confident.

Greenaway leaned in towards him, 'now, you're a scientist, and psychologist, based at London University and you say you can explain to us how this trick is done?'

'Indeed I can Kerry,' he said with false modesty and a broad smile. He reached into his jacket pocket and took out a good-sized cork with a needle stuck into its centre and placed it upright on the coffee table in front of them. Then, he reached into his inside pocket and took out a small square of paper, which he placed on the table and folded it in half, and then again. Scoring the folds to ensure they clearly creased the paper. He opened the folded paper and pinched it in the centre where the folds crossed with the thumb and forefinger of both hands. This created a sort of indentation which he then used to balance the piece of paper on the needle in the upright cork. He sat back and looked up with a smug smile.

'Our very own psi wheel,' said the Professor.

He then looked over to his right, off the set, and nodded. In response to this an assistant brought on what looked like an ordinary lidded coffee cup, of the sort that are sold in most coffee shops. He took hold of this with both hands and turned back to Greenaway, still smiling.

'You see Kerry,' he said in a slightly superior manner, 'it's important to remember that there are only four fundamental forces in the universe. And this has nothing to do with alleged powers of the mind and everything to do with thermodynamics.'

Having said this, he took a brief sip of his coffee, placing the cup to one side and sat forwards, placing both hands below and to either side of the paper balanced on his version of the psi wheel. After just a few seconds the square of paper clearly began to rotate. There were gasps and cheers from the audience as this was relayed on the large screen.

'Wow!' cried Greenaway, looking very impressed. She quickly looked back to the camera. 'Ladies and gentlemen, I hope you can see this. Professor Wells is . . . somehow, moving this psi wheel without actually touching it. It's amazing.'

Wells removed his hands from beneath the paper psi wheel and it immediately stopped moving. He straightened up and sat back on the sofa looking very pleased with himself.

Greenaway looked at him inquisitively, 'ok Professor, how *did* you do that?'

Wells, still smiling, explained. 'As I said, it's got nothing to do with the paranormal. It's simply thermodynamics. The coffee cup your assistant gave me is full of very hot water. I held onto that for a few seconds and then placed my very warm hands near the paper, though of course being careful not to touch it. The hot air from my warmed hands would naturally rise, it's simply the rising hot air from my hands that causes the paper wheel to spin.'

There were groans of understanding and other sounds of disappointment from the audience as they began to realise how the trick was done.

'So, no mind control?' asked Greenaway.

Smiling and shaking his head Prof. Wells said, 'there's no such thing as mi . . .'

He was interrupted by someone from the audience shouting, 'it's moving!'

The large screen behind Greenaway and Wells was showing the image of Barry's psi wheel, which could now be clearly seen to move, very, very slowly.

With surprising speed Greenaway was up and over to Barry's side. As soon as she reached him she placed a hand on his shoulder, leaning over to look down at the psi wheel. Her touch and movements distracted Barry instantly and the wheel immediately stopped moving. Barry gritted his teeth in frustration at the interruption.

'Hmm,' said Greenaway in a disappointed tone, shaking her head slowly, 'doesn't seem to be moving.

'Bu. . .' began Barry who was immediately interrupted by Greenaway's light mocking tone.

'Perhaps you should ask Professor Wells to show *you* how to do it Barry,' she said. This got a laugh from the audience as the image on screen continued to show Barry's stationary psi wheel. Greenaway looked back over to where Wells was sitting, 'so, it's all down to thermodynamics then Professor?'

Wells nodded, 'yes. And if any of your viewers are interested in trying this on their friends at home they can check out my YouTube channel which explains how these so-called mind tricks work.'

Greenaway stood up straightening her jacket and smiled to the camera. 'Well ladies and gentlemen, that's about all we have time for this evening.' She indicated Wells over on the sofa, 'please join me in thanking Professor Andrew Wells,' she then pointed back towards Barry, 'and Mr Barry O'Donoghue.' The audience applauded.

'Next week,' continued Greenaway, 'we'll be meeting a young woman who claims to have had a near death experience and a seven-year-old boy who says he can recall events from a previous life.' These titbits of what was to come were greeted with loud gasps of delight, cheers, and more applause from the audience.

'Until then, good night and thank you for watching' said Greenaway smiling into the nearest camera. The moment was held as the applause continued. Then someone to the side called out 'and . . . we're done'. The main lights came on and the camera lights went out as the recording ended.

Barry remained standing by the table which displayed his psi wheel. He was silently fuming. Despite all the distractions, and worry over not being able to perform, he felt that he'd just begun to make some progress and get the thing moving when she'd come over and distracted him. He was feeling annoyed and aggrieved about the whole event. They hadn't allowed him any time to relax prior to coming on. He wanted to tell Greenaway that she'd distracted him, and that the two set-ups were not comparable because his was set up beneath a clear plastic box to precisely rule out the idea that air movements could cause the mobile to turn. He put his head in his hands for a moment and stood there contemplating what he could do and how this must have looked. He thought about his friends, which made him look up towards the audience. All those he could see above the glare of the lights were in the process of leaving their seats. Looking among them he caught Steve's eye in the front row, who smiled weakly and gave him a thumbs-up sign. Besides Steve, Alice and Helen both attempted encouraging waves. However, despite their actions he could see the disappointment in their faces. Worse, he thought he saw pity reflected in Helen's face and was sure that she winced when their eyes met.

Meanwhile, Greenaway had now moved away from him and was again surrounded by various assistants all talking about how the show went. He shook his head and sighed feeling deflated and defeated. Just then, another assistant approached him and asked if he'd like to join the cast and crew for an after-show drink backstage? The assistant hinted that Greenaway might even make an appearance.

Barry was annoyed, frustrated and, if truth be told, a little ashamed of himself for not being more assertive and making sure he'd had the conditions he needed. It was his once chance, he remonstrated with himself, to show others what he could do. Now, they'd just see that he couldn't do anything. His anger, and shame, did not make him feel like he wanted to spend time socialising. He turned to the assistant, 'No thanks,' he said disconsolately, 'I'd just like to go home.'

'Oh,' said the assistant, a little deflated, 'err, ok. Did you have a coat or a jacket?' she asked. Barry told her where he'd left his things, and she only took a couple of minutes to retrieve them for him. The assistant then led him backstage and along a corridor towards a door marked "Exit".

Barry followed the assistant, all the time thinking back to his performance and coming up with various justifications as to why it hadn't worked as well as he'd hoped. It had worked a bit though, he thought, in an effort to try and justify to himself that the event wasn't a complete disaster. Surely people would've seen his mobile *had* started to move. He knew someone had shouted out, just before that bloody Greenaway had distracted him. He hoped that Steve and the others had seen it. His thoughts once again turned to his friends in the Kulagina Club, particularly Helen. At their last meeting he'd really felt that he'd managed to impress her. Not something he was usually good at. He groaned inwardly at the thought of seeing them all and trying to explain what happened.

As they reached the exit the assistant opened the door and stood to one side, 'here you go,' she said.

Barry just nodded a silent thank you and walked out into the chilly damp evening air, pulling his jacket tight in around himself, in an effort to provide some much-needed comfort.

∞

The following Tuesday Barry was making his way home from work after another particularly difficult day. He was feeling very pissed-off with life in general, as someone at the warehouse had seen his attempts on TV and made sure everyone knew about, what they all thought of as his failed efforts at some form of psychic trickery. He'd had to listen and put up with all the usual banal and unfunny jokes about mind reading, spoon bending and psychic phenomena. Being the butt of all these jokes had done nothing to improve his mood and Thursday was fast approaching, along with the next meeting of the Kulagina Club. He didn't know what to do. He'd never missed a meeting since they'd started but now he'd give anything not to have to go and face his friends. Since his less than dazzling appearance on EtE he'd received supportive text messages from both Steve and Alice, but not heard anything from Helen.

On arriving home at his bedsit, he made himself his usual cup of tea and just sat in the dark feeling very depressed and sorry for himself. He couldn't see a way out. Work was crap but he needed the money. The KC meeting loomed but he wasn't sure he could face it.

It was with these dark thoughts whirling around his head that he heard the front doorbell go downstairs. He wasn't expecting anyone and hoped to God it wasn't Steve or Alice. Though, a small part of him hoped it might be Helen. It would give him an opportunity to explain things to her in private, away from the others. He heard the woman downstairs answer the door and then footsteps on the stairs outside followed by a brisk knock at his door. His heart leapt at the thought of Helen coming to see him. He got up from the bed, and walked over to the door, stopping briefly to switch the light on, he opened the door. He was surprised to see a youngish man in a dark suit standing there.

'Ah,' said the man, 'Mr Barry O'Donoghue?' he asked.

'Ye'es', answered Barry cautiously.

'I'm sorry to bother you at home Mr O'Donoghue but it's taken me a while to track you down after your appearance on EtE.'

'I'm not interested in coming back!' he said with barely concealed anger.

'Please,' appealed the man, taking a small step forward and placing his foot in the doorway, 'hear me out. I'm not from EtE, I simply got your contact details from one of the assistants there. My name is Dr James Preston and I head up a research facility just outside Cambridge that explores anomalous behaviour.'

Barry stood there for a moment, unsure how to respond. He felt a little conflicted. Initially, he'd been annoyed at the mention of EtE but then became cautiously interested once he'd heard the phrase, "research facility" and "Cambridge". 'What do you want with me?' he asked.

'Do you mind if I come in?' asked Dr Preston.

Barry stood for a moment thinking, then slowly moved aside and indicated the one chair over by the small table. 'Have a seat,' he said as he walked back over to the bed and sat down.

Preston smiled gratefully, made his way across the bed-sitting room to the chair and sat down.

The two men sat looking at one another for a few seconds before Preston began.

'I saw your performance on EtE,' he said.

Barry shook his head, 'it's not a trick,' he said sullenly. 'They didn't give me enough time. Plus I wasn't able to relax beforehand. It just . . . it just all went wrong.'

'But I did see you move the mobile,' said Preston with interest.

Barry looked up. Brightening considerably. 'Yeah, I'd just got it going before that . . . that woman,' he said, 'came over and interrupted me.'

'The question is,' Preston said with a glint in his eye, 'do you think you can you do it again?'

Barry looked cautiously at him. 'What d'ya mean?'

Preston reached into his jacket pocket and took out a small business card. He briefly rose and took a step towards Barry, holding out the card as he did. Barry partially rose from the bed and took the card, reading the inscription. It said '*Dr James Preston*, *Head of Anomalous Behaviours Research*, and then gave a Cambridge email and telephone number.

'What do you want with me?' he asked.

'We,' said Preston, sitting back on the chair, with a bright cheerful smile, 'want to offer you a job.'

Barry sat back on the bed, shocked. 'A job,' he echoed as he re-read the card. Then with a suspicious look asked, 'doing what?'

'Working as a Research Associate on the team, exploring precisely the sort of behaviours you exhibited on that programme.'

Barry couldn't believe it. He heard the phrase 'Research Associate' and thought it sounded grand. He instantly imagined himself in a white lab coat with clipboard. He wasn't sure what it involved but had a good inkling that it would be much better than picking in a warehouse.

Preston continued, 'we believe you are uniquely placed to help us examine these aspects of human behaviour.'

'In Cambridge?' queried Barry quietly.

'Yes, though there is a re-location package as part of the offer. I just wanted to come and see you in person so that you could see that the offer is genuine and I'd be able to answer any questions you may have about the role.'

He couldn't believe it. It seemed the answer to all his prayers. It also seemed too good to be true which made him very cautious. However, after the two men had spent a little more time chatting about the role and its responsibilities Barry was starting to believe this might just be true. It would also be a way out for him. He could get away from this bedsit, away from the warehouse job and all the idiots that worked there and away from the Kulagina Club. This last thought gave him mixed feelings. On the one hand he wasn't keen on facing Steve and Alice, or Helen, again, but on the other hand being part of the club had been the only thing that kept him going. Also, he felt uncomfortable about the idea of letting the others down. He certainly felt conflicted.

They ended their meeting with Barry agreeing to think about the offer and promising to get back in touch within the next week to give Preston an answer.

It was some months later when Dr James Peterson was again meeting with Sir Carmichael Harrington to provide him with an update of their progress.

'James,' said Harrington with what seemed like genuine pleasure, 'please,' he said waving one arm towards the comfy chairs, 'come in and have a seat.'

Once both men were seated James began. 'You've had a chance to look at the report?' he asked.

'Oh yes, quite intriguing,' said Harrington. 'How did Mr O'Donoghue take to the relocation?'

'Like a duck to water,' responded James smiling. 'He was very happy to move. I think he'd been looking for a way out of his situation for some time.'

'Indeed,' smiled Harrington.

'Have you had a chance to review the recording,' queried James.

'Yes, I must say his performance is quite impressive. Do you have any idea yet how he's doing it?'

James frowned a little in dismay, showing how perplexed he felt. 'No.'

There was a moments silence as the two men sat in thought before James continued.

'At least, not fully. We do know that just prior to him moving the object there's a burst of high frequency gamma activity in the anterior region of his brain.'

'What do you think it means?'

'It's difficult to say at this moment in time. But it may be an indication of some form of hyper-connectivity occurring across multiple regions of the brain.'

Harrington simply nodded slowly as if in thought.

'We will of course know more as the trials increase but its possible that this hyper-connectivity allows the brain to develop multiple feedback loops which greatly enhances its processing capabilities.'

Harrington was pleased with the caution James was showing in terms of his explanation. He favoured the slow and steady approach.

'However,' continued James, 'we still don't know how that would enable him to move a physical object without touching it.'

'Perhaps the connections are not physical,' mused Harrington.

'Hmm, yes, that's possible of course,' responded James. 'With that in mind I have people exploring the idea of panpsychism and the notion that if consciousness were a fundamental force then the interaction, if it can be called that, may be one that is occurring at the level of consciousness itself.'

Harrington nodded in encouragement and was pleased to hear about the progress being made. 'Excellent,' said Harrington briskly, ending that part of the conversation. He then turned and picked up another buff-coloured folder from the coffee table and handed it to James saying, 'here is a report of a young woman who claims to have psychic healing abilities.'

James took the folder and opened it to briefly scan the documents inside.

'You'll find all you need in there to begin surveillance and possibly, if it turns out to be true, to help recruit another . . . associate to your team.'

Harrington rose from his chair and James quickly mirrored him, closing the folder and placing it under his arm.

'Keep me posted on your progress,' said Harrington, indicating that the meeting had now come to a close.

James nodded smiling, 'certainly sir.' Then left the office.

Harrington walked back over to his desk slowly thinking to himself of the various reports that were now coming in. Odd, he thought to himself, we seem to be getting more healers now than anything else. I wonder whether this is some sort of reflection of the current state of the world.

4

I Know What I Saw

The bus pulled into the station and headed towards its allocated bay. As soon as it had stopped many of the passengers were up and out of their seats forming a queue in the aisle to get out of the door at the front. Grace looked up and decided to wait for a moment, she wasn't in a rush. As the other passengers began to move forward and exit the bus, she gathered her shopping bag and made sure her coat was done up. After a few moments she stood and joined the remaining passengers as they all made their way off the bus.

As she passed by the driver at the front of the bus, she offered a cheery, 'thank you.' Something she noticed that fewer and fewer people seemed to do nowadays. She stepped off the bus and made her way to the town centre, weaving amongst the milling crowds of shoppers and day trippers. Grace was a lean woman of seventy-six, with short silver curls where once she had long black locks. She had a kind face, although deeply lined and had bright hazel eyes that still held a hint of mischief.

The town was busy, as usual, and it took her just over an hour to get the few small things she wanted from the department store, where she also stopped briefly for a small coffee and a fruit scone. Having got the things she needed she headed for the bakery before returning to the bus station. She was pleased that the town still had a bakery, so many didn't now, as the supermarkets seemed to take over. Upon arrival at the small independent bakery stoor she opened the door and took a deep breath. The sweet smell of fresh bread and cakes was something she really enjoyed, and it briefly transported her back to her childhood. Triggering long-cherished memories of visits to the local baker's shop with her mother. As these memories began to fade, like the echo of a past once lived, she moved to wait in line whilst the young woman in front of her ordered a selection of cakes. Once the assistant had placed the cakes in a cardboard box, and tied it up with string, she took the woman to the other end of the counter so she could pay.

Grace continued to wait, looking over the cakes, and trying to decide whether to get an apple turnover or a Bakewell tart. As she mulled over this seemingly difficult decision a face at the window caught her eye. She looked over – it was Lilly! She was a little shocked and surprised, but pleasantly so. Lilly and she had been friends since their early twenties but had lost touch in recent years after Lilly had moved away to the coast to help look after her sister who'd fallen ill. She smiled and waved at Lilly. Ooh, she thought, it will be such a treat to catch up with Lilly and hear all about what she's been up to. She could clearly see Lilly's gently smiling face. It was then that she noticed Lilly wasn't wearing a coat. That's odd, she thought, it's really quite chilly out. She also thought it a bit odd that Lilly hadn't waved back. It was obvious the woman could see her; she was smiling directly at her. All in all it gave Grace a very odd feeling.

'Can I help you?' asked the assistant, her voice interrupting Grace's thoughts.

Grace turned to the middle-aged woman behind the counter, 'oh sorry, I was just waving to a friend,' she said, nodding back to the window to indicate the spot where Lilly had stood.

But Lilly wasn't there.

Grace frowned, feeling a little perplexed. She looked around to see if Lilly had come into the shop or moved to look in through the other window. That's odd, she thought, why wouldn't she wait for me.

'Can I help you madam,' said the assistant again, this time raising her voice as if Grace was deaf.

'Oh, I am sorry,' flustered Grace. 'I, . . . oh – er, yes, can I have a Bakewell tart and a small granary loaf please?'

As the assistant began to put together Grace's order, she looked around again to see if she could see Lilly. But there was no sign of her anywhere.

'If you'd like to come this way and pay at the till please,' said the assistant, speaking loudly and clearly to ensure she was heard.

Grace moved to the end of the counter and paid for her goods and then put them in the top of her shopping bag. As she left the baker's she looked up and down the street to see if she could spot any sign of Lilly. Surely, thought Grace to herself, she wouldn't just leave without saying hello. She reached into her pocket and checked her mobile phone in case Lilly had left her a message. The phone came to life in her hand letting her know that she had no new messages.

The whole event left Grace feeling very out of sorts. It played on her mind as she made her way back to the bus station and all the way back home.

Once Grace had arrived back home, hung up her coat and unpacked her shopping, she decided to sit down with a cup of tea and a slice of the Bakewell tart she'd just purchased. She carried her teacup and small plate with the tart into the lounge and sat in her favourite chair beside the rear window.

She often sat here so she could look out at the trees and the flowers in the garden. It was her window on the world and a place she enjoyed sitting in the afternoon. However, now, as she sat down and put her tea and cake on the table beside the chair, she looked not outwards through the window but inwards, at her memory of the day's events.

Grace hadn't seen Lilly for about five years now, ever since she'd moved to the coast. They'd stayed in touch initially but over time the phone calls had become less and less frequent, until eventually they just petered out altogether. Grace shook her head frowning as she wondered why Lilly hadn't hung around and waited for her to come out of the bakers. Surely, she thought, she can't be annoyed with me for not keeping in touch. It wasn't something either of them had planned, it was just one of those things. Yet Grace still had this odd feeling about the event, which was hard to describe and just left her with a general sense of unease. She shook her head briskly and decided to try and put the event from her mind. Sitting back, she picked up her tea and smiled in anticipation of her sweet treat.

Later that evening she sat in the lounge watching the early evening news on the BBC. It all seemed to be bad news. It always seemed to be bad news nowadays. She couldn't understand it, and it was something that had annoyed her over the years. It was as if they could only report the bad things that had happened in the world. Which she knew, meant you'd end up having a distorted view of the world you lived in. Weren't news broadcasts supposed to present a balanced view she thought crossly. Why do they insist on this continuous onslaught of negativity. With a combination of anger and frustration she switched the TV off and reached across to pick up a copy the local newspaper – *The Kent Herald*. At least here, she thought, she'd find some more local and upbeat stories.

The headline story told of a local celebrity who'd be switching on the Christmas lights this year. There was also news of a well-known wine merchant developing a multi-million pound winery in the heart of the Kent countryside. She smiled as she read this, thinking how nice it might be to have local wines. As she read through the paper she stopped and scanned through the obituaries. It was more a spot check, than morbid curiosity. She'd noticed that as she got older, thinking about death, and the death of those near to her, was just something that became more a part of her everyday experience.

Just then her eyes caught one of the notices. Everything seemed to stop for a moment. Her mouth went dry, and her breath became shallow as her heartbeat quickened, thumping against her chest. The notice said Lilly had died. She read through the notice, slowly and carefully:

Ms. L. PATTERSON. The death of Ms. Lilly Patterson, aged 78 years, occurred on November 4th at the infirmary, after a long and painful illness. The funeral took place on Saturday, at St. Mary's Cemetery and was officiated by The Rev. J. Treadwell.

Once she'd finished reading through for the second time, she let the paper drop to her lap. She couldn't believe it. She couldn't understand it. She picked the paper up again and looked at the date in the notice. The 4th of November, but when was that. She got up quickly and walked out into the kitchen to check the calendar that was pinned to the wall by the fridge. The 4th of November was two weeks ago. Still shaken, she made her way back to the lounge and sat down again. How can this be, she thought, feeling distinctly unnerved.

Ah, she thought, an idea occurring to her after she'd thought about it for a while. It could be a different Lilly

Patterson. After all, who's to say there must be only one person in the world with that name she reasoned. She picked the paper up again and scanned the notice. It made no mention of where this Lilly Patterson had lived, and she wasn't familiar with St. Mary's cemetery. As she sat there, she began to think, who could she call that might know? As she thought this the answer immediately popped into her head – Joan!

Grace knew that Joan had been a long-time friend of Lilly's sister before she fell ill and that she very likely would have kept in touch as her husband Eric had been a good friend of Lilly's younger brother Nigel, as they both went to the same bowls club, over in Ashford. Now, she thought, where did I leave that mobile phone. She got up again and went back to the kitchen. Finally, after a brief but fruitless search of the kitchen she found the mobile on the hall stand where she must have put it when she arrived back home earlier. Taking the phone, she returned to the lounge, and with trembling fingers, accessed her contacts list. Once she'd found Joan's number, she pressed call.

The phone rang three times before an elderly woman's voice answered slowly, 'Hello.'

'Oh, hello,' said Grace somewhat shakily, 'is that Joan?'

'Yes.'

'It's Grace Worthington here.'

There was a moments silence. Then the other woman responded more warmly, 'oh, Grace, its good to hear from you. I haven't heard from you in quite a while. Is everything ok?'

Grace wasn't sure where to start or what to say.

'I'm so sorry to bother you,' she began, 'but I've just been reading The Herald.'

She got no further.

'Ah yes,' said Joan sadly, 'the notice about Lilly.'

'So, it was – it was, Lilly,' said Grace in little more than a whisper.

'Yes, so sad. I'm sorry you didn't know it was . . .'

The conversation ran on for a few minutes as Joan filled Grace in on the details of Lilly's final days. Grace responded as best she could, but she wasn't really listening. It was as if a part of her mind was operating on automatic pilot, making the necessary noises in response to Joan's words. Grace allowed the mostly one-sided conversation, to go on for a couple of minutes before finally excusing herself and hanging up.

She sat there in silence for a few minutes, trying to process what she'd now had confirmed. That Lilly was dead. Had died, in fact, two weeks ago. She just couldn't reconcile that information with the knowledge, the certainty she felt, that she'd seen Lilly that afternoon, outside the bakers.

She felt she needed to talk to someone about this. To try and help her understand it. She looked down at the phone in her hand, scrolled through until she found Ana's number and pressed call.

'Hi mum,' said Ana, 'how's things?'

'Oh, Ana,' said Grace in a voice distraught with emotion. 'I've just had some . . . some very shocking news.'

∞

The following Wednesday evening found Grace, sitting alone in her lounge, still unable to shake the odd experience of the previous week. The radio was on in the background, but she was only partially listening as she waited for Ana and Peter to arrive. Thinking about her two children helped to provide some comfort and in doing so brought a weak smile to her face.

Ever since Grace's husband Anthony had died a few years previously, Wednesday evening dinner had become a regular family event, and one that Grace looked forward too. Being of a generation that reserved praise, she didn't say it very often, but she was proud of her two children. Ana, with her PhD in psychology, now lecturing at the local university, and Peter, who was the head chef of a local restaurant in town. It was primarily because of Peter that they met at all, and on a Wednesday at that. Out of the two, Peter had always been the more sociable one. Always out with friends, or off to live events somewhere. Whereas Ana was the quieter, stay at home, more studious one. It was Peter who'd first suggested the three of them getting together for dinner. It wasn't a surprise that he'd suggested they meet over dinner, it was obvious from his big build that he was someone who enjoyed his food. It also gave him an opportunity to cook for them both, something else he always enjoyed, and he could show off new dishes or try out new recipe ideas on them both. Also, Wednesday evening was one of the few times that Peter didn't have to work late.

The ring of the front doorbell interrupted Grace's thoughts and she quickly got up and made her way out and along the hall to the front door. Opening the door, she saw Ana standing there. Ana was short and round, with a dark bob of hair and light hazel eyes. These lit up when she saw her mother. 'Hi mum.'

Grace smiled in greeting. 'Hello love,' she said.

Ana stepped into the hall and gave her mum a big hug. 'Is Pete here yet?'

'No not yet,' answered Grace as she took Ana's coat and hung it up with the others on the wall beside the door.

'Huh, no surprise. He's always late,' complained Ana.

'Come into the lounge and we can sit in the warm,' said Grace, not responding to Ana's barbed comment. 'Do you want a cup of tea, or something?' she asked.

'Hmm, not yet,' said Ana. 'Probably best to wait and see what he's cooked for us.'

'You look tired,' said Grace, noticing the dark shadows beneath Ana's eyes and the increasing lines on her brow. 'How are things at work?'

'Arrgh! Don't get me started on work,' responded Ana, with a shake of the head. 'I want to hear all about this . . . this experience you had.'

'Well, I wanted to wait and then I could tell you bo . . .'

She was interrupted by another ring of the doorbell. Grace left again to open the door to her son. Unlike Ana, everything about Peter was large. His bulky frame, his loud jovial voice, and his big smile.

'Hi Mum!' he boomed through his open visor, as she opened the door on him. His motorcycle helmet and leather jacket added to his size, making him fill most of the doorway. 'You take these,' he said handing her two heat bags containing their food for the evening, 'and I'll get out of this gear.' He came through the door, turned slightly and then closed it behind him.

'Why didn't you get a taxi?' asked Grace, as she carried the bags of food to the kitchen 'rather than having to carry these on . . . on that bike.' Grace was not a fan of motorcycles and couldn't understand Peter's fascination with them.

'It's fine,' said Peter, 'they easily fitted in the top-box.'

Grace, thin lipped, said nothing. This was a topic they'd both been over many times and through some unspoken agreement generally avoided in order to keep the peace.

Meanwhile, Peter took off his helmet, placed it on the floor beneath the coats and then took off his large black leather jacket and hung it next to Ana's long coat. Once he'd taken his calf-length motorcycle boots off he made his way along the corridor and into the lounge.

'Hi sis,' he said with a big smile, enveloping Ana in his arms as she stood to greet him.

'Ok Pete, how's things?' she asked, almost disappearing beneath his large arms as he wrapped them around her.

'Yeah, good. We've been working on introducing a new classic range of desserts,' he said as they both sat down.

'How can classic desserts be new?' queried Ana.

Unperturbed, Peter just grinned. 'Because,' he responded with a smile, 'we haven't done 'em before – that's how.'

Ana smiled, in spite of herself. Peter was one of those eternally cheerful people who always looked on the bright side.

Grace then entered the room, 'I've put the dishes in the oven to warm through,' she said. 'Do either of you want a drink before we eat?'

'That can wait,' said Ana quickly, 'I want to hear about this experience you had.'

'Err, oh yeah, me too,' said Peter, with slightly less enthusiasm. 'But, we can listen and drink at the same time – can't we?'

'Wine or beer?' asked Grace with a knowing smile.

Both responded immediately, with Ana asking for beer and Peter asking for wine.

Grace smiled and nodded in acknowledgement, leaving the room to fulfil the drinks order.

Peter looked back at Ana as he made his way over to the settee. 'So, how's life at the Uni?' he asked, sitting down and wriggling a bit in an effort to make himself comfortable.

Ana sighed, her shoulders slumped, and shaking her head slightly, said, 'mad. I'm working all the hours and still not getting enough done.'

'Don't worry, soon be the Christmas break.'

Ana smiled wryly, 'oh joy. Two weeks of marking.'

Peter's smile was a little forced as he looked over at his sister. Though he rarely admitted it, and never to her face, he too was proud of her. He knew how hard she'd worked to get into university and then the scholarships and the PhD. But he couldn't help wondering if all that effort was really worth it.

'Here we go,' said Grace, entering the room with a beer for Ana and two glasses of red wine. One for Peter and the other for herself.

Once they were all settled Ana wasted no time in returning the conversation back to Grace's experience. 'So,' she said, 'tell us about this . . . this experience.'

Grace took a sip of her wine and then began to tell them both of her experience at the bakers the previous week. The story didn't take long to tell and as she finished, she looked at them both, trying to gauge their reaction.

Peter spoke first, which wasn't unusual. 'What do you think Sis?' he asked, 'you're the expert.'

Ana made a wry face and shrugged. 'It's obvious,' she answered, 'it wasn't Li . . .'

'No!' interrupted Grace, more fiercely than she'd meant to. 'I know what you are going to say. That I made a mistake. That it wasn't her, just someone who looked like her. But that's rubbish. I've known,' she faltered for a moment, 'I'd known' she continued emphasising the change in tense, 'Lilly for years. It was her. It wasn't someone who looked like her – it was her!'

'Hmmm,' nodded Peter thoughtfully, as he took a gulp of his wine. 'Ooh, this is good' he said with a smile and some hope of decreasing the tension in the room.

Momentarily distracted Grace also smiled. 'I'm glad you like it,' she responded.

'Mum,' appealed Ana, shaking her head slightly in disagreement. 'Think about it. There must be thousands of people who live in and around the town. It's obvious that given those odds there's likely to be at least one person who looks . . .'

She got no further as Grace interrupted again, though more gently this time. 'No Ana,' she said firmly. 'I know you mean well, but it wasn't just seeing her, it was the feeling I had. I can't explain it. It was odd, as if somehow I knew, or a part of me knew that this was . . . that it was odd, or off in some way. Oh,' she shook her head and shrugged a little. 'I can't explain it. But it was her, I know it was.'

Peter, ever the mediator, said, 'well, you do hear of such things don . . .'

He got no further before Ana interrupted sharply, 'things,' she said, 'what *things*?' she queried, her voice rising.

Peter struggled for a moment. 'Well, you know. Like, when you think about someone you haven't seen for ages and then out of the blue you get a phone call from them.'

'No,' said Ana with stern emphasis. 'That's salience bias.'

'What?' jeered Peter. 'You just made that up,' he laughed.

'No,' responded Ana with a slight shake of her head. 'It simply means that you think about people you haven't heard from lots of times, and they don't call you. But you only remember the times when they *do* call.'

'Yeah,' persisted Peter, 'but lots of people have seen . . .'

'Seen what?' interrupted Ana, her voice rising again along with her temper. 'Seen people who died two weeks ago! No, I'm sorry. I don't think so.'

Peter tried to placate Ana's growing annoyance. 'But you've got to admit Sis, we don't know everything.'

'Oh, not that old chestnut,' groaned Ana. 'Of course we don't know everything. No one is saying we do. But,' she took a breath, 'just because we don't know everything, doesn't mean we start jumping to conclusions about . . .'

'Do you mind!' reproached Grace mildly. 'I am still here you know. And, Ana, I know you're a psychologist and all that, but I was there, and you weren't and there's nothing wrong with my eyesight or my mind, thank you very much.'

'Mum,' consoled Ana. 'I didn't mean that . . .'

'Let's just leave it there for now,' said Grace, more calmly than she felt. 'I've told you what happened, now let's go and have some dinner. But I will tell you this,' she said with grim determination, 'I know what I saw.'

It was the following Wednesday evening, when Peter and Ana were again due for dinner. However, somewhat surprisingly Peter had arrived first and was now sitting with Grace at the kitchen table studying an open laptop.

'Ah, here it is,' said Peter, indicating with a nod of his head that he'd finally found what he'd been searching for. Grace, who was sitting beside him pulled her chair in closer so she could see what he was referring to.

'Here,' said Peter. 'It's called an after-death communication, or ADC[1], and it's . . .' he leaned in towards the computer and read the text. 'It's when an experient,' that's you mum he said smiling, 'either sees, feels or senses the presence of a deceased person.' He straightened up and looked at Grace.

'Well, I certainly saw something,' said Grace, 'and there was definitely a very odd feeling about it.'

'See, I told you. And look, there's loads of stuff on it here,' he indicated with a click of the mouse. 'Look, there are different types, and lots of people have written in about their own experiences.'

Grace put her arm around him and leant her head on his shoulder. 'Thanks love,' she said.

'And,' he said, now grinning broadly, 'there's a section here where you can buy books and everything.'

'Click back on to that bit that had people's experiences,' said Grace, sitting more upright now and leaning in to see the screen more clearly.

Peter clicked back to the relevant webpage and let Grace read through some of the anecdotal reports that people had sent in. The two of them sat there in silence for a few minutes while Grace read through these accounts. After a few minutes however, the silence was broken by the sound of the doorbell. Grace looked up and said, 'that'll be Ana. I wonder what she'll make of all this?' she said with a nod towards the open laptop. She got up from the kitchen table and went off to let Ana in. Meanwhile, Peter continued browsing the site. He found the personal accounts much more interesting and was engrossed in them when he heard Ana's voice echoing from the hall. 'Bloody hell! you mean he's here before me.'

Peter looked up and turned as Ana entered the kitchen. 'Hi Pete,' she said, 'this is a first.' She walked over to where he was sitting and gave him a quick hug. Even though she was standing she only just topped his height as he sat there.

Peter smiled, happy to see her, but there was a reticence in his movements that portrayed an element of guilt, and she was quick to notice it.

'What have you got there?' she asked, nodding at the open laptop. 'Don't often see you with a computer.'

'He brought that along for me,' said Grace as she re-entered the kitchen and moved back to her chair beside Peter, pointing at the screen as she sat. 'Peter's found some interesting things out about, what were they called, DC's . . . or something?'

Peter response was slightly hesitant. 'They're called ADC's.' There was a brief silence as Ana waited for an explanation. 'It means,' he continued, 'an . . . an after-death communication.'

Ana's shrill voice rang out. 'A what!?'

'It's when people have experiences,' said Grace, working hard to keep her tone of voice neutral and calm. 'Like the one I had. Where they see someone . . .' she hesitated momentarily, 'someone who's dead.'

Ana dropped her head, and her shoulders slumped. 'Not this again,' she groaned.

'But look,' pleaded Peter, 'there's loads of stuff about this on the internet. There's books and loads of people have written about their own experiences, and there's this website that deals with research and stuff.' He clicked another webpage, 'see, it's called the after death communication research foundation[2].'

Ana's response was scathing. 'Of course there's loads of stuff about it. It's the bloody internet for Christ's sake!' Her voice quickly rising as her temper flared. 'You can find anything on the internet! Thousands of people on the internet think the Earth is flat – but that doesn't make it real!' She took a deep breath and held up her hands as if trying to placate them. 'Look, why are you turning some simple coincidence, or mistaken identity, into something major?'

Grace sat bolt upright in her chair. Her hands tightly clasped and her jaw clenching, she took a deep breath. '*Do you mind*,' she said, emphasising each word. 'I happen to think that the experience, which happened to me by the way, *was* something major.' She leant back a bit, her thin-lipped expression one of mild annoyance. 'And I'll thank you not to swear Ana,' she added.

'Mum,' intoned Ana in appeal. 'All I'm saying is that you need to be careful about believing what you read on the internet.'

'Ana,' said Grace more calmly than she felt, 'I'm very proud of you and what you've done – you know that. But you don't know everything. This . . . this happened to me, and despite what you may think it wasn't a coincidence or a case of mistaken identity.'

'All I'm saying,' said Ana with emphasis, 'is that you need to be careful about believing stuff on the internet.'

Grace stiffened a little, her face taking on an air of forced calm that was betrayed by the tightness of her lips. 'Don't you think I know that,' she said, 'I'm not completely gullible you know. And yes, when it happened it did make me question my sanity. After all, you just don't go around seeing dead people. This is real life, not the films. And yes, I was shocked. At first, but now, after reading some of this,' she indicated the laptop, 'I feel a bit more . . . more relieved.'

'Relieved?' queried Peter.

Grace relaxed a little, unfolding her arms and smiling a little wryly, 'yes,' she said. 'I don't know if I can explain, but when it happened, I was shocked. It was unexpected and I didn't know what to make of it. But after reading some of these accounts. From people who've had similar experiences to me, it makes me feel . . . well, more at peace really. I mean, I don't know what happens when we die, but seeing Lilly makes me think that perhaps it's not all bad. Maybe there is something more – and maybe we'll never know,' she added quickly, 'but that's not the point. It makes me *feel* better – less afraid of death.'

There was a moments silence as the word death hung in the air. The three of them sat motionless, stilled by reflections of mortality.

Peter shuddered. 'How about we get those dishes out of the oven,' he said, quickly changing the subject.

Grace nodded and rising, went over to the oven to take out the dishes Peter had brought over earlier.

'Nice try,' said Ana, sotto voce to Peter, as she moved to help with the plates and cutlery.

The meal that evening was a more sombre occasion than previous dinners. Both Grace and Peter made attempts to lighten the mood and maintain a civil atmosphere, but Ana continued to make it clear throughout that she wasn't happy with the situation.

Two days later Ana was still feeling a little irritated by the previous Wednesday's family dinner. In particular, she was annoyed with Peter for making a big deal out of it all and for showing mum all that stuff online. She shuddered momentarily as she thought about how many times she'd warned him about blindly believing what he read online. Deep down however, she knew he was just trying to help mum deal with her odd experience. She knew he didn't really have a bad bone in his body. Her irritation slowly turned to frustration as she thought about how gullible he could be when it comes to online information. She began to wonder if she'd been just a little too harsh with him and resolved to try and ring him later just to see how he was.

Later that day, having just finished giving her weekly lecture on cognitive models in psychology, Ana left the lecture theatre and began to make her way back to her office on the other side of campus. As she walked out of the exit by the refectory she looked up and was surprised to see Peter standing on the other side of the quad. She felt her step lighten as she smiled and waved at him.

Peter stood there, dressed in his black leather jacket, holding his helmet. He smiled and waved back to her.

It was odd she thought that they could fall out over something so trivial, when generally they had such a good relationship. Just then a voice behind her interrupted her thoughts.

'Excuse us Dr Worthington,' said a young female student.

Ana turned to see two female undergraduates earnestly clinging on to a selection of books and looking slightly anxious. Ana sighed inwardly. Other lecturers had joked about running the gauntlet of students after a lecture. Some even went so far as to take obscure and meandering detours to avoid them, but Ana always liked the idea that someone not only enjoyed her lecture enough to formulate a question but might also want to know more.

'Yes,' said Ana with an encouraging smile. 'What can I do for you?'

The two students looked at each other momentarily and then one took the lead, saying, 'we've just come from your lecture on models of memory, and we wondered,' here the speaker looked to her friend for support, who nodded in encouragement. 'We wondered if it would be possible to book a tutorial with you so that we could just go over some of the material from the lecture?'

Ana's face brightened. 'Yes of course. If you check my online calendar, you'll see my office hours posted up and all you have to do is book a slot.'

'Oh, great, thanks,' the two girls chorused, now looking slightly less stressed. They both smiled and turned to leave.

'Oh,' added Ana calling after them, 'when you book the slot, if you could just identify which issues you want me to cover, that will help us to structure the session.'

'Ok,' the girls responded in unison.

She turned back and resumed her journey. However, as she looked back across the quad she saw that Peter had now gone. She frowned, wondering why it was he couldn't have waited for her. It was odd. He didn't usually come and see her on campus. Her resolve to call him later and straighten things out strengthened. However, once back in her office, she noticed that her mobile, which was still on her desk, showed four missed calls from her mother. That was unusual. Odd, she thought, seems to be the day for unusual events.

Ana sat down at her desk and began to work through the endless stream of emails whilst at the same time pressing re-dial on her phone to call her mother back. The phone only rang twice before a voice answered.

'Oh, Ana, is that you?' Grace whimpered in a voice heavy with emotion.

'Mum!' responded Ana, concern echoing in her voice. 'Are you ok? What's up?'

'Oh, Ana, I've been calling and calling . . . its, its Peter.'

Ana froze. There was a sinking feeling in the pit of her stomach.

'Ana? – Ana?' called Grace, the distress now clearly evident in her voice. 'Are you still there?'

Ana didn't want to think. To let her mind race along the corridors of possibility. She worked hard to rein in her thoughts and control her feelings. Matter-of-factly asking, 'what is it mum?'

'I've had the police round,' there were sobs now. 'Oh Peter . . .'

Exasperation turned to worry and then quickly to anguish. 'Mum! – what is it? What's happened?'

The sobs quietened into sniffling, it's – it's Peter,' sniffed Grace. 'He's been involved in an accident.'

Silent shock followed this announcement.

'Oh Ana!' howled Grace, now not trying to hold back her tears. 'He died this morning.'

Bewildered alarm echoed in Ana's voice, 'but – but that's impossible.'

'Oh, Ana,' Grace cried, 'I know. I couldn't believe it. But there was a road accident. The police said a truck had swerved to avoid a cyclist and ran straight into Peter on his motorbike. They said,' she sobbed, 'they said, he would have been killed instantly.'

Ana sat in confused anguish. She tried to picture Peter as she'd seen him only moments ago in the quad. She clung to this image of stability as she faced a surging wave of grief.

'But that's not – that's impossible,' cried Ana. 'I've just seen . . .' Then it struck her. The dawning realisation of what had just happened was a hammer blow to her heart. She cried out in despair.

'Oh Mum,' she wept. 'I've – I've just seen him.'

∞

5

Unintended Intentions

Professor Norris sat reading the report. Despite his somewhat shabby brown suit and unkempt silver hair he was known to have an excellent mind and be a fair judge when it came to the research conducted in his unit. As he finished reading the report he sat up and took off his small reading glasses, rubbing the bridge of his nose, he looked across towards the two men sitting attentively on the other side of the desk. They were both young, although all the post-doctoral researchers seemed young to Norris' eye now. However, the elder of the two, Dr Steve Matlock, was lean with cropped, almost shaven fair hair and bright blue eyes. Whereas his companion, Dr Tom Oakridge, was more solidly built, almost stocky, and had dark curly hair with light green eyes.

'Well done gentlemen,' said Norris with a slight nod of the head, as if emphasising his appreciation of the results heralded in the report. 'It seems that the cellular trials indicate a clear benefit for using…' he stopped and reached back to the report, 'what was it again?'

'The drug is called QuixSoma,' said Steve, straightening his back and sitting even more upright.

'Ah yes, QuixSoma,' said Norris replacing the report on his desk. He sat for a moment stroking his short beard as if pondering what to say next. The moment played out, increasing the tension across the room to a level that was almost palpable. The cause of this tension was the fact that the two young research scientists had now completed their initial trials with the drug and needed Professor Norris' permission to move on to the next phase. A phase that would necessitate the use of live animals and hence required the permission of the head of department. They all knew the ethical, and moral issues involved with using live animals, and didn't take such decisions lightly.

'Well,' continued Norris in a sombre thoughtful tone, 'I see no reason not to move on to the next phase of the trials.' There was a moments silence, then he added, 'I'll approve the live specimens immediately and you should have them by the end of this week.'

'Thank you,' said both researchers in unison.

'Keep me posted on the outcome,' said Norris handing the report back to Steve, indicating clearly that the meeting had now come to an end.

'Of course,' said Steve, as he and Tom nodded in agreement.

Both researchers left Professor Norris' office feeling very happy with themselves. The project was progressing well, and the early results were positive. Both were hoping that this would lead to better things. Ideally, in the form of permanent contracts. They were also hopeful that the results of the live trials, if as good as the previous in vitro trials, could be published in a prestigious scientific journal. Something that would significantly help their prospects in obtaining the, much sought after, permanent contracts.

As the two men walked along the corridor back to their lab Steve turned to Tom. 'When do you think we should start the live trial?' he asked.

'Now that we have approval, and if we can get the live samples by the end of this week, I'd think we should be able to start sometime next week,' answered Tom.

'Agreed,' said Steve smiling.

'However,' said Tom with a slight frown, 'I think we should include a wound reduction protocol as this will provide a more explicit indicator of the drug's . . .' he was about to say success but just stopped himself in time and instead said, '. . . effect.'

'Hmmm,' Steve replied nodding slightly. 'Also,' he added, 'we could euthanise a sub-set of each group and collect fibroblast[1] counts and run histological evaluations to provide additional indicators of the drug's impact.'

Both men continued along the corridor in thoughtful silence as they made their way back to their lab, mulling over the next phase of the study in their minds and thinking about the possible outcome.

∞

The following week found Steve and Tom working busily in their lab, preparing a group of twenty-four male Wistar rats. These are rats that had been specially bred for use in the fields of medical and biological research. The group of rats they had obtained were all the same age and of approximately the same weight. With each rat housed individually in its own PVC container this enabled the researchers to control the temperature, lighting and access to food and water for each of them.

The protocol required all rats to be sanitised and then receive an anaesthetic injection. They would then be lesioned, or wounded, along the central back part of their spines. Technically known as the dorsal cervical region. This wound would be produced using a trephine punch, or small circular surgical saw, that would remove a precise section of skin from each of the rats. The rats would then be randomly allocated into two groups. One that would receive the healing drug

QuixSoma – the treatment group, and the other remaining as an untreated control group.

Tom was responsible for the initial steps of the procedure with Steve taking over to administer the drug treatment.

'All initial steps complete,' said Tom, once he'd finished lesioning the final rat.

'Ok, if you randomly separate them into two groups,' said Steve, 'I'll take the treatment group through and administer the intervention.'

Tom carried out his tasks diligently and competently. Gently separating the rats into two groups and placing markers on each of their PVC homes to indicate which condition the rat was in. He then placed the PVC containers of the treatment group on an aluminium trolley so that Steve could wheel them into the next lab to receive the treatment. The remaining rats, that formed the control group, he placed on another trolley to return them to the housing section, which was in a separate room down the corridor.

'All done,' said Tom, indicating the trolley with the rats in the treatment group.

'Thanks,' said Steve, and wheeled the trolley out through the swing door and into the next lab. He set each of the PVC containers, containing a still sleeping rat, on the bench ready to receive the treatment injection. He then opened the central drawer and took out two sealed packets of syringes. He broke the seal on each packet and placed the empty syringes on the tray beside the containers. As he was about to reach out to the med cabinet for the drug he felt his phone vibrate in his pocket. He reached in his pocket, took out his phone and checked the alert message on the screen. It was from his wife Elena.

'*Urgent! call back asap,*' it read.

Steve frowned, a little concerned but not overly worried, he opened the phone and tapped the screen to call his wife. The phone only rang once before the concerned and somewhat stressed voice of his wife answered.

'Steve, is that you?'

'Hi Ellie,' said Steve cautiously, 'what's up?'

'Oh Steve, it's your mum, she's had a fall.'

For a moment Steve just stood there. The news had shocked him, and like an unpleasant cold shower it had washed away all thoughts of rats, drugs and protocols. Only to be replaced by despondent gloomy thoughts of what this could mean.

'Wh - what?' he mumbled. All the while thinking – 'a fall, that could mean anything. She could've fallen off a chair, fallen over, fallen down the stairs, or fallen in front of a car.'

'It's-your-mum,' repeated Elena, emphasising each word slowly.

Steve felt a knot tighten in his stomach and a light headedness, as if he'd stood up too quickly. His voice cautious and calm asked, 'when?'

'About twenty minutes ago,' answered Elena quickly. 'She rang me as soon as she could get to a phone, but I don't have the car today – which is why I rang you straight away.'

The fact that Elena and Steve shared a single car, each taking it in turns to use it, was an ongoing bone of contention in their relationship.

'Has she called the emergency services?' asked Steve.

'Yes, but they say it will be at least an hour before they can get to her.'

'Shit!' exclaimed Steve, 'an hour. What . . . why?' he spluttered, not sure what to say next.

'Apparently, she's not top priority,' answered Elena.

Steve mentally shook himself to gain control of his emotions and growing anger at the treatment of his mother. 'Ok,' he said, sounding calmer than he felt. 'I'll leave right away, and I should be able to get there in about twenty minutes.'

The relief in Elena's voice was clear, 'ok great. I'll text her to let her know you're on your way.'

'Ok, thanks. I'll just square things here with Tom and I'll be on my way.'

'Call or text me as soon as you get there,' requested Elena.

'I will. Thanks love, I'll speak soon, bye.' With that Steve hung up, leaving the rats in their PVC containers where he'd laid them out and quickly went back to the main lab to find Tom. On entering the main lab however, he found it empty. Apparently, Tom had taken the control specimens back to the housing section. He quickly walked through the side exit towards the housing section and as he did so he saw Tom coming back towards him.

'Tom, I'm really sorry but there's been a family emergency. My mother's just had a fall and I need to get over there asap.'

Tom looked a little shocked at the news but responded well. 'Go,' he said, 'I'll finish up here.'

'Thanks!' called Steve, turning to make his way quickly to the main exit. 'Oh, I've left the treatment group in med lab 2,' he added as he half walked half ran back along the corridor.

'Don't worry,' Tom called after him, 'go. I'll sort things out here. Just call me if you need anything.'

'Thanks,' shouted Steve, now running down the corridor towards the exit.

Tom stood for a moment watching as Steve made his way out of the main exit. He hoped that everything would be all right. He shook his head slightly as if to dislodge the unpleasant thought of Steve's mother having some sort of accident and made his way back to med lab 2. As he entered the lab he could see that Steve had laid out the containers with the anaesthetised rats and had left two empty syringes in the tray beside them. Tom smiled to himself, thinking that Steve had obviously finished administering the drug treatment but not had time to clear away the used syringes. He picked up the two empty syringes and dropped them neatly into the nearest sharps box and then put the PVC containers back on the trolley to take them back to the housing section.

Later that day Steve called Tom to let him know that his mother had eventually been taken to hospital and had suffered a bruised hip bone, which while painful and debilitating, was not as serious as it could have been. Tom was relieved and again made an offer of help.

'Thanks anyway,' said Steve turning down Tom's offer, 'but it will mean I need to take her home and then stay with her for the next few days just to make sure she's ok.'

'Don't worry,' said Tom. 'Everything here is set. All I have to do now is monitor the samples over the next four to six days.'

'Thanks,' Steve said again, 'I really appreciate it, and if you need anything from me just call.'

'I will,' said Tom, 'just make sure your mum's ok.'

'Ok, I'll be back in again about the middle of next week.'

Tom smiled to himself, 'great, I'll have the initial results for you by then.'

'Ok, look forward to seeing them. And . . .' Steve hesitated, 'thanks Tom, I really appreciate it.'

'Relax,' said Tom, 'it's all under control.'

∞

For the next few days, while Steve helped nurse his mother back to health, Tom was kept busy at work with a variety of other tasks. However, Tom was very keen for their live animal trial to show a positive effect – even more so now that he was going to be solely responsible for the data collection and analysis. He quickly began to think of the treatment group of rats as 'his group' and spent every spare minute he had thinking about them.

First thing each morning he'd wonder how 'his group' were doing and in his mind's eye he would picture their wounds healing nicely. Throughout each day, whenever he had a spare minute, he'd spend a few moments thinking about his group of rats and how well they'd be doing compared to the controls. At the end of each day, when he was relaxing at home, his mind would again turn to his group of rats, and he'd think about how well they would be healing. He became so focused on the live trial that his partner, Rebecca, began to remark about his distracted nature.

As part of the data recording process, he took digital images of the wounds from each rat on the second, fourth and seventh days after injury. This provided clear and accurate images so that they could measure the diameter of the wound and map its reduction over time. On the fourth day he also euthanised half of the rats from each of the two groups, as this would allow tissue samples to be collected from around the wound site. These samples were treated, coloured, and then placed on slides to enable them to be able to carry out fibroblast counts.

It was the following week, as Tom was completing his analysis of the data from the digital images and slide samples, when Steve returned to the lab. As Steve walked into the lab Tom looked up from his computer with a big smile on his face.

'How's it going?' asked Steve.

'It goes,' answered Tom, raising his eyebrows and grinning, 'particularly well.'

The two men looked at each other for a moment.

'Well,' said Steve, 'don't keep me in suspense. Do you have the initial results or not?'

Tom sat for a moment without responding, enjoying the feeling of smug superiority that knowledge of the results gave him.

Steve made a move towards the computer. 'Do I have to run the analysis myself,' he moaned.

'Ok, ok,' said Tom raising his hands to ward Steve off. 'Have a seat and listen to this.'

Steve moved over to a nearby chair, took a seat and looked on expectantly.

Tom sat back in his chair, looked up at the ceiling as if trying to remember something and took a breath. 'Digital images show a forty-six percent improved reduction in wound healing area for the treatment group.'

Steve whistled, his face brightening.

'But that's not all,' continued Tom. 'Cellular analysis also showed a thirty-five percent increase in fibroblasts in the treatment group'.

'And both these changes are significant[2]?' asked Steve.

'Oh yes. Both very highly significant,' answered Tom.

'Yes!' whooped Steve punching the air.

There was a moments silence as they both sat there looking at each other with large grins on their faces. Their thoughts turning to the publications, job offers and research projects they might get invited to work on, given their success with this project. At that moment the future seemed bright indeed.

'What do you think?' asked Tom, smiling broadly, 'Nature or The Lancet?' he said, naming two of the most prestigious scientific medical journals.

'Ha-ha!' laughed Steve, 'we still need to write this up.'

Tom made a wry face to suggest that this was a mere trifle in the process of them getting their just rewards.

'By the way,' asked Steve, now relaxing back in his chair, 'what dosage did you use for the treatment group?'

The instant silence that followed this question was both tense and awkward.

Tom frowned with a mixture of concern and confusion. 'Wh . . . What?' he queried.

'The dosage,' repeated Steve, 'what did you use? It must have been reasonably high to get over forty percent reduction in wound . . .'

'But,' interrupted Tom, 'but, *you* gave them the treatment.'

Now it was Steve's turn to look confused. He sat upright and then leant forwards. 'No, I left the treatment group in the med lab and asked you to finish them off for me when I had to rush off.'

'What! I thought you'd already given them the drug,' moaned Tom.

Steve grimaced and shook his head, 'no. I'd only just begun to lay out the syringes.'

Tom screwed his face up in annoyance. 'I thought you'd given them the treatment and just hadn't finished clearing away the syringes.'

'Hold on a second,' said Steve raising both hands slightly. 'Are you saying that we have a treatmnt group – a treatmnt group that improved significantly more than the control group by the way – but a treatment group that, well, that . . . that didn't receive any treatment?'

Tom nodded slowly and then put his head in his hands, emitting a low groan of despair.

'But how can that be?' challenged Steve. 'Are you sure you didn't . . .'

'Absolutely sure,' said Tom sitting back up and shaking his head in response to the unanswered question.

The two men looked despondently at one another, each trying desperately to understand the situation and simultaneously hoping that it wasn't what they now thought it was.

Tom's shoulders dropped, his expression one of distaste. 'Are *you* sure you didn't have time to . . .' he asked, making a vague stabbing gesture with his hand to indicate injecting a drug.

Steve grimaced. 'Unfortunately, yes. I think I would have remembered injecting twelve rats.'

'But – but, I don't understand it,' said Tom falteringly. 'The data clearly shows an effect for the treatment group.'

'It just doesn't make sense,' responded Steve. 'And what we have to find out now, is why?'

∞

The odd pattern of results had left the two researchers feeling somewhat at sea. They both found it hard to fathom how, or why, such an effect could have emerged for the treatment group alone. After they had both spent some time grumbling in disbelief Steve suggested they go back and review each step of the protocol, to try and understand if there was any possible contamination of the treatment group. This only took them a couple of hours but neither of them could see any possible way a contaminant could have interacted with the treatment group alone. They didn't feel any further forward and in an effort to try and resolve the impasse Steve tried to reason it out.

'Do you think there's any possibility that someone else in the lab could have . . . could have.'

'Could have what,' scoffed Tom, 'interfered with our sample?' Even as he said it, they both knew it was almost impossible. One of the most sacrosanct rules of working in any lab was that you don't interfere with anyone else's research.

The two researchers sat opposite one another looking dejectedly at the data sheets spread between them that Tom had now printed out. The hard copies, showing the beneficial outcome for the treatment group, seemed to mock them as they sat there in confused bewilderment.

Steve put down the sheet he was re-reading. 'Ok, let's just go back over every step one last time.'

'But we've already done that,' moaned Tom.

'I know, I know. But we need to be sure that we haven't missed anything. And I mean anything. No matter how small or how trivial we may think.'

Tom sat back in his chair, looked up and closed his eyes as he recalled the sequence of steps each of the groups of rats had gone through. At the end of his recital the room was silent as they both sat thinking.

Steve looked across, 'so the treatment group didn't receive anything that the controls didn't also receive?'

Tom looked down at the floor now, shaking his head in weary resignation. 'No, I've already told you. Nothing.'

Steve persisted, 'they weren't the focus of anything unusual?'

Tom sat still for a moment lost in thought. On hearing the word focus his mind turned to his own thoughts of what he'd called his group of rats. He frowned as he thought about and almost instantly rejected the idea . . . almost . . . His brow furrowed and he grimaced as he tried to articulate what was going through his mind. He looked back at Steve, 'well . . .' he began, unsure of how to proceed.

Steve cautiously asked, 'well . . . what?'

Tom grimaced. He was struggling to put his thoughts into words. 'Well, not so much the focus of anything specific – but I did spend a lot of time thinking about them.'

Steve frowned a little. 'In what way?' he asked.

Tom shifted in his seat. It was clear that he felt a little uncomfortable with this line of reasoning. 'Well, you know. Thinking about them getting better,' he shrugged. 'I would imagine them healing and that the results would be – well, would be . . . what they are,' he finished lamely.

Steve rocked back in his chair now, thinking for a moment. 'How often?' he asked.

'Hmm, quite often actually. Rebecca even commented on how distracted she thought I was.' They both sat in silence for a moment, contemplating the possibilities.

'But come on,' pleaded Tom. 'What are you saying?'

Steve raised his hands in a placatory gesture, 'I'm not *saying* anything,' he said. 'But you know what Norris always says.'

'Yes,' said Tom, mimicking Professor Norris' deep baritone, 'a good scientist is one who remains critical yet open minded.'

'Exactly,' said Steve, 'and we just need to keep an open mind here.'

Tom made wry face, 'yes but not so open that . . .'

'No,' interrupted Steve quickly. 'You can't put limits on how open you're prepared to be. That's the point.'

The two men looked at each other, then they looked away, each deep in thought.

Tom shrugged. 'So, what *are* you saying. That me thinking about the rats, *somehow*,' as he said this, he made air quotes with both hands, 'helped them get better.'

'Tom,' Steve appealed, 'don't turn it into a straw man argument.'

Tom looked a little shamefaced as he smiled back, 'ok, ok, sorry.'

'All I'm saying,' continued Steve, 'is that we need to be open to the possibility that such a thing *could* happen. After all, we're scientists, aren't we?'

'Damn right,' answered Tom nodding in agreement and happy to be on more familiar ground.

'So, what I suggest we do is examine this possibility, in order to either help us make sense of what's happened here, or to rule it out.'

Tom made a wry face and looked uncomfortable.

'Ok?' asked Steve, wanting to hear Tom's explicit agreement.

After a moment Tom shrugged, 'Ok with me.'

'Right then,' continued Steve, now taking the lead. 'To begin with each of us needs to spend the next twenty-four hours searching the literature to find out if there's any evidence to support such a notion. If not, we can simply rule this idea out and move on – agreed?'

'Agreed,' said Tom, nodding more enthusiastically now.

'Ok, let's meet back here tomorrow at 4pm after we've both had a chance to search for any possible clues in the literature.'

∞

The following day at 4 o'clock Tom could be found in the lab sitting at his desk with a selection of scientific articles spread out before him. He'd meticulously sorted the articles into three piles and then sat back in his chair, linking his hands behind his head, he let out a large sigh. He sat for a moment just staring at the ceiling and trying to digest some of what he'd spent the morning reading. He shook his head in bewilderment.

Just then, Steve entered the lab, carrying a selection of articles and a couple of books. He walked over and sat at his desk, which was next to Tom's. He dumped the articles and books on his desk and looked over at Tom with a wry smile and shook his head.

Tom leant forward in his chair, put his head in his hands, and swore, 'shit!'

'Hmmm,' nodded Steve in agreement.

'Ok,' added Tom, sitting up now and looking across to Steve. 'First, I just want to apologise.'

'What for?'

'Well,' answered Tom, 'when you mentioned this idea yesterday, I thought it was just a lot of nonsense. But now . . .' he shrugged.

'And now . . .' echoed Steve.

'I'm not sure what to think. I mean, I wasn't familiar with any of this research. It's not exactly standard course reading for cellular biologists.'

'I know,' said Steve, amusement twinkling in his eyes. Then adding wryly, 'maybe it should be.'

Tom let out a small laugh. 'When I first came across the human studies of . . .' he faltered.

'Energy healing[3],' offered Steve with a smile.

'Hmm . . . ok, energy healing,' agreed Tom. 'Well, when I first came across the human studies I thought, no problem. This is just a placebo effect.'

'Really,' interrupted Steve, 'even with the double-blind random allocations?'

Tom looked a little uncomfortable. 'Well, it was difficult to see how else you could account for the data.'

Steve ummed and ahhed a bit, suggesting that whilst he didn't necessarily agree with Tom's interpretation, he didn't want to tie himself down to a specific interpretation, just yet.

'Anyway,' continued Tom, 'despite the positive findings I thought the human trials could still be accounted for in terms of a placebo effect. But, once I'd read the animal studies and then the in vitro studies – I mean!' he almost shouted in disgust, 'in vitro studies. There's just no way that the data could be accounted for in terms of a placebo effect.'

Steve nodded in agreement. 'Are you saying you think that energy healing,' as he said these words Tom winced noticeably, 'is real?'

'Don't you?' asked Tom defensively.

Steve nodded tight lipped. He reached out to his pile of papers, pulled one out and held it up. 'Did you read the meta-analysis by the Northampton group[4]?'

'Meta-*analyses*,' said Tom emphasising the plural aspect of the word.

'Ah yes, sorry, meta-analyses.'

'Yes,' answered Tom forlornly.

Steve opened the article he was holding and searched through for the quote he'd highlighted with a yellow marker pen. 'Ah, here it is,' he said, folding over the page. 'Overall, the effects of energy healing tend to be small but are significantly positive.' Having finished reading the quote he closed the article and flung it back on his desk.

The two researchers sat in silence for a moment trying hard to think about the implications of the evidence they'd read. Tom was first to break the silence with a plaintive plea.

'So, what do you think we should do now?' he asked.

'We'ell,' said Steve slowly, 'if, and it's a big if,' he added quickly, 'if that's what it is then I say we test it. We run another trial, but this time with three groups. A drug treatment group, an,' he stopped for a moment and grimaced a little, 'an energy healing group, and a no-treatment control group.'

'O – kay,' agreed Tom cautiously.

'However,' Steve said seriously, and looking directly at Tom, 'it's imperative that you try to recreate the feelings and intentions you had during the first trial.'

Tom nodded in understanding but made a wry face. 'I'm not sure I can.'

'But it's essential that you try,' emphasised Steve. 'We need to try and re-create the same conditions as we had in the first trial.' He waited for Tom to respond whilst looking at him expectantly. After a few moments Tom seemed to come to some sort of resolution.

'Ok, I'll give it my best shot.'

'Excellent!' cried Steve, reaching over to place a hand of encouragement on Tom's shoulder. 'Let's go and see Norris to get the next batch of rats sorted and set up the trial.'

∞

It had taken some diplomatic negotiation by Steve and Tom to explain to Professor Norris why they needed another, larger group of rats to run a second trial. Telling him that there had been a possible confound in the data of the original trial was true – though they had neatly talked around precisely what that confound might be. Once the second live trial had been agreed they set it up in a similar way to the original trial, only this time with an extra group that were targeted to receive what Steve called, energy healing. Tom called this group his energy group and did his very best to focus his thoughts on them throughout the trial. He was so successful that once again Rebecca asked him if everything was all right at work, as he seemed very distracted.

It was just over a week and a half later when they had finished running their second trial with the three groups of rats. As before, Steve let Tom run the data analysis, just to ensure that this trial was completed in a way that was as similar to the previous one as possible. It was late on the Thursday afternoon when Tom returned to their shared office with the print-out of the results. Steve had been waiting impatiently for the past hour, trying, and failing, to distract himself by reading back through the articles on healing that they'd both amassed. As Tom entered the office Steve looked up expectantly from the article he was reading for the third time.

'And?' he asked impatiently.

Tom sauntered over to his desk, sat down and handed Steve the printouts. 'Well,' he said with an affected nonchalance, 'there's good news and there's . . .' he hesitated for a moment, searching for the right word, 'and there's . . . other news.'

'Ha!' Steve burst out. 'What's the good news?'

Tom answered in a deliberately neutral voice, 'the drug treatment group showed a forty-three percent wound reduction compared to eleven percent in the controls.'

Steve nodded eagerly, 'not bad.'

'In addition,' continued Tom, 'fibroblast counts were forty-one for the drug group and thirteen for controls.'

'So,' interjected Steve, 'the drug treatment group showed a significant improvement compared to controls.' There was a moments silence as he thought about the results, then quickly added, 'tell me these differences were significant?'

'Yes,' answered Tom, 'very significant.'

'Excellent,' cried Steve. 'And the . . . er the, other news?'

Tom closed his eyes for a moment and leant back in his chair as if this would help him recall the figures. 'The energy group showed a thirty-seven percent wound reduction, with a fibroblast count of thirty-one.' He opened his eyes now and looked back at Steve, 'both, again, significantly better than the controls[5].'

Steve frowned in thought for a moment and then asked the all important question.

'And the difference between the drug treatment group and the energy group?'

Tom shook his head, 'nope, nothing.'

'But a difference in effect size[6] surely,' appealed Steve.

'A small but non-significant difference,' answered Tom solemnly.

'Ok,' said Steve, now leaning back in his chair as he attempted to summarise the findings, 'so we have a drug treatment group and an energy healing group that both show significant improvements compared to a no-treatment control group – correct?'

'Yep,' responded Tom in a resolute voice.

Both men sat in quiet contemplation for a moment, thinking about the implications of these results and what they should, or could, do with them. Tom, looking forlorn and despondent, was the first to break the silence.

'What do you think we should do?' he asked, as their dreams of publishing in Nature or The Lancet slowly slipped away[7].

After thinking for a moment Steve shrugged, shook his head and then laughed lightly in mild amusement. 'You wouldn't believe it.'

'What?' asked Tom.

Steve took a sharp breath and looked up decisively, 'well, there's only one thing we can do.'

Tom cocked his head to one side, eyebrows raised in question.

Steve grinned, 'publish the results in the Journal of Complementary and Alternative Medicine.'

There was a moments silence as the two men sat facing each other, contemplating the impact this would have on their respective careers. Tom shook his head, then his shoulders began to shake. After a second or two he began to laugh as he thought about the influence of his unexpected intentions. Steve shrugged, joining in, he laughed good naturedly as he leant forwards and clapped Tom on the shoulder in a gesture of solidarity.

∞

6

Harmonic Resonance

Roy Woodall had worked as deputy director of digital information at the office for national statistics, or ONS as everyone called it, for over eighteen years. As such, he was used to seeing requests for information come down through the chain of command. In that sense the file containing the request, which lay on the desk in front of him, was not unusual. It had originated from the Home Office and asked for some detailed information and analysis regarding levels of crime in a number of regions, as part of what was called a *policy reflection process.*

Roy sat for a moment, drumming his pen on the file as he thought. He was wondering which of his senior analysts he should give this particular task to. After a few moments he seemed to come to a decision and reached across the desk for his phone. He punched in a short number and waited. It was answered before the third ring, which made him smile as he thought about how efficient this particular analyst was.

'Emily, its Roy,' he said by way of introduction. 'I've a new request just in from the HO and I'd like you to deal with it if you can.' Emily responded by letting him know that she'd be happy to take on the project and that it would fit nicely around the other research and analysis she was currently involved in. That was another thing Roy liked about her, her can do attitude. She rarely said no to a project and always delivered.

'Ok,' said Roy, bringing the conversation to an end. 'If you could pop by my office this afternoon at four, we can go through it together and agree a strategy etc.' As he finished, he put the receiver back on its cradle and sat back in his chair nodding gently to himself.

Later that afternoon, at precisely four p.m., Emily knocked on his door.

'Come!' he called.

Emily opened the door, 'hi,' she said. 'I just came by to pick up that request from the HO.'

'Have a seat,' said Roy, pointing to the chair on the other side of his desk. As she sat down, he sorted through the folders on his desk, picking out the relevant one and handing it over to her.

'This,' he began to explain, 'is a request from the HO as part of some policy review, and they want us to try and find out why several regions in the south and east are exhibiting anomalously low levels of reported crime compared to their surrounding areas.'

'Hmm, a mystery,' responded Emily raising her eyebrows. She picked up the folder, opening its flap and removed the papers from inside.

'You'll see,' he nodded at the papers she was now holding, 'that the figures they give indicate some quite clear differences across the regions of interest.'

The two of them then spent the next twenty minutes discussing the many and varied factors that were known to influence such statistics, mapping out a plan of action and agreeing a timescale and deadline. At the end of this discussion Emily nodded in agreement and replaced the papers in the folder.

'Anything else?' she asked brightly.

Roy shook his head, 'no, that's it.'

'Ok,' she said. Then, rising from her chair she nodded her thanks to Roy and left to return to her own office, which was two floors down, on the second floor.

∞

Nine days later Emily sat at her desk, her head in her hands, as yet another statistical model showed a null result. She stirred herself, sitting back in her chair, looking up at the ceiling and breathing out in heavy exasperation. She'd spent the previous few days constructing a number of time series analysis models, which could be used to identify possible predictor variables, and none of them could identify a significant predictor variable for the given reductions in crime across the regions of interest.

She examined all the usual predictors, including the number of police officers as well as the number of crime prevention officers on record. She also included any changes to local and/or national police interventions and campaigns. Then, she'd checked the crime rates in nearby areas to see if it was simply a case of reported crime shifting across local authority boundaries – nothing. Following this, she created an additional batch of models that included general weather patterns, including changes in temperature, precipitation, and humidity, all known to influence reported crime rates. Again, nothing. She then added in factors such as time of day, time of year, number of daylight hours, employment levels, election cycles, both local and national. All failed to identify a clear predictor of the anomalous crime rates.

She was starting to feel less sure of herself now, as it didn't usually take this long, or require such detailed examination, to identify a useful predictor. Determined however, not to be beaten by what she now saw as a direct challenge, she created a new batch of models that included variables such as the number of grammar schools across the regions, reported education attainment levels, reported bankruptcies, divorce rates, and then added in child and infant mortality rates, just in case. Still nothing. In a near desperate attempt she tried again, this time adding in the phase of the moon. Crazy as it sounds, she'd read somewhere that phases of the moon could affect people's behaviour and thought that it would be worth a try given that her options were very clearly running out. However, this too, failed to produce a model identifying any clear predictor.

She slumped in her chair. It was getting late now, and she was feeling irritated and frustrated. This had never happened to her before, and she wasn't enjoying the experience. She sat for a moment staring into space, trying to think of any variable that she might have missed somehow. A light frown creased her forehead as she struggled to come up with anything.

Just then, her mobile phone began to vibrate, calling her attention away from the construction of hypothetical statistical models towards more mundane matters. She leant forward and reached over to pick it up. There was a message on the screen from Amy, her best friend, saying that she and some others were meeting up in the Two Brewers pub at eight o'clock and that Emily should come along. She sat there with the phone in her hand, thinking about what to do next. She noted the time on the phone's face, it was six fifty-five p.m., and she was starting to feel a bit peckish. Pursing her lips she thought about stopping by at the local Pret to get a sandwich and then joining Amy and the others at the pub. Right now, that seemed like a good idea, and perhaps time away from the problem might help. She frowned in thought as she tried to recall what it was called when you give yourself a break from trying to solve a particular problem and just let it percolate in the back of your mind. The frown lifted as realisation dawned, ah yes, that's it, she thought, incubation.

Having made her decision, she briefly texted Amy back saying she'd be there just after eight. Then she reached over and shut down her computer, tidied her desk and left to get her dinnertime sandwich before heading over to the pub.

∞

Later that evening Emily sat with her friends in the pub. Having failed completely to stop thinking about the problem she was facing at work, she was currently sitting with her second glass of chilled wine, attempting to explain it to Mike. Mike, who lectured in psychology at the local university, had come along primarily to see Amy and spend time with her, as he really liked her and wanted desperately to get to know her better. Hence, he was only partially listening to Emily as she went into lengthy, and he thought with some irritation, tedious detail about what she'd done and how she couldn't understand why none of the models she'd created showed any clear predictors. He tried to play his part in the, mostly, one-sided conversation by adding in the odd, 'oh,' or 'hmm, interesting,' every now and then, but really just wanted Emily to shut up and go away, so he could talk to Amy – ideally alone. It was then that he noticed that Emily had finally stopped talking. He smiled a little, relieved that she seemed to have eventually run out of steam. However, he then noticed that she was looking at him, eyebrows raised in expectation, as if waiting for some response. Panic quickly took hold as he tried to replay in his mind what he thought she'd just said. It was no good. He'd been thinking about how beautiful Amy's smile was and wasn't listening at all to what Emily was saying. His mind raced as he realised he needed to find a suitable response, and fast. He quickly replayed the topic in his mind and was pleased when an idea suddenly occurred. Tilting his head slightly to one side, in a feigned show of interest, he asked, 'what makes you think you've considered all the possibilities?'

Emily rolled her eyes in irritation, 'well obviously I haven't considered *all* the possibilities have I,' she answered. 'I mean, if I'd considered *all* the possibilities I would have found the right predictor – wouldn't I?'

Mike tightened his jaw and produced a thin-lipped smile at Emily's precise and over literal interpretation of his question.

Emily, seemingly unaware of Mike's irritation, continued, 'I've just considered all the possibilities I could think of. That's why I was asking whether you had any ideas?'

Ah, Mike thought, relieved now to at least know what the question was that he'd been asked. He took a moment and nodded sagely, as if giving the matter some deep thought. All the while wondering how she'd react if he made an excuse to go to the bar, get a drink and then come back and went over to sit by Amy.

'Well?' demanded Emily, interrupting his thoughts of Amy, again.

It was perhaps this interruption that made him blurt out in irritation, 'well maybe they all meditate more or something.'

'What!' scoffed Emily, laughing.

Mike thought quickly. He couldn't understand why he'd said that. It had just sort of come out. Still, now he'd said it he felt that he should at least offer some sort of justification for it.

'Seriously,' he said with a solemn face that hid his frantic efforts to try and recall what that seminar had been all about. 'We had this chap give an online seminar recently, as part of the integrative research programme, and he talked about how when groups of people get together and meditate crime rates can go down.' He thought for a second, 'or something *like* that,' he added.

'Ha, ha, ha,' laughed Emily, taking a large sip of her wine. 'You're kidding.'

Mike frowned, his irritation with this whole pointless conversation growing. He shook his head, 'no,' he said in all seriousness. 'It was called. . .' he hesitated for a moment trying hard to recall what the effect was called that the speaker had been referring to. 'Something like "rishi effect", he said vaguely.

Emily stopped laughing, though still looked sceptical and repeated the phrase, 'rishi effect?' she queried.

Mike scrunched his face up a bit, 'not that, but something like that,' he replied rather lamely.

Emily looked at him warily as if he were offering to sell her something.

Mike shrugged, 'or like that. But something to do with meditation. Look it up on Google Scholar,' he added. Then quickly asked her, 'would you like another wine?' before she had a chance to say anything else.

Emily looked at her half-full glass and thought about the journey home. 'Ah, no, thanks,' she said.

'Well I do,' said Mike with a heavy sarcasm that Emily completely failed to notice. So saying, he got up and made his way over to the bar. She remained where she was, watching his back recede across the room, pondering what he'd said. Eventually, she came to a decision and reached into her bag for her mobile phone. Opening the web browser, she tried to check online and then realised she needed to sign-in to the pubs free wi-fi. Annoyed at this additional step she quickly agreed to the never read conditions and waited for her mobile to show it had connected to the internet. Once connected, she opened the browser again and typed in Google scholar and then in the search bar typed in "rishi effect". Various articles came up with 'Rishi' as a named author but nothing about crime reduction or meditation. She tried again, this time extending the search query to "rishi effect and crime reduction". Again, nothing of any relevance showed up. She frowned a little as she began to wonder if Mike had been having some sort of joke at her expense. How, after fruitlessly searching for this alleged effect, he'd laugh and say it was all just a joke. Gritting her teeth in a last determined attempt, she typed in the words "meditation and crime reduction". Instantly, a raft of publications came up, all with titles suggesting that meditation was somehow preventing violent crime. There was also something called the "Maharishi Effect[1]" that was mentioned in a number of the publications. Initially she felt bewildered. Somehow, it seemed easier to accept the possibility that this was a joke than to entertain the notion that it could be real. She sat for a while scanning through the various publications, marking those of interest and downloading copies of those that were available. After about twenty minutes she'd collected just over a dozen articles all linked to the idea that meditation was in some way responsible for reducing crime[2]. She emailed the articles to her work account and then closed the phone, frowning now, as she wondered what this Maharishi Effect was and how it could possibly influence crime. She took a final sip of her wine, emptying the glass, and decided that tomorrow she'd find out what this was all about.

∞

It was late afternoon, two days later, as Emily sat and looked across her desk at the papers and notes she'd made. She'd painstakingly read every article that she could find that mentioned this meditation effect, and in the process had also chased up a variety of additional references. She was determined to try and get to the bottom of this seemingly bizarre effect. Having now read all that she could find on the subject she felt that she had a reasonably good understanding of the issues. However, it had been an intellectual rollercoaster of a ride and in the last forty-eight hours she'd moved from scepticism, through incredulity, to settle finally on astonishment. More and more she began to feel like Alice, having fallen down the rabbit hole. Only to emerge in a strange and absurd alternate universe where scientists in peer reviewed publications made startling claims suggesting that meditation was somehow linked with reductions in crime.

In addition to this, from her reading of the various publications, not only was there evidence that meditation was linked to reductions in crime, but it was also linked to reduced levels of international terrorism, and international conflict, as well as reduced levels of mortality. What she found most astonishing about these effects was that that those doing the actual meditating didn't even need to be thinking about reducing crime, or mortality rates, or whatever. It was as if these effects occurred by themselves, as a sort of by-product of the meditation process.

It was as she read through the material, trying to understand how such a thing could occur, that she came across the suggested cause. Apparently, these reductions in crime, violence, mortality etc. were supposed to occur when a certain number of people in the area learnt to meditate. According to the arguments made in the scientific papers, that number needed to be around one-percent of the local population. And, when around one percent of the population learnt to meditate, and did this regularly, it would somehow produce a shift in the level of their own conscious mind, away from everyday things and towards a more transcendent level of consciousness. It was this supposed shift in consciousness that would somehow radiate outwards, producing a change in the surrounding region towards a more orderly and harmonious level of functioning. It was, she'd read, this increase in coherence and harmony of the collective consciousness that had a positive influence on the quality of life in society in general which in turn led to reductions in violence and crime.

Although she'd read this argument through several times, it didn't make it any easier to accept. She felt distinctly uncomfortable about the use of terms such as coherence, harmony, and in particular collective consciousness. They all seemed so vague, so nebulous. She silently groaned to herself as she leant forwards and put her head in her hands. What the hell was collective consciousness supposed to be, she thought. The trouble with such terms is that there seemed to be as many definitions as there were people who expressed an interest in the topic. And these definitions ranged from a shared set of values or beliefs that a community had, to a collection of knowledge and imagery that every person is born with and is shared by all conscious beings. She had the distinctly uneasy feeling that it was the latter of these definitions that the researchers were referring to in the articles.

She felt that she could have easily dismissed all of this if it wasn't for the data from the most recent models. Having decided to accept the possibility, albeit small, that meditation could in some way influence violence and crime, she had initially fact-checked the regions of interest to find out whether they had local meditation groups that met on a regular basis. After checking local authority amenities in each of the areas she was able to establish that every region of interest offered regular classes in group meditation. When she'd discovered this it sent a tingle of nervous excitement through her. On the one hand, things seemed to be falling into place. On the other hand, the idea seemed so outlandish that it made her a little apprehensive. Nevertheless, she continued with the work, abiding by the long-lived mantra of just "following the data". The credo of "just follow the data" had been one she'd lived by her whole life as a scientist. She knew how important it was not to jump prematurely to conclusions. Not to let her own biases and preconceived ideas or pre-constructed theories blind her as to what might really be going on. But this was the first time she'd ever felt apprehensive about where it might be taking her.

Once she'd identified that each of the regions offered the relevant meditation practice sessions, she then constructed a new statistical model, with this as the primary predictor. The data report for this model was now up on her computer screen and she'd been staring at it for the past three minutes. It clearly showed that this new model accounted for just over ninety-eight percent of the variance.

She'd found her predictor.

It just wasn't one she'd been expecting. And now she was faced with the dilemma of what to do with this information. She knew she couldn't ignore it, the model showed that meditation clearly and significantly accounted for the unusual reductions in violence and crime in the regions of interest. But to write a report stating that, even after all she'd read, seemed so at odds with her view of the world and how things worked.

A slight smile slowly dawned on her face as she thought about what "her view of the world" was and what this really meant. As she thought about this more and more she was reminded of her old statistics Professor. Of how he used to drum with his hand on the lecture podium to emphasise a point he'd made in almost all of his lectures, that a good scientist is *someone who remains critical yet open minded*. Of how important that 'open' component was to the ongoing growth and development of science and understanding. New growth, new knowledge and new understanding were only possible when the mind was open to them.

Reflecting on these topics her smile broadened a little, as she realised with the honesty that is inherent in all good scientists, that she'd been critical but not very open to the possibility that meditation could have such an effect. It just didn't fit in with her expectations. Her preconceived expectations, of what meditation is, or does. Feeling more at ease with herself now, she looked back at the piles of papers and notes, then back to the screen with the results. Sitting forwards in her chair she reached over to the keyboard and pulled up Microsoft Word. Once she'd created a new report file she began to type.

∞

At the end of the following week Emily was once again making her way upstairs to Roy's office on the fourth floor. She had a good instinct as to why she'd been called. By now he'd have received her report on the meditation effect and its impact on violence and crime and would no doubt want to discuss it with her before they sent it back up the chain to the HO.

As she reached his office she stood for a moment, taking a deep breath and calming herself. She reached up and knocked.

'Come!' echoed a loud voice from within

She turned the handle and entered the office. Roy was sitting behind his desk, which was still covered with various papers and reports. He looked up at her smiling.

'Ah, Emily,' he said, 'thanks for coming by.' He waved a hand at the chair opposite him, 'please have a seat.'

Emily entered the office, closing the door behind her and moved over to the indicated chair. Sat and waited.

Meanwhile, Roy reached out to one of the trays on his desk and extracted a buff-coloured folder and from this took out a report. Emily could see it was the one she'd written. Roy placed the report on his desk, face up and took a deep breath, and then sighed.

Looking directly at Emily he said, 'we can't publish this.'

Emily didn't speak. She wasn't sure what to say. She looked down at her feet for a moment, then back up at Roy. Frowning slightly, she finally asked in a quiet voice, 'why?'

She could see the muscles working in Roy's jaw as he clenched and unclenched his teeth. It was a habit of his when thinking. He looked up toward the ceiling. 'Can you imagine,' he began, 'what the tabloids would say if a Minister of the Crown were to tell the public that meditation can reduce violence and crime.'

Emily waited. She hoped this was a rhetorical question.

'They'd have a field day,' Roy continued. 'You could just imagine the headlines. "Minister says 'Om' to violent crime", as he said this he made air quotes with both hands.

Emily smiled in spite of herself and continued to wait in silence. She wasn't sure what to say. The evidence was there. The model clearly showed that meditation was the best, the only, predictor.

Roy gently patted the report in front of him. 'What we need to do,' he said, 'is find a way to . . . to present this in a way that is more . . .' he searched for the right word, 'acceptable.'

Emily frowned slightly. She couldn't understand what he was getting at. Her analysis was clear. If anyone else ran the stats using the data she had, she was certain they'd come up with the same results.

'Now,' began Roy, 'I know how conscientious and thorough you are. I've seen the appendices with the list,' he smiled briefly, 'the long list, of possible predictors that you'd managed to rule out.'

Emily waited.

'But,' he said, 'can you be sure that this . . .'

'There was a very high probability . . .' responded Emily interrupting him.

'Ah,' interrupted Roy quickly, 'but can you be *certain*.'

Emily caught the emphasis. 'Well, no. Of course, I can't be . . . certain.'

'Precisely!' agreed Roy with emphasis.

'But there is a very high, and very statistically significant probability . . .' Emily began.

Roy interrupted again, 'but you can't be certain.'

Emily clenched her jaw in annoyance and grimaced. 'You know,' she said carefully, 'that science doesn't do certainty.'

'Exactly' responded Roy. 'So, while you think you've identified the *probable* cause it could in fact be some other, unknown variable, that we haven't looked at.'

There was a moments silence as Emily thought through this point. 'But I've examined every other possible variable that I could think of,' she said. 'The appendix extensively lists the . . .'

'Yes, I've seen the appendix,' he interrupted with a rueful smile. 'And my point is that whilst you may *think* you've identified the best predictor, you can't be certain.'

Emily decided to speak plainly, she knew that Roy would appreciate that more. 'Now you're just playing with words,' she said.

'No,' he said. Then, placing his hand on the report he continued, 'and you need to work with me on this in order for us to be able to use what you've found. But we need to present it in a way that is . . . is more acceptable.' He thought for a moment and then added, 'what we need is some sort of phrase that's syntactically correct but semantically light. Something we can use to describe the data.'

Emily looked a little unsure.

'You know,' he said, 'something that people can use to describe what's going on but doesn't necessarily explain why. A place holder. You know . . . like . . .' he looked around his office momentarily, as if he were trying to locate something. 'Like ... placebo.'

'Placebo,' she repeated, frowning as if she'd misheard him.

'Yes, placebo,' he answered.

Emily's frown deepened. 'But,' she struggled, 'but placebo . . . I mean.'

'Yes, I know,' agreed Roy, 'you think you can explain what it is.'

'But I can,' complained Emily.

Roy cocked his head to one side, smiled ruefully and raised his eyebrows. 'Really,' he said, 'so tell me?'

A little taken aback Emily thought for a moment. Then answered, 'its when an inert substance, like a sugar pill, is given to someone and it produces an effect, simply because they *believe* that it will.'

'Ha!' laughed Roy. 'Perfect.'

Now Emily looked confused.

Roy leant forward in his chair and placed both palms down on the report as he tried to explain. 'My point is that you haven't *explained* it, you've simply *defined* it.'

Emily thought for a moment, trying to fully grasp what he meant.

'It's like dark matter, or dark energy,' he said. 'Placebo is a just a place holder term we use to describe effects we don't currently understand.' He let that point sink in for a moment before continuing. 'I mean, we're talking about your belief influencing the outcome of something here, right?'

Emily nodded slowly in mute agreement.

'Well, why don't we call it the *mind over matter effect* then?'

'Well,' began Emily, 'that sounds a bit . . .'

Roy nodded, 'precisely. And so, we use the term placebo. Ask anyone if they can explain the placebo effect, and explain mark you, and they'll invariably define it for you, thinking that they've explained it.'

Emily sat for a moment. Thinking hard and trying to pick holes in Roy's argument. But the more she thought about it the more she realised he was right. These terms that were used to describe such effects don't explain them at all. They simply defined them. She wondered for a moment why this was the case. Why everyone seemed to accept that a definition was an explanation.

Roy interrupted her train of thought. 'How about unidentified demographic anomaly,' he offered, tapping the report on his desk. 'We could use the acronym UDA.'

Emily sat back momentarily. 'UDA,' she said uneasily. 'Won't people think we're trying to link it to the Irish paramilitary?' she asked.

'Ah,' nodded Roy. 'Ok, not UDA, but something like that.'

Emily looked down at her feet again. Concern creasing her forehead. 'But,' she began hesitantly, 'but, aren't we being disingenuous?' she asked.

'What do you mean?'

'Well, if we published this report showing that meditation has a clear link to reductions in violence and crime then those regions that currently don't offer such an option might well re-think their strategies and this could have much wider beneficial effects.'

Roy looked across at her. He liked Emily, she was a good researcher. Conscientious to a fault and diligent, but he was a little disappointed that she could still be so naïve. 'Let me make this absolutely clear,' he said with slow emphasis. 'This report in its current format is going nowhere.'

The disappointment on Emily's face was clear. Her heart sank a little as she realised that he was right, and that people would find it hard to believe, or, more likely wouldn't believe it at all. It irritated her. She wanted to make a stand for science. Decisions, she thought should be informed by evidence, not by short-sighted biased and closed-minded beliefs. However, she also knew that he could just as easily get someone else to re-write the report.

Roy meanwhile was sitting thinking hard. Looking at Emily through half-closed eyes trying to come up with some sort of compromise. 'Ok, how about we identify a short list of demographic variables which *includes* meditation among them? We could refer to them as "selected demographic anomalies"' he smiled, 'hmm, SDA could work.'

Emily's shoulders sagged a little in resignation. 'If we tell people it's the SDA they'll think we're referring to Seventh-Day Adventists,' she said with a weak smile.

'Christ!' he retorted. Then realising what he'd just said quickly added, 'oops, sorry about that. No pun intended.'

Emily let out a brief snort of quiet laughter.

Roy grinned, raising his palms and eyebrows he asked, 'well? If you work with me on this, I'm sure we can identify a useful phrase that would convey what we want and could include meditation.'

Emily nodded slowly. She knew this was the best offer she was likely to get. 'Ok,' she answered.

'Right!' Roy said, clapping his hands together. 'Let's map out a list of candidate variables and then we can go from there.'

The two of them spent the next forty-five minutes discussing possible variables and combinations of predictors along with potential acronyms that might be used to help convey what they both wanted.

∞

Later that same night Emily met Amy at their favourite pub and re-told the story of her findings, the report, the meeting, and finally the revisions that she'd agreed to, over a glass of wine.

'I mean,' said Emily for the umpteenth time, 'I know it's weird, but I think we have a duty to report the findings as they are.'

'Hmmm,' responded Amy, taking a large sip of her wine.

'Wouldn't you rather want to know the truth,' she demanded, 'rather than some . . . some edited and sanitised version?' She took an angry glug of her wine.

'Hmmm,' nodded Amy.

'After all,' continued Emily, 'how are things going to change if we don't let people make informed decisions based on the evidence.'

'Hmm-hmm,' agreed Amy.

It began to dawn on her that Amy's continued non-committal responses might indicate that she wasn't fully focusing on the key issues of the discussion. Which was odd, she thought, as she'd felt sure she'd explained them to Amy at least three times now. She looked over at Amy. 'Are you ok?' she asked.

'Hmmm,' Amy nodded smiling dreamily.

Emily frowned a little. Unsure how to react to this surprising response.

'Mike and I have started seeing each other,' said Amy, failing to hide a big grin.

'Oh,' said Emily, making a wry face. Weird, she thought, she hadn't seen that coming. She thought back to the last time they were all together. It was in this very same pub. She tried hard to think back to that evening but couldn't recall Mike showing any interest in Amy. Odd really, she thought frowning a little, she was sure that she'd have noticed if he had. After all, she was usually pretty good at picking up on the subtle cues that others missed.

Amy, still smiling, interrupted her thoughts by asking, 'so what are you going to do now?'

Emily looked across at her and shrugged. 'The only thing I can do,' she replied. 'Learn how to meditate.'

7

Time to Act

The noise of the underground washed over him as he stood with his back to the tiled wall, trying to distance himself from the other passengers, as they crowded onto the platform. Standing there he felt an element of uncertainty. Unsure which train he was supposed to be getting, or where he was going. Thinking felt effortful and slow. His thoughts seemed to elude him, hiding in the fog of his mind. He felt it more than thought it. He wasn't *going* anywhere; he was exactly where he needed to be. But the feeling brought anticipation with it, and an element of fear. A hollow ache in the pit of his stomach. He knew this feeling well, they were old friends.

He felt her before he saw her. As if an invisible string tugged his heart and caused him to look up. He watched, but from a distance. As if he were watching himself watch her. She walked past in front of him. Who was she? Why did she feel so familiar? As she passed, he felt the icy grip of fear close around his heart. Apprehension and anxiety rained down on him like a cold shower. This was wrong. Something about this was wrong. He could feel his body start to tremble. His breath came in short gasps, as with a supreme effort he turned his head to follow her.

As she approached the main entrance to the subway a large group of students pushed their way onto the platform, sweeping others back before them like a mini tsunami. The knock-on effect was to push back those already on the platform. The crowd moved like a single entity, jerking to one side. People cried out in a mixture of fear and anger, the girl was pushed out beyond the edge. She reached out screaming as she toppled.

Realization dawned, filling him with familiar dread. He knew this. He'd seen this before. Nooo! he cried out in the silent vaults of his mind. But no one heard, no one cared. He didn't want to see this again. Not like this. He tried to shut his eyes but felt paralyzed with fear. He couldn't breathe. It was as if his throat had closed to stop him calling out. His heartbeat pounded in his ears as he strained to draw breath. Mouth open, gasping, choking. The dread, the fear. He felt himself topple forwards and fell . . . into darkness.

Gasping and covered with sweat Grant sat bolt upright in bed. He shook his head slowly, trying to dislodge the faded images of his dreams. Tears rolled down his face as he took a few breaths to try and steady himself. His throbbing heart a pounding reminder of what he'd felt. Slowly, he toppled back onto his side and curled into a foetal position, wrapping his arms around his legs in an effort to try and provide the comfort he so desperately craved.

It had happened again. He couldn't understand why he was having these dreams, these . . . nightmares. The other, yes, but why these? He knew something needed to be done. Adam was right, he needed to see someone.

It was later the following week when Grant walked through the open door of the medical centre and made his way over to the reception desk. Behind the desk sat a plump, middle-aged woman with short grey hair, large round glasses and a cheery face.

Looking up she asked, 'Can I help you?'

'Grant Stevens,' said Grant. 'Here to see Dr Wentworth.'

'Date of birth?' she asked. Grant gave it to her, and she took a moment to look up his details on the computer screen in front of her before nodding. 'Ok, if you'd like to have a seat over there,' she indicated a small waiting area with a selection of comfy chairs. 'Dr Wentworth will call you in a minute.'

'Thanks,' he said. Then turning, he sauntered over to the waiting area. Nodding in acknowledgement to the one other person waiting, he took a seat. As he sat there, he started going over the sequence of events in his head. The accident, like a magnet, always pulled his thoughts in that direction whenever his mind wasn't occupied. It had been almost a year now and he still had trouble sleeping. He also had trouble concentrating at work. He wasn't sure if talking about it would help but he'd tried medication and all it seemed to do was dull the pain. But it was still there, still part of him, and he knew that he needed to move past this. He knew that to get his life back he needed to move on, to let the past go. He desperately wanted to live again – he just wasn't sure he deserved to.

His thoughts were interrupted by a short dark-haired woman in a navy trouser suit coming over and asking, 'Mr Stevens?'

He stood and smiled weakly in acknowledgement.

'If you'd like to follow me please,' she said, turning and walking back along the corridor towards an office at the end. As Grant walked behind her he felt a mixture of apprehension and hope. On reaching the office she stood to one side and indicated that he go in ahead. He stepped through the door and noticed the desk and chair off to the right with two smaller armchairs on the left. The two armchairs had been slightly offset so that their occupants, whilst clearly able to look at each other, would not be facing directly at one another.

'Please have a seat Mr Stevens,' she said indicating one of the small armchairs to the left. He took a seat in the one nearest to him and the woman, after gently closing the door behind her, moved over, and sat in the chair in front of him. Once seated she placed the file of notes she'd been carrying on her lap. 'Let me introduce myself. I'm Dr Anita Wentworth and you can call me Dr Wentworth or Anita if you prefer, whichever makes you feel more comfortable.'

Grant nodded, saying, 'please call me Grant.'

'Well, Grant,' her gaze flicked down to her notes for a second, 'I see you work at the University.'

'Yes,' he said. Then, answering the unspoken question said, 'I work in the IT department.'

'How long have you been there?'

He drew breath and thought for a moment. 'About eighteen years.'

'And you live alone?' she queried.

A pause and then, 'yes,' he answered quietly.

'And on your file it says that you're still having trouble sleeping and that you've started to experience recurring nightmares.'

He nodded silently.

She paused for a moment. Her eyes flicked as she pursed her lips in thought. 'And this began after the accident?' she enquired.

Another silent nod.

Her voice was gentle, caring. 'Perhaps we could begin,' she said, 'with you telling me about the accident in your own words.'

Grant sat for a moment; head bowed. He knew that this was what he'd come for, but he was afraid. Ever since that day, he'd felt such an overwhelming flood of grief and despair. Guilt, at not being the man he so desperately thought he should have been. And so much anger at the seeming injustice of the world. And he'd bottled it all up. Hid it away behind a wall of distractions, propped up by fear. Now, the pressure scared him. He couldn't understand how so much emotion could be contained in one person. He wanted to let go of the pain, let go of the anger. But there was just so much of it, he was afraid that if he were to open up, he'd be drowned in a flood of tears that would engulf him. That if the tears washed away his grief and guilt, there'd be nothing left.

'In your own time' she said, gently coaxing him along.

He began rocking gently back and forth, clenching his jaw, his hands urgently wrapping themselves around one another, trying to grasp on to something he couldn't touch. He opened his mouth to speak but all that came out was a loud sob. Then, the tears began to fall. Streaming down his face, he screwed up his eyes, as if this could hold them back. His body shook, wracked by loud sobs of grief too long held.

She allowed him time. Then, leaning forward she passed him a box of tissues. He grabbed a couple and noisily blew his nose, apologising for his behaviour.

'You don't have to be sorry,' she gently reminded him.

He shook his head. Wiping fresh tears away with another handful of tissues. 'I think sorry is all I have left,' he said quietly. He sat for a moment trying to regain some sort of composure. Then drew in a shuddering breath and began to relay his story.

It had happened just over a year ago he told her. He'd been on a night out with Sarah – his girlfriend. And he'd got upset about her flirting, or so he thought, with one of the other guys in their group. He knew it was silly. That she wasn't really the sort of person who flirted with other men, but his insecurities just got the better of him. He'd made some sarcastic remark which she'd challenged. This led to a heated discussion which almost turned into a full-blown row. The consequence of this was that, in the taxi, on the way home, Sarah had got in the front seat next to the driver leaving him to sit alone in the back. This had annoyed him. As if a gulf was already opening up between them. Irritated by this small slight he then ignored her during the ride. This didn't seem to bother Sarah who made light conversation with the driver, which only irritated him more. Then, out of nowhere, a truck hit the side of the car, almost ripping it in two and killing the driver and Sarah instantly. Later the paramedics had told him that he'd had a miraculous escape, as the rear of the car had remained largely intact and all he'd suffered were some minor cuts and bruises. He didn't feel miraculous, he felt horrified. Sure in the knowledge that *if* he hadn't shown such petty jealousy at the club, Sarah would have sat in the back with him and she'd still be alive. The accident had removed from his life of the one thing he truly loved, only to replace it with shame and regret.

Once he finished, he sat there wiping his eyes with the last of the tissues from the box.

'Did the nightmares begin immediately after the accident?' she asked.

Grant shook his head. 'No, it was some time after.'

She waited.

'It was about a month or so,' He added. 'At first it was just the accident. Over and over. The events leading up to it and then ... then ...' He couldn't bring himself to say the words.

'What changed?' she asked gently.

He sighed. 'Then I started to see other people in accidents. In my dreams I mean,' he explained.

'The same type of accident?'

'No, all different types. Some major accidents like . . .' the unspoken point hung in the air between them for a moment. 'And some, just minor accidents.'

'How did this make you feel?'

'Scared . . . at first' he admitted. 'I thought I was just sort of re-living the . . . the accident. But just somehow seeing other people in it. As if, seeing other people in it would make it better.' He took a shuddering breath and tried to explain. 'You know, as if that would make it less . . . less meaningful to me. But then I wondered if I was just seeing accidents, I mean danger, everywhere.'

He paused for a moment, leant forwards a little and placed his head in his hands.

She allowed him time. After a while she gently queried, 'you said, at first?'

He sat back, raising his head and taking a deep breath in an effort to steady himself. Shaking his head slightly he responded. 'Now, just an overwhelming feeling of helplessness.'

They spent the rest of the session talking about his thoughts and feelings associated with the accident. Dr Wentworth explained that dreams were sometimes a way for the brain to try and make sense of random events, particularly traumatic ones. Also, that they were likely to change as he faced the thoughts and feelings he'd been suppressing. On his way out of the centre, after the session had ended, Grant admitted to himself that he did feel a bit better for sharing. Though he was still unsure about the dreams. As was the case with dreams, they seemed so real. He shrugged and thought that next time he met with Adam, his best and only remaining friend, he'd ask him about it.

∞

'Try switching it off. . .' said Adam holding up his pint.

'And then back on again,' responded Grant in their time-honoured way, clinking his pint glass with Adam's as he said it. The toast had started out as a joke, as they both worked in IT, but despite the cliché, the *try switching off and then back on again*' mantra was one that everyone in IT knew well and either loved or loathed. And it was still surprising how many times it just seemed to do the trick. The two friends had agreed to meet that Friday after work for a drink at the White Hart, which was a favourite of theirs as it served a good pint of Doom Bar. They were currently involved in discussing the best sci-fi films that had made the transition from book to screen. It was a topic they'd often debated over a beer, or three.

'Well, I thought the Foundation series was a pretty good adaptation,' argued Adam, referring to Apple TV's recent attempt to screen Asimov's classic.

Grant took a sip of his beer and thought for a moment. 'Yeah, but it was only the first book,' he pointed out.

Adam shrugged. 'Of course. They've got to wait and see if they can get enough viewers to make the next two.'

There was a moment's silent supping as the two friends contemplated how the second and third instalment of the Foundation series should play out.

'I still think Hoyle's "*Black Cloud*" would make a good film,' offered Adam.

'What about "*The Player of Games*",' responded Grant.

'Ahh, now you're talking.'

There followed a few minutes where the two men discussed the merits of having sentient AI systems as part of a screen plot. As this part of the discussion came to an end Grant stood and asked, 'same again?' Picking up the now empty glasses.

'Yeah, ok,' answered Adam.

It was a few minutes later that Grant returned with two fresh pints of Doom Bar and two bags of crips. Placing the beer and crisps on the table he sat looking thoughtful.

Adam noticed the slight change in Grant's demeanour and asked, 'you ok?'

Grant frowned a little in thought. He screwed up his face, as if he'd tasted something unpleasant. Then, nodding back towards the bar, he said, 'that bloke at the bar.'

Adam turned slightly in his seat to be able to see the man Grant was referring to. The man was in his late forties and sat at the bar with his back to them, but Adam could clearly see that the man's left forearm was encased in a cast of some sort.

'I'm sure he was in my dream,' finished Grant quietly.

Adam looked back. The shock clearly evident on his face as he tried to laugh off the situation. 'Are you kidding,' he said. 'You're dreaming of men?'

Grant shook his head and rolled his eyes in mild annoyance.

'You want to get out more mate,' continued Adam. 'That, or get yourself a –'. He stopped, instantly regretting what he'd almost said. An uncomfortable silence hung between them for a moment. In an attempt to move things on Adam reached for his pint and took a large swig. As he replaced his glass on the table he looked over at Grant.

'I'm sorry mate,' he said with genuine concern.

Grant just shrugged and shook his head, as if to indicate that it was no big deal. Then said, 'I'm serious.'

'About what?' asked Adam.

'About that bloke being in my dreams.'

Adam couldn't help himself, he groaned in dismay. 'Grant, you've got to let it go mate,' he said.

'But I'm telling you I dreamt of that man having an accident and injuring his wrist.'

'It's just coincidence,' suggested Adam. 'Do you know how many people live in London?' he asked.

Grant shrugged, 'about nine million.'

'Exactly!' cried Adam. 'And if only about zero point zero, zero one percent of them injured their wrists last week it'd still be more than one person a week. Which means you could dream of someone injuring their wrist in any week of the year and there'd be someone, somewhere in London, that had.'

'Yes, but I dreamt of *that* man,' argued Grant, nodding towards the man still sitting at the bar.

'When?' Adam said sharply.

'Err, I think. . . no, it was Monday night,' answered Grant.

'Ok,' said Adam in exasperation, 'how'd he do it?'

Grant looked down at the table for a moment, trying to recall the details of the dream he'd had. Frowning slightly with the effort he said, 'I think he was about to step out into the road when one of those e-scooters shot past in front of him. It didn't touch him but the momentum of it sort of spun him round, and he tripped and fell back onto the pavement, and as he fell, he put his hand out. His left hand. And, when he fell on it, he broke it.'

Once Grant had finished telling the story of his dream Adam took a long pull on his beer and the two of them sat there in silence for a moment.

'Well,' said Adam putting his near empty glass back down. 'Now you've got to ask him how he did it now.'

'What!' exclaimed Grant.

'Well, you think you dreamt of him.'

Grant looked back defiantly.

'So, you've got to find out if you were right.'

'But I can't just walk up to a stranger and ask them why they have a cast on their forearm,' whined Grant.

Adam slowly shook his head in disbelief.

'You ask him,' appealed Grant.

'Why me,' complained Adam, 'it's your dream.'

'Well, you find it easier to talk to people,' murmured Grant. Then smiling added, 'besides, it's your round.'

'Oh, very funny,' Adam snorted. He shook his head slowly and then got up from his seat. 'I don't know. The things I do.' And with that he picked up the now empty glasses and made his way over to the bar, positioning himself next to the man on the stool with the cast on his arm.

Grant watched with interest how Adam nodded to the man on the stool as he ordered their drinks. Then, with an ease that Grant envied, he struck up a conversation with the man. He couldn't hear what they were saying but knew that they were talking about the man's cast as he raised his left arm as he spoke as if to show Adam what it was he was talking about. A few minutes later Adam returned with two fresh pints of beer and a mild look of concern on his face. Grant was eager to know what they'd talked about. 'Well?' he asked with raised eyebrows.

Adam sat, and before responding lifted his glass and took a large swig of the light brown liquid. 'Oooh, that's good,' he said, smacking his lips in appreciation.

'Well!' demanded Grant with some agitation.

'Alright, alright,' cried Adam, holding his palms out in a placating gesture. He pursed his lips in thought for a moment. 'It wasn't *exactly* like you said,' he responded.

Grant raised his eyes in question.

'According to our man,' Adam nodded back to the man on the bar stool, 'an e-scooter *did* in fact hit him, just as he was about to cross the road.'

'What?' exclaimed Grant.

'But apart from that,' Adam shrugged, 'it was roughly as you said.'

Grant took a moment to let that sink in. 'Bloody hell,' he said, the colour draining from his face.

'Could still be a coincidence,' Adam pointed out in a rather half-hearted manner. 'Or just a lucky guess,' he added. But the slightly haunted look on his face suggested that he didn't believe this either.

'Bloody hell,' repeated Grant in a dazed manner. Then, looking directly at Adam he asked, 'so what do we do now?'

Adam shrugged. 'I don't know. Though, if you're going to start dreaming of future events could you let me have tomorrow's Lotto numbers please,' he said with a grin.

'I'm being serious,' complained Grant.

'So am I,' cried Adam. 'This time next week we could be millionaires!' he said with a short laugh.

Grant looked at him in disbelief. 'Are you kidding?'

'Ok, ok,' countered Adam, quickly seeing that he might have overstepped the mark a bit.

Grant continued to sit in silence for a few minutes. Sill feeling dazed by the revelation. 'That's. . . that's just weird,' he said, his face now shifting to mirror the concern that Adam had shown earlier. 'What do you think it means?' he asked.

Not sure what to say Adam simply offered a tight-lipped smile and a shrug.

For a few minutes the two men simply sat drinking their beer in silence. Each contemplating the implications of what it might mean if someone were able to dream of future events.

'Well, I've got to make a move,' said Adam at last, draining his pint.

Grant nodded in understanding.

As he rose to leave Adam looked down at Grant's concerned face. 'If you're really interested why don't you look up online to see if there's anything about. . .' he thought for a moment, finally saying, 'this sort of thing.'

'Hmmm,' responded Grant.

'You never know,' encouraged Adam.

The two men said their goodbyes and Adam left, leaving Grant sitting deep in thought, slowly sipping the dregs of his final pint. It wasn't a bad idea, he thought to himself as he watched Adam make his way out of the side door. Once he'd finished his drink, he resolved to have a search on the internet and see what he could come up with.

∞

At work the following week Grant spent every spare moment he had searching online for information on, or about precognition, and in particular precognitive dreams. What surprised him was that he found a lot more information than he'd originally expected. He also found it challenging to his way of thinking. One of the things he liked about working in IT is that things were either right or they weren't – there was no hazy middle ground. But the more he read about precognition the more he came to realise that it was all hazy middle ground. A lot of information was available on various websites, one site in particular, called the PSI Encyclopaedia[1], seemed to be a mirror of Wikipedia, and acted as a comprehensive online resource, providing lots of information about individual researchers and topics related to paranormal phenomena.

Grant absorbed the information eagerly. He'd read that precognition was generally thought of as obtaining information about a future event *before* it happens. There were many case studies illustrating just how this occurred, including the infamous case of President Lincoln dreaming of his impending death. The various discussion forums also went into lengthy detail arguing about the counterintuitive and paradoxical nature of precognition. That, for example, you never saw the milk separate from your coffee, or eggs unscramble themselves. Many in the chat forums used such arguments to deride the notion that precognition was anything more than a deluded fantasy. There were also those that argued that knowledge of the future was impossible because it led to odd paradoxes. The many and varied examples were often related to travel. How, the argument went, could someone *see* that their future travel plans led to disaster if, on seeing this, they changed their plans and then didn't make the journey. Grant had to read through this a few times just to get his head around it. He understood the logic of this, and it made, or seemed to make good sense to him. However, he'd also read a survey showing that almost half of the people asked had changed their travel plans at some point due to, what the researchers called, an intuitive sense that something bad would happen[2].

Digging deeper he came across research papers suggesting that such premonitions provide the person with a glimpse into *possible* futures rather than a single future set in stone. That the human mind has the potential to transcend the normal boundaries of time and peek at these possible futures, only one of which may emerge, depending on which course of action the person takes. There were other, slightly more esoteric ideas, suggesting that the four dimensions that we are all familiar with, are themselves encapsulated within higher dimensions and that, again, the conscious mind may be able to access those higher dimensions and in doing so see past, present, and future simultaneously. Reading such material Grant would often groan in despondency, unsure he'd ever really find any clear answers. One answer he was encouraged by was the frequency with which people reported dreaming about future events. According to one survey he'd read it was almost half of all those who took the survey. This made him feel less odd knowing that a good many others had also had similar experiences.

Towards the end of the week, he felt as though he'd read enough material and now wanted to talk it through with someone. The question was who? To help him deal with the issue he sat and wrote a list of all the names he could think of. Writing lists was something he generally did when trying to deal with any situation. He liked lists, they helped to map out clearly what assumptions were made, what the goal was, what steps needed to be taken, and so on.

The list hadn't taken long to produce. It only had three names on it. His therapist, someone he knew in the psychology department of the university and finally, Adam. At least he had options he thought, smiling to himself.

∞

At his next therapy session Grant tentatively raised the issue of his dreams with Dr Wentworth. It was always Dr Wentworth, never Anita. He also liked clear boundaries.

'Well,' she said in response to his query, 'dreams are often a way for the brain to bring together the various events of the preceding day and consolidate them into your long-term memory.'

'What about recurring dreams?' he asked.

'It depends,' she answered cautiously. 'Recurring dreams can often, though not always, represent some underlying stressor in your life.'

They both sat in silence for a moment as each of them thought about the accident that neither had mentioned.

'What about dreams of the future?' Grant asked tentatively.

'Hmmm, well that's not really an area that I'm familiar with. I know that there are anecdotal reports of such things ...' she tailed off. There was another short silence before she asked, 'do you think your dreams are of the future?'

Grant felt conflicted. He did want to talk openly about his dreams, especially about the possibility that they might be premonitions. And he liked and respected Dr Wentworth, but if all she knew about them was based on anecdotal reports then he might be better off speaking to someone with greater expertise in the area. Taking a moment to decide he then shook his head. 'Nah, not really. Just wondered if such a thing were possible.'

'Who knows,' she smiled. 'Now, tell me about your week,' she said, deftly steering the conversation back to him.

The following week at work Grant had arranged to meet with Dr Ivan Sorensen, one of the psychologists on campus he'd met a few times when helping him with various computer issues. Grant knew that Ivan was a cognitive neuroscientist, which to Grant meant he lectured on the brain, and stuff like that. So, he thought he'd be a good person to chat to. They'd agreed to meet for an afternoon coffee in the senior common room. As they made themselves comfortable in the plush armchairs Ivan kicked off the conversation.

'So,' said Ivan with a smile, 'how can I help you?'

'I've been trying to find out about the nature of dreams,' answered Grant.

'Ha! – you and the rest of the world I shouldn't wonder.'

Grant smiled at the enormity of the question. 'Yes, but do we know what dreams are?'

'We'll, the generally accepted notion is that dreams are simply the events of your day that your brain is working to consolidate into memory.'

'Nothing more than that?'

'What do you mean,' asked Ivan with interest.

'Well, what about the idea that dreams can be meaningful.'

Ivan frowned a little as he heard this and shook his head. 'No, I'm not sure about that.'

Grant's shoulders sagged a little in disappointment.

'The problem with attempting to interpret dreams,' offered Ivan, 'is that there are too many unknowns.'

'What do you mean?'

'Well, think about any type of dream. The images that occur could represent something that happened to you during the day. Or, something earlier, or the image could have some special meaning to you and would be meaningless to anyone else.'

'So, I suppose,' suggested Grant, 'that would mean that each person would need to interpret their own dreams?'

'Yep,' nodded Ivan.

'Hmmm. But what about dreams of . . .' he hesitated for a moment. 'Dreams of future events?'

'Ha!' Ivan snorted. 'Now we're really out there with that sort of stuff.'

Grant waited, a little uncertain of what to say next.

Ivan shook his head. 'No, we need to be careful not to fall into that trap.'

'What trap?' asked Grant.

'The illusion that people sometimes dream of future events.'

'So, you don't think that happens then?'

'Ha ha ha! No way. It's just salience bias, poor recall, wishful thinking or a combination of all three.'

'Is there any research on the topic?' Grant asked, slightly disingenuously, given that he'd spent the previous week searching out and reading as much material as he could.

Unfortunately, Ivan was rather dismissive, 'nothing useful,' he said. Then added as an afterthought, 'that I'm aware of anyway.'

Grant was a little disappointed. He'd read a lot of material over the past nine to ten days. Ok, some of it was online and anecdotal but quite a lot *was* published in journals and books. He wondered how Ivan could be so sure. Or at least so dismissive without knowing about the research. He decided to try again.

'But I thought there was some research on precognitive dreaming,' he tried.

Ivan screwed his face up in thought. 'There may have been something done in the sixties and seventies, probably in the States,' he offered. 'But I don't know of any research looking at precognition or precognitive dreaming now.'

'What about research into something called retroactive priming[3]?' Grant asked, offering up a term he'd come across in his research. 'Have you ever come across that?'

Ivan puckered his mouth and shook his head again. 'No, never heard of it.'

The conversation paused for a moment as both men sat in silent contemplation.

Ivan shrugged, 'you could check out,' he frowned as if in thought. 'Ah yes, Edinburgh I think it was. They hold a Chair in parapsychology – only university in the UK that does[4]. They *might* be able to tell you a bit more,' he said rather vaguely. 'As I say, not really my area.'

The conversation then moved on to more mundane matters, which included the latest round of IT upgrades which seemed to cause no end of disruption. They both bemoaned the upgrades which seemed only to make life more difficult and complicated. Later, when Grant had returned to his office, he thought about what Ivan had said, and Googled Edinburgh University. He spent a few minutes searching through their website until he found the parapsychology department and fired off a quick email asking if they had any information on precognition, and in particular dream precognition.

At the end of the week Grant had arranged to meet Adam in their favourite pub to see what he thought of it all. As it was, because of a last-minute problem with the campus server he was running slightly late and he could see Adam already seated at a table with two glasses of beer in front of him. One full and the other only two-thirds full. Grant was full of apologies as he arrived.

'Sorry mate,' he said, taking the seat opposite, 'problems with the server.'

'Twas ever thus,' responded Adam philosophically. He moved the full pint over to Grant and lifted his own glass. 'Try switching it off. . .'

Grant lifted his pint, '. . . and then back on again,' he responded with a smile. They clinked glasses and then both men took long satisfying sips of their beer.

Adam was first to replace his glass on the table. As he did so his face shifted from a look of relaxed geniality to one of mild concern. He looked over at Grant asking cautiously, 'so your email said you had something to tell me.' But before Grant could answer Adam quickly added, 'it's not about your bloody dreams again, is it?'

'Well,' began Grant, having second thoughts about telling Adam what he'd found out.

'Did you speak to anyone at the uni about this?' inquired Adam interrupting his thoughts.

'Well, er, . . . yes actually. In fact, I spoke to my therapist first, but she wasn't really aware of the research . . .'

'You mean there is some research?' sneered Adam interrupting him.

Grant gritted his teeth in mild annoyance and looked down at his feet. He took a breath and tried to reflect for a moment on the whole thing and how crazy he'd initially thought it all was. Until that was, he'd started having these weird dreams. Until he'd spent time reading some of the research he'd found and some of what he'd been sent from the researchers in Edinburgh. Until now. He decided to appeal to their friendship.

'Look, trust me,' he began, 'I know how weird this all sounds.'

Adam nodded emphatically, taking another sip of his pint.

'But just hear me out,' pleaded Grant.

After a few seconds Adam conceded with a nod, 'ok, you have the floor.'

'Well, as I say, I did speak to my therapist initially, but she didn't seem to know much about it, so I asked one of the psychologists at the uni.'

'What a good idea,' said Adam with a smug smile.

'Ok, yes, I know that's what you said I should do, but anyway, I asked this guy I've met a few times on campus, and I knew he lectured on brain stuff, and thought he'd be able to offer some help.'

'And did he?'

Grant screwed his face up a little. 'Hmm, some. Well, he didn't really know much about the topic himself, which was odd because he seemed so sure that it was all a lot of nonsense.'

'What's odd about that?'

'I don't know. It just felt weird that he was so sure it was all rubbish without even knowing any of the research.'

'Ha ha ha!' laughed Adam. 'I don't think a lack of knowledge has ever stopped an academic from telling you what they think.'

'Sad but true,' conceded Grant, smiling wryly. 'Anyway, the point is, that whilst he didn't seem to know much himself, he did give me a useful pointer. Apparently, there's a department at the university of Edinburgh where a group of researchers focus specifically on this sort of stuff.'

'What ESP and all that?'

'Yep.'

'Hmm,' responded Adam, 'nice work if you can get it.'

'And so, I pinged off an email query to them and within a couple of days one of their researchers had got back to me. In fact, I've been talking with her for the ...'

'Ooh, a her is it?' asked Adam, perking up instantly.

Grant rolled his eyes. 'Just leave it will you.' There was a moments pause before Grant continued. 'So, I've been talking to this researcher via email, and she's been really helpful. She's given me lots of interesting information, links to various sites and recommendations for books. I mean, that's what's so weird about it all really.'

'What do you mean?'

'Well, not that I found – or rather, have been shown – lots of information about the topic, but that there is so *much* of it.'

'Why's that weird?' asked Adam.

'Because Ivan – that's the psychologist I spoke to – well, Ivan didn't seem to know anything about it.'

'Why is that surprising?'

'I don't know. I just thought he'd know something about it. I mean, don't they teach this sort of thing in undergraduate psychology courses?'

'Shouldn't think so.'

'But then how can they argue that there's no evidence for ... for whatever it is, if they've never looked at it?'

Adam grinned. 'Didn't we just have this conversation? You know what academics are like. They know an awful lot about very little but once you get beyond their specialist subject, they're as ignorant as the rest of us.'

'Hmm,' responded Grant thoughtfully. 'Still, makes you think doesn't it?'

'No,' responded Adam finishing his beer, 'it doesn't, and I've found that beer helps a lot with that.' He smiled at Grant. 'Another?' he asked, nodding at Grant's almost empty glass.

'My round,' said Grant.

'Even better,' smiled Adam, handing him his empty glass.

It took Grant a few minutes to get them both another pint and a couple of bags of crisps. Returning to the table he carefully placed the beers down and then threw one of the packs of crisps to Adam, who deftly caught it.

Adam looked at the bag of crisps. 'I still can't get used to cheese and onion in blue bags.'

Grant smiled. This topic was another of the many ongoing conversations they'd had over the years about how things had changed, and in their shared opinion, not always for the better. 'No neither can I – I mean, what's that about. Everyone knows cheese and onion should be in a green bag.'

'I blame the Americans,' said Adam.

'Why?'

'Stands to reason doesn't it. They made us change marathons into snickers. . .'

'And what the hell does snickers even mean?' demanded Grant. 'Always makes me think of a sniggering laugh. I mean, there's nothing chocolaty about that.'

'Whereas marathon,' offered Adam, 'clearly speaks of a nourishing chocolate bar with a hazelnut in every bite.'

'You're thinking of a topic,' said Grant. 'The marathon, or snickers,' he said the word with a sneer, 'has roasted peanuts.'

'You sure?'

'Yep.'

'Hmm,' conceded Adam.

The two men each took a sip of beer and reflected for a moment on the changing nature of the world around them. Wondering why, as they so often had, that it needed to change and whether it was in fact the nature of change that they railed against.

The moment came to an end with Adam asking, 'so, these researchers at Edinburgh, they gave you some good info then?'

Grant settled into his chair. 'Ooh yes. I mean, did you know there's a society in London called the,' he looked up in an attempt to recall the information. 'It's called the Society for Psychical Research[5].'

'Psychic research?' teased Adam, 'sounds like a contradiction in terms to me.'

'Very droll,' responded Grant. 'Anyway, this organisation has been going since the late eighteen hundreds and they've loads of information about all sorts of things. They publish a scientific journal, and a magazine, and they have a library in West Kensington which you can visit.'

Adam raised his eyebrows in mild surprise.

'Anyway,' continued Grant, 'I went along there and found out quite a bit. I've made some notes.' So saying he reached over to his jacket and extracted a small notepad. Opening the pad, he began. 'Apparently some people think that precognition is in fact the only form of . . .' he consulted the pad, '. . . of psi[6].'

'Sigh?' queried Adam.

'It's spelt p-s-i and I'm not sure if its short for psychic or something else, but it's a sort of general term that means all the different forms of . . . of weird stuff,' he added. 'But it's interesting that some of these scientists think it's the basis of all the different forms of psi.'

'In what way?' queried Adam.

'Well, think about telepathy for instance. That's supposed to be about one person communicating with another by thought alone, yes?'

Adam nodded in agreement.

'Well, according to these researchers, you can more easily account for any findings from such studies in terms of precognition. Because there's a time, at the start for example, when one person might be trying to think about what the other one is thinking about, when they *don't* know what that other person is thinking. But, at the end, they're told whether their guess, or whatever you call it, was right or not. So now they *do* know what the other person was thinking. And these researchers say that this is simply precognition.'

'Hmm,' said Adam, interested now despite his earlier protestations. 'Seems that this precognition is more complex than I thought.'

'Ha!' laughed Grant. 'You haven't heard the half of it. There's even different types of precognition[7].'

'What do you mean?'

Grant consulted his notepad again. 'Well, there's something called unexplained anticipation, which is the idea that you can somehow anticipate what's going to happen. Then, there's precognitive preference and avoidance, retroactive priming and something called presentiment. Which is doubly weird, as this is when your body, or your physiology, reacts in some way before a stimulating event.'

'You're kidding?'

'Nope. It's all there in the books and journals. And listen to this. One researcher has even done some of this work with animals[8].'

'How?'

'I think it was with birds. Apparently, he shows them random images and hidden among the random images is a picture of a predator – such as a snake. And he's found that the birds respond to the image of the snake *before* they see it.'

'Whew,' responded Adam. 'How weird is that?'

'I know. That's what I mean. There's just loads of stuff about this. And then, of course, there's work on dream precognition[9]. Which, supposedly, is one of the most common forms of precognition.'

'Really?'

'Yeah. I came across a couple of surveys and they put the numbers at between forty to fifty percent of the population.'

'Wow!' responded Adam in surprise. 'More than you'd think.'

A thoughtful silence followed Grant's summary as both men turned their attention back to their beers. After a few minutes Adam finished his crisps and neatly folded the bag into itself, placing it back on the table. Then looking over at Grant he asked, 'so, is that what you think your dreams are, precognitive?'

Grant shrugged a little, screwing his face up in thought. 'I don't know. Maybe, yeah.'

'Why?'

'It's weird. I mean, I've had dreams before, but these *feel* different. And remember that guy at the bar with the broken wrist. That wasn't a coincidence.'

'Ok,' conceded Adam, 'but why now?'

Grant looked confused.

'I mean,' continued Adam, 'why do you think you're suddenly having dreams about the future now. After all, as you say, you've had lots of dreams before. What's changed?'

Grant thought for a moment. They both knew what he was thinking about. He let out a deep sigh. 'I think it was the accident,' he admitted.

'So, you think that because you were in an accident you're now dreaming of random strangers in accidents?' To be fair Adam was trying to remain neutral, but he was finding it hard to hide his incredulity.

'Yes. . . no – I don't know,' responded Grant in a slightly confused manner. Then added, 'maybe.'

'Do you dream of the same person, or the same accident over and over?' asked Adam.

'No, well – sometimes. It depends. Sometimes they repeat and sometimes they don't.'

'And have you ever tried acting on them?'

'What do you mean?'

'Well, if they're dreams of future events,' said Adam, 'why don't you try and change one?'

Grant's face registered a mixture of bewilderment and shock. It was simple, but it wasn't something he'd really thought about. For some reason the idea scared him a little and he wasn't sure if this was because trying to do something about them would prove that it was all a lot of nonsense, or that it wasn't.

'Something to think about,' said Adam as he finished the last of his drink.

Grant nodded and hemmed a cautious agreement.

'Well, I've got to go,' said Adam, now standing. He turned to go, stopped, and then turned back to Grant. 'Seriously, have a think about it.' He shrugged, 'what have you got to lose?'

With that the two men said their goodbyes and Adam made his way out of the pub leaving Grant deep in thought about what he should do next.

∞

Once again, he heard the noise of the underground and felt the tiled wall at his back. The feeling of dread began earlier this time, as if there was a sense of urgency to it. The mixture of anticipation and fear made his heart pound in his ears. He wanted to keep his eyes closed but it was as if his body was no longer under his control. His head moved up and his eyes followed her as she walked by in front of him. The intense feeling of wrongness almost overwhelmed him this time. He began to tremble, his breath coming in short gasps.

He watched her approach the entrance. Saw, again, the oncoming rush of people pushing the crowd back and out. Her cry . . . which turned into a scream.

He was clenching his teeth so hard his jaw ached. In a determined effort to move forwards, to do something, he strained against the unseen barrier that held him locked in place. He could feel his heart pounding with the effort. Not this time, he thought. Not again. Slowly, his fear began to turn to anger at the thought of remaining helpless. With a supreme effort of will, crying out through gritted teeth, he managed a step forward.

Choking for breath Grant sobbed as he instantly came awake. He could feel the tears on his face and his heart thudding against the wall of his chest. He choked back another sob as he fell back onto the sweaty sheets moaning in despair. Slowly, he rolled onto his side, curling into a ball as he wrapped his arms around his legs. Laying in this position, Adam's words echoed in his mind, *"why don't you try and change one – what have you got to lose?"*

∞

It had been a tough week for Grant. He'd had the dream about her twice more that week and each time the feelings seemed more intense. This was disturbing his nights and as a consequence he was often tired and distracted at work. More than once that week colleagues had asked him if everything was all right. He'd always smiled politely and made up some excuse but inside he felt a growing anguish. He didn't know what to do. He'd thought about it more and more all week. Especially, Adam's words. But he didn't know which underground station he was dreaming of. He'd tried hard to try any recall details of the station but nothing about it seemed familiar to him.

Later that evening, as he made his way home on the northern line, he managed to squeeze himself into a small space to the left and back, by one of the carriage doors. From this position he was able to surreptitiously scan the faces of the other passengers for any signs of familiarity. He didn't recognise any of them. He became so engrossed in searching the carriage for any sign that one, or more, of the passengers would be familiar, that he missed his stop at Camden town. It was only as the train was pulling out of the station, the signs on the station wall floating by his window waving him goodbye, that he noticed. Oh, shit! he thought to himself, angry at having missed his stop. Not only was this whole thing disrupting his sleep, it was also impacting on his work and now he'd missed his bloody stop. Just perfect, he groaned. The icing on the cake. He looked up at the tube map on the upper wall of the carriage to check the route back. It only took a few seconds for him to realise that if he got off at Kentish town, he'd be able to double-back on the next train to Camden. A few minutes later he arrived at Kentish town, exited the carriage through the nearby door and made his way up and over the line to the southbound platform.

As he walked onto the southbound platform he felt a tingle of recognition. His steps slowed as half-dreamed memories drifted through his mind. He closed his eyes and listened. The sounds of the other passengers echoed a remembrance heard only in his dreams. He stopped for a moment, then moved to one side, standing with his back to the wall. Reaching back with both hands he felt the smoothness of the ceramic wall tiles. The feeling of familiarity was almost overwhelming.

Gently, he raised his head to see her walk by once again in front of him. This time however the reality of it was palpable. In that moment he knew. Instantly, fear gripped him, holding him in place like an invisible vice. For a moment he felt the panic rise in his chest, squeezing his dry throat. He felt sick with fear.

Then he remembered.

The last time he'd had the dream he'd moved. Only a single step. But he'd taken it. That knowledge, that feeling, took root in his soul and gave him comfort. A feeling of peace descended, wrapping him in a calm embrace. Then, a jolt ran through his body like an electric shock, and he somehow shifted. He was no longer standing on the platform. He was looking down, watching himself standing there. With a serene, detached casualness, he watched as his body moved along the platform towards the edge. Time and motion seemed to slow down. He followed the movements of the crowd as they were swept back and watched as she was pushed towards the edge. Saw her cry out and heard her scream as she began to topple outwards. With a dispassionate interest he felt the movement of his arm, and saw this reflected in his body as it reached out and took hold of her outstretched hand. Their hands locked.

He watched as his body pivoted against the pull of her weight, swinging her round and back onto the platform. A tingling jolt, a shift in perspective and time returned with the noise of an angry crowd and the screaming brakes of an incoming train.

People crowded round and in, shouting out, asking if she was ok. A man dressed in a London Transport uniform began to push his way through the crowd, urgently asking if she was alright, whilst appealing to the surrounding passengers to stand back and give the girl some space. The push and pull of the crowd jerked him sideways and their hands parted. Unnoticed, he slipped out and away from the crowd and made his way along the platform, to the far end, away from all the noise and the commotion. With each step his pounding heart began to slow, his short gasping breaths easing, becoming deeper, as his trembling body began to relax.

Standing alone, with head bowed, he tried to block out the surrounding noise. Focusing only on the jumbled events in his mind. Some that seemed so real, some he thought had happened and others – he wasn't sure. He closed his eyes in an effort to calm the chaos of his thoughts. Just breathe, he thought. Just breathe. He wasn't sure how long he'd been standing there, but he slowly became aware of a familiar sensation in his chest. The feeling tugged at him, causing him to raise his head.

She was standing there – directly in front of him.

As their eyes met, she smiled. 'Bloody hell!' she exclaimed, smiling more broadly now as she shook her head in disbelief. 'That was . . .' she hesitated. 'I'm . . .' she took another breath, 'I'm still shaking,' another pause. 'My God, you saved . . .'

'Are you ok?' he interrupted, not wanting to hear her say the words. The thought of saving her still scared him and he wasn't sure he could live up to the idea of it.

She nodded, still a little breathless. Then smiled again. 'What's your name?'

It took him a moment. He had to swallow before he could respond. 'Grant.'

She reached down into her bag and pulled out a pen. Then, grabbing his right arm, she lifted it and began to write on the back of his hand. 'I'm Kelly, and this is my number.' As she finished writing she lowered his arm but continued to hold it.

Standing there, their hands touching, the moment stretched time.

'Call me,' said Kelly, her face lighting up. 'I owe you a beer.'

He nodded, not trusting his lips to convey the words in his heart.

'Ok?' she asked, wanting to be sure he'd got the message.

'Ok,' he mumbled.

'Just make sure you do.' With that she turned and headed back along the platform to the exit. As she walked, she looked back once, smiling as she did so.

He watched her leave and stood for a moment trying to calm himself down. Three minutes later the next train for Camden pulled in and he boarded, moving between the other passengers, being careful not to smudge the number printed on the back of his right hand. The rest of the journey home was uneventful but with each passing minute he felt a lightening of his step. He also became conscious that he was smiling. It felt good. He felt good. He hadn't felt this good in a long time. He thought about what had happened and about telling Adam. His smile broadened. Adam's not going to believe this, he thought. Then he thought about her number. Briefly looking again at the scrawled ink on the back of his hand he wondered how long he should wait before calling.

That night, for the first time in a long time, Grant spent a long night in a deep and dreamless sleep.

8

A Change of Heart

Glennis opened the door to find a large man in his mid-fifties, reasonably well dressed, lightly tanned with thinning grey hair. It took her a moment to recognise him as the man who'd put the offer in on her house.

'Oh, Mr Stevens,' she said, 'please do come in.'

The man smiled affably, 'please call me Harry,' he said, 'everyone does.'

Glennis led him back through the hall to the living room, which was sparsely furnished and had a distinct chill in the air, now that she could no longer afford to have the central heating on for long. Glennis, a widow of seventy-nine, had no children and was essentially alone. She'd lived in her cottage for the past thirty-six years, but it had become increasingly difficult to manage, what with her meagre pension and very little left of the savings she and Robert, her husband, had squirreled away over the years. Since he'd died four years ago, she felt as though she were on a downward spiral. Over time more things seemed to need doing around the house, which she couldn't really afford. As they were left, they invariably built up and multiplied, adding to her worries. It wasn't that she wanted to sell. She didn't. She had many happy memories associated with her home and was very reluctant to leave. But she also worried about being able to cope. And now, with everything going up except her pension she knew she needed to do something. She thought it was a stroke of luck that Mr Stevens had got in touch with her at about that time to see if she was interested in selling the place. Apparently, he was a property developer, among other things.

Of course, it wasn't luck. Or at least not good luck for Glennis. It was a network of people who kept an eye and ear out for such properties and let Harry know what the situation was with the owner. Old woman, living on her own, struggling to make ends meet. And the cottage had a lot of potential, Harry could see that immediately. Oh yes, it was luck all right. And all of it was with Harry.

As the two of them sat, Harry opened a large buff-coloured folder he'd been carrying. 'Well, Mrs MacMillan,' he began, but she interrupted.

'Please, call me Glennis.'

He smiled, he could be charming when he needed to be and now, he knew, a bit of the old-world charm and good manners would go a long way to increasing the profit on this deal. 'Ok, Glennis. Well, I've had the reports back from the surveyors, electricians, plumbers and builders.' He sighed for a moment, made a wry face and shook his head slowly with the seeming air of one very sorry to impart bad news. 'And it's not good news I'm afraid.' He let that point sink in for a moment, watching her as she looked down at the floor in embarrassment.

She sighed heavily and shrugged her shoulders a little. 'I knew it needed a bit of work,' she said in a voice that still held some hope that a good price could be obtained.

Shaking his head Harry said, 'I'm sorry but it's a bit more . . . actually it's a lot more than a "bit of work".' He watched her out of the corner of his eye as he began to remove the various reports from the folder. As he handed her the reports, he noticed the tightening of the jaw and glint of tears in her eyes, which she quickly wiped away and attempted to mask by blowing her nose on a tissue. Perfect, he thought. Get her on the back foot and then push gently.

'As you'll see from the initial surveyor's report there's quite a lot of substantial work that needs to be completed to bring the electrics and plumbing in line with current regulations.' He then switched topic quickly, not giving her much time to absorb each point he made. 'You'll also see on page seventeen that they noted damp in the rafters, which could also mean an additional extensive survey and the replacement of roof timbers.' Switching again, but back this time, 'and on page nine you'll see that they note possible indicators of damp and mould around the windows and doors, which would require all frames to be changed to the more modern UPVC ones.'

He continued in this fashion for some time. Going over points, building regulations and standards, some more than once. Stressing how bad the condition of the cottage was and how much work, and cost, would be needed to bring it up to something that would equate with modern living. Whilst only some of these issues were true, all of them had been exaggerated because that's what Harry had paid for. Sadly, for Glennis, it was a list of her worst fears. As if all the worries she'd hidden away or ignored over the years had finally been brought out into the light. She also felt ashamed that her home had fallen into such disrepair. That there were so many things wrong also seemed to emphasise to her how badly she was coping and merely confirmed that she needed to do something.

Once Harry had finished going over all the points, he sat back a bit and allowed Glennis a little time to think and reflect. Then, working hard to affect an air of concerned interest he leant forward. 'There's a lot here Glennis,' he emphasised.

She sat in silence, nodding slowly as if trying not to admit the inevitable.

Now, he thought. Time for the winning tactic. 'I'm wondering whether you should think again about selling.'

She frowned, and her voice wavered as she asked, 'what do you mean?'

He held up the reports in one big fist and shrugged. 'With all of this work, there's no way you'll be able to get the price *you* want.' He waited for a moment. It was important to stress that it was the price she wanted and not what he was prepared to give. That way she wouldn't be thinking about asking someone else, because it was her price that was wrong. 'Perhaps you should re-think selling and just have the work done yourself.' He knew this was out of the question given her financial situation.

'What would happen,' she asked meekly, 'if I just decided not to have this work done?'

Harry made a rocking side-to-side gesture with his head, 'well, these problems . . .' important now to use the word problems instead of work. 'They won't go away.' A short pause then he added, 'and could of course cost you more in the long run.'

Glennis sat in silence for a moment with head slightly bowed as if in defeat. He knew now was the moment to back off and leave her to her thoughts.

'I think it's probably best if I leave you those copies,' he nodded at the ones she held loosely in her lap, 'and give you time to re-think your options.' The word was options, but the tone was price. 'And once you've made a decision give me a call and we'll go from there.'

'Oh, thank you Harry,' she said gratefully. 'I do appreciate what you've said.'

'No problem,' he said cheerfully.

So saying, they both got up from their chairs and Glennis led him back out through the hallway to the front door. After saying goodbye, she returned to the living room and sat for a while on her own, trying desperately to think about what she could, or should do. As she sat there, alone, her eyes spoke with salty tears of sadness at where she'd ended up. Her options were limited she knew, and time was passing. It wasn't a great time to be selling, what with interest rates on their way up and inflation running at an all-time high. But she wasn't getting any younger and she'd seen a retirement flat that had a live in warden in one of the new developments at Meadowcroft Park which would be perfect. Deep down she knew what it was that she was going to do, but she was honest enough to realise that she just needed a little time to accept what this would mean. That it would mean having less money, less to live on. But at least she could live in a place that might be warm, didn't need lots of maintenance, and where she might not feel so lonely. She wiped the tears from her eyes and took a deep breath. Sometimes, she thought, you just have to have faith in the decisions you make.

'Ok,' said Harry, into his mobile phone, as he stood in the designer kitchen of his well-furnished home. 'I'll get on to my solicitor right away and get things moving.' There was a short silence as he listened to what the other person was saying. 'Ok, thanks Glennis, I'll be in touch.' He pressed the call-end button, gently put the mobile on the worktop and then fist pumped the air whilst doing a little jig. 'Yes!' he cried, 'reeesult!'

'What's that love?' asked Rita, his wife.

'The deal on Bramble cottage,' he answered with a big smile. 'Looks like it'll all go through.'

'Ooh,' she said with a smile, 'well done.' She looked at him with fondness, thinking it was good to see him happy. A part of her also knew that if he'd made a good profit on some deal or other then it could well mean a night out, possibly a new outfit for her. Or even something more expensive. She beamed as the thought of a shopping trip for something special ran through her mind. Rita was a petite woman in her late forties who spent a lot of time, and a substantial amount of Harry's money, on making sure she looked good. She'd maintained her figure over the years with the help of membership at an exclusive local spa and gym. Her slender frame, usually well-tanned and pampered, always looked good in the latest Versace dress, and Jimmy Choo heels.

'How about dinner out tonight?' Harry asked, then added, 'to celebrate'.

'Oooh,' she cooed,' delighted at the opportunities this would present. 'Perfect.'

'We could invite Cathy,' he added. His voice hopeful.

'Aw no!' complained Rita. 'She'll just moan the whole evening.'

Cathy was Harry's older sister. She'd been widowed five years ago when her husband, Eric, had died of cancer. Since then, she rarely ventured out and her health had deteriorated. Harry was genuinely fond of his older sister and could still recall her looking out for him when they were kids. Roles which had reversed a long time ago now. It was true however that she tended to moan a lot whenever they took her out. Which wasn't conducive to an evening of celebrations.

'How about Michael and Jennie?' offered Rita. 'We've not seen them in a while.'

Harry looked down in thought for a moment. Mike was an old friend from school and they'd not seen each other for a while and it would be good to catch up. He shrugged, 'ok, I'll call them and see if I can get us a table tonight at *Chez Marcel.*'

Rita squealed with delight, thinking that the deal must have been successful to be going there. 'Right, I'll just ring Carol at the salon to try and fit in a quick wash and set.'

'Why?' he asked, 'you look great to me.'

She rolled her eyes in a melodramatic way and shook her head. 'Trust me, if we're meeting with Michael and Jennie I need to look better than this.'

Harry shook his head in wonderment but smiled indulgently.

Later that evening the four of them were seated at a round table at the plush restaurant enjoying a good, if somewhat overpriced, dinner. Harry and Michael had been at secondary school together and somehow, despite the different paths they'd taken over the years, had maintained their friendship. Michael now worked as a manager for one of the large out of town retail stores and his wife Jennie worked as a part-time teacher at the local primary school. Harry liked to spend time with them because he always found it easy to talk to Mike about anything. There was also a strong element of comparison to their relationship which always made Harry feel better. He liked to think about them both coming from the same background but that he'd made significantly more of his life than Mike. Bigger house, his and hers Mercedes, luxury holidays every year. It helped of course that Harry and Rita didn't have any children. They only needed to think about themselves, something both of them were quite good at. It's not that Harry hadn't wanted children, but that Rita couldn't conceive. And, over time, it had just been one of those things that just wasn't to be. So, they'd made do with the various distractions money could buy them. Mike and

Jennie in contrast had two girls, Annie and Sarah. Both now at university, one studying medicine and the other engineering.

Harry smiled contentedly as the waiter brought him and Mike large brandies and cleared away the remaining plates from the table. As they both took appreciative sips of their liqueur Harry winced a little as he felt a slight discomfort in his chest. The unpleasant feeling passed as he looked across to see Rita looking stunning in what he was sure was another new dress. He knew how much she liked to show off new outfits and there was a part of him that also enjoyed showing her off. It always made him feel good to see other men eye Rita when she was wearing one of her dresses. Right now, she was busy telling Jennie about some spa treatment she'd recently tried that Jennie absolutely had to try, knowing full well that such luxuries were well beyond Jennie's means. As he sat there for a moment thinking about Mike and Jennie a small frown appeared on Harry's face. The evening had been a good one and the food had been excellent, but Mike had been a little more reticent than usual. A little slower to laugh and drinking a little more than usual. It made him wonder if Mike and Jennie were having what was euphemistically called "marital problems". He hoped not. The warm fuzz of alcohol helped him to feel magnanimous as he leant in towards Mike and spoke quietly.

'Is . . .,' he asked cautiously, '. . . is everything ok with you and Jennie?'

Mike looked puzzled for a moment, then his face brightened. 'Ha!, no.' Then quickly added, 'I mean yes. Yes, we're fine.'

Harry's face mirrored the concern in his voice. 'It's just that you seemed a bit . . . a bit off this evening that's all.'

Mike looked down for a moment and sighed. He shook his head slightly. 'It's just the girls.'

'Nothing wrong with them is there?' asked Harry quickly. He'd always felt very fond of Mike's girls and there were moments, when he saw them with Mike, that he wondered whether he and Rita shouldn't have tried harder. Or tried something else.

'No, no, nothing like that. They're both doing fine. More than fine in fact, both really doing well.'

Harry smiled, relieved to hear it.

'It's just that with both of them now studying in London their grants barely cover their living expenses and we're both worried about the amount of money they're expected to borrow to get through it all.'

Harry, who'd never gone on to higher education found university finances a mystery. He could understand the necessity and the benefits of going to university to train for a professional career, such as doctor or engineer, which was one of the many reasons he'd always felt close to Mike's kids. He could appreciate what it was they were trying to achieve. But he couldn't understand a system that enslaved them into tens of thousands of pounds of debts in the process. He quickly realised his thoughts had wandered a bit as Mike was still speaking.

'. . . decided to sell the Jag,' Mike finished mournfully.

Mike's bombshell startled an automatic response. 'You what!?' exclaimed Harry.

Mike grimaced a little. 'Jennie and I have been through everything. We just don't have any other way of raising a chunk of money.'

Just over eight years ago Mike's father had died and left him a classic 1968 Jaguar Mk II. It was a beautiful car and Mike had spent the intervening years restoring it with a love and care that was rarely seen but easily appreciated. In order to make a little bit on the side he sometimes hired it out for weddings and special occasions. It was Mike's pride and joy and the fact that he was considering selling it clearly indicated that financial times were indeed tough for them.

'That's why,' continued Mike, faltering slightly, 'I just thought I'd ask you. See if you knew of anyone that might be interested in such a car.' The question was "anyone" but the subtext was "you".

Harry did feel a little sorry for Mike, knowing how much he adored the Jag and he could see that selling it might enable them to help support Annie and Sarah for a bit. However, he couldn't help feeling slightly superior in the knowledge that his finances were in a much better state. It also occurred to him that if he played this right he might be able to make a few quid for himself. He was after all a businessman first and foremost and couldn't resist the opportunity to make a bit on a side deal.

'Well,' responded Harry screwing his face up in thought. 'As you know, cars aren't really my forte.'

Mike's face fell a little.

Meanwhile Harry was sure he'd be able to sell the car given his extensive contacts, if only he could get a good price from Mike. However, he knew he couldn't buy the car directly from Mike because haggling over the price of that particular item could seriously jeopardise their friendship. He'd need someone he could trust to buy it for him – at least on paper – so he could then sell it on. Such men were called straw buyers. He'd used straw buyers before, in his property dealings and could think of a couple of people who'd be willing to help out, for a small bonus of course. He looked back at Mike. 'But I may know a bloke or two who would be interested.'

Mike perked up a little on hearing this.

'Why don't you leave it with me and I'll put the word out and see if I can drum up any interest.'

'Ah, thanks Harry,' Mike sounded relieved.

'As I say, not really my thing, but if I can find someone, I'll give them your number and they can get directly in touch with you. If that's ok with you?'

'Yes, yes, of course.'

They both smiled now. Mike, relieved in the hope that Harry would be able to help him out and Harry because he was sure he'd be able to make something out of this. Harry raised his now empty glass. 'Fancy another?' he asked.

'Why not.'

'How about you two?' Harry asked the women, 'anything else?' They both requested top ups on their wine and Harry called the waiter over to fulfil the various requests. A few minutes later they were all sitting relaxing with their drinks. This time, as Harry took a sip of his brandy he grimaced and shifted his head to the side. Rita noticed the odd movement and asked if he was ok. Harry grimaced, turning his head from side to side. 'Necks a bit . . .'

Still smiling, but concern clearly evident in her voice, Rita reached out a hand and placed it on his shoulder. 'You should take it easy,' she said, 'get yourself a massage.'

Harry nodded and smiled, 'hmmm.' He was feeling a little light-headed, which was odd because he hadn't drunk that much. As he sat there the thought of drinking any more made him feel a bit queasy, so he gently placed his glass back on the table and sat back in his chair closing his eyes for a moment to quell rising dizziness. He could feel beads of sweat on his forehead as his breath came in short gasps.

Noticing the colour draining from his face Rita leant forward, 'Harry, are you ok?'

'What's wrong?' asked Jennie, seeming to note for the first time that Harry was struggling to breathe.

Harry attempted to make a short placating gesture with his hands. 'It's ok,' he grimaced, getting unsteadily to his feet, 'I'll just. . .' and then with a gasp he toppled to the floor, grabbing his left arm and crying out in pain.

'Oh my God!' cried Rita, rising so quickly her chair fell backwards.

Mike had already dug out his mobile and was calling for an ambulance. The last thing Harry could remember was an incredible pressure on his chest making it difficult to breath and then . . . darkness.

∞

Events slowly shifted into focus as Harry became aware of what was going on around him. For some reason he seemed to be looking down on the backs of a medical team as they frantically worked on someone he couldn't see. Weirdly, as his mind shifted to each of the medical team he could hear their thoughts, as if they were speaking aloud. Their anxieties and tensions, their concerns about the patient's health, and for the lead doctor whether it was going to be possible to resuscitate the patient again. A nagging curiosity edged Harry forward to see who this patient was. As he looked down, one of the nurses shifted to the side to clip a bag of clear liquid onto a stand. The liquid dripped into a tube that was connected to the arm of the patient laying on the bed. Harry moved forward slightly to get a better view. It was with a detached curiosity that he realised he was looking down . . . at himself.

There was no shock, no fear, just an odd feeling of seeing his body lying on a bed as if it were someone else. As he looked at the body on the bed, he had the feeling he was looking at a favourite old shirt or jacket. Something he'd worn many times but had now, simply discarded, because he no longer needed it. He wondered if this meant he was dead. Something he'd not given much thought to during his lifetime. Despite the feelings of tension and anxiety he could sense from the others in the room he felt an overwhelming sense of peace and tranquillity. He began to wonder what would happen next. As he did so he became aware of a pinprick of light forming up to his right.

He felt himself begin to drift towards this tunnel of light. Slowly at first and then with increasing speed. Movement then became a blur as he was pulled into the tunnel which seemed to hold a bright living light at the end. Despite the odd and unusual nature of the events unfolding he continued to feel completely calm and at peace. The feeling of moving incredibly fast lasted for a while, but it was difficult to say precisely how long it lasted. Then, with no discernible shift in the feeling of movement he became aware that he had emerged from the tunnel and was being held, bathed in a bright golden light. The intensity of the light was almost overwhelming, but strangely reassuring and comforting. Despite its brightness he found that it was possible to look directly into it and feel nothing but pure unconditional love. It felt like coming home to a place only partially remembered. The intense feeling of love and comfort held him there for a while as he soaked it up hoping he'd never have to leave again. As these thoughts passed through his mind the intensity of the light receded a little forming a wide circle around him, leaving behind a figure, standing, or floating, directly in front of him.

He took a moment to recognise her because for some reason she seemed to be younger now and radiated love and health. Despite these differences he knew with an absolute certainty who it was. 'Cathy!' he called out with his mind. 'Are you dead too?' Despite the nature of the question, it held a hope that they would be reunited.

Cathy smiled at him with a gentle expression of love. Despite the fact that she made no moment with her lips she spoke to him, as one mind speaks directly to another, telling him that there was something he needed to see. It wasn't a command, more in the way of a gentle instruction.

Harry looked on in serene anticipation as multiple images began to form all around him. As he focused on them, he realised that each image was playing out a different episode from his past. All seemingly showing key points that had occurred during his life. He watched again as he made his first deal, the one where he'd made enough money to start his own property development business. But it was more than just watching. When he looked, he felt drawn into the episode and he re-experienced, re-lived, every aspect of it in a sort of immersive-vision. He completely absorbed himself in the various deals he'd done, the houses he'd bought, the cars, and the luxury trips with Rita. Re-living and re-experiencing each one seemed to emphasise to him just how good his life had been and how successful he truly was.

Eventually, the images slowly faded, and Cathy was again in front of him, smiling. Once again, her mind spoke to his with a firm but loving encouragement. 'No,' her voice echoed in his mind, 'you need to watch again.'

Harry looked on as multiple images again formed all around him. He could see all the unique points in his life, but somehow it was different now. Each thought, every intention, all acts were laid bare. He not only saw but felt the greed and selfishness of his actions with a clarity that was both obvious and incomprehensible. Obvious because it was so undeniable, and yet incomprehensible because it didn't fit with his own view of himself. Unable to shift his gaze away from the images he continued to feel the reactions and responses of those he'd cheated in any, and every way. And, like ripples in a pond, how these negative actions and emotions had spread out to others. Showing how his actions had impacted on those he'd never even met. He saw his life now as the epicentre of a storm of darkness, reaching out to crush and overcome those that came within his reach. The overwhelming inhumanity he'd shown to others during his lifetime threatened to drown him in a sea of despair. However, gentle tendrils of light reached out and embraced him, filling him with unconditional love. He knew with a certainty beyond reason that he wasn't being judged. He was simply seeing his life for what it really was.

He saw a thousand missed opportunities to do something good for someone and couldn't understand why he'd let those moments pass. Saw more plainly and more clearly how simple acts of kindness were worth more than all the deals he'd ever made. That he'd falsely measured success by the amount of money he'd accumulated in his life, when he should have been cultivating love and nurturing it in others. He saw with a clarity beyond expression how an act of unconditional love could light the world. That the true meaning of life was simply, love, in all its forms.

After some time, the images faded, and Harry remained embraced in the light. It had been difficult for him to watch the events of his life play out in this way. To see himself, not as the success he'd initially thought, but as someone who'd seemingly and simply missed the point. He wasn't sure how long he remained there but eventually he became aware of Cathy standing in front of him, radiating love and understanding.

He looked up at her and formed the words in his mind. 'What now?'

Her response was instant. 'That's up to you.'

He nodded to indicate the images that were no longer there. 'I'm a better man than that.'

Again, her words were filled with loving kindness, no hint of judgement. 'I know.'

'I can do better.'

'It's your decision.'

'I want to do better.'

She nodded. 'Ok. Remember this, it'll help.'

With that, the light intensified around him and there was a feeling of being pulled backwards extremely fast. He instantly became aware that he was lying on a bed with a tube up his nose and wires attached to his chest and left arm. It felt as if someone were sitting on his chest making it difficult to breathe. He felt panic rise in his chest. Slowly however, the pressure began to lift, making breathing easier.

'Patient's beginning to stabilise,' said a disembodied voice.

'Good,' said another, 'I think we're through the worst of it.'

That was the last thing Harry heard before drifting off into a peaceful, morphine induced sleep.

∞

Some time later, Harry slowly came round, as if surfacing from a deep sleep, to realise that he was lying in a bed and there were things, cables, and tubes, attached to his left hand and arm. Gently, he opened his eyes, blinking as he did against the bright light of day. Raising his head slightly he looked around and began to wonder where he was. As this thought occurred to him, he suddenly remembered. His seemingly surreal journey and the events that had unfolded caused an anxious reaction. He felt dizzy and his heart began to pound. He lay back on the bed and closed his eyes for a few minutes taking several slow deep breaths to calm himself. Once he felt more in control he thought back to what had happened. Part of him wanted to ask the obvious question – was any of it real? But as soon as the question formed in his mind, he knew with a certainty that eclipsed the feeling of lying on a bed in a hospital, that it was. It had happened. And, it had happened to him. He lay there for a while thinking back to what had occurred. As he did, he could hear a nearby nurse checking the monitor beside his bed. He slowly opened his eyes and turned his head towards her, smiling. As soon as she noticed he was awake she smiled back.

'Good morning Mr Stevens,' she said brightly. 'Nice to have you back with us.'

With effort, he produced a quiet groan, 'hmmmm.'

'Doctor Piatelli will be along later to check on you,' she began, but noticed that he'd slipped back into unconsciousness, so simply took her readings and left quietly.

Much later that day when Harry awoke again, he was feeling distinctly better. More rested and relaxed. This time as he opened his eyes he saw Rita sitting beside his bed. As he moved his right hand towards her she let out a cry of delight followed by a stream of questions.

'Ooh, Harry, you're awake. How are you feeling love? Are you in any pain, do you want me to call a nurse?'

He smiled gently as she babbled for a few minutes to cover her nerves. Shaking his head at her request to call a nurse he simply asked for some water to ease his dry throat. Rita dutifully poured him a small cup of water from the bottle beside his bed and held the cup to his mouth as he took a few sips. The cool water soothed the tension in his throat making it easier to breathe and speak. Meanwhile Rita was still talking about what had happened.

'. . . and we had to wait ages for the ambulance. I've a good mind to complain to the hospital about that. Thank God Mike was so quick to call. One of the paramedics said that he'd probably saved your life by calling it in so quickly. I don't know what the other diners thought. Oh, the manager was so sweet. He just told us to get you to hospital and not worry about the bill, or anything.'

Harry closed his eyes for a moment. Thinking back to the dinner with Mike and Jennie now somehow made it all seem so long ago and so far away. So much had happened. So much had changed. Or perhaps, he thought, he'd changed in response to what had happened. Nevertheless, he felt a fire had been lit within him. A burning desire that created an urgency to tell everyone what had happened to him. What he'd seen and what it meant to him and could mean to others. He wanted . . . no, he needed to share his experience. He couldn't keep it bottled up, the pressure was just too great. Rita's chattering voice brought him back to the moment.

'. . . and the staff were so helpful. Oh my God I thought you'd died in that restaurant.'

'I think I did,' Harry whispered, interrupting her monologue.

Rita looked shocked. 'Don't say such things' she pleaded. 'The important thing is that you're back and you're on the mend.'

'No, I'm serious,' Harry persisted. 'I think I died.'

'Harry!' she wailed, 'don't, please. My God it was bad enough having to watch you suffer a heart attack I don't want to hear you talking about . . .' she couldn't quite bring herself to say the words. '. . . about, that.'

'But,' he began to explain, 'I had . . . I had this . . .'

'I know!' she interrupted, 'I was there. And I don't want to go over it all again. Ever. Please.'

He didn't have the energy at the moment to argue with her but did feel a little saddened and deflated by the fact that she didn't seem to want to hear what had happened to him. He took a breath and tried a different tact.

'What's happened to Cathy?'

Rita frowned for a moment. Then, looking back at Harry asked cautiously, 'what've the nurses told you?'

'Nothing. Why, what's happened?'

She clenched her jaw reflexively as she considered what to say and how much to tell him. But Harry pre-empted her.

'I saw her,' he said simply.

'What!' she cried.

'I saw Cathy.'

'What the hell are they showing you your dead sister for,' she cried.

Harry's shoulders slumped as he collapsed back into the bed, nodding to himself. 'I knew it.' It was more acceptance than surprise. As if, her words had simply confirmed something he'd known for himself, deep down. Strangely, he didn't feel any sense of loss or grief just a feeling of joy as he pictured her in a place of light and love. However, Rita's angry words brought him back.

'You wait till I speak to . . .'

'No,' he interrupted, 'I saw her when I . . . when I,' he faltered. Taking a moment to catch his breath he gripped Rita's hand and looked into her face. 'Look,' he pleaded, 'I need to tell you something, and I just need you to listen for a bit.'

He told her everything. About seeing the medics working on his body, about moving along a dark tunnel and floating in the light. How it had been the best feeling he'd ever had in his whole life and how he could have easily just stayed there wrapped in the bliss of that light. Then he told her about meeting Cathy. He even told her about the two life reviews and how this had made him see things differently and want to do things differently from now on. It felt good to talk about his experience because trying to keep it bottled up wasn't really an option. It was as if the experience had built up a tremendous pressure inside of him and the only way to relieve that pressure was to tell others about it. To share the experience with as many as he could. And he felt good at being able to share his experience with someone close.

Rita, however, listened to his story in silence, her face remained a pale mask. Eventually, he broke the silence.

'Well,' he asked, smiling weakly, 'what do you think?'

She looked slightly worried. 'About what?'

His smile turned to a frown. He couldn't believe how she could say such a thing. 'What do you mean . . . what!' he exclaimed, his voice rising.

'Harry,' she appealed, stroking his chest gently with her hand, 'don't start getting worked up, you need to keep calm.' He simply groaned in response and they both sat in silence for a moment before he tried again.

'Well?'

Rita shook her head and shrugged a little. 'Oh . . . I don't know.'

'What do you mean you don't know,' he sounded incredulous.

'Well, I don't,' she complained defensively. 'I mean . . . what do you want me to say. It could be anything. You were seriously ill. Who knows what effect that can have on you.'

He lay there feeling a little shocked that she could so easily disregard his experience.

Rita continued. 'I mean, it could have been a dream . . .'

'It wasn't a dream' he interrupted hotly.

'Ok, ok, calm down. You need to rest, not stress yourself out about what might have happened during . . .'

'There's no "might have",' he snarled, 'it happened.'

'Look Harry,' she appealed to him, 'you've been seriously ill and the only thing I can think of right now is thank God you survived. It doesn't matter what happened before, the important thing now is to focus on getting better.'

He felt deflated by her indifference to what had happened to him and tried to reconcile his thoughts and feelings by reflecting on how he'd have reacted if someone else had told him they'd experienced such events. He knew how odd, or weird, it all sounded. But he also knew that it wasn't just a dream. In fact, it had felt more real than real. He couldn't explain it, but he was certain that something had happened to him, something amazing.

Rita squeezed his hand and looked at him longingly. 'And I just want things to get back to normal.'

He smiled a brief tight-lipped smile and squeezed her hand in acknowledgement, nodding slightly. All the while, thinking that he wasn't sure things would ever be the same as they were before. It was the first inkling Harry had that those close to him might not see, or be willing to see, things the way he did and that this difference could produce a rift between them.

∞

Over the next few days, as Harry recovered, he tried talking to a variety of people about his experience. Initially, he'd tried talking to the doctors about it, but they'd been cautiously dismissive. Instead, they suggested to him that what he'd most likely experienced was a combination of a lack of oxygen to the brain, which would have disrupted his conscious experience, and a chemical stress response, which would have led to the release of certain chemicals in the brain called endorphins. And these endorphins would act like a natural morphine, producing feelings of intense pleasure.

Harry felt mild annoyance at having his experience pathologized in this way and when he tried pressing the matter further they politely yet firmly suggested that he make an appointment with the hospital therapist if he wanted to "talk through" what had happened to him. This did nothing to improve his mood and made him feel somewhat despondent. He knew it was hard to believe, he still struggled with it himself at times, but he also knew it was real. It wasn't some brain abnormality, or some side effect of the heart attack. He'd seen himself on that bed and he'd travelled . . . somewhere, and seen things. Felt things. The feelings were so positive and intense he wanted others to feel them, to know what it was he'd experienced. But he knew his words were woefully inadequate. He wasn't even sure such an experience could be captured in words.

In the intervening days he'd tried a number of times to broach the subject with Rita each time she visited but he could see that she clearly felt uncomfortable with the whole thing. Anytime he mentioned it she did her best to either ignore it or change the subject quickly in the hope of avoiding any discussion. This seemed to open up the growing rift between them and he was saddened to feel them moving apart in this way.

It was on his last day in hospital, as one of his regular nurses was taking his blood pressure for what he hoped would be the last time, that he let out a heavy sigh. The nurse frowned a little as she adjusted the cuff on his arm and looked down at him.

'That's a big sigh,' she said, 'why so glum? I thought you were heading home today.'

Harry looked at her. She was an attractive woman who looked to be in her mid-forties with golden hair pulled back and the bluest eyes he'd ever seen. He was caught off guard for a moment by how pretty she looked. It was only when she made a querying hemming noise that he realised he'd been staring at her for a few minutes without answering.

'I'm sorry,' he smiled, reddening slightly with the embarrassment of having been caught staring like a besotted schoolboy. 'It's not that. I am looking forward to getting out of here.'

'Ooh thanks,' she grinned. Her smile seemed to brighten her face.

'No, no, I didn't mean . . .' he faltered.

'Only joking,' she smiled again.

He shook his head. 'It's not that,' he repeated, 'and I'm more grateful to you,' then quickly added, 'to all you nurses, more than I can say. It's just that . . .' he faltered again, not sure whether he should say anything.

'Hmmm,' she enquired, raising her eyebrows as she removed the cuff from his arm.

And then, without quite knowing why, he told her. About seeing himself from above, about travelling along a dark tunnel towards a light. His meeting, and his life reviews. It just seemed to pour out of him with an ease that was unfamiliar and yet strangely comforting. He couldn't understand why he was telling her. It was as if a separate part of him had taken over and decided to act on his behalf. He felt slightly dissociated from the whole process, as if he were partially watching himself tell this nurse all about his experience. All the while he felt this odd, gentle tugging sensation in the centre of his chest. At first he wondered if he was having another heart attack but the sensation wasn't unpleasant. It felt like something gently vibrating within him, but he couldn't understand what it was. All the while, he told her about his experiences, she stood there politely listening. Once he'd finished, she remained standing with pursed lips, deep in thought. Then, shifting her head to one side said, 'sounds like you had some sort of NDE to me.'

'An N what?' he queried.

'It's N-D-E,' she spelt the letters out, 'and it means a near death experience[1].'

His face brightened. 'Wow! Do you think that's what happened to me?'

She shrugged a little, 'well, I can't say for sure of course, but it does sound like it. Look,' she took a pad from her apron pocket and made a few notes, tore off the paper and handed it to him. 'I've written down what NDE means and included a website that,' she hesitated for a moment, '. . . that I know has been set up for people who've had similar experiences. I'd say have a look there and see how you get on.'

Harry took the proffered piece of paper and carefully read through her annotations noting the website address. 'I will,' he said gratefully. 'Thanks very much.'

She smiled again, 'happy to help. Now, get some rest and I'll leave you in peace.'

'Hold on!' he quickly called, causing her to stop and turn back. He noted her name badge and the name printed on it.

'I just wanted to say thank you . . .err, Mrs Edwards.' He knew he was fishing but hoped it wasn't as obvious as it felt. Again, it felt as if part of him were acting automatically, somehow outside of his conscious intention.

'You're welcome,' she responded lightly, 'and it's Ms Edwards by the way, but you can call me Penny.' With that she turned and headed back out of the ward.

∞

Later that day as Harry arrived home, he became a man on a mission, and his mission was to find out as much as he could about NDEs. He began by firing up their home computer and checking out the website that the nurse had given him[2]. He was both surprised and impressed. The website contained a wide variety of resources, including lists of interesting books[3], research articles about the phenomenon, community chat groups which included reports from others who'd had similar experiences, as well as listing various meetings and talks. When he expressed disbelief at the amount of information, Rita asked him what it was he was up to. Unfortunately, when he told her she became coldly distant and immediately told him that she needed to go out, as she'd booked a late appointment at the salon. He felt a little despondent about her avoidant reaction but knew he'd be able to search through the material in peace if she wasn't around so, half distracted by what he was reading, told her to go and have a good time.

The more he searched and read about NDEs the more surprised and perplexed he became at the amount of information that was available on the topic. He couldn't understand why more people weren't talking about this, or why it wasn't common knowledge. Over the next few weeks he spent every waking moment reading accounts, searching out and ordering books on the topic, watching videos of others who'd had similar experiences and chatting with some of them via the various internet chat rooms.

He found it tremendously exciting to learn about the topic and every time he came across something new or interesting, he'd share it with Rita, in the hope that she'd learn to develop a similar fascination for the topic. He told her that the NDE often contained a selection of key elements, and that only some people experienced all of them[4]. Whilst others might not have the same experiences, and still others could have similar experiences but in a different order. He enthusiastically informed her that NDEs were very likely more common than most people thought because people were often afraid to say anything for fear of being thought weird or crazy. A feeling he could very easily empathise with. He delighted in telling her that NDEs were reported in many cultures from around the world, and by people from all walks of life. They even had NDE reports from children[5].

Unfortunately, Rita remained stoically disinterested in the topic and did her best to avoid listening to him, in her words, rant on about bloody death. More than once over the course of those few weeks she lost her temper and they both ended up shouting at each other. She couldn't understand why he was so obsessed with something that was linked to death and he couldn't understand why she couldn't see how fascinating this was and what it meant to him. Rather than bringing them together it seemed that every new fact he learnt and tried to share acted like a wedge, driving them further apart.

The final straw came for Rita when he asked her if she'd like to accompany him to one of the NDE group meetings. He'd hoped that if she could meet others who'd had similar experiences it may help her to see things differently. She couldn't believe it when he asked her if she'd like to come along.

'Why the bloody hell would I want to come along and listen to a load of people I don't know talk about something I'm not interested in!' she screamed.

'Because it's important to me!'

'What about me?' she cried. 'What about the business?'

He was bit taken aback at this last comment as she'd never shown any interest in his business dealings before. Though he had to admit to himself that he'd been neglecting his business for the past few weeks. It's just that he wasn't interested in it anymore.

He shrugged, spreading his hands. 'The business is fine,' he said, 'it'll run ok without me.'

'Oh yeah!' she responded, 'and for how long?'

He wasn't sure what to say.

'Harry,' she appealed to him, 'I just want things to go back to the way they were before . . .' she still couldn't bring herself to say it.

This was a phrase he'd heard time and time again. It was as if she wanted to remain in the past and he wanted to move forwards into the future. Their pathways diverging, now seemingly incompatible. He'd heard it so many times now, his anger got the better of him and he lashed out.

'Well, I don't bloody well want things to be like they were before!' As soon as he'd said it they both knew a line had just been crossed.

Her tear-stained face looked at him with a mix of anger and fear. 'Well, what do you bloody well want!'

He breathed deeply, working to bring his anger under control. 'I want,' he said with forced calmness, 'things to be different. I want to *do* things differently.'

'And what about me?' she cried.

Harry looked down at the floor for a moment. He wasn't sure what to say. Over the previous few weeks he'd made every effort to include her in his pursuit of this topic but she'd always rejected it out of hand. And each time it had felt as though she'd been rejecting him. Never listening to what he had to say and using every excuse she could, to get away once he started talking about it. Deep down, he knew what it meant and where they were headed but he didn't yet have the courage to face it. He simply shrugged and muttered, 'I don't know.'

'Aaarrrgh!' she screamed storming out of the room.

But left alone there, listening to her stomp up the stairs, he knew.

They both did.

∞

In the following months Harry continued to make an effort to include Rita in his new-found interest. In part out of a deep sense of guilt that all of this was really his fault. He'd been the one who'd changed, she hadn't asked for any of it, and made it clear time and again that she wasn't interested in it either. The final stroke came when Harry told her that he was thinking of selling the business, and that he thought it would be a good idea if they got rid of the two cars and downsized from their large house to something smaller. Rita wept openly and he felt more guilty than ever. He hadn't wanted to cause her pain, but he knew he couldn't live this way anymore. He needed to find new meaning in his life, and it wasn't based on how big his house was, or how large his bank balance was.

Before the end of that year Rita and Harry had agreed to separate and begin the necessary steps involved in starting divorce proceedings[6]. Overall, the process, whilst still onerous, had been more amicable than he'd anticipated. In part this was because he let Rita keep the house and provided her with a small but sufficient annuity. This was primarily because of the guilt he felt at being the one to change. He knew he was no longer the man he was when they'd met and whilst *he* wanted to change, she'd wanted that old version of him back. But as far as he was concerned, that version of him had died that day at the restaurant. He'd also found it rather refreshing not to worry or care about the money. An approach which was definitely unique for him. Not that he was going to be poor, not by a long shot. The sale of the business and most of his assets had provided them both with an enviable level of financial security that would last them the rest of their lives. He'd also kept Bramble Cottage for himself and was keen to move in and turn it into a home. However, before he started on that he knew that there were still some things that he had to do. Things that needed to be put right.

It had been a busy few weeks for Harry and it had required a lot of effort to track down the various people he needed to find. Many of them had moved and some had even changed names because it was so long ago. But each time he'd been successful he knew it was the right thing to do. He'd never felt so good about anything in all his life. Now, there were just two more to deal with.

Mike answered the door and was genuinely please to see Harry standing on his doorstep.

'Harry,' he cried enthusiastically, 'why didn't you tell me you were coming round?'

Harry smiled a greeting. 'Hi Mike.'

'Come in, come in.'

'No, no, it's ok,' said Harry. 'I won't stay, I've just come to drop something off.'

'Are you sure,' asked Mike.

'Yeah, yeah,' he nodded. 'Maybe next time.'

Mike frowned a little. 'Look, Harry,' he hesitated for a moment, 'I'm sorry to hear about you and Rita.'

'Thanks mate,' said Harry. Then, reaching inside his jacket he pulled out an envelope and handed it to Mike.

'What's this?'

Harry raised his eyes and grinned. 'Open it.'

Mike gently tore open the envelope and removed the cheque from inside. His eyes scanned the small piece of paper. 'What!' he exclaimed, 'are you kidding.' He made a gesture of returning both the cheque and envelope to Harry, 'I can't take this.'

Harry still grinning pushed them back. 'You bloody well can, you saved my life.'

'No, Harry, I can't. I didn't. This isn't . . .'

'Anyway,' interrupted Harry, 'it's not for you.'

Mike frowned looking back down at the cheque to re-read his name on the payee line. 'But . . .' he began.

'It's for Annie and Sarah.'

Mike looked on in stunned silence.

'You know I've sold the business,' queried Harry.

'Yes,' responded Mike.

'Well, this is just a little something from the proceeds and I'd like you to use it to help support Annie and Sarah whilst they're studying at uni.'

'Harry,' Mike choked, 'I don't know what to say. . .'

'Say you'll bloody well give it to the girls for me.'

Mike beamed, shaking his head a little. 'Harry . . .' there were tears in his eyes now.

'Don't bloody start!' cried Harry, 'you'll set me off.'

Mike reached out a hand and Harry took it. They shook hands, and then after a moment's hesitation gave in and embraced, patting each other on the back as they did, both now with tears in their eyes.

'Just promise to let me know how the girls get on,' requested Harry.

'I will,' responded Mike. 'And I'll let them know this is from you.'

'Thanks. I promise I'll be in touch again soon. Oh, and there's a card in there as well from an old contact who'd be interested in hiring out your jag if you've still got it?'

'I have,' said Mike, grinning sheepishly. 'Never quite got round to selling it.'

'Well don't. This bloke will give you a good rate for every hire and he should be able to put enough work your way over the year to enable you to keep it and make sure it's kept in good condition.'

Mike, still smiling, shook his head in disbelief. 'Thanks, I really appreciate that.'

'My pleasure. Besides, you can use it to take us both to the pub next time.'

'Agreed,' Mike grinned.

'I'll see you later,' said Harry, waving and turning to make his way back along the pathway towards the road.

'Thanks Harry,' Mike called out after him.

Harry felt good. In fact, he felt better than he had done in a long time and often found himself walking around with a big smile on his face. As he made his way back to the car he checked the address of the last place he needed to go. It was part of a new development over by Meadowcroft Park. Thirty minutes later he arrived at the building and parked in one of the visitor bays. He then made his way to the warden's office on the ground floor. Once there he made enquiries for a Mrs MacMillan and was told that she occupied flat number thirty-four on the second floor. He made his way up the stairs found the door to thirty-four and knocked firmly. After waiting for a minute or two the door slowly opened to reveal the elderly woman who'd sold him Bramble Cottage.

'Hello, Mrs MacMillan,' he said in a slightly over loud and cheerful manner. 'I don't know if you remember me but I'm ...'

'Yes,' she interrupted, 'you're the young man who purchased my cottage. Mr . . . ah, err, I'm sorry I can't quite remember your name.'

He smiled to think of himself as being a young man. 'Mr Stevens. But please, call me Harry. And yes, it's about that, that I wanted to speak to you.'

She frowned for a moment, 'is everything ok?' she asked, the concern clearly evident in her voice.

'Yes, yes. Nothing bad, trust me. Just a small matter that needs to be settled.'

'Would you like to come in?' she queried.

'If that's ok,' he nodded in answer, 'it'll only take a minute and I don't want to disturb you.'

'Oh, don't worry about that,' she smiled, 'I don't usually get many visitors.' She stood back from the door and waved him in, 'please, come on through.' Once inside she led him to a small lounge off the short hallway. 'Please have a seat,' she indicated a chair. Harry took a seat and waited for her to get comfortable in the chair opposite. Once seated she looked a little concerned and asked again, 'there's nothing wrong is there? With the cottage I mean?'

'Oh, no,' responded Harry smiling. 'In fact, it's quite the opposite.'

She looked a little bewildered.

'You'll remember that when I purchased the cottage from you we had to re-negotiate the price due to the work that needed doing.'

She nodded unenthusiastically, 'yes, quite a bit of work as I recall.'

'Well, it turns out that on closer inspection some of that work,' he faltered. This was the moment. Did he spin her a story or could he face her with the truth? He already knew the answer, he just needed an extra minute to steel himself for what might happen. He looked across at her, shrugged a little and spread his hands. 'Actually, Mrs MacMillan . . .'

'Please call me Glennis,' she said.

'Ok. Well, actually . . . Glennis, that's not strictly true about the work that needed to be done on the cottage.' He took a deep breath and sighed. 'In fact, I had those traders inflate the work and estimates needed as leverage to bargain the price down.' In the ensuing silence he waited for a reaction.

Tight-lipped she shook her head slowly. 'I did think there was rather a lot of work that I hadn't expected.'

Harry made a wry apologetic face. 'It's something I've used in the past to help in negotiating a good deal.'

She smiled slightly. 'I do understand. You are, after all, a businessman. But . . . but why are you telling me this now?'

'Because,' he said, 'we re-negotiated the price based on those . . . err, estimates.'

She nodded. 'Hmmm.'

'But, given that those estimates were exaggerated you should have received a fairer price for the cottage.' As he said this he reached inside his jacket and took out a small brown envelope and rising from his seat leant across and handed it to her.

She took the envelope and asked, 'what's this?'

'That,' he nodded at the envelope, 'is the balance that I owe you given our original agreed price.'

She opened it and removed the cheque from inside. Reading it her face lit up. 'Oh my goodness,' she seemed quite taken aback. 'Are you serious?'

'Absolutely.'

Disbelief echoed in her voice as she asked, 'and this … this is for me?'

'Yep,' he beamed, watching the realisation of what this would mean for her dawn on her face. It was like watching the sun rise on a spring morning. And it felt very good.

Suddenly she looked back at him, confusion etched on her face. 'But … but why? I mean, you have the cottage. You didn't need to do this. There's no legal requirement for you to do anything like this.'

Harry gently shook his head in disagreement. 'Actually, I think I did need to do this.'

'But why?' she asked again.

'Because,' he responded with a light shrug, 'it's the right thing to do.'

She seemed slightly breathless with the shock of what he'd done. 'Oh my goodness. This is a lot of money.'

'Well it's yours now.'

'I don't know what to say,' she smiled, shaking her head gently with tears in her eyes.

'Oh bloody hell,' he moaned, 'say you won't cry otherwise you'll only set me off.'

She looked across at him, her face alight with emotion. 'And I'll thank you not to swear,' she said with a wry smile.

He grinned back. 'Sorry about that. Just enjoy it. It's only what you deserve.'

'But I still don't understand why?'

'Let's just say that I had a change of heart.'

'Well, I'm very grateful. This will certainly change my life,' she said waving the cheque at him.

'And Glennis,' he asked gently, 'would it be ok if I popped by from time to time just to see how you're getting on?'

Her smile broadened, 'yes,' she said, slowly nodding in approval, 'I'd like that.'

∞

Harry was sitting in the kitchen of Bramble Cottage thinking back on the things he'd done over the past few weeks. It had felt so strange going back, re-visiting people and deals from the past. But each time he'd corrected those past events he knew it had been the right thing to do. Though one of the things that still surprised him was how everyone seemed to cry and how simply he'd end up crying along with them. He'd never thought of himself as being particularly emotional before, but now each time he sorted something out, the other person would start to tear up and he'd be off. When this first happened he was bewildered. After all, he'd profited from these deals, and in some cases by quite a lot of money. He thought that going back and trying to set things right might make people hate him for what he'd done. But they all seemed so grateful for what he was doing now. It made him wonder whether there was an element of forgiveness in such actions, both from others and from himself.

As he sat there, his mind returned to the kitchen and he looked around at the work underway. It still looked a bit like a building site, but he knew that the various changes and upgrades he was having done would turn it into a great home. However, as this thought occurred to him he experienced an odd feeling in his chest. It was a distinct feeling that something was missing from the cottage. That something else was needed to bring it alive and turn it from a house to a home. Strangely, he had this nagging feeling that he knew what the answer was but couldn't quite put his finger on it. As if, somewhere, he'd seen it, but couldn't quite recall where.

He shook his head gently in an effort to dislodge these odd thoughts and then reached across to his laptop, which was on the counter in front of him, and opened it up. After entering his password, the operating system booted up and reloaded the last screen he'd been looking at. It was the NDE website. Not really focusing on anything in particular he clicked on the various links, surface reading the material he was now so familiar with. It was only after a couple of minutes that he found himself staring at one of the screens. It was one headed *Founder,* and he frowned a little in consternation as he slowly became more aware of the information on screen. He couldn't remember seeing this screen before and he was sure he'd clicked on every link. Still, he thought, might be a new addition. He scrolled smoothly down the screen, reading about the founder and how she'd set up the site because her father had experienced an NDE and didn't have anyone to talk to about it. That with the help of friends and colleagues she'd set up the site to provide a community support network. Then, his hand froze on the touchpad. The screen now showing a picture of this benevolent founder. He knew he'd seen her before, but it took him a few minutes to remember where because she was out of context, or, more accurately, out of uniform. It was the nurse who'd given him the website details all those weeks ago. As he thought back to that moment, he remembered her deep blue eyes. As the picture of her face formed in his mind, he felt a gentle tingling in his chest. Not knowing why, or for how long, he starred at the picture on screen.

∞

It was the following week and Harry's third visit to the hospital. The first time he'd been there he couldn't find anyone he recognised or who'd talk to him or tell him anything. Fortunately, the second time he went he found a familiar nurse who swallowed his story of wanting to give a thank you card and chocolates to one of the nurses who'd helped in his recovery. However, she told him that the person he was trying to find wasn't on shift that day and that he'd need to come back in two days. Hence, on his third visit he knew she'd be there. Also, after quite a bit of careful checking and planning he'd timed his visit to coincide with her lunch break and knew that she'd be in the cafeteria on the first floor.

As he entered the café he felt a knot of nervous tension tighten in his stomach. Scanning the diners, he saw her sitting alone at a table beneath one of the windows on the far side of the room. Despite feeling slightly sick he forced himself to walk over to her table. As he arrived she looked up, recognition lit her face.

'Hello,' she smiled in recognition.

'Hi,' he grinned. 'Is it ok if I join you?'

'Of course,' she said, nodding at the chair opposite.

He sat down and for a moment they simply stared at one another. He was momentarily spellbound again by her deep blue eyes and wasn't sure what to say. But then, as if a valve opened in both of them, they talked. Simply, freely, openly and honestly. They shared, and it brought them closer, beginning the subtle process of bonding. Time, inevitably, stole the moment from them and she eventually looked at her watch, saying that her lunchbreak was almost over, and she needed to get back to the ward.

'Can I see you again,' he asked quickly. Afraid that if he didn't say it now, he might never have the courage to say it.

Her face lit up and she supressed a smile. Raising her eyebrows she asked, 'are you sure? Most men run a mile when they find out I've got two teenage boys.'

He smiled, shaking his head gently. 'I'm not most men.'

'No,' she agreed thoughtfully, 'I don't think you are.'

Slowly, he reached across and laid his hand on hers. Their touch was electric and in that moment he knew. Knew with a certainty beyond belief what the cottage needed, what he needed. A family. Family – the most fertile ground to nurture and cultivate love he could think of. He smiled as he thought how his life was going to be very different from now on. It was a good feeling.

9

Distant Call

A light buzz of conversation, interspersed by raucous laughter, flowed across the university quad, providing a clear indication that the students were enjoying the sunshine. Despite the fact that it was mid-June, and most if not all undergraduates had long since left for the summer, the quad was still busy with postgraduates who remained to work on campus over the summer period. Two of these postgraduates, both women in their late twenties, were seated at one of the bench-tables deep in discussion. Alexandra, the shorter of the two, who had a distinct Greek appearance, with shoulder length dark curly hair and large brown eyes was explaining to Samantha, whose pale skin echoed pale blue eyes and fair hair, how she'd been trying to find ideas for her research project.

'Remember what Dr Wheeler said about finding ideas in controversies,' said Alexandra.

Samantha nodded.

'Well, I spent some time online searching for possible controversial topics and came across two that I think are interesting. The first is something called *"power posing"*'.

'Ha ha!' snorted Samantha, 'Alex, you're kidding, you've just made that up.'

Alex shook her dark curls vigorously. 'No, honest. It's where you stand in a posture that's supposed to be associated with being powerful and this is supposed to help you feel more confident and assertive.'

'Oh, you're kidding me,' groaned Samantha.

'No seriously Sam. You just stand with your feet apart and your hands on your hips and this is supposed to make you feel more powerful. That's why it's called power posing.'

Samantha shook her head slowly, looking doubtful. 'And does it work?

'Ah well,' said Alex grinning. 'That's the question isn't it.'

Samantha laughed lightly.

'The evidence,' continued Alex, 'is . . .' she faltered for a second.

'Controversial' offered Sam with a smile.

Alex made a wry face. 'Oh very funny. I was going to say, the evidence is inconsistent. Some argue that this really works and others say it's all a load of nonsense.'

'Academics,' groaned Sam. 'Don't tell me, they suggest that more research is needed.'

'Precisely,' answered Alex with a smile.

Sam leant back on the seat for a moment, closing her eyes she turned her head up towards the bright sunlight. Her voice as soft and slow as the summer breeze. 'Hmmm, this sunshine is great.'

'Makes me think of home,' said Alex.

Noting the hint of wistful sadness in her voice Sam worked to bring the conversation back to their projects. 'You said you had two ideas. What's the second one?'

'Ah yes,' Alex quickly sorted through her notes and pulled out a piece of paper covered with annotated markings. 'It's part of something called *embodied cognition* and it's all about how holding a pen in your mouth can make you happier.'

'What you mean like this,' said Sam popping the pen she had in her hand into her mouth.

'No,' said Alex with a shake of her head. 'You have to hold it sideways, almost as if you were trying to bite into it, like corn on the corn.'

Sam changed the position of the pen in her mouth '. . . ike ish?' she asked. Holding the pen in her mouth as she spoke.

'Yes, exactly.'

Shaking her head Sam removed the pen. 'Why?'

'Because, when you hold the pen in your mouth sideways like that it's supposed to make your face mimic a sort of smile. Apparently, when you hold the pen that way, you're using a lot of the same facial muscles that you'd normally use when you smile, and this provides your brain with feedback which sort of says, I'm smiling, so I must be happy.'

'Sounds like circular reasoning to me,' noted Sam.

'No,' said Alex with a grin, 'I think you'll find it's called neural priming.'

There was a moments silence as the two friends simply enjoyed sitting in the warm sunshine.

'So have you come up with anything?' asked Alex as she put her papers back into her folder.

Sam grinned mischievously. 'Oh yes. Like you I spent a lot of time online looking through the articles on Google Scholar and the online resources of the library trying to find something that was controversial but also interesting.'

'I think my ideas *are* interesting,' complained Alex in mock aggrievement.

'You know what I mean,' placated Sam. 'And for what it's worth so do I. Actually, I think both your ideas sound fun. But I couldn't find anything that *I* found interesting . . . until I came across an area of psychology called parapsychology.'

Alex shook her head slowly. 'What's that?'

'It's an area of psychology that deals with . . .' she hesitated for a moment. 'Well, it deals with what I can only describe as all the weird stuff.'

'Such as?'

'Such as clairvoyance, precognition and telepathy.'

'Wow!' Alex's surprise was clear. 'That does sound weird.'

'And when I came across it, I knew that this is what I wanted to do my project on.'

'What clairvoyance?' asked Alex.

'No,' answered Sam sharply, 'not clairvoyance. I want to do a study on telepathy.'

Alex screwed her face up a little. 'What's the difference?'

'Ha!' Sam snorted, 'start with the easy question why don't you.'

Alex grinned back and shrugged.

'Well, as far as I can tell clairvoyance is about obtaining information about *things* in a . . .' she raised her hands to make the typical air quotes, '"non-usual" way, but telepathy is about a sort of *mental communication* where one person gets information from the *mind* of another.'

'So, it's like mind reading then?' queried Alex.

Sam grimaced a little as her head made a gentle side to side rocking motion. 'I'm not sure. The more I read about it the less sure I am that information is *transferred* in any real sense.'

Alex now looked confused. 'Huh?'

Sam shrugged. 'A lot depends on how you try and account for the effect.'

Alex thought for a moment before asking, 'do you think it's real?'

'What?'

'Telepathy. I mean, do you think people can read other people's minds?'

Now it was Sam's turn to think. It was a question she'd become increasingly familiar with, as almost every time she'd mentioned the topic people responded with genuine interest and wanted to know if it worked or not. 'Before I'd read this research, I'd probably have said no.'

'And now?' asked Alex with interest.

Sam screwed up her face in thought. 'We'ell, there's a lot of published research on the topic. Which is odd in a way because we don't get to cover any of this stuff in the lectures. And there's much more than I would have thought and certainly more than I'd expected.' The slight exasperation in her voice was evidence of the hours she'd spent reading through the many journal articles and book chapters.

'And have you spoken to Wheeler about this yet?' asked Alex.

'No. I've got a meeting with him tomorrow. And I've been reading up on it as much I can for the past couple of weeks to prepare for it.'

Alex smiled good naturedly. 'In that case, good luck'.

'Thanks,' Sam nodded and smiled back.

∞

The following day Sam met with Dr Adam Wheeler to discuss ideas for her research project. It was a meeting that they'd both prepared for, with the hope of a good outcome. However, it became immediately clear from their conversation that a good outcome might not mean the same thing for both of them. Something that was evidently clear from Dr Wheeler's initial response to her proposed topic.

'You want to do what!?' he cried out, the incredulity in his voice unmistakeable as he collapsed back in his chair, a mild look of shock on his face.

Sam worked to remain calm by holding on to the folder she had in her lap. 'I want to conduct my project on the topic of telepathy, using a modified ganzfeld procedure[1],' she repeated.

Wheeler frowned for a moment, lost in the disappointment that one of his best students wouldn't be producing a publication that he could put his name to. Or at least, a publication that he'd *want* to put his name to. Shaking his head slightly he looked over at Sam as she sat opposite him. 'You do realise that this is supposed to be a *scientific* research project,' he said emphasising the word scientific.

His condescending tone irritated her. 'What makes you think studying telepathy isn't science?' she asked.

'Ha!' he snorted, responding without giving it any thought, 'the whole topic is more . . .' he looked around the office as if searching for the right word, '. . . more pseudoscience than science.'

The muscles in Sam's jaw tightened as she bit down a retort. 'Why would you think that?' she asked, working hard to keep her tone level.

'Well, there's no real evidence for any of . . .' he waved his arms about as if to encompass all the research on the topic, 'this, is there?'

Sam opened the folder she had on her lap and removed one of the journal articles that she'd printed out from the library. Leaning over she handed the article to Dr Wheeler. 'This is a recent review article showing that, overall, the evidence for telepathy is greater than would be expected by chance[2].'

Wheeler gingerly took the article, only deigning to give it the briefest of glances. Holding the offensive article, he immediately became defensive. 'But such effects, if real, are often simply noise in the data and rarely, if ever, replicated.'

Sam took another article from her folder. 'This is a recent meta-analysis of thirty different studies, all working to replicate the effect of telepathy, and they found a target hit rate of just over thirty percent, when chance would predict twenty-five[3].'

Wheeler took the second article. 'Hmm . . . mm,' his tone still unhappy. However, he slowly began to realise that he was backing himself into an uncomfortable corner. To give himself a little thinking time he pretended to skim through the article, all the while wondering why one of his brightest students wanted to waste her time on such nonsense. He groaned inwardly as he became aware that in truth there was very little he could do to dissuade her from going down this particular rabbit hole. Then with a growing horror it dawned on him that if he did agree to supervise her on this topic it would be all round the department by the end of the day. In the ever-hallowed halls of academia reputation was everything and he didn't want his tarnished by association. He briefly wondered whether he'd be able to say that this was a topic outside of his area of expertise and as such she might be better off with one of the other members of the academic staff. This was the subtle language of academia, which translated into *"I'm not interested in what you're interested in, so go away and find someone else who is"*. But after a moment's thought he realised everyone else would say the same thing, and besides, it was always a nightmare trying to shift research students. Understanding slowly dawned, like a bleak sun struggling to be seen through the grey clouds of winter. As he continued to sit there ruminating over the problems this could create for him, he became aware that Sam was waiting for some response from him. Seeing no way out he tried to calm himself by taking a deep breath. Then, sounding more open minded than he felt, and ignoring completely what he'd just said, he took on an affected air of magnanimity. 'Ok, Tell me about your project idea.'

Sam brightened and sat a little more upright. She then consulted the papers and notes she had in her folder. Once arranged in order she looked back up and began to explain. 'So, telepathy is the ability of . . .'

'The *alleged* ability surely,' interrupted Wheeler pedantically.

Sam did a quick double take of her notes and despite the nervous feeling in the pit of her stomach managed to retain a calm outward composure. 'Well, when you look at the evidence, I think it would be fair to say that there is certainly something unusual going on.'

Wheeler remained silent, making a sour face as if to suggest he could taste the unpleasantness of what might be going on, and really didn't want any part of it.

'Anyway,' Sam continued, 'telepathy is the ability for one person to communicate directly with another via a . . .' she consulted her notes again, '. . . a non-usual route.'

'Hmmm,' said Wheeler with a wry smile, 'you can say that again.'

Sam's face reddened slightly as she read on. 'Such communication can be mental in the sense that information may be transferred from one mind to another. Or it may include feelings, emotions and intentions. Apparently. . .' she stopped and looked up to ensure that Dr Wheeler was following her and saw that he did at least seem to be listening. Encouraged, she quickly resumed reading her notes. 'Er, apparently, the idea or notion of telepathy, that one person has or can receive information from the mind of another, is one of the most common[4] paranormal experiences and is likely influenced by the many reported accounts of crisis calls.'

Wheeler frowned. 'What's a crisis call?' he asked.

'This is when one person reports hearing the cry, or call, of a loved one, or someone very close to them, who's very far away and in danger at the time of the call,' answered Sam. 'It's often associated with a strong feeling that the person making the call is in some sort of danger or may have been involved in an accident or may be ill.'

There was a moment's silence as this information sank in.

'Hold on,' said Wheeler, breaking the silence. 'I thought you said you wanted to test . . .' he hesitated for a moment, searching for what he considered to be a more appropriate word. 'Test this *effect* using some sort of *ganz-field* . . . or something.'

'Yes,' replied Sam smiling slightly to herself at his mispronunciation. 'It's called the *ganz-feld* approach. But I wanted to give you some background before I got to that.'

Wheeler made a wry face and nodded cautiously. 'Ok.'

Sam started to feel a little more at ease as she continued. 'Crisis calls may be common, or at least commonly reported, but it's really difficult to test for them because of course we can't put people in a crisis.' She briefly looked up at Wheeler to see him smile slightly at her attempted humour. 'Which has meant that over time researchers have developed a variety of ways to try and test for telepathy.'

'Assuming it exists in the first place,' Wheeler quickly added.

Sam decided not to respond to his comment and continued with her explanation. 'So, over time researchers have generally used paradigms that require people to work in pairs. For example, one person in the pair would act as the sender and the other as the receiver. Then, during the test both partners would operate in different locations, such as separate rooms, and have no physical contact at all throughout the experiment. The sender would be shown a random image or piece of text and the researchers would then test to see if the receiver could pick up on this either by simply saying what's on their mind at the time or by identifying the target from a set of images or words. And they've tested these sender-receiver pairs using different types of approaches which has included tests where the receiver is in an altered state of consciousness.'

'And why is that?' asked Wheeler.

Sam took a moment to find the relevant information in her notes before responding. 'Well, it's because there's a sort of assumption that when the receiver is in an altered state of consciousness that this might make it easier for them to come up with the correct target information.'

'Yes, but why?' persisted Wheeler, smiling now at what he perceived was a key weakness in her line of reasoning.

Slightly flustered Sam searched through her notes and papers, until she found the article she was looking for. 'Ah, yes, here it is,' she said with clear relief in her voice. Briefly flicking through the pages, she came across the highlighted piece that she wanted and began to read. 'The argument is that this altered state helps to enhance what's called the signal-to-noise ratio. The idea is that the telepathy signal is small, or weak, and that by reducing all external stimulation, or noise for the receiver, you improve the chances of that person identifying the telepathic signal.'

'Hmmm,' mumbled Wheeler. 'And how precisely do you want to test this . . . this idea.'

Sam smiled as she thought of her idea, and how pleased she was when it first occurred to her and when she'd checked and realised that no one else had tried this yet, how excited she was to try it out. 'Well, you know how you said in the lecture that we should try and use the resources from the department?'

Wheeler nodded slowly in response.

'I thought we could use the virtual reality kit[5] to place the sender in a specific setting rather than simply show them a static image and that this might create a stronger reaction in them, which would make it easier for the receiver to pick up the signal and pick out the target.'

Wheeler considered the plan for a moment. Despite his initial concerns and lack of enthusiasm for the topic, he had to admit that Sam's idea was a good one. He felt himself being slowly drawn to the topic. 'Hmm . . . the VR kit eh?' Then, his interest growing, he asked, 'what sort of VR settings would you use?'

'In the past they've used lots of different images, but we don't have a large database of VR clips, so I thought we'd stick to the positive stimulating experiences we have on file.'

'Give me an example,' he said, a chink of enthusiasm breaking through the initial disapproval.

'Well, such as riding in a hot air balloon, or going on a rollercoaster, or skiing down a mountain.'

'And would you show these clips to the . . . the er . . . what was it again, the receiver?'

'No not the receiver, the sender,' responded Sam. 'Rather than show the receiver clips I thought we could show them a set of four or five images, each of which would relate to the specific event that the sender was experiencing in VR.'

'Like the ones you've just mentioned.'

'Yes. And then they'd have to pick out the correct target image representing the experience their partner was having.'

Wheeler was now clearly on board with the design and procedure, and it was with genuine interest that he asked, 'but if the receiver is looking at sets of images how can they be in an altered state?'

'Ah yes,' admitted Sam with a brief smile. 'They won't be in the traditional full immersive state, but we can still shield them from all sounds and other physical distractions.'

'And you think that providing a more stimulating experience for the sender might,' he thought for a moment. 'Might, off-set this issue in terms of the strength of the . . . the er, signal.' He still couldn't quite bring himself to say telepathic signal.

Sam shrugged and smiled. 'I'm not certain of course, but I do think it's a possibility.'

Wheeler thought for a moment. His mind checking the various aspects of the method to see if he could spot any glaring errors.

Sam interrupted his thoughts by adding, 'and I've checked the literature, and no one's ever used VR in a telepathic study before.'

Upon hearing this Wheeler's face slowly developed into a smile. The idea of being the first to try something, even when the topic area was one he'd initially considered suspect, appealed to his ego. 'Never done before, eh?'

The two sat in silent contemplation for a few moments. Then, Wheeler seemed to come to a decision and with a slightly embarrassed smile said, 'sounds like a good idea.'

Sam's face lit up and she smiled in relief. Happy that her idea had at least been accepted.

As Wheeler handed the journal articles back to her he said, 'just run it through the usual ethics committee, but I don't see any issues here.'

Sam nodded, please with herself.

'Then, once you've got ethical approval,' he continued, 'you can get started with recruitment etc.'

They looked at each other for a moment. Both now thinking that the outcome of the meeting may have been a good one after all.

Sam gathered her papers back into the folder and stood to leave. 'Thanks,' she said, still smiling.

Wheeler simply nodded. As he watched her leave, he began to wonder what, if anything, she might find.

Over the following weeks Sam worked hard to obtain ethical approval for her study and set up the relevant equipment in two separate labs. She then spent time identifying pairs of friends that she could recruit as participants and once ethical approval had been given began running the study. It took time and was a lot of hard work. Managing pairs of participants, making sure that they didn't have any contact or communicate with each other during the study, and keeping everything on track was more difficult than she'd imagined. But it was also a lot of fun and the people taking part seemed to enjoy the process too.

Once she'd had the prerequisite number of people complete the study it was closed, and she began the process of checking and analysing the data. This was a fairly straightforward process but also the part of the study that Sam had simultaneously most looked forward to and dreaded. She knew that research wasn't just about obtaining meaningful, or what was generally referred to as "statistically significant" results. That it was about the process of uncovering the truth. And that a null result, was still a result. She also knew that despite the fact that everyone said this, what they all really wanted were statistically significant results. So, once she had her results and had re-checked them for accuracy, she arranged another tutorial with Dr Wheeler to discuss her findings.

It was later that same week when the two of them met again in Wheeler's office. Upon entering Sam walked over and once again sat in the chair opposite. Taking a set of notes from her folder she arranged those detailing the results of her analysis.

This time Wheeler was cautiously interested. 'So,' he asked, 'how did it go?'

Sam told him about the lab set-up and the use of the equipment, making mention of the help she'd received from the technical support team. Then, with a wry grin she told him how challenging it had been to herd the various participants from room to room and the difficulties involved in keeping them apart throughout the study.

Wheeler was keen to know the outcome so asked, 'and what were the results?'

This was the bit Sam had been building up to. She tried, and failed, to suppress a grin. 'Analysis shows that the receivers were more accurate than chance at identifying the target image.'

His interest piqued Wheeler leant forward. 'How much more?'

'Just over ten-percent higher than chance,' responded Sam, now smiling broadly.

'And I take it from your grin that this is a significant difference?'

'Yes,' answered Sam, smiling more broadly now, 'very.'

There was a brief pause as they both sat and let this information sink in.

'Ok,' said Wheeler, 'let's just take a step back here.' This was something Sam had heard him say many times when he wanted to go through the details of something to get a clear picture of what was going on. 'So, you're saying that you had sender-receiver pairs, housed in separate rooms. And when you put the sender in a VR setting and simultaneously showed a set of images – by the way, how many images were in the set?'

'Five,' responded Sam confidently.

'Ok, so the chance rate would have been one in five, or twenty percent. And you're saying that when the receiver saw this set that they were able to select the correct target image at a rate that was significantly higher than chance.'

Sam nodded. 'Yes.'

'Hmmm.' Wheeler screwed his face up a little as he spent a moment deep in thought.

Excited and yet apprehensive Sam waited to hear what he'd have to say. She didn't have to wait long.

'And I presume that you would suggest that such a finding is indicative of . . .' he searched for an appropriate word, couldn't think of an acceptable alternative and finally gave up and bit the bullet, 'of . . . some form of telepathy?'

Sam's smile widened and she nodded. 'I think so, yes.'

Wheeler sat in silent thought for a moment. His jaw working slowly as if he were chewing over the result, trying to grind it down into something more acceptable. Eventually, he sat back in his chair clapped his hands together and rubbed them in a "let's get this sorted" manner. 'Ok,' he said with deliberate care and precision, 'take me through every aspect of the method. I want to know who the participants were, how you recruited them, any interesting demographic information. I then want a clear explanation of the materials and how you obtained them and from where. Then take me through the procedure again, step by step.'

Sam nodded in understanding and reached into her folder for her notes. This was standard practice in any given situation when a significant finding emerged. The researchers would go back over every aspect of the method and try to pick it apart to ensure that it stood up to scrutiny and that the finding, if still there at the end, was in fact the result they thought it was, and not just some methodological error that they'd overlooked or failed to notice. With this in mind the two of them spent the next ninety minutes going over every aspect of the study, scrutinising in detail the various aspects of the method. Nevertheless, once they'd done this the result remained the same. Now, both feeling a little drained from the expended effort of thinking intently about the various details of the study, they sat back and relaxed in their respective chairs and allowed a contented silence to descend.

Again, it was Wheeler who broke the silence. Though this time in a much more collegial tone. He was even smiling slightly. 'Ok,' he asked, 'so how do you account for it?'

Sam frowned a little. 'What do you mean?'

'Well, according to your results you've found an effect.'

She nodded.

'And your argument is that this effect represents some form of telepathy.'

'Hmm mmm,' she agreed, still nodding.

'Well, that's the effect,' he said. 'So what's your explanation?'

Sam's frown deepened. She thought that telepathy *was* the explanation and now Wheeler seemed to want her to provide something more. She shrugged a little in confusion. 'I'm not sure what you mean.'

'Well, you say you've found an *effect*,' he said, emphasising the word effect. 'But that's not an explanation. You need to offer some sort of explanation for this effect. How, for example can you account for it?'

Slightly aggrieved now at what she considered his unfair focus on what she thought was a less important secondary issue, her buoyant mood started to fade. She began to feel overshadowed by doubts about how, if at all, she'd be able to explain the effect. 'Err, I'm not sure.'

The brief silence that followed this remark seemed to cast a veil of gloom over the original exciting result.

'In that case,' he proposed, 'I'd suggest you go back to the literature and try to think about how you could best account for the finding.'

It wasn't a dismissal, but Sam clearly caught the tone suggesting that the meeting had come to an end. 'Ok,' she nodded, gathering up her notes and putting them back into her folder. She then stood to leave.

Wheeler nodded. 'Once you've got a clearer idea of how to account for the effect get back in touch and arrange another tutorial.'

Despite being slightly annoyed Sam nodded in grateful relief at the offer of additional discussion and help. 'Ok, thanks.' With that she left his office feeling somewhat deflated but determined to find a way to account for her result.

Wheeler watched her as she left, knowing that he'd set the bar higher than he normally would but also sure that she'd be able to overcome it. She was, after all, one of his best students and she'd found something . . . well, something interesting. He smiled to himself as he wondered what she'd be able to come up with that would help her account for her unusual result.

∞

It was a couple of weeks after they'd discussed the results of the study that Sam and Dr Wheeler met, once again in Wheeler's office. He watched with interest as she entered with a seemingly triumphant air and sat in the chair opposite. He smiled slightly, interested to hear what she'd have to say. 'You look pleased with yourself.'

She nodded in satisfaction. 'I think I've got a good explanation for my telepathic result,' she said as she sorted through the notes from her folder.

Wheeler sat back in his chair, spreading his hands. 'Ok, let's hear it.'

Sam took a moment to retrieve the relevant material from her folder, handed Wheeler a copy of one of the articles and then began. 'This is an article that outlines the view that consciousness is fundamental. It's essentially a form of panpsychism . . .'

Interrupting, Wheeler frowned, leaning forwards. 'Pan what?'

Sam was prepared for this. 'Panpsychism,' she smiled. 'It literally means that the mind, or *psyche*, is everywhere – *pan*.' She waited for this information to sink in before continuing. 'Essentially, everything has a mind.'

Wheeler snorted in derision, almost laughing. 'Ha! Do you mean that this has a mind,' he said as he waved a hand over his desk.

Looking back at her notes to ensure that she was on the right track Sam responded cautiously. 'Err . . . yes.' She reached down and selected another article, handing it to him as she continued. 'This article, which is written by a top neuroscientist by the way, argues that everything has a mind, or consciousness, and that the only real difference is the complexity of that mind[6]. Which is based to a large extent on the complexity of the object. Brains being very complex have a high level of mind or consciousness, whereas...' she pointed at Wheeler's desk, 'your desk has a very low level of complexity and as such a very limited mind.'

Wheeler looked very doubtful and was shaking his head slightly. 'Are you saying that everything is based on... on some form of consciousness?'

Again, Sam responded cautiously after re-checking her notes. 'Erm, yes.' She waited for a moment in case he had anything else to say. However, she could see that he was busy scanning the summary of the article she'd just given him. As he read his eyebrows rose and a look of mild surprise appeared on his face. He pursed his lips in thought as he took note of the publication date for the article.

'Is this a recent idea?' he asked.

'Not really,' she answered. 'I think it originally stemmed from the Greeks and over time it's just... sort of gone out of fashion.'

Wheeler frowned at the term fashion. Disliking the idea that anything as frivolous as fashion could find a place in the hallowed halls of science.

'However,' continued Sam, 'it's an old idea that does seem to be gaining in popularity.'

'And so,' he proposed, 'you think, or rather this view that consciousness is ...' he grappled for a moment before Sam came to the rescue.

'That consciousness is fundamental. Yes.'

'Hmm. But that means what precisely?'

Briefly looking down at her notes again she scanned for the highlighted points she'd made earlier. 'I think it means that consciousness, rather than being reliant or based on physics, chemistry and biology is something that operates at a more fundamental level.'

'Ookay,' said Wheeler still sounding unconvinced. 'If, and it's a big if, but *if* we accept this view then how does it account for . . . for your result?'

Sam brightened, feeling a bit more on solid ground with this. 'Ah, yes. Well, if we take the view that consciousness is fundamental, not only would the result make sense but it's what you'd expect to see.'

Wheeler's frown deepened, 'why?'

Warming to her subject Sam continued. 'Because, if consciousness *is* fundamental then each pair of participants we ran in our experiment are not separate components of consciousness but are rather different aspects of the same underlying consciousness.'

'Ahh,' sighed Wheeler understanding slowly dawning.

'And in this case telepathy wouldn't, or rather shouldn't, be seen as the,' she moved to make air quotes with both hands, '. . . *"transfer"* of information from one distinct mind to another, but rather as the sharing of information between two minds linked by an underlying consciousness.'

'Hmmm,' Wheeler murmured, nodding slowly. 'And you think that this . . .' he was interrupted then by the phone on his desk ringing. Its harsh tone breaking up the atmosphere of studious interest and bringing them both back to a seemingly less mysterious reality. 'Oh, er, sorry about this,' he said as he turned back to his desk to answer it. He picked up the receiver with a brief response. 'Yes, hello.' Time passed and Sam could just hear the tinny voice on the other end. Meanwhile Wheeler's face darkened. 'Ok, he said with an urgency that was new and palpable. 'I'll leave straight away and get there as soon as I can.' He replaced the phone and turned back to Sam. 'I'm sorry about this Sam, but it's a family emergency.'

Sam's eyes widened. 'Oh, err, not a problem.'

'I've got to go, my daughter's at the hospital.'

'Oh my goodness. I hope she's ok?'

Wheeler looked genuinely worried. 'I don't know,' he shrugged.

Just then Sam realised that for the first time she was seeing him as a person, as a father, and not just as another tutor who marked her work. It made her feel disoriented for a moment, but she quickly recovered. 'Of course,' she said, gathering up her papers and quickly stuffing them back into her folder. She stood to leave.

'As soon as I've sorted this I'll be in touch and we can discuss this . . . further,' he assured her.

'No problem,' she said. 'I hope everything works out ok.'

He smiled weakly. 'Thanks.'

As Sam left his office, he grabbed his mobile phone and texted his head of department to let her know he'd be away from the office that afternoon. Then, pausing just to grab his jacket he left his office to make his way over to the car park.

∞

Less than thirty minutes later Adam Wheeler was entering the A&E of the local hospital having just left his car in the nearby car park. He made enquiries at the reception desk and was told that his daughter Chloe had been admitted earlier. It was a sentence no parent ever wants to hear about their child, and he had to steady himself for a moment before getting directions from the receptionist. Then with a grim determination and a sinking feeling in the pit of his stomach he quickly made his way along the corridor to find her. As he half walked half ran along the corridor memories of Chloe played out in his mind's eye. Like every parent before him he begged and bargained with every deity he could think of to ensure that she'd be ok. He finally arrived at the waiting area, slightly breathless and sweating from the exertion and the stress, to see Rachel, his wife, pacing over by the vending machine.

'Rachel,' he called in a dry croaky voice heavy with emotion. As soon as she heard him, she turned and almost ran into his open arms.

'Oh Adam!' she cried.

They stood for a moment locked in one another's arms. The embrace supporting them both, holding them up, and together. His eyes spoke a greeting as he thought how much he loved her, loved them both. This thought brought him quickly back to Chole. 'Tell me, he said urgently, 'is she ok?'

Still in his arms Rachel moved her head back and wiped her own tears with an already damp tissue. 'Yes,' she sniffed. 'I got her here in time.'

'What is it?' he asked, 'what happened?'

Rachel emitted a nervous laugh as more tears came, shaking her head she looked up at him. 'Appendicitis.'

'But she's ok?' he pleaded insistently, 'she's not in any danger?'

Rachel shook her head before finding the words to respond. 'No, no, the doctor said that we were in time. They're just performing a . . .' she searched for the right words. 'An appendectomy, I think the called it.' Adam relaxed a little as he leant in towards her and buried his face in her hair, hugging her with a ferocity born of the fear of possible loss. Standing there, he breathed in her scent. Its sweet delicate fragrance helping to calm his wildly beating heart.

After a moment Rachel moved back from the embrace to look at him. Her tear-stained face smiling weakly with relief. 'They said she'd be about an hour, and they'd probably have to keep her in overnight.'

'Why?' he demanded. Concern showing on his face.

'Just for observation I think,' she reassured him.

'And you,' he asked looking into her eyes, 'are you ok?' She nodded slightly and smiled back at him, and he knew in that moment, as he had in so many others during their lives together, that he loved her with an energy that was beyond words.

'It's the shock, I think,' she said, sniffing slightly. 'Or after shock, or whatever it's called.'

He tried to sooth her. 'Well, it's a good job you were there.'

'But I've gone over it again and again,' she cried. 'What if I hadn't. I mean, what if I didn't?' This somewhat confusing narrative brought with it another burst of tears as Rachel once again buried her head in his chest, leaving him feeling a little bewildered.

He took a moment to steady himself and then, with a gentleness that spoke of a deep and enduring love, slowly lifted her head from his chest. 'Rachel. What is it?'

She shook her head as if trying to dislodge an uncomfortable thought and wiped away the tears. 'I'm sorry . . .'

'Don't be sorry,' he interrupted. 'You have nothing to be sorry about.'

'It's just,' she shrugged a little, 'it's just that I keep going over the "what if's" and wondering what might have happened if . . .'

He shook his head gently. 'Let it go,' he soothed. 'Just be thankful you were there . . .'

'But that's it,' she sobbed, 'I wasn't there.'

There was a moment of confused silence as he thought about this. 'But – hold on. You said.'

'I wasn't there,' Rachel interrupted quickly, 'I was at work.'

His frown of confusion deepened. 'So, what – did, did Chloe call you?'

Rachel let out a short burst of almost hysterical laughter. 'Ha!'

'So – she called you . . .'

'No,' moaned Rachel. 'I mean. . . possibly . . . yes. Oh, I don't know,' she cried.

Separating slightly but still holding onto her gently he looked directly into her face. 'Just tell me what happened.'

Rachel was shaking her head and looking very uncomfortable. 'It sounds crazy,' she complained. 'I think it is crazy, and I've gone over it again and again in my head.'

'Just – tell me what happened,' he repeated gently.

She looked down and took a deep breath as if to steady herself before looking back at him. 'Ok. Well, I was at work.'

He nodded in encouragement.

'We were in a meeting. Me and Janine, and Harry from planning. It was about that new development on the Sandhurst bypass. Anyway, that doesn't matter. The point is, we were in a meeting. And . . . and this is where it gets a bit weird.'

He smiled gently, nodding for her to continue.

She looked down at the floor again as if afraid to see the reaction in his eyes. 'I know how this sounds. But it was a feeling.'

'A feeling?' he echoed.

'Well, it started as a feeling.' She twisted her body back and forth in agitation as she struggled to find the right words. 'I can't explain it,' she said eventually. 'It was just this . . . this feeling. And I've never felt anything like it before. All I can say is that I knew. I absolutely knew, beyond words, beyond anything, I *knew* that this feeling was real.'

'Ok,' he reassured her.

'And . . .' she broke off for a moment choking back a sob. 'And then, then I heard Chole's voice calling me.'

'Her . . . voice?'

'I know,' she wailed. 'I'm at the office right – I mean, how can I hear my daughter's voice when I'm at the office and she's at home revising?'

Adam stood there for a moment. Not sure what to say or do. Eventually, he broke the silence. 'What did the voice . . .' he checked himself, 'I mean, what did Chloe say?'

Still avoiding his gaze Rachel responded. 'I heard her cry out in pain and . . . and she called my name. And I knew. In that moment I knew. I don't know how, or why, but I knew that there was something wrong, and that I had to get to my daughter.' There was a brief pause before she continued. 'And so, I left. I walked out of the meeting – god only knows what Janine and Harry thought. I drove home as quickly as I could and I found Chloe curled up on her bed in pain complaining of a severe stomach ache.' Another pause. 'I called 111 and after I'd gone through the symptoms with them, they advised me to take her to A&E.' She took a deep steadying breath. 'And, well, you know the rest,' she shrugged. She waited for a moment, but Adam remained silent. Slowly, as if still afraid to look him in the eye she raised her head, and her voice now held a note of defiance. 'I know how this sounds. You'll think I'm mad, or I've made it all up. Or . . .'

'No!' interrupted Adam, sharper than he'd intended.

His response made her look up at him. She could see the colour draining from his face as he soundlessly mouthed something. Now it was her turn to be concerned. 'Adam, are you ok?'

He shook himself a little as if bringing himself out of a stupor and smiled. 'Oh my god!' he said, 'it was a crisis call.'

She frowned. 'A what?'

His shoulders slumped a little as he relaxed, and his smile became a short gentle laugh. 'It was a bloody crisis call,' he repeated shaking his head as if he didn't believe his own words.

Her voice was hesitant. 'A . . . a crisis call – what's that?'

Looking back at her he grinned now, as his voice took on the relaxed timbre it always did when he was trying to explain something. 'A crisis call is when you hear the call of a distant loved one in your mind.'

'So, you don't think I'm mad then?' she queried.

'Hahaha. No, I don't. In fact,' he stopped for a moment thinking back to his meetings with Sam. 'In fact, I have it on good authority that crisis calls are one of the most commonly reported telepathic experiences that people have.'

The disbelief in her voice held an undertone of hopeful relief. 'Really, is that true?'

'Oh yes,' he answered. 'It's true.'

∞

10

Broken Filter

The click of the boiling kettle echoed in the empty kitchen, snapping Martin out of his reverie. He was in his late fifties, with a short crop of silver hair. Tall and lean, he had the careworn look of someone thrown one too many curve balls by life. Lifting the kettle, he reached across and filled his mug with boiling water, making sure to hold down the teabag with his spoon. Once he'd finished making his tea he reached up and took down the biscuit jar, taking out a couple of shortbread fingers, he placed them on a small plate. He smiled as he did so, recalling the countless times Jennie had moaned at him for taking biscuits into the lounge without a plate.

'You make the crumbs, you clean them up,' she used to say. The irritation in her voice often at odds with the smile on her face.

God, how he missed that smile . . . how he missed her.

The instant caught him off guard, allowing a flood of memories to well up in his mind. He had to stand still for a moment, clenching his jaw and holding on to the worktop to steady himself from the onslaught of grief that threatened to overwhelm him. He took a couple of deep breaths, trying to suppress the sinking feeling in the pit of his stomach that had become all too familiar over the last three years. Breathe, he kept telling himself over and over. Just breathe. In, then out. Gradually, the feelings subsided, and he gently shook his head as if to dislodge the unwelcome but dearly loved memories, making a sort of huffing sound as he sighed heavily.

He still missed her even though it was three years ago that the cancer finally took away what he considered to be the best part of his life. Shaking his head slightly, he took the plate of biscuits and his tea back into the lounge, put them on the small table beside a smart cream leather recliner, what he'd always called his "thinking chair", and sat down. He sat in silence for a moment, gathering his thoughts and then reached down to pick up the magazine he'd been reading. It was the latest edition of *British Chess Monthly*. He'd really begun to get into chess. Trying to learn the various openings with their odd sounding names. The gambits, middle game strategies, and end game battles. The famous games, the chess problems and interviews with the world's Grand Masters. He loved the idea that, despite the fact it was possible to know precisely what move each of the eight major pieces and eight pawns *could* make, the possibilities grew exponentially with each move and became almost impossible to predict beyond a few moves in. It amazed him how something so seemingly simple could become so overwhelmingly complex and endless. To an extent, it was the unending possibilities and permutations that he liked about chess, because he could lose himself in them. It reminded him of his time working as a chief engineer, always facing problems, and having to come up with solutions. The challenge of a new problem had always been something he enjoyed, along with the time pressure that often went alongside it. He liked to immerse himself in a problem and allow his mind to work on finding the right solution. Always feeling sure that a solution was there, he just needed to find it. It was simply a case of figuring it out. And he was good at it. In fact, he was much better at dealing with engineering problems than he was with people. Something Jennie would invariably remind him when they were at loggerheads about something Roger, their son, had done and how best to deal with it.

After Jennie's death however, he felt as though the wind had been knocked from his sails. He just couldn't find it in himself to care about the work anymore. It all just seemed so, small, and the problems, the endless problems, now seemed so trivial in comparison to what had happened. He knew it was a mistake to blame his work for what'd happened to Jennie, but he'd felt that it had taken him away from her over the years. As if somehow, it had stolen precious time from them both. Though deep down he knew that he'd been the one that had prioritised work over family. That he could have, should have, spent more time with her, and Roger, when they'd had the time. That he should have told her he loved her. Loved them both. But saying those three words wasn't something that came naturally to him. He thought it was obvious. Implied by his actions, his caring, by the fact that they were still together after all these years. That he didn't need to say it. But he was wrong. He knew now, that the weight of words unsaid, could be a heavy burden to carry. After her death, work had made him feel guilty by a sort of association. It wasn't rational, it wasn't even honest. But he'd ended up leaving, taking early retirement, as a way of trying to avoid the pain and ignore the guilt.

Not long after this James, his best friend, had encouraged him to try and develop some new hobbies and interests. One of these was chess. Ever since, chess had become his way of dealing with life. Though he sometimes wondered if he'd just swapped one avoidance strategy for another. But perhaps that was enough, for now anyway. To try something new. Change the routine in the hope it might change the way he felt.

Part of him had hoped, perhaps unrealistically, that it might be something he and Roger could play together. And that this might be a way for them both to find their way back to each other. As if playing a game of chess would provide Roger with a sufficiently good reason to visit. The thought of Roger made him look up at the family picture on the mantelpiece. It had been taken many years ago, when Roger was still at university, and all three of them were smiling, seemingly happy. He frowned slightly as his gaze fell away and he wondered what had happened in the intervening years to turn that happiness into . . . into what he had now. A long-distance relationship where Roger worked in London and rarely, if ever, called or visited. The time between these points of contact expanding, filled by the intervening years, making it ever more difficult to bridge a growing gap and reach one another. A heartfelt sigh escaped his lips as he began to wonder how it had come to this, but the falsehood dissolved instantly, bringing him up sharply. He knew the reason. The sigh hadn't just been one of sadness, it contained an element of shame as well. Shame for the way he'd acted and the way he'd treated Roger over the years. It wasn't that he didn't love his son, he did. It was simply that he wasn't very good at telling him or letting him know that he loved him. Martin was an advocate of what he considered to be, tough love. Always pushing and never praising. Failing to realise that his approach, whilst often very tough, failed to contain much in the way of love. Jennie used to make a point of saying that he needed to be more considerate or risk pushing Roger away permanently. And he always said that he would, and he meant it. He really did. He was going to ease up just as soon as Roger had finished his A-levels, or graduated, or established himself in his chosen career. But there always seemed to be one more thing Roger needed to do. One more goal in life that, according to Martin, he needed help to achieve. Unfortunately, this focus on things to come had made him blind to the things his son *had* achieved. Never more so than when, two years after graduating from university, Roger had finally qualified as an architect. Martin was proud of his son, but he just didn't know how to tell him. As such, his reaction was the same as it had always been. To not get too carried away, as there's always more to do, always more to learn. At the time he'd played it down with a thoughtless quip, that it wasn't such a great deal, as architects just drew things, and that it was the engineer's that built them. Even now, the shame of those words haunted him. He didn't know why he'd said it, but he could still remember the look in his son's eyes when the words came out. And now, now it was too late to take them back. Too late to take it all back. Jennie had always said that if he wasn't careful, he'd lose the only son he had – and she'd been right. It hadn't helped that with her death he'd also lost the one thing that had held them together.

With a deep sigh, full of regret, he returned his gaze to the magazine laying in his lap. Looking at the chess problem on the page he groaned to himself as he wondered what sort of chess manoeuvre would be needed to get him out of this mess and back on track with his son. After a few minutes lost in thought he decided to take a break and reached over for one of the biscuits. Instead of dunking the biscuit, he did what he'd always done, and took a small bite followed by a sip of tea, allowing the hot tea to dissolve the biscuit in his mouth. He'd always liked the feeling of this as much as the taste. It was as he took his first bite of the biscuit that *it* happened.

A searing pain at the back of his head and the world around him shattered into a myriad of images and sounds that surged through him. The shock of it made him gasp for breath as his hands reached up to cradle his head, dropping the cup and the remainder of the biscuit. Fortunately, the majority of the hot tea splashed onto the magazine in his lap. The cup falling first onto his lap and then, as he fell forwards, with head in hands, rolling onto the carpet. The images and sounds in his mind were overwhelming. He felt bombarded. Caught up in a whirling cacophony of information which threatened to overload and drown him. He shook his head in an effort to try and focus, but this just made the images whirl around him, making him feel dizzy and sick.

It was as if the world had suddenly pixelated into an infinite number of elements reaching out in every direction. With each pixel showing its own scene along with soundtrack and emotional overtones. His breath came in short gasps as he tried to focus. But each time his vision alighted on one of the seemingly infinite pixelated scenes surrounding him he saw, heard, and felt, every aspect of what was being shown. The overwhelming rush of information was staggering and made him feel sick. He tried to squeeze his eyes shut but failed, as if somehow he was being forced to experience it all, in every way. In an effort to contain the pressure he held both hands to the sides of his head, fingers pressing into his scalp. The landscape around him was shifting and moving continuously, as each of the infinite pixelated scenes rushed up to and around him, as if they were all vying for his attention.

Part of him wondered whether he might be having some sort of heart attack. The instant this occurred to him he immediately thought of Jennie. As he did, time seemed to slow, expand and stretch, like an elastic band pulled taught. A pixelated scene appeared in front of him. As he looked into it, he gasped. It was Jennie. She was just standing there, smiling back at him. But she was different somehow. As he stared, he became aware that there was no trace of the cancer that stole her away. In fact, she looked healthy and radiant. Though her lips didn't move he heard her voice clearly in his head.

'It's ok Martin, I'm here.' Bathed in a diffuse glowing light she smiled at him. He couldn't take his eyes off her. The love they shared welled up in him, the ache in his heart matching the pain in his head. Her soft gentle voice echoing in his mind. 'Don't worry, you're not alone.'

The pain in his head momentarily forgotten, he tried to reach out with both hands to embrace her.

Still smiling, she gently shook her head. 'Soon,' she said. Then she seemed to come forwards, the image of her clarifying and intensifying as she raised her hand, finger pointing towards him. Her voice still gentle but encouraging. 'Just don't leave it too late to tell him how you feel.' Then, with a slight nod she receded back into the light.

He wanted to cry out, he couldn't lose her again. The pain, both physical and emotional, was intense. But at that instant time seemed to return with a sharp snap. Quickly shifting the landscape around him again into a whirling cacophony of intense light, colour, sound and emotion. It was as if he simultaneously occupied two worlds. One, close up unreal and bizarre, containing an infinite number of pixelated scenes all playing out before him, continuously shifting and changing. Creating an overwhelming whirlwind of information. The other, seemingly far away, real and mundane. He could feel his physical body, which felt a long way off, slip from the chair onto the floor. A part of him fought to move it. To stand, move upright, or crawl. He knew that if this was a heart attack or some other sort of seizure he needed to try and get some help quickly and that meant getting out of the house. He focused on ignoring all that surrounded him. The sights, sounds and emotions. Thinking instead of getting his physical body outside.

Recalling the layout of the room and working hard to focus his attention he managed to get his physical body upright and moving out towards the hall.

'Left and straight. . . left and straight' he repeated to himself over and over, knowing that this would get him to the front door. He felt his body stagger forwards and come up against the door. Once there he grappled with the latch twisting and pulling at it in what seemed like ineffectual attempts to grab something elusive rather than simply turn a lock. After a couple of attempts he managed to get the door open and pulled it roughly inwards causing it to swing back with the edge hitting him in the face. His eyes watered and his nose felt wet, which produced a strange metallic taste in his mouth as he staggered out onto the front path.

As he lurched outside his neighbours, Margie and Dennis Crompton, were returning from their weekly food shopping trip. Margie was walking back from the car with a shopping bag in each hand. She looked up briefly as she saw Martin emerge from his door.

'Morning Martin,' she called out cheerfully, barely glancing at him before looking back towards her front door. When he failed to respond however she frowned slightly and looked again. Then she noticed that his shirt front and trousers seemed to be wet, which was unusual as Martin always took pride in his appearance. She then noticed that his face was bleeding, or was it his nose, and he was making small, odd gurgling noises.

Concerned she called out. 'Martin,' her voice rising in pitch. 'Martin, are you . . .'

But before she could finish the sentence Martin swayed forward and collapsed onto the front lawn.

'Oh my God! Dennis!' she cried, looking back over her shoulder to the parked car. 'Dennis, call an ambulance. Martin's just collapsed. I think he's had a heart attack.'

∞

Two days later Martin lay awake in bed at the local hospital and for the first time in his life, he was contemplating his fate. The previous twenty-four hours had been a long and arduous series of tests, including multiple CT scans, an endless ream of questions, and various blood tests. Though once the scan results had eventually come back it hadn't taken the doctors long to identify the problem. In fact, it had been quite easy to spot the large tumour in his brain, which showed up as an ominous black mass in the back of his head. What was hard was the fact that it couldn't be treated. They'd told him it was a sub-cortical malignant growth. Which, they explained, meant that it was so deep in his brain, that they'd end up doing more harm than good trying to get to it. The fact that it was malignant also meant that it was growing and spreading. So, the take home message seemed to be that it was bad, and it was only going to get worse. All in all, the doctors had been very good at explaining it to him. Answering all his questions and softening the blow with an outline of treatment options. It was this latter point he found initially confusing. He couldn't make sense of the idea that he'd been diagnosed with terminal brain cancer which they'd made clear that they couldn't cure, only to then have them talk about treatment options. To Martin's literal engineering mind, treatment meant solving the problem. It took him a while, and some persistent questioning, to eventually find out that whilst they couldn't cure him, they still had a duty of care to provide any, and all, possible treatment options. He remembered feeling a bit bewildered at this notion and putting the young neurologist on the spot.

'Sorry, I just want to check this. So, there *are* treatment options?' asked Martin.

The consultant neurologist smiled, nodding politely. 'Oh yes.'

'But . . . but, these treatments won't *cure* the cancer in my brain?'

The neurologist looked a little uncomfortable and broke eye contact. Looking down at the floor he shook his head gently. His voice heavy with regret as he responded. 'Ah, no. I'm afraid not.'

Despite his irritation Martin felt a little sorry for the doctor. He knew it can't be easy to give people such bad news, and he wasn't trying to make the doctor's life difficult, he just couldn't understand the point of offering treatments that everyone knew would be ineffective.

The doctor kindly explained however, that it was more a question of palliative care now.

Palliative care. Another new term that Martin had to learn, which meant not curing but managing the symptoms and pain in the time he had left. Essentially, trying to make his last days and months as comfortable as possible. Discussing this they'd asked him about close family and whether he'd like them to inform family members about his illness, but he'd made it clear that he only had a son and he wanted to be the one to tell him. Though precisely how he would do this he wasn't sure.

Now, as he lay there in bed, he thought about what had happened. The whole thing had been quite a shock and he still couldn't make sense of the experience he'd had, seeing, or thinking he'd seen, Jennie. Was it real, or had he imagined it? Despite going over it again and again in his head he still wasn't sure. And the memory of it now seemed to have faded. As if it were something far away or had happened a long time ago. And he was sure that she'd spoken to him, but he couldn't remember what she'd said.

He'd asked the doctors about his experience when they were going through the diagnosis with him, but all they'd said was that in such cases, as the tumour spreads, it can often put pressure on different areas of the brain which can activate various thoughts and memories. But it just didn't make sense. He'd never seen Jennie like that before. She'd looked so healthy, and he'd never seen her bathed in light. How could a tumour in his brain stimulate a memory he'd never had. When he'd pressed the doctors about it, they just told him that any problems in the brain can produce a variety of strange thoughts and feelings and it was best not to dwell on them. But he had a hard time letting it go. It had felt so real. As if she were talking to him, telling him something. Something important.

As he lay there, he thought about Jennie. For possibly the first time he wondered where she was now. It was a strange thought because ever since her death he'd just thought of her as 'gone'. Missing from his life. Leaving a great big Jennie shaped hole behind. It hadn't really occurred to him to wonder where, if anywhere, she might be now. Thinking about it now made him feel a little selfish. As if he'd only seen her loss in terms of what it'd meant to him. Which, he realised with a degree of self-reproach, was exactly how he had seen it. Like most people of his generation Martin didn't consider himself particularly spiritual or religious. The only times he'd attended church had been for christenings, weddings, and funerals. And like most people of all ages, he hadn't given much thought to what happens when we die. As if somehow thinking about it might make it more likely to happen. When, in fact, he realised with a certain amount of irony, it was the only certainty in life we all share. Also, he wasn't sure what to make of his experience and how, if at all, he could make sense of it. It all seemed so . . . so intangible, he wasn't even sure where to begin. As he thought about what might happen, he tried to simplify it in his head, to make it easier to think about. He liked things to be clear and straightforward and he reasoned, logically so he thought, that either nothing happened, and you just die and that's the end of it. Or . . . and it was a big 'or', or something happened. But what that something could be he just didn't know.

As he thought about this now it occurred to him that he should talk to James about it. He knew that being a psychologist James had a long-standing interest in the mind and what he called 'all that stuff'. After all, he'd raised the subject once or twice during their many chess games. But as he thought about this he also remembered, with a degree of shameful guilt, that whenever James had raised the matter, he'd either shut down the conversation abruptly or changed the subject. Shaking his head with a wry smile he knew now that he could no longer avoid the issue. Thinking back, he realised that he might also owe James an apology for his behaviour. He also wondered whether James would be able to shed any light on his experience regarding Jennie. Yes, he thought, James was definitely someone he should speak to, and soon.

Thinking of the people he needed to speak to, immediately led him back to Roger. He wasn't sure at all how to deal with this. And he had this nagging feeling at the back of his mind that Jennie had mentioned something about Roger. But for now, he couldn't recall what she'd said. He wished she were here now. Jennie had always been the one Roger had talked to. The one he'd shared confidences with. They both just seemed to be able to talk easily with one another. Not something he'd ever managed very well. It wasn't that he didn't love his son. He did. He just thought it was something that was so obvious that it didn't need mentioning. Like gravity. Throw a ball up into the air and gravity makes sure it always comes back down to Earth again. The fact that Roger was his son seemed to him clear evidence that he loved him. Obviously, he loved him. He was his son. Did he really need to say it? According to Jennie he did, and more than once they'd had what he called 'heated words' about it. As he looked back now, he realised that he'd often avoided the issue. Now, true to form he thought that the best way to deal with it would be to deal with it later. Right now, he wanted to talk to James. Having made his decision, he reached for his phone and punched in James' number.

∞

It was visiting time the following evening when James arrived at the hospital ward. The same age as Martin he was slightly shorter in stature, though still retained a thick head of dark hair which complemented his dark brown eyes. He was well built but not overweight and always prided himself on being well dressed. Today, he was wearing his trade-mark Gap khaki trousers and a smart blue linen shirt with dark brown leather boating loafers. As he appeared in the doorway his face held an unfamiliar frown as he scanned the small ward for Martin's bed. As soon as he spotted it his face lightened and he smiled in recognition as he made his way over.

'Hi Marty,' he said with false brightness, taking his seat on the small hard chair beside the bed. 'You look like shit,' he grinned.

Martin laughed lightly. 'Thanks. I've certainly felt better.'

James laid a couple of paper bags on the bed. 'I brought you some fruit,' he said as he upended the bags to reveal their contents, 'and some chocolate.'

'Thanks Jim, you're a life saver,' said Martin. 'The food in here's bloody awful.'

'I think its all part of the strategy. You know, to get you out of the ward sooner,' responded James, smiling.

'Trust me, I'd much rather be at home.'

James frowned a little. His face mirroring the concern in his voice. 'So, what happened?' he asked.

Martin sighed and shrugged, as he made a vague gesture with his hands, not sure where to begin. There was a moments silence as the two old friends just looked at one another, concern and care evident in their faces.

'Well,' began Martin, 'it just came on suddenly the other day.' And he went on to tell James what had happened and the diagnosis that the doctors had given him after the various scans and tests. It didn't take long. When he mentioned the brain tumour James looked a little stunned and swore softly under his breath, shaking his head in disbelief. His discomfort increased markedly when Martin then told him that there were no treatment options, and it was now a case of palliative care. Once he'd finished both men sat in grim silence for a few minutes.

'And . . . and there's nothing they can do?' asked James quietly. The disbelief evident in his voice.

Martin shook his head. 'Nope.'

'Did they give you any indication of how long?'

'Six months, tops,' responded Martin.

There was a moment's silence before James asked, 'so, what do you want for your last Christmas present then?'

'Hahaha,' laughed Martin, the dark humour helping them both to cope with the awkward situation and going some way to relieve the tension. 'How about a new brain?'

'Sorry, fresh out of brains,' responded James with a wry smile.

'Typical,' complained Martin.

James frowned momentarily. 'Have you told Roger yet?' he asked.

Martin looked down at the bedclothes. 'Ah, no,' he said, 'not yet'.

'Bloody hell Marty! You've got to tell him.'

Martin nodded in agreement. 'Yes, yes, I know.' He knew James would ask, not only because he was Martin's oldest and best friend, but also because he was Roger's godfather.

James looked concerned. His face took on a stern and tight-lipped expression.

'I will, I will,' said Martin, recognising the signs of a potential dispute. 'I'm just not sure how. . .' he left it hanging for a moment.

'Just call him,' said James.

Martin grimaced slightly and looked down, a little ashamed. His voice was softly reticent. 'I'm not sure he'd pick-up,' he said.

'Of course he would,' blustered James. 'Look do you want me . . .'

'No!' interrupted Martin. 'No. I'll do it. Leave it with me, I'll figure out a way to speak to him.'

The two friends avoided looking at each other. Each lost for a brief moment in their own discomfort.

Still shaking his head as if he didn't want to believe the news about Martin's illness, James spoke quietly in a voice tinged with regret. 'I'm so sorry Marty, I just feel so bloody helpless.'

'It's not your fault Jim,' said Martin with a shrug.

'Just let me know if there's anything – anything I can do,' emphasised James.

'Thanks,' nodded Martin. 'That means a lot because I'll need you to help out after . . .' he faltered for a moment. The unspoken words hung in the air for a moment as they each contemplated what they meant. 'Well . . . you know,' he finished lamely.

James nodded. 'Anything, just ask.'

Martin frowned in thought as he shifted in the bed to make himself more comfortable. 'Well,' he said cautiously, 'there is, or there might be, something you could help me with.'

'Anything,' responded James quickly. 'Just name it.'

'Well, you're a psychologist right.'

'Ha!' snorted James, 'nice of you to remember.' Then as he saw the concern on Martin's face he quickly added, 'yes, yes I am.'

Martin seemed to be thinking about what to say, as if unsure of himself, which was unusual. 'It's just that, when I collapsed, something happened.'

'What?' asked James wondering cautiously where this might be going.

Martin, still unusually cautious took a moment before responding. 'Just let me tell you about it first and then you can tell me what you think . . . ok?'

James shrugged. 'Ok.'

Martin then began by telling him how, when he'd collapsed, the world seemed to fragment into lots of different images. And how, if he looked at any one of them, he could experience everything that was going on in it. How he could see, hear, touch, smell and feel everything that went on. As if it was happening to him right there in that moment. That it was so real and so intense. How there seemed to be an endless number of these images moving around him and trailing of in every direction. And finally, how he'd met Jennie and she'd talked to him, but he couldn't quite remember what she'd said. When he'd finished speaking both men sat in silence for a moment as if trying to absorb the fullness of Martin's narrative and come to terms with what it could mean.

After a minute or so Martin broke the silence. 'What do you think . . . what do you think that could have been?' he asked.

James made a wry face. 'Well, we need to be cautious and remember that you'd suffered some sort of episode . . .'

'It wasn't an hallucination,' interrupted Martin quickly. 'It was real.' The statement hung like an accusation in the air between them. As if he were daring James to challenge him.

James made a placating gesture with his hands. 'You mean it felt real to you.'

'No! – it was real,' cried Martin. 'As real as sitting here with you.'

'You're lying down,' James noted pedantically.

'Oh ha-ha. You know what I mean. Ok, as real as lying here being patronised by you.'

This time it was James' turn to smile. 'I'm not saying I don't believe you,' he began. 'I'm just saying that we need to be cautious.'

'Why?' challenged Martin. 'What possible benefit could there be for me to make this up? I've got enough on my plate for the moment without adding going mental to the list.'

'We don't use the term *mental* anymore,' James pointed out patiently.

'Look – I'm dying. I can say what I want,' responded Martin petulantly.

James shook his head in disagreement. 'We're all dying, you just have a clearer idea of when. So, no – you don't get to act like an arse just because of that.'

There was a moment of awkward silence as both friends looked at one another. Then, Martin smiled ruefully and shrugged a brief apology. 'Ok, sorry.'

'By the way,' James said matter-of-factly, 'did you know that a recent government poll showed that if you ask people whether they'd like to know the date and nature of their death around forty percent of 18–25-year-olds say yes. But that this decreases to around twenty percent for those over fifty-five[1]. Weird eh – you'd expect it to be the other way round.'

Martin thought for a moment before responding. 'Not really. The closer you get the less you want to think about it.'

James screwed up his face. 'Really, you think so?'

'Yes,' said Martin with a slight hint of exasperation. 'Now, if we can just get back to what happened to me.'

'Ok,' James shrugged. 'Just saying.'

'Well, you know about the mind and all that,' stated Martin. 'How would you explain what happened to me?'

'Hahaha!' laughed James. 'You do realise that the phrase – "the mind and all that" – has kept smarter people than me occupied for centuries.'

'Yes, but there must be a theory or best explanation for the mind that you know of?' said Martin.

James sat back in his chair and thought for a moment. 'Well, that depends.'

Martin groaned. 'Spoken like a true academic.'

'These are deep questions,' complained James, 'the fact that we've been asking them for centuries should give you some idea of how complex they are and how difficult it might be to answer them.'

'But there must be some sort of answer,' countered Martin, the hope clearly evident in his voice.

'We'ell,' began James. 'The currently agreed view is that the mind, or consciousness, is an emergent phenomenon of the brain.'

'So, the doctors were probably right then?' queried Martin. 'When they said that my experience was probably the result of the tumour impacting somehow on my brain.'

'Well,' responded James, 'as I say, that's the most commonly held view, at the moment.'

There were a few seconds of silent contemplation before Martin took the bait. 'Ok, what do you mean by, at the moment?'

James grinned broadly, warming to his subject. 'Well, as I say, the current focus is on the brain, but it hasn't always been that way. The early Greeks for example put the centre of your mind in your heart because when you place your hand on your chest you can feel something move, your heartbeat. And they thought this movement was important and signified the centre of your being, or self. This was called the cardiac hypothesis and at that time the brain was seen as nothing more than a radiator used to cool the blood.'

'Ha!' snorted Martin as he heard this. 'You're kidding?'

'Nope,' replied James shaking his head. 'It wasn't until later that Plato moved the seat of the mind from the heart to the head.'

'Hmmm,' nodded Martin, as if agreeing that this was a sensible course of action.

'But he only did that,' said James, 'because the head was seen as being closer to heaven.'

'You're making this up,' grumbled Martin, sitting upright in agitation.

'I assure you I'm not,' responded James.

'So now everyone agrees that the mind is based on the brain then?' asked Martin.

James shifted in his chair, getting comfortable and made a side-to-side rocking movement with his head. 'Well, as I say, that's the dominant view but it's not the *only* one.'

Martin groaned audibly. 'But don't you psychologists carry out tests and things to prove that the mind is based on the brain?'

'For a start people aren't just data producing machines,' reproached James. 'Something you might want to keep in mind the next time you talk to Roger.'

Martin gritted his teeth but decided to say nothing for now and let that one go.

'Also, we try to avoid using the word *prove* as it has too much of a note of finality to it.'

'What!' Martin burst out. 'But surely the whole point of the research you do, the never-ending research you do,' his voice heavy with sarcasm, 'is that you prove things?'

'No,' said James shaking his head gently. 'It's more subtle and complex than that.'

'It feels as though you're making it more complex,' complained Martin.

'On the contrary,' responded James, 'you're just beginning to understand that's its more subtle than you thought it was.'

'What do you mean?'

'Well, the problem with the word *proved* is that it has the note of finality to it. As in, we've proven X and that's it – job done, and we can all go home.'

'Ha!' snorted Martin. 'No wonder you don't like using it – you'd all be out of a job.'

James made a wry face. 'Very droll. The point I'm trying to make,' he continued, 'is that it mistakenly suggests that we know all there is to know about something[2]. That we've fully understood it and that our current view, or the way we're currently thinking about it is right and it always will be.'

'But that sounds like a good idea,' said Martin.

'Ok, but let me ask you this,' replied James. 'Is the Earth flat?'

'No,' Martin quickly answered. 'But I did hear that there are people on the internet…'

'Yes, yes, I know,' interrupted James sharply, 'but for the sake of simplicity we're going to ignore the idiots on the web.'

Martin shrugged, 'hmm, ok.'

James continued. 'Does the Sun go around the Earth?'

'No.'

'Are germs real?'

'Yes.'

'Does the Earth's crust move creating boundaries of tension that can lead to earthquakes?'

'Err, yes, I think so,' said Martin, a little less sure of himself now.

'And can your brain grow new brain cells?'

'Ah, er, I don't really know. Possibly,' answered Martin truthfully.

James smiled. 'The answer's yes.'

'Ok, ok, but what is the point of all these questions?' asked Martin.

'The point,' said James with emphasis, 'is that what we thought was proven to be true at one point in time, later turned out to be completely wrong. As we gathered more data, made more observations our understanding of something improved. And because of this our ideas about what was *proven to be true* had to be changed as the new findings didn't fit in with the old view. Leading to something called a paradigm shift – and it's happened many, many times in science. Sometimes because of a build up of new evidence, sometimes because the "old guard" die off, and sometimes both.'

'Die off,' snorted Martin, 'are you serious?'

'Absolutely,' confirmed James. 'In fact, it was Max Planck who famously said that science progresses one funeral at a time.'

'So, what you're saying is that science doesn't prove things with certainty because our understanding of it, whatever "it" may be, can change.'

'Exactly,' nodded James.

'And the idea that the mind is based on the brain might be the current best view, but it's not the only one and it could change as new information comes in.'

'Precisely,' agreed James.

'Hmm,' nodded Martin thoughtfully. What are the other ideas then?' he asked.

James looked up and leant back in his chair for a moment. 'Well, there's panpsychism, which is an old idea that seems to be coming back, and then there's the brain as filter theory.'

'Pan – what?' asked Martin.

But just then a nurse popped her head into the room to let everyone know that visiting hours would come to an end in five minutes. Their conversation interrupted, the two friends looked at one another and James shrugged as Martin made a wry face. There was a feeling that neither really wanted to end the conversation, but both knew that their time for now was up.

'Will you be able to come tomorrow night?' asked Martin.

James nodded, 'yeah, of course. Let me know if you need anything.'

'I will, thanks.'

James rose to leave but then stopped. He stood for a moment beside the bed as if unsure how to get out. He looked down at Martin, his voice quite but firm, 'you know what I'm going to say don't you?'

Martin nodded in understanding, 'I will. I just need to figure out how best to do it.'

'Just don't leave it too long,' said James. He leaned over the bed and the two friends briefly hugged before James made his way out of the ward.

Later that night Martin lay in his bed trying to get comfortable as thoughts of his illness, along with images of Jennie and worries about Roger intermingled with ideas from his conversation with James. Again and again, he went over the idea that the mind is simply the brain, and because his was suffering the effects of a tumour his mind would, quite naturally, be traumatised. And it was this trauma that produced the hallucination or hodge podge of random memories pieced together in a confused way. When he reflected on this it did seem like the most straightforward explanation, but for some reason he found it hard to accept. The things he'd seen, and the way he felt told him that it was more than this. It had to be. Or did it? A part of him realised that, given his condition, it could all be wishful thinking. The eternal hope of seeing Jennie again. The notion that life did have meaning and purpose beyond this physical existence. He just wasn't sure. But the feelings he'd had during his experience were different somehow. It wasn't just *what* he'd seen, it was the feelings he had as well. They were so intense, vivid, somehow feeling *more* real than real. Also, he was certain that he'd never seen Jennie looking like that before and couldn't understand how it would be possible to remember something he'd never seen before. It was as his mind stumbled uncertainly over these ideas that *it* happened again.

It began with a sharp stabbing pain in the back of his head, making him feel simultaneously sick and dizzy. Gasping for breath he felt himself falling, down through the bed, down and down as he flailed about in desperation. Fear began to grip him as he felt a lack of control over what was happening to him. Then, tossed like a leaf on the wind, he felt himself shift violently, first in one direction and then another. He tried to open his eyes to see what was going on around him and as he did the world around him shattered into an infinite number of pixelated scenes. Though it was a little more familiar it was no less shocking. It was as if every fleeting thought had come alive, been captured, and was being reflected back in high-definition immersive reality. As before, whichever way he looked pixelated scenes rushed up to him, immersing him in their reality and threatening to overwhelm him with their content. It was a maelstrom of chaos and confusion. He felt afraid and the child in him longed for a safe harbour in this storm of colour, sound and emotion. As the fear threatened to overwhelm his mind a pixelated scene rushed up and enveloped him. Time paused for a moment as the scene before him revealed his parents. They both looked younger than he remembered them, and both were smiling and happy. Confusion and shock stole his breath and his voice. He stared dumbly at them for moment. The thought of parents, of family, made him think of Roger and instantly he was spun around as another set of scenes rushed him. As this set of scenes surrounded him, he saw multiple pixelated images of Roger. Some young, some old, some where he was alone and others where he was with what looked like family. Briefly, he noticed that the scenes containing the younger Roger were clearer, more colourful and more defined. Whereas those where he seemed older, with family, were hazier, and opaque. The pixelated scenes all veered off at different angles as if they represented distinct pathways away from this point in time. As Martin looked at the scenes containing his son, he felt a sadness and heartache at the distance that had grown between them and wished that Jennie was there to help. As soon as his mind thought of Jennie he was shifted again, spun and dropped, pulled and pushed, buffeted on a sea of chaotic images until time once again seemed to stretch and slow as a pixelated scene halted in front of him. Staring he saw instantly the same glowing image of Jennie that he'd seen before.

In desperation he called out, 'Jennie!'

Her image moved forward slightly, becoming sharper, more defined. Again, her lips didn't move but her voice, gentle and comforting, echoed in his mind. 'It's ok Martin, everything will be alright.'

He shook his head in bewilderment and confusion.

'There is still time,' he heard her say in a voice edged with hope.

'Time for what?' he wailed. 'What is this?'

'It's up to you,' her voice echoed. 'It's always been up to you.'

'I don't know what you mean,' he cried.

She smiled gently and moved back into the misty light. 'Just make sure you don't leave it too late to tell him how you feel.'

'Jennie!' he sobbed as he watched her disappear back into the hazy light.

Instantly the scene around moved again. This time the fractured, pixelated scenes all seemed to shift away from him, as if pulling back. Then with a sharp snap they instantly reversed direction and hurtled toward him, engulfing him, drowning him in images, sounds, smells and feelings. Like a gently flickering candle attempting to remain alight in a hurricane his mind was overwhelmed, and all went black.

∞

It was visiting time the following evening as Martin lay recovering in his bed, waiting for James to arrive. His latest experience had worried the doctors, increasing their concern about the impact his tumour would have on his health. Strangely, for Martin, his latest experience had increased his confidence that something unusual but meaningful had happened to him and that it wasn't just an hallucination. Nevertheless, visiting time arrived, as did James, carrying a small bag and dressed in his usual khaki trousers, this time sporting a bright red short-sleeved shirt. Martin nodded in recognition as James came into the ward and made his way over to Martin's bed to take the ready placed chair beside it. On reaching the chair however, James stood for a moment, placing a hand on Martin's shoulder. He nodded, smiling with genuine affection. 'Good to see you Marty,' he said.

Martin smiled in return, clearly pleased to see his old friend. 'Thanks for coming.'

'No problem,' said James as he sat in the chair and placed the bag on the bed.

'Hmmm,' said Martin eyeing the bag, 'more chocs and fruit?'

James smiled a little. 'Ah, well, just the chocolate this time,' he said as he upended the bag to spill its contents onto the bed. 'And a book.'

Martin looked with pleasure at the three large bars of dark chocolate, each with a different filling. One had hazelnuts, the second had ginger and the third contained mint. 'Ooh they look good,' he said picking up and inspecting each of the bars in turn. 'Dark chocolate, my favourite.'

'Thought you might like a treat,' said James.

'And the book?' enquired Martin.

'After our last conversation I thought this might help a bit.'

Martin picked up the book and read the title. 'Is this about the mind and stuff?' he asked as he turned it over to skim read the reviews on the back cover.'

James smiled and nodded. 'Sort of, yes.'

'Interesting, thanks,' he murmured, flicking through it briefly. 'I'll just put it here,' he said as he leant over and laid it on the cabinet beside the bed, 'and have a better look at it later.' Then sitting back upright he reached over to the chocolate bars, picked up the one with hazelnuts in and tore it open. As he broke off a large piece of chocolate he looked back at James. 'Would you like a piece?' he asked.

James shook his head, 'no thanks. You go ahead.'

Just before Martin put the chunk of chocolate in his mouth he looked directly at James. 'It happened again,' he said.

'What, your . . .' James hesitated for a second, 'your odd experience,' he finished.

'Hmm-mm,' nodded Martin, mouth now full of chocolate.

'Was it the same as before?' queried James.

Martin chewed and swallowed before answering. 'Not exactly. It was similar, but this time I recall seeing my parents, and Roger.'

'Did it feel the same?' asked James.

'Yes. It felt just as *real* as last time,' he answered, placing heavy emphasis on the word real as if challenging James to question him about it. However, James didn't rise to the challenge, he just sat there thoughtfully. 'And I saw Jennie again,' continued Martin.

'Was that the same as before as well?' asked James.

Martin shifted as if trying to get comfortable and grimaced a little. 'I'm not sure. It felt similar and again I had the feeling she said something. Something important. But I can't remember exactly what it was. It's as if I can recall generally what happened but not the details.'

'A bit like a dream,' said James.

'It *wasn't* a dream,' responded Martin indignantly.

'I'm not saying it was a dream,' soothed James quickly. 'Just, *like* a dream, that's all. You know, how you can have a dream and it seems so real and so vivid and yet when you wake up it seems to fade away, and a few minutes later you can't even remember what it was about.'

'Hmm,' intoned Martin, only partially appeased.

'Anything else you remember?' asked James quickly, keen to move the conversation on.

Martin thought for a moment and frowned. 'Something about time,' he said, 'but I'm not sure what it was.'

'Did you tell the doctors?'

'No.' Martin's response was quick and again held a note of challenge, as if daring James to question his judgement.

The two friends sat for a moment, each lost in thought as to what this could all mean and what to make of it. Martin broke the silence. 'You were the one who said that our understanding of the mind wasn't complete.'

'True,' said James, nodding.

'That there needs to be some sort of paradigm shift or something. And it would lead to a different view, something about pans – something or other.'

'Panpsychism[3],' corrected James.

'Is that what the book's about,' asked Martin nodding towards the book on the bedside cabinet.

'Not only that,' answered James, 'but it does include information on that approach, among others.'

'But you never explained what it is,' complained Martin.

'Ah yes, well,' responded James sitting a little more upright in his chair. 'It literally means mind is everywhere. It's an old idea really that seems to be undergoing a sort of renaissance. The central point is that consciousness, or mind, is a fundamental aspect of the Cosmos.'

James waited for a moment for this point to sink in.

'Clear as mud,' groaned Martin.

James smiled in response. 'Ok, think of it this way. What's the basis of reality?'

'What do you mean?' asked Martin.

'Well, what are you made of?'

'Are you serious?'

'Yes – what are you made of?'

Martin thought for a moment. 'Ah, err ok. Erm, cells,' he answered cautiously.

'And what are those cells made of?' asked James quickly.

'Err, the cells are made of molecules I think.'

'And they are made of what?'

'Atoms.'

'And then?'

'Protons and electrons I think,' answered Martin, 'my biology was never that good.'

'That's ok,' said James. 'But what about the electrons and protons. What are they made of?'

Martin shook his head, 'I don't know.'

James smiled. 'So, just think about it for a moment. All the way down, from cells, to atoms, to electrons. At some point you reach the bottom. The fundamental level of reality.'

Martin nodded in silence to show he was following James' line of thought.

'Now imagine that that fundamental level of reality is conscious experience. Mind, if you like, though different people have given it different names they all essentially mean the same thing. That mind, or Mind with a capital 'M', isn't derived from physical reality, but is more primary, more fundamental than that.' He waited for a moment to see if Martin had any questions. But it seemed that Martin was still following him, so he continued. 'As I say, people have given this fundamental level of Mind various names. And it's important to step back for a moment here and realise that we're using language to try and describe an abstract idea and that the language we use might very well constrain us or limit our thinking in some way. But we have to use language to describe it, so we just need to be aware that the words we use are really just place holders. Nothing more.'

'Ah!' interrupted Martin, 'is that why the book's called *Dark Cognition*? Because like the terms *Dark Energy* and *Dark Matter* it's just a place holder to suggest that something is going on here, but we just don't know what it is.'

'Exactly,' smiled James, nodding enthusiastically.

'Ok,' said Martin cautiously, 'that sort of makes sense.'

'Now,' continued James, 'as I say people have given this fundamental level lots of different names such as *proto-consciousness, zero-point field,* or the *collective-consciousness,* but I particularly like the more neutral term *field of consciousness,* so we'll stick with that for now.'

'Hold on,' interrupted Martin, thinking he'd spotted a flaw in James' argument. 'If everything is built up out of this, this field of consciousness, that would mean that everything is conscious.'

James nodded, 'yep.'

Martin laughed derisively, 'hahaha. You've got to be kidding.'

'No, no, wait,' pleaded James. 'Don't fall into the trap of thinking that there's only one type of mind or consciousness.'

'What do you mean,' asked Martin looking sceptical.

'Well, think about it,' urged James. 'We've come to accept the possibility that our pets have minds, yes?'

'Er, yes. Ok, I'll grant you that.'

'Even though they are very likely different from our minds – yes?'

'Hmm-mm,' agreed Martin cautiously.

'By the way,' James went on, clearly enjoying himself as he defaulted to lecture mode, 'did you know that a lot of the early research relied on something called the *mirror test*[4] to identify whether an animal was self-aware or not.'

Martin shrugged in a noncommittal manner.

'What happens,' James explained, 'is that researchers would put a mark, or sticker of some sort, on the forehead of the animal and then put it in front of a mirror to see if it would realise that they're looking at themselves and reach up to remove the mark or sticker from their own forehead.'

Martin simply frowned, not sure where this was going.

'However,' said James, 'the point is that the test is biased.'

'What do you mean?' asked Martin.

'It's visually biased. A test that relies on vision, created by a visually dominant species – humans.'

'And?' queried Martin.

'Well, dogs for example often fail the test. As do very young children by the way. They often don't pass the mirror test until about the age of two. But, if you were to run the test based on smell, dogs would very likely pass and humans would fail.'

'Is there a point to this?' asked Martin somewhat irritated.

'Yes,' said James earnestly. 'It shows that how you classify mind can depend on the base of your argument. And the findings from the young children also suggest that mind, or consciousness, changes over time.'

'Oh-kay,' said Martin, still not sure what the point was.

'And this is important,' said James, noting Martin's continued uncertainty, 'because we need to be careful how we define mind and not fall into the trap of thinking that there's only one type of mind, and that it is somehow fixed, and doesn't change over time.'

'Ok, I grant you that,' responded Martin, 'but, cats, dogs, even babies,' he said with a smile, 'are all alive.'

James smiled at this. 'Yes, but again you need to be careful of not falling into the trap of thinking that mind has anything to do with biology, or life. If, Mind is a fundamental aspect of the universe then everything, and I mean everything. This bed, that table, the lamp, even the book I've just given you. All have an aspect of mind.'

Martin lay in his bed looking very sceptical. 'That,' he said, shaking his head slowly, 'I find very hard to believe.'

James nodded in understanding. 'I'm not saying it's easy,' he said. 'To an extent it challenges the way we think about mind, or the basis of mind at least.'

'How,' asked Martin.

'Well, think about it. All your life you've been told that mind equals brain. Or to a great extent anything that has a mind *must* have a brain.'

Martin nodded slowly.

'And here I am suggesting that this view is certainly limited, and in fact it may well be wrong.'

'Ahh,' sighed Martin as if understanding was slowly dawning. 'Are we back to that paradigm shift thing again?'

James nodded. 'To an extent,' he said. 'We just need to be aware of our limited understanding of mind and not allow this to define and restrict the way we think about it.'

'I still find it hard to accept,' said Martin.

'Well, changing people's minds is never easy,' responded James with a grin.

'But', continued Martin, clearly struggling to accept the ideas he'd heard. 'If mind is based on this fundamental level of reality wouldn't everyone's mind be the same?'

'Good question,' smiled James, happy to see that Martin was thinking about it. 'But you're falling into what I call the "either/or" trap.'

Martin made a wry face, 'oh,' he said sardonically, 'and what's that?'

'You're thinking that mind is "either" based on this fundamental level of reality "or" it's based on the brain. Which is just limiting the way we think about things, when it might be better to think in terms of "both/and".'

Martin's look was one of slight confusion. 'But that's what you said,' he complained.

'Not quite,' answered James. 'I said that mind, that's Mind with a capital M, may well be the fundamental level of reality.'

'But that's what I …' began Martin before James interrupted him.

'Hold on, just let me finish,' continued James. 'I said Mind was the fundamental level of reality. But your mind, that's mind with a small 'm' by the way, is an interaction between your brain and that fundamental level of Mind.' He waited a moment to give Martin time to think about it before continuing. 'Which brings us on to the idea of the brain as filter model.'

Martin screwed his face up mild irritation. 'The brain as what?'

'Filter,' responded James. 'Right now, the dominant view is that the mind, or your mind anyway, is solely produced by your brain. But, rather than take this extreme view you could think about your mind as the possible interaction between your brain and this more fundamental level of Mind. In this way your mind is *related* to your brain but not *solely* reliant upon it.'

Martin's face remained confused. 'I'm not sure I follow.'

James thought for a moment, trying to come up with a useful analogy that might help. 'Ok, think about your phone.'

'My phone,' Martin's voice held a note of incredulity.

'Yes, your phone. It's just an analogy,' he explained, 'but it might help. Now, you can access a whole range of information from the internet via your phone – right?'

'Yes,' responded Martin.

'But that information isn't held on your phone, is it?'

'Err, no.'

'So, the information you can see on your phone is the result of an interaction between that phone and the internet.' James watched to see if this made sense. Martin took a moment but then slowly nodded in agreement. 'Well, imagine that your mind is based on the interaction between your brain and that more fundamental level of Mind. In this way there will be a unique aspect to your mind, unique to you because your life has shaped your brain, quite literally. But also, this individual or unique aspect of mind can also interact with a larger or wider aspect of Mind that operates at a more fundamental level. And in this way *your* mind is based on *both* your brain *and* the more fundamental level of Mind.'

Martin lay there for a moment lost in thought before he hesitantly queried, 'so, it's like my mind.' He faltered, struggling with the words. 'My ah, individual or unique mind, is made up of different levels of mind, based on both my brain and this other more fundamental part of . . . of mind?'

James shrugged and his voice remained non-committal. 'Different levels, different aspects, different dimensions. Again, these are just words we're using to describe abstract ideas, but yes, something along those lines.'

'But if everyone is linked to this fundamental Mind in some way' queried Martin, 'wouldn't that mean we'd all be part of the same . . . the same, oh I don't know what to call it,' he complained.

James nodded. 'Yes, it would. And you can call it whatever you want. The same network, the same system, the same *uber-Mind.*'

'Wow,' echoed Martin quietly. 'Imagine it. Everyone. All connected, part of the same network.'

'Hmmm,' agreed James. 'Makes you think doesn't it.'

Martin nodded slowly.

'For a start,' continued James, 'we might treat each other with a bit more care and respect.'

'Phew!' sighed Martin heavily. 'Sounds more like philosophy than science.'

'To an extent it is,' responded James, 'though I'm not sure the distinctions between those topics are as clear as you might think.'

'What!' exclaimed Martin. 'Are you telling me this is all just . . .' he faltered for a moment. 'Just words,' he spluttered. 'Ideas. That there's no evidence for this?'

James snorted with laughter. 'Hahaha. There *is* no single piece of evidence that can be used to identify consciousness. After all, prove to me you have a mind.'

Martin frowned for a moment not quite sure how to respond.

'Well?' demanded James.

Martin thought for a moment and then shrugged, unsure. 'Well, I could tell you.'

'So could a computer,' countered James quickly.

'But you could measure . . .' Martin faltered for a moment, not sure exactly what could, or should, be measured.

'Measure what,' asked James trying hard not to sound too scathing. 'Your brain activity?'

'Well, surely that would tell you something,' said Martin.

James' voice now held a hint of sarcasm. 'Oh yes. It would tell me that there's a correlation between your brain activity and your behaviour – whoop!' he exclaimed, the level of sarcasm now reaching substantially higher than just a hint.

'Well . . . well surely that would tell you something,' cried Martin.

'Beyond the fact that there's an association between your brain activity and your behaviour – no!' answered James curtly. 'And, as every first-year undergraduate student knows, or at least should know, correlation does not imply causation.

So, we'd still be no closer to knowing whether your brain produced the information or simply relayed it from elsewhere.'

A little annoyed now Martin complained, 'are you saying that there's no way of ever knowing which of these ideas of the mind are right?'

'Not at all,' responded James.

'Well, what can we do then?' asked Martin a little aggrieved.

'We look for evidence that challenges the status quo,' said James. 'Findings that are anomalous, which means that they are difficult, or seemingly impossible to explain, using the current paradigm. That is, the one where mind is based only on the brain. Such findings, when they become unavoidable and undeniable often lead to this paradigm shift we've been talking about. And to find evidence that challenges such a view we need to look to the very edge of our knowledge and understanding, to what some may call the fringe of science. And a good example of this is the field of parapsychology.

Martin grimaced. 'Parapsychology?'

'Yes, not the best term I know,' replied James. 'And you wouldn't believe the amount of time and energy that's been spent, or perhaps wasted, on debating that. However, it's a general term and for now we're stuck with it. Other terms include psychic and psi ...'

'Psychic!' interrupted Martin loudly. Oh you are kidding me. I thought that was all a load of nonsense. That there's no real evidence for any of that ...' he faltered for a moment before finishing, 'for that stuff.'

James looked a little crestfallen as he replied, 'sadly that is a common, a *very* common, misconception.'

'You mean there *is* evidence for it?' challenged Martin.

James nodded towards the book on the bedside cabinet. 'That's why I brought you that.'

Martin looked back over towards the book frowning a little. 'Humph! If that's true I'm surprised you only brought one.'

'Well, you always were a slow reader,' said James with a smile. 'And I had to keep in mind that you only have limited time.'

Martin's eyes widened in shock, he looked back at James, momentarily unsure how to respond to what he'd just heard. Then, after a brief silence, he shook his head and laughed. It was a loud, genuine laugh full of humour and good nature. 'Bastard,' he said sotto voce.

James simply shrugged and ginned back. 'The point is,' he continued, 'if we take the view that Mind is fundamental and your individual mind is able to interact with it in some way then not only do the anomalous findings of parapsychology become more understandable but to some extent, they're exactly what you'd expect to find[5].'

'What do you mean?'

'Take telepathy for example.'

'You mean sort of mind reading?' queried Martin.

'Well, sort of,' said James, in an effort to keep things simple. 'One of the biggest stumbling blocks in trying to account for telepathy has been how information could transfer from one mind to another. What is the signal, so to speak.'

Martin nodded in mute understanding.

'However, rather than seeing it as the transfer of information from one distant mind to another you could see it as the sharing of information between two linked aspects of a more fundamental Mind.'

'Like two phones communicating or sharing information via the internet,' said Martin.

Pleased that Martin had kept with his original analogy James smiled and nodded in agreement. 'Yes. Something like that.'

Martin also smiled, pleased that his use of the analogy had made sense.

'And other areas,' continued James, 'such as remote viewing and clairvoyance could also be accounted for in terms of accessing shared information from the fundamental level of Mind. Also, if we accept this idea that Mind is fundamental then there's no distinction between mind and matter, which could account for psychokinesis – the ability to move things with the mind alone.' James stopped for a moment. Aware that he'd covered a lot of points and he wanted to give Martin time to absorb what they'd talked about and allow him the opportunity to ask questions. He didn't have to wait long.

'What did you call all this stuff, parapsychology?' queried Martin.

'Yes, that's right,' answered James.

'So,' queried Martin cautiously, 'is it just the findings from this area that this model of mind would account for?'

'Crikey!' exclaimed James. 'I don't have all the answers you know.'

Martin's smug smile seemed to take heart at this response.

'In fact,' continued James, 'it's important to be aware that this view of Mind as fundamental doesn't answer all questions and even raises some of its own. Such as, how exactly do we, or our minds, interact with this more fundamental level and is it possible to influence this in some way. To strengthen it perhaps. But in answer to your question – no. This idea of Mind as fundamental could also explain findings from other areas of science. For instance, it might help explain the accounts of those who report a spiritual connection to a greater whole[6]. It might also explain why some gifted people or geniuses are the way they, possibly because they have greater access to this fundamental level of Mind[7]. Interestingly, in the medical literature, there's something called terminal lucidity[8] which is starting to get a lot of attention. It's where dementia patients, very close to death, show a return to normal levels of thinking and memory.'

'Why's that unusual?' asked Martin.

'Well, if you think about it,' responded James, 'their brains have suffered because of their dementia and may have deteriorated quite a bit. But then, just at the end, their memories and language skills seem to return to normal again.'

'But why is that a problem?' persisted Martin.

'Because there's been no recovery in the brains of these patients. They're still suffering from dementia . . .'

'But, how . . .' interrupted Martin.

'Exactly!' proclaimed James, now interrupting Martin. 'How can they now show normal, or nearly normal, thinking and memory if their brains are still damaged by the dementia?'

Martin shook his head slowly and shrugged.

'Perhaps,' offered James, 'because such information is not reliant on their brains.'

'You mean . . .' said Martin, the unfinished sentence left hanging in the air between them.

It was James' turn to shrug. 'The honest answer is that we just don't know. But its certainly difficult to account for if you take the view that their thinking is solely reliant on their brain – which has suffered serious damage.'

'Phew!' exclaimed Martin.

'Hmmm,' agreed James.

The two men sat for a while thinking through some of the implications of the issues they'd been discussing. After a few moments Martin broke the silence. 'If the brain acts as a filter, what would happen if it was damaged?'

'What, the brain?' asked James.

'Well, both I suppose. What if the brain were damaged which in some way damaged this filter thing.'

James sat in silent thought for a moment. 'You're thinking of your tumour?' he said. It was more statement than question, but Martin silently nodded. James shook his head slowly, his voice softened, becoming more cautious and reflective. 'I don't know. I mean, can you imagine? Everything. And I mean everything. And not just everything you've experienced, but everything everyone, every*thing*, has ever experienced. It would be. . .' he faltered for a moment trying to find the right words. 'It would be . . . overwhelming.'

'Like the world around you had shattered into an infinite number of pieces,' said Martin quietly. 'With each one trying to tell you a story that involved sight, sound, taste, touch, smell – in fact every sense you could image.'

The two men starred at each other.

'Information overload,' said James softly.

'Hmm,' agreed Martin nodding slowly.

'Do you think that's what's happening to you?' asked James seriously.

Martin shrugged. 'I don't know. But it certainly felt overwhelming.'

Just then the nurse came onto the ward to remind them that visiting hours were almost up. As they heard this the two friends looked at one another and smiled. Martin shrugged a little, still unsure how to express the feelings he had. 'Look, I really appreciate you talking to me about . . . about, all of this,' he said.

'No problem.'

'It's really helped,' said Martin with a brief smile.

James nodded towards the book on the bedside cabinet. 'As I say, have a read through that. It'll give you better idea of these topics along with some of the evidence from the field of parapsychology.'

The two friends remined staring at one another for a moment, sharing the silence and simply enjoying each other's company. Eventually, James stood. 'If you need anything just text or call.'

'I will, thanks,' said Martin.

James remained standing at the bedside for a moment, as if waiting to be given his leave. He sighed heavily and looked down at Martin. 'You know what I'm going to say don't you?' he said with a wry smile.

Martin nodded slowly and smiled back.

'Just don't leave it too long to tell him,' he said.

As he heard these word Martin's face paled, and he felt a tightening in his chest. It was as if a veil had been lifted, a barrier removed, and he heard the words Jennie had spoken to him echoing around his mind. *Just don't leave it too late to tell him how you feel.* It all came flooding back. The meetings with Jennie, her words, her messages, and her urging him to do something. He let out an audible groan and leant back against the pillows closing his eyes.

'Are you ok,' asked James, concerned about Martin's reaction.

It took a moment for Martin to respond, as his mind was distracted with thoughts of Jennie and mixed feelings of loss and regret. 'Hmm, what,' he answered after a moment. 'Oh, yes. I'm fine. Just a little tired,' he smiled weakly.

'Ok,' said James still frowning with concern. 'But call if you need anything ok?'

'I will, thanks.'

Concern making him reluctant to leave James remained standing by the bed. 'Right, as long as you're sure you're ok?'

Martin nodded, 'yeah, I'm fine. Thanks.'

'See you tomorrow then,' said James.

'See you tomorrow,' agreed Martin.

James leaned in over the bed and the two friends briefly hugged before he stood again, nodded one last time and then turned to leave.

Martin watched him walk out of the ward and as he did his thoughts returned to Jennie's words. Her voice echoing in his mind. *It's up to you*, he heard her say. *It's always been up to you*. And perhaps most poignantly of all – *Just don't leave it too late to tell him how you feel*. He lay there for some time, his mind reverberating with the power of these words. Initially, they stirred up intense feelings of remorse, guilt, and sadness, at the missed opportunities, and at what might have been. He could see a pathway opening up before him, leading to a dark place of heartbreak and despair. Knowing that it would be all too easy to give up and fall forwards. But then, he recalled the hope in Jennie's voice. Realising, that it is during our darkest moments that we need to focus on the light ahead to help guide us along our way. Focusing now on Jennie's voice, he let it guide him up and out of such dark thoughts, showing him what could still be. At first, he thought he didn't have much to offer but then smiled as he realised, he had the greatest gift anyone *could* give – time. Because when you give someone your time, you literally give them a piece of your life. Understanding and acceptance filled his heart, as he realised with a certainty beyond words, that he wanted to give the rest of his life to Roger. He took a deep breath and released a calm sigh of contentment as he reached over to his phone to make the call.

Notes

Lost and found

1. The term *remote viewing* was originally coined by researchers Russell Targ and Harold Puthoff and refers to a paradigm that generally involves a remote viewer sitting in a room or lab whilst a confederate goes outside to visit a randomly identified pre-set location. The aim is for the remote viewer to try and describe the geographical location and context of the confederate. Alternatively, the remote viewer may simply be given a set of map coordinates and asked to describe what is at that location.

Targ, R., & Puthoff, H. E. (1974). Information transmission under conditions of sensory shielding. *Nature, 251*, 602-607.

2. The International Remote Viewing Association has a good online resource site at: https://www.irva.org/

Silver futures

1. There are several different types of remote viewing. For example, there is *outbound remote viewing* – which involves someone travelling to a site; *coordinate remote viewing* – which involves being given a set of map co-ordinates, as well as *associative remote viewing*. For those interested you can find a good outline of these and a summary of evidence in Chapter 4 [*Clairvoyance and Remote Viewing*] of my book: Vernon, D. (2020). *Dark cognition: Evidence for psi and its implications for consciousness.* Routledge.

2. The book by Paul Smith [Smith, P. (2015). *The essential guide to remote viewing: The secret military remote perception skill anyone can learn.* International Press] is an excellent starting point for anyone interested in finding out more about this topic.

3. The magazine *Aperture* covers a range of features related to remote viewing, including articles, historical comments, and book reviews. It can be found online at: https://www.irva.org/library/aperture

4. Despite sounding like an episode of the popular TV series the *X Files,* Project Stargate is real. Given its controversial nature it should come as no surprise that there has been much that's been written about it. Possibly the best and most comprehensive summaries have been written by Ed May and Sonali Marwaha, see below.

May, E., & Marwaha, S. B. (2018). *The star gate archives: Reports of the United States governments sponsored psi program, 1972-1995. Volume 1: Remote Viewing 1972-1984.* Jefferson, NC: McFarland.

May, E., & Marwaha, S. B. (2018). *The star gate archives: Reports of the United States governments sponsored psi program, 1972-1995. Volume 2: Remote Viewing 1985-1995.* Jefferson, NC: McFarland.

5. The International Remote Viewing Association, or IRVA, represents a group of interested scientists, practitioners, and lay-people. The society promotes the responsible use and development of remote viewing. Anyone interested should check out their website at: https://www.irva.org/

6. This is an excellent book by one of the leading researchers in the field of parapsychology and is well worth a read.

Radin, D. (2009). *The conscious universe: The scientific truth of psychic phenomena.* HarperOne.

7. This work based on predicting the price of silver over a period of weeks has been widely reported in many publications and a good account can be found in Russel Targ's book, see below.

Targ, R. (2012). *The reality of ESP: A physicist's proof of psychic abilities.* Wheaton, IL: Quest Books.

8. ARV is not a simple panacea for getting rich quick – so just be careful what you do with your money. A good example of research showing null results which led to the loss of money over time is that led by Debra Katz:

Katz, D. Grgic, I., & Fendley, T. W. (2018). An ethnographic assessment of project firefly: A yearlong endeavour to create wealth by predicting FOREX currency moves with associative remote viewing. *Journal of Scientific Exploration, 32*(1), 27-60.

Spinning wheels within wheels

1. There are many meta-analyses from the field of parapsychology, each usually focusing on a different area, but all coming to the same conclusion, that an effect is evident and such behaviours are real. I've outlined some references below for those interested:

Bem, D., Tressoldi, P., Rabeyron, T., & Duggan, M. (2015). Feeling the future: A meta-analysis of 90 experiments on the anomalous anticipation of random future events. *F1000Research, 4.*

Schmidt, S., Schneider, R., Utts, J., & Walach, H. (2002). Remote intention on electrodermal activity: Two meta-analyses. *The Journal of Parapsychology*, 66(3), 233-235.

Storm, L., Sherwood, S. J., Roe, C. A., Tressoldi, P. E., Rock, A. J., & Di Risio, L. (2017). On the correspondence between dream content and target material under laboratory conditions: A meta-analysis of dream-ESP studies, 1966-2016. *International Journal of Dream Research*, 10(2), 120-140.

Storm, L., Tressoldi, P. E., & Di Risio, L. (2012). Meta-analysis of ESP studies, 1987-2010: Assessing the success of the forced-choice design in parapsychology. *The Journal of Parapsychology*, 76(2), 243-273.

2. The psi wheel refers to a device that usually, though not always, involves a balanced folded pieced of paper on a needle or pin that's stuck into a cork. The aim is to get the balanced paper to *turn* using only your mind/thoughts. However, as anyone will see if they Google this it can be moved using simple thermodynamics. Nevertheless, there are more robust versions that involve lightweight wheels balanced on pins that are hidden inside sealed containers that adepts try to move with their minds.

3. Probably one of the most notable cases of macro-PK is that alleged to be attributable to the Russian Nina Kulagina. According to Henry (2005) she could move small objects on a table as well as alter her heart rate. During such mental effort Kulagina was reported to have lost up to three pounds in weight because of the level of concentrated energy required to complete the task. However, due to lack of support from the Russian authorities at the time investigations of Kulagina's alleged abilities often took place in her home or in a hotel

room with far from ideal controls. Nevertheless, some have suggested that such behaviours were seen and filmed without any apparent trickery. It's not possible to say with certainty what she could or couldn't do but if you look on YouTube, you'll no doubt find an old clip of her doing her stuff – which is certainly thought provoking.

Henry, J. (2005). Psychokinesis. In J. Henry (Ed.), *Parapsychology: Research on exceptional experiences.* (pp. 125-136.). Hove, East Sussex: Routeledge.

4. The use of random event generators, or REGs, forms part of what is often referred to as micro-PK, as it refers to the attempted mental influence of small objects or REGs which often require inferential statistics to identify non-random patterns. Hence, the evidence is more statistical and inferential than perceptual. Part of the logic of such an approach is that it may be 'easier' to influence such small targets as it requires less energy. There are many published reports showing effects of PK on REGs, I've listed some below:

Bosch, H., Steinkamp, F., & Boller, E. (2006). Examining psychokinesis: The interaction of human intention with random number generators - A meta-analysis. *Psychological Bulletin, 132,* 497-523

Radin, D., & Nelson, L. D. (1989). Consciousness-related effects in random physical systems. *Foundations in Physics., 19,* 1499-1514

Radin, D., Nelson, L. D., Dobyns, Y., & Houtkooper, J. (2006). Reexamining psychokinesis: Comment on the Bosch, Steinkamp, and Boller (2006) meta-analysis. *Psychological Bulletin, 132,* 529-532.

5. This refers to the excellent work led by Dr Eric Dullin from the Psychophysics and Cognitive Dissonance Laboratory (LAPDC), Poitiers, in France. Along with collaborator David Jamet, they have reported on some very interesting and positive PK effects using a very simple version of the *psi wheel*.

Dullin, E., & Jamet, D. (2018). A methodology proposal for conducting macro-pk test on light spinning objects in a non-confined environment. *Journal of Scientific Exploration, 32*(3), 514-554.

I know what I saw

1. An After Death Communication, or ADC, generally refers to a *spontaneous* event during which a living individual may see, feel, hear, or simply sense the presence of someone deceased. Other terms include post death contact. They are, according to leading researcher Julie Beischel, one of the most common types of experience regarding contact with the dead. For those interested in finding out more details I've included a couple of useful references below:

Beischel, J. (2019). Spontaneous, facilitated, assisted, and requested after-death communication experiences and their impact on grief. *Threshold: Journal of Interdisciplinary Consciousness Studies, 3*(1), 1-32.

Klugman, C. M. (2006). Dead men talking: Evidence of post death contact and continuing bonds. *OMEGA-Journal of Death and Dying, 53*(3), 249-262.

Wright, S. H. (1999). Paranormal contact with the dying: 14 contemporary death coincidences. *Journal of the Society for Psychical Research, 63*(857), 258-267.

Though widely reported the ADC represents a significant challenge to the current scientific paradigm – after all, it's not really possible to randomly allocate someone to have a spontaneous experience in the lab.

2. The After Death Communication Research Foundation (ADCRF: https://www.adcrf.org/index.html) is an online community consisting of scientists and lay-people interested in the phenomenon. It provides some useful resources and a space where people can share their stories of ADC's.

Unintended intentions

1. Fibroblasts play a crucial role in regulating skin physiology, helping to repair wounds.

2. Statistical significance is a term used by scientists to identify whether a result is more likely due to chance or some other factor of interest, such as a treatment intervention. When a result is 'statistically significant' it generally means that the outcome was, with a high degree of probability, not due to chance. Hence, making it more likely that the result was due to the intervention. As such, a statistically significant result, often referred to simply as a 'significant result' suggests that something important is going on.

3. Energy healing is a catch all generic term that encapsulates a range of different techniques, such as Johrei, Reiki, Therapeutic Touch, Qigong and Prayer. According to the National Centre for Complementary and Integrative Health (NCCIH) if refers to the channelling of healing energy, often through the hands of the practitioner, into a client's body to restore health. However, it should be noted that it is not clear at this time precisely what this 'energy' is, or where it comes from. A good summary of the findings from these areas can be found in Chapter 8 (Energy Healing) of my book (Dark Cognition).

4. This refers to some excellent research led by Professor Chris Roe from Northampton looking at the efficacy of what they called 'non-contact' healing.

Roe, C. A., Sonnex, C., & Roxburgh, E. C. (2015). Two meta-analyses of noncontact healing studies. *Explore, 11*(1), 11-23.

5. I deliberately chose an 'animal' study for the story because of the placebo problem. When talking about energy healing sceptics often try to dismiss the findings by arguing that there's "nothing there" and its all really a "placebo effect". However, the placebo effect cannot account for the various effects shown when based on animal studies or those showing beneficial effects on bacteria used for in vitro research. I've listed some relevant publications below for those interested in finding out more.

Abe, K., Ichinomiya, R., Kanai, T., & Yamamoto, K. (2012). Effect of Japanese energy healing method known as Johrei on viability and proliferation of cultured cancer cells in vitro. *The Journal of Alternative and Complementary Medicine., 18*(3), 221-228.

Bengston, W. F., & Krinsley, D. (2000). The effect of the "laying on of hands" on transplanted breast cancer in mice. *Journal of Scientific Exploration., 14*(3), 353-364.

de Souza, A. L. T., Rosa, D. P. C., Blanco, B. A., Passaglia, P., & Stabile, A. M. (2017). Effects of Therapeutic Touch on healing of the skin in rats. *Explore, 13*(5), 333-338.

Rubik, B., Brooks, A. J., & Schwartz, G. E. (2006). In vitro effect of Reiki treatment on bacterial cultures: Role of experimental context and practitioner well-being. *Journal of Alternative & Complementary Medicine, 12*(1), 7-13.

6. Alongside statistical significance researchers sometimes (it really should be always) also look at what they call the "effect size". This is an objective and standardised measure showing the magnitude of any effect. This is important because, whilst significance can tell us that a result is different in a meaningful way it doesn't say 'how' different. That is, an effect can be significant but very small. As such, when looking at the effect size we are asking what is the strength, or size, of the effect or treatment.

7. For those outside of the academic world it might sound odd that certain scientific journals might be unwilling, or less likely, to publish results from the field of parapsychology. After all, science is supposed to be objective. Unfortunately, whilst the paradigm of science may be objective, it is sometimes undertaken and enacted by people who are not. A good example of the negative bias shown when people read about parapsychology was reported by Bethany Butzer when she examined how people would evaluate two identical studies – one alleged to be from the field of parapsychology and the other from the field of neuroscience. Unsurprisingly, for those all too familiar with the biases shown by Journal Editors and Reviewers, the results showed that participants rated the neuroscience study as significantly stronger and more valid than the parapsychological one – despite the fact that they were identical.

Butzer, B. (2020). Bias in the evaluation of psychology studies: A comparison of parapsychology versus neuroscience. *Explore, 16*(6), 382-391.

Harmonic resonance

1. According to Maharishi Mahesh Yogi, who developed the Transcendental Meditation (TM) technique, if a number

of individuals participate together in such meditative practice this will have a wider beneficial effect on surrounding life and society. The suggestion is that TM encourages the individual to shift their conscious mind away from the everyday waking state to a distinct transcendent level of consciousness and this will radiate outwards producing a transition in society towards more orderly and harmonious functioning. In honour of the developer this is more generally referred to as the *Maharishi effect*. Interestingly, it's not that the individuals practicing TM do so with the specific intent of reducing crime or violence. The effect is often seen in terms of an emerging result of TM or a by-product of its practice. For those interested in finding out more I've outlined some useful references below.

Borland, C., & Landrith, I. G. S. (1976). Improved quality of city life through the Transcendental Meditation program: Decreased crime rate. In D. W. Orme-Johnson and J. T. Farrow (Eds.), *Scientific research on the Transcendental Meditation program: Collected papers* (Vol. 1, pp.639-648). Rheinweiler, West Germany: MERU Press.

Morris, B. (1992). Maharishi's Vedic Science and Technology: The only means to create world peace. *Modern Science and Vedic Science, 5*(1-2), 199-207.

Orme-Johnson, D. W. (2003). Preventing crime through the Maharishi Effect. *Journal of Offender Rehabilitation, 36*(1-4), 257-281.

2. Over time quite a substantial amount of research has been conducted to show that the Maharishi effect (ME) has been associated with reductions in crime, international conflict as well as reducing mortality rates. Again, for those interested I've provided some key references below.

Dillbeck, M. C. (1990). Test of a field theory of consciousness and social change: Time series analysis of participation in the TM-Sidhi program and reduction of violent death in the U.S. *Social Indicators Research, 22*, 399-418.

Dillbeck, M. C., & Cavanaugh, K. L. (2016). Societal violence and collective consciousness: Reduction of U.S. homicide and urban violent crime rates. *SAGE Open*(April-June), 1-16. doi: 10.1177/2158244016637891

Dillbeck, M. C., & Cavanaugh, K. L. (2017). Group practice of the Transcendental Meditation(R) and TM-Sidhi(R) program and reductions in infant mortality and drug-related death: A quasi-experimental analysis. *SAGE Open*. doi: 10.1177/2158244017697164

Orme-Johnson, D. W., Alexander, C. N., Davies, J. L., Chandler, H. M., & Larimore, W. E. (1988). International peace project in the Middle East. *Journal of Conflict Resolution, 32*(4), 776-812.

Orme-Johnson, D. W., Dillbeck, M. C., & Alexander, C. N. (2003). Preventing terrorism and international conflict. *Journal of Offender Rehabilitation, 36*(1-4), 283-302. doi: 10.1300/J076v36n01

Time to act

1. The Psi Encyclopaedia is a free-access online encyclopaedia of psychical research hosted by the *Society for Psychical Research* (https://psi-encyclopedia.spr.ac.uk/).

2. This is based on a survey conducted in the USA by June Mack and Larry Powell. They found that, of those that responded, over half reported experiencing dream-based premonitions. Fifty three percent reported premonitions of

future events that they claim later occurred and forty five percent reportedly changed their travel plans as a result of an 'intuitive' sense that something may occur.

Mack, J., & Powell, L. (2005). Perceptions of non-local communication: Incidences associated with media consumption and individual differences. *North American Journal of Psychology, 7*(2), 279-294.

3. Retroactive priming refers to the idea that exposure to target material in the *future* can influence your response to it in the *present*. It was made popular by the eminent psychologist Professor Daryl Bem who wanted to create simple tests that other psychologists could use to explore such effects. I have attempted to elicit such effects a number of times, both in the lab and using online studies, and only met with partial success. I've identified a few key references below for those interested.

Bem, D. J. (2011). Feeling the future: Experimental evidence for anomalous retroactive influences on cognition and affect. *Journal of Personality and Social Psychology., 100*, 407-425

Vernon, D. (2017). Exploring precall using arousing images and utilising a memory recall practise task on-line. *Journal of the Society for Psychical Research., 81*(2), 65-79.

Vernon, D. (2018). Test of reward contingent precall. *Journal of Parapsychology, 82*(1), 8-23.

4. Rather sad but true that Edinburgh University is the only UK based university to offer a Chair in parapsychology. It was created in 1985 and is now referred to as the Koestler Parapsychology Unit (https://koestlerunit.wordpress.com/research-overview/).

5. The Society for Psychical Research (SPR) was established in 1882 in London, and it was the first scientific organisation to examine claims related to paranormal phenomena. It publishes a quarterly magazine and scientific journal (Journal of the Society for Psychical Research). I have been, and still am a member and Council Member of the SPR and was honoured to be able to work as Journal Editor for two years between 2018-2020. The society holds various study days, online webinars (which I often host) and annual conferences. For those interested in finding out more check out their website at: https://www.spr.ac.uk/home

6. This is a proposal put forward by researchers Sonia Marwaha and Ed May.

Marwaha, S. B., & May, E. C. (2016). Precognition: The only form of psi? *Journal of Consciousness Studies., 23*(3-4), 76-100.

7. A good summary of these different types of precognition and an outline of evidence can be found in Chapter 5 (Precognition) of my book *Dark Cognition*.

8. This is based on the research conducted by Fernando Alvarez showing that when Bengalese finches are randomly presented with a selection of images, they exhibit displays of alarm *just before* the image of a predator is shown, compared to a non-threatening control image.

Alvarez, F. (2010). Anticipatory alarm behavior in Bengalese finches. *Journal of Scientific Exploration, 24*(4), 599-610.

9. Dreaming about possible future events (i.e., dream precognition) is more common than most people think. For instance, surveys by Erlender Haraldsson and Michael Schredl

have shown that around 38% of those responding say that they've experienced at least one precognitive dream, and this rises to around 50% when student populations were sampled.

Haraldsson, E. (1985). Representative national surveys of psychic phenomena: Iceland, Great Britain, Sweden, USA and Gallup's multinational survey. *Journal of the Society for Psychical Research, 53,* 145-158.

Schredl, M. (2009). Frequency of precognitive dreams: Association with dream recall and personality variables. *Journal of the Society for Psychical Research, 73,* 83-91.

Dream precognition research has evolved away from lab-based research to allow participants to dream at home, record their dreams and then later upload them to a website and/or identify the target they were supposed to be dreaming about. The research group led by Michael Schredl has found some interesting effects using this type of paradigm.

Schredl, M., Götz, S., & Ehrhardt-Knutsen, S. (2010). Precognitive dreams: A pilot diary study. *Journal of the Society for Psychical Research, 74*(900), 168-175.

However, it is important to point out that research on dream precognition has not always been successful in eliciting clear and robust effects (see Mossbridge & Radin, 2018 for a review).

Mossbridge, J. A., & Radin, D. (2018). Precognition as a form of prospection: A review of the evidence. Psychology of Consciousness: Theory, Research, and Practice, 5(1), 78-93.

Nevertheless, the most recent meta-analysis conducted by Lance Storm and colleagues concluded that dream precognition is a genuine effect that is not governed by the specific experimenter or laboratory, the necessity to monitor rapid eye movement (REM), the type of target, agent and perceiver arrangements or the number of choices available in a target set.

Storm, L., Sherwood, S. J., Roe, C. A., Tressoldi, P. E., Rock, A. J., & Di Risio, L. (2017). On the correspondence between dream content and target material under laboratory conditions: A meta-analysis of dream-ESP studies, 1966-2016. *International Journal of Dream Research, 10*(2), 120-140.

A change of heart

1. The term *Near-Death Experience* (NDE) was first made popular by Dr Raymond Moody in his book *Life After Life,* which outlined the various experiences reported by patients who'd suffered cardiac arrest.

Moody, R. A. (1975). *Life after life.* San Francisco: Harper.

2. This is based on the excellent website of the *International Association for Near Death Studies* (IANDS) and can be found at: https://iands.org/

3. There have been many books written about NDEs, some by individuals who have had an experience themselves. I can't list them all, so I've provided what I consider to be some very good and readable sources below.

Bailey, L. W., & Yates, J. (Eds.). (1996). *The near death experience: A reader.* New York.: Routledge.

Parnia, S., & Young, J. (2013). *The Lazarus effect: The science that is rewriting the boundaries between life and death.* London: Rider.

Rivas, T., Dirven, A., & Smit, R. H. (2016). *The self does not die: Verified paranormal phenomena from near-death experiences.* Durham, NC.: IANDS.

van Lommel, P. (2010). *Consciousness beyond life: The science of the near-death experience.* New York: HarperOne.

4. Chapter 10 (Near-death experiences) of my book *Dark Cognition* provides a good summary of the phenomenology and classification of the NDE.

5. This is based on the excellent research by Melvin Morse who has led the field in exploring the NDEs of children.

Morse, M. (1983). A near-death experience in a 7-year-old child. *American Journal of Diseases of Children, 137*(10), 959-961.

Morse, M. L. (1994). Near-death experiences of children. *Journal of Paediatric Oncology Nursing, 11*(4),139-144.

6. Unfortunately for many, the disruptive changes brought about by experiencing an NDE can often lead to divorce between couples. With research showing that the divorce rates of couples, where one has experienced an NDE, are much higher than normal.

Christian, S. R. (2005). *Marital satisfaction and stability following a near-death experience of one of the marital partners.* University of North Texas, Denton, Texas (unpublished doctoral dissertation).

Distant call

1. Ganzfeld is a German term that refers to the *whole field* and represents an approach in psi research that is thought to improve the signal to noise ratio in telepathic communication by reducing all sensory input for the receiver.

2. This is based on the findings from dream telepathy research by Simon Sherwood and Chris Roe.

Sherwood, S. J., & Roe, C. A. (2003). A review of the dream ESP studies conducted since the Maimonides dream ESP programme. *Journal of Consciousness Studies.*, *10*(6-7), 85-109.

3. This is based on telepathy research using the ganzfeld paradigm by Lance Storm, Patrizio Tressoldi and Lorenzo Di Risio. They reported a hit rate across thirty studies of 33% when chance would predict a hit rate of only 25%.

Storm, L., Tressoldi, P. E., & Di Risio, L. (2010). Meta-analysis of free-response studies, 1992–2008: Assessing the noise reduction model in parapsychology. *Psychological Bulletin,* *136*(4), 471-485.

4. According to a survey conducted by John Palmer the feeling of receiving information from the mind of someone else is one of the most commonly reported psi type of experiences.

Palmer, J. (1979). A community mail survey of psychic experiences. *Journal of the American Society for Psychical Research.*, *73*, 221-251

5. This idea is based on some research I conducted with a couple of postgraduate students at Canterbury Christ Church University. We put the *sender* in a virtual reality headset and had them experience positive, stimulating events. Such as skiing down a mountain or parachuting out of a plane. We hoped that this might make it easier for the *receiver* to identify the correct target – and we were right.

Vernon, D., Sandford, T., & Moyo, E. (2020). Using virtual reality to test for telepathy: A proof-of-concept study. *Journal of Scientific Exploration, 34*(4), 683-702

6. This idea is based primarily on the work of eminent scientist Guilio Tononi and his Integrated Information Theory (IIT).

Tononi, G., & Koch, C. (2015). Consciousness: here, there and everywhere? *Philosophical Transactions of the Royal Society B: Biological Sciences, 370*(1668), 20140167.

Broken filter

1. This was based on a YouGov poll reported in 2018. The details of which can be found online here: https://yougov.co.uk/topics/society/articles-reports/2018/10/29/would-you-know-when-youll-die

2. The idea that science can sometimes take a dogmatic approach and argue with a level of certainty that may be unfounded is very nicely outlined in Rupert Sheldrake's book *The Science Delusion*. For anyone interested in exploring the possible dogmas of science I would thoroughly recommend Rupert's excellent book.

Sheldrake, R. (2012). *The science delusion: Freeing the spirit of enquiry*. London: Hodder & Stoughton.

3. The idea that the mind (*psyche*) is found everywhere (*pan*) is an old idea that seems to be undergoing a renaissance. The key point is that rather than think of consciousness as something that is based *on* either physics or biology, it is seen as operating at a more fundamental level. Unsurprisingly, much has been written about this approach and I've outlined some useful references for those interested below.

Chalmers, D. (2015). Panpsychism and panprotopsychism. Consciousness in the physical world: *Perspectives on Russellian monism, 246*(2003), 102-154.

Goff, P. (2017). *Consciousness and fundamental reality.* Oxford University Press.

Koch, C. (2014). Ubiquitous minds. *Scientific American Mind,* 25(1), 26-29.

4. The *mirror test* has long been used in both human and non-human animal research to ascertain self-awareness. However, it is far from certain that it provides a simple index of consciousness. I've provided some references below for those interested in finding out more.

De Veer, M. W., & Van den Bos, R. (1999). A critical review of methodology and interpretation of mirror self-recognition research in nonhuman primates. *Animal Behaviour, 58*(3), 459-468.

Gallup Jr, G. G., Anderson, J. R., & Shillito, D. J. (2002). The mirror test. *The cognitive animal: Empirical and theoretical perspectives on animal cognition,* 325-333.

Suddendorf, T., & Butler, D. L. (2013). The nature of visual self-recognition. *Trends in Cognitive Sciences, 17*(3), 121-127.

5. This, in essence, is the argument made in the final chapter of my book *Dark Cognition*. It is one that many researchers, both within the field of parapsychology and beyond, are coming to. I've outlined some useful sources below.

Schwartz, S. A. (2015). Six protocols, neuroscience, and near death: An emerging paradigm incorporating nonlocal consciousness. *Explore, 11*(4), 252-260.

Tressoldi, P. E., Facco, E., & Lucangeli, D. (2016). *Emergence of qualia from brain activity or from an interaction of proto-consciousness with the brain: which one is the weirder? Available evidence and a research agenda. Available Evidence and a Research Agenda.* Article available at SSRN: https://papers.ssrn.com/sol3/papers.cfm?abstract_id=2765331

6. This is based on a report by Etzel Cardeña and colleagues. I've given the reference below for those interested.

Cardeña, E., Lynn, S. J., & Krippner, S. (2017). The psychology of anomalous experiences: A rediscovery. *Psychology of Consciousness: Theory, Research, and Practice, 4*(1), 4.

7. According to Olivier Brabant gifted individuals may simply have greater access to a wider realm of information. This could be due to a stronger link or bond between the individual and the wider field of consciousness, or fundamental Mind.

Brabant, O. (2016). More than meets the eye: toward a post-materialist model of consciousness. *Explore, 12*(5), 347-354.

8. Terminal lucidity, which is also sometimes called *paradoxical lucidity*, refers to the mental clarity shown by those suffering from some form of dementia or neurological disorder shortly before death. Given the state of the brain at this stage it challenges the notion that thinking/language/memory etc. are reliant solely on the brain. Although it has been known about for some time it is only in recent years that it has been receiving additional attention for what it may be telling us regarding the nature of consciousness. I've provided a couple of references below for those interested.

Delorme, A., Radin, D., & Wahbeh, H. (2021). Advancing the evidence for survival of consciousness. *Bigelow Institute for Consciousness Studies*. Article available at: https://www.bigelowinstitute.org/wp-content/uploads/2022/10/delorme-radin-wahbeh-survival-consciousness.pdf

Wahbeh, H., Radin, D., Cannard, C., & Delorme, A. (2022). What if consciousness is not an emergent property of the brain? Observational and empirical challenges to materialistic models. *Frontiers in Psychology*, 5596.

Acknowledgements

First and foremost, my heartfelt love and thanks to Annie Morris. Without whom none of these stories would have seen the light of day. Annie, your love, kind heart and encouraging words of support inspired and humbled me. That day was a turning point for the book, for me and, as it turned out, for us. It would take me another book to tell you how much you mean to me and even then, I feel my words would fall woefully short. All I can say is that to the world you may be one person, but to me, you are the world.

Enduring thanks and love to Alessandro Paolieri, Sabina Hulbert and Lara Hulbert for the love, laughter, support and pizza! I don't think I would have survived without you all. You've been there for me so many times – thank you! Thanks to Greg Fitzgerald for listening to me and my ideas, for guiding me, and for the many stimulating conversations we've shared over coffee. Looking forward to sharing many more. Thanks to Gary O'Mahoney for sticking by me all this time and providing much needed coffee and support.

Thanks to Tracy Spratt and Lynn Nichols-Pike for reading early drafts and providing useful feedback, insights and support.

Special thanks to Mads Carlsen and Signe Amdi Hansen for your kind support, friendship, shared adventures, and Camino coffee. You both helped me a lot when I was stuck with a particular story line and I'm forever grateful for that, and your friendship. Buen Camino!

Thanks to Zofia Weaver for taking the time to proofread and help edit the book, spotting the many errors I didn't see and making the narrative much clearer. Special thanks also to Dean Radin, Graham Nicholls, Callum Cooper and Paul Smith for their supporting and encouraging words, very much appreciated. Finally, thanks to Stella Lee and the team from White Magic Studios with their help and support and patience with my endless questions, changes, and edits.

* 9 7 8 1 8 3 5 3 8 2 3 4 9 *